A THRONE OF SWANS

KATHARINE & ELIZABETH CORR

HOT
KEY
BOOKS

First published in Great Britain in 2020 by
HOT KEY BOOKS
80–81 Wimpole St, London W1G 9RE
www.hotkeybooks.com

A CIP catalogue record for this book is available from the British Library.

ISBN: 978-1-4714-0875-5
Also available as an ebook

1

This book is typeset using Atomik ePublisher
Printed and bound in Great Britain by Clays Ltd, Elcograf S.p.A.

Hot Key Books is an imprint of Bonnier Books UK
www.bonnierbooks.co.uk

For Mum and Dad, who encouraged us to
read *everything*. (EC)

For Victoria, who told me *Swan Lake* would make a
great starting point for a story, and was totally right.
(KC)

Surrounded by unspeakable deeds, I am forced
into something terrible.
I know my rage. It cannot go unacknowledged.
But amidst the terrors I will not resist this ruinous
path . . .

ἐν δεινοῖς δείν᾽ ἠναγκάσθην·
ἔξοιδ᾽, οὐ λάθει μ᾽ ὀργά.
ἀλλ᾽ ἐν γὰρ δεινοῖς οὐ σχήσω
ταύτας ἄτας . . .

Sophocles, *Electra* vv.221–4, trans. Georgie Penney

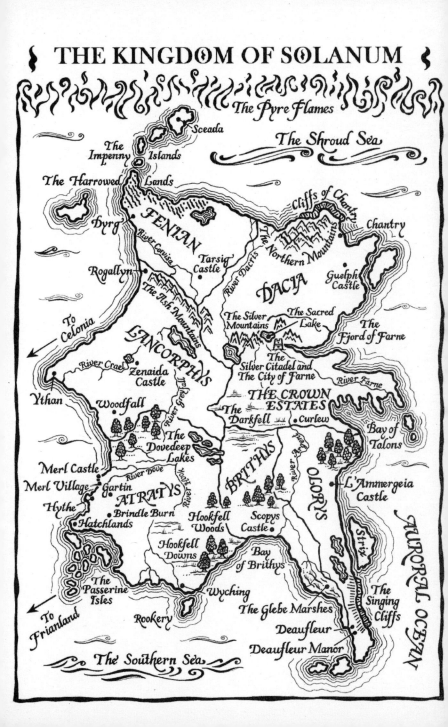

THE KINGDOM OF SOLANUM

The Pyre Flames

The Shroud Sea

Sceada

The Impenny Islands

The Harrowed Lands

Cliffs of Chantry

Chantry

Dyrg

FENIAN

The Northern Mountains

River Corisa

Tarsig Castle

River Dacris

DACIA

Guelph Castle

Rogallyn

The Silver Mountains

The Sacred Lake

The Fjord of Farne

To Celonia

LANCORPHIS

The Ash Mountains

The Silver Citadel and The City of Farne

River Farne

River Crael

Zenaida Castle

River Tolega

THE CROWN ESTATES

Ythan

Woodfall

The Darkfell

Curlew

Bay of Talons

The Dovedeep Lakes

BRITHYS

L'Ammergeia Castle

Merl Castle

River Dove

OLORYS

Merl Village

Gartin

ATRATYS

River Livel

River Ammel

Hythe

Brindle Burn

Hookfell Woods

Scopys Castle

Strix

Hatchlands

Hookfell Downs

Bay of Brithys

AURORAL OCEAN

The Passerine Isles

Wyching

The Singing Cliffs

To Frianland

Rookery

The Glebe Marshes

Deaufleur

Deaufleur Manor

The Southern Sea

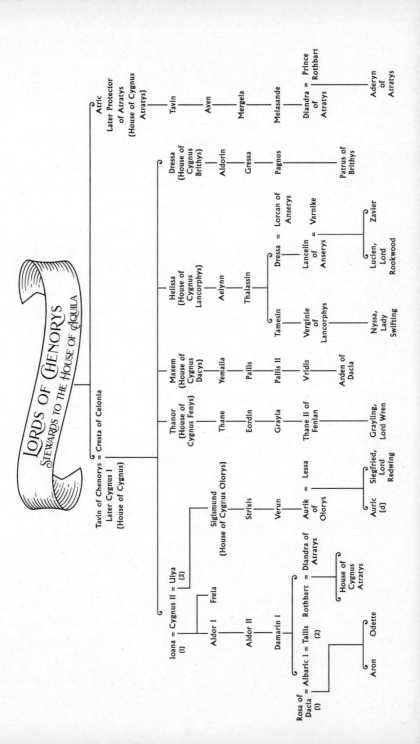

Prologue

It is nearly midnight, and my father is dying.

The physicians continue to scurry around him, grinding up herbs with pestles or chanting over their poultices. But the lavender-scented smoke of the fire can't mask the odour of decaying flesh. Candlelight can't conceal the laboured breath, the claw-like fingers clutching convulsively at the bedclothes. He pushes the nearest doctor away, irritable, and beckons me closer.

The doctors mutter about infection. Still, I obey. As I balance on the edge of the massive oak-framed bed, my red silk skirts are like a spill of blood in the dimness. I lean in, holding tight to one of his hands.

'This . . .' he gestures to the weeping sores on his chest and shoulders, 'a mistake. I . . . stayed too long. And the contagion . . .' His speech is thickened, as if his tongue is swollen. 'I'm sorry, Aderyn.'

I understand him. The sickness that has ravaged one of our port towns for the last month has led to quarantine and death.

My father – to help his people, or in the cause of science, or both – stayed with the afflicted, hoping to discover a cure. He has gambled his life in pursuit of knowledge before. But this time he lost. And now – now he wants absolution. I try to tell him that all will be well, that the doctors might still find a way to save him, but the lie catches in my throat. Instead, I stare into his clouded eyes and murmur, 'I know. It's late, Father. You should rest.'

But he shakes his head and grits his teeth, blinking, trying to focus. 'I want you to . . . stay here, once I'm gone. Stay in the castle.'

His words are not new. I've been confined within our castle and the peninsula upon which it stands for years. So many years that I long ago stopped asking when I would be allowed to leave. I have learned that it is possible to stand in the open air with the wind on my face and still suffocate. That it is possible to command others and still be a prisoner.

'You must stay –' He breaks off in a paroxysm of coughing; a servant darts in and wipes the blood and spittle from his chin. 'Stay here, where it's safe. Promise me.'

Perhaps this sickness is finally claiming his mind. If I never leave, I cannot do what will be required of me. And I cannot believe my father truly expects me to become my own jailor, trapped behind these walls through an oath of my own making.

But I am wrong apparently. He grips my upper arm tightly, pulling himself up, the pressure of his fingers still painful despite his loss of strength. 'Promise me, Aderyn. You know I love you. All I want is –' he gasps with pain – 'to protect you.'

'I know you love me, Father. And I love you too.' But I make no promise. I won't lie to him now.

Mercifully he does not notice my omission. He sinks back into the mattress, eyelids fluttering as the clock begins playing the chimes that lead to the hour. 'Good. You'll understand eventually, I hope. And finally . . . finally, your mother . . .' The words fade into silence.

'Father? What about her? Please, if there's anything you haven't told me, anything . . .' My voice seems to be coming from a long way away. I shake his shoulder. 'Father . . .' The doctors cluster round and I am moved gently to one side as they check pulse and breathing and heartbeat.

And then someone is closing his eyes, and drawing the sheet up over his face. The clock strikes the hour.

'Your Grace?'

For a moment, I don't understand. I think, *My father is dead. He can't answer you.*

But the servant repeats the question. 'Your Grace?'

And then I realise: he is addressing me. I am no longer a seventeen-year-old girl who can spend her time exactly as she wishes. I'm no longer merely Lady Aderyn. I am Her Grace, Protector of the Dominion of Atratys, sole mistress of Merl Castle and all the lands that belong to it.

Somehow, in the space between the end of one day and the start of the next, everything has changed.

For the next week or more, I seem to be submerged, looking out at the world from inside a bubble of my own grief. Grief; anger; pity. For my father. For myself. I take care that no one else should know. I walk and speak as normal, eat and sleep at the appropriate times. The dressmaker brings mourning

3

gowns, and I try them on; I give my red dress, that had been my favourite, to a servant. Lord Lancelin of Anserys, our steward, sets before me suggestions for my father's Last Flight – food, music, people to be invited – and I make a show of reading through his lists. But the scratches of ink on the pages convey no meaning to me; I agree to everything so that I might be left alone. When I am alone, I sit and stare at the waves breaking against the familiar granite rocks beneath the castle, stare until my eyes are sore. I listen to my own breathing, crushed into immobility by the ache in my chest, the onslaught of this second loss. And so, the time passes.

The day of the Last Flight comes. My father may have ignored the rigid etiquette of the court while he was alive, but his death brings its own set of demands. I am dressed in my new black gown – high-collared, with long sleeves that almost hide my hands – and from somewhere in the vaults my maid produces a heavy mourning diadem of jet and silver. She sets it on top of my dark hair; the clips dig into my scalp. When I arrive at the jetty, the guests – castle inhabitants, tenant farmers and local lords, mostly – are already assembled, a mass of shadow like so much inky seaweed cast up on the shoreline. There are the required number of speeches and songs, and then my father – like my mother, and their parents before – is laid in the high-prowed boat that awaits him and pushed out into the current. At the last minute, a fire is set among the dry kindling piled around the body. Red flames swarm. And as they do, the honour guard steps forward. Each member a noble, representing his or her family, they are dressed in long black cloaks.

One by one, they hand their cloaks to the leather-garbed servants. For a moment, each noble shivers, naked in the chill morning air. And then, they change.

Cranes, cormorants, ravens and rooks, herons and falcons – the air fills as each person shifts seamlessly from human to bird. Birds far larger, far more dangerous than their namesakes that live in our forests and fields. Together, the transformed nobles follow the blazing boat out to the sea. So many different types of bird. But no swans.

Now my father is dead, I am the only swan here.

And I do not fly.

One

I'm sitting at the large desk in my study. A new room this; my father conducted business in the long gallery, under the dead gaze of our ancestors' portraits. Like most of our kind he walked as he worked, orbited by servants taking notes or carrying stacks of paper; it's easy for your leg muscles to wither if you spend much of your life on the wing. The steward pauses in his pacing and raises one forefinger – a sure sign that he has thought of another argument.

'You only came out of mourning last week, Your Grace. Only four days ago. To hasten to the society and pleasures of the court the moment you are no longer wearing black . . . Some might consider it unseemly. Demonstrating a lack of respect for your late father.'

'They might. But I am out of mourning, and I'm not proposing to go to court tomorrow. We both know my visit will take some time to organise; I see no reason for delay.'

A muscle twitches in the side of my lord steward's lean face. 'And I see that you are determined to leave Merl and your dominion as soon as possible.' He raises an eyebrow. 'Regardless of my attempts to persuade you otherwise. Regardless of the fact that there is so much to be done here and now in Atratys, Your Grace.'

The sound of singing floats up from the courtyard. Abandoning our quarrel, I go to the tall, arched windows and open the casement wider. There are servants working in the kitchen gardens, walking to and fro between the vegetable beds with hoes and wheelbarrows. Leaning outward, I turn my face to the sun, trying to catch the stray beams just lighting up the angle of the wall, wishing I was outside. On a fine morning like this my father would have summoned me to walk beside him through the castle grounds, testing me on my knowledge of Atratyan plants and crops, teaching me about those we export, entertaining me with tales of his visits to other dominions and the differences he found there. Places I'd never been allowed to see for myself.

'Your Grace . . .'

'I've been shut up here long enough, Lancelin. I know I have responsibilities –' I cast a guilty glance at the piles of paperwork that take up at least half my desk – 'but I won't be gone long. And it's the court. I would have spent at least two years there by now, in the ordinary course of things –'

'But your situation is not ordinary, Aderyn.' The use of my given name surprises me into silence. My steward pinches the bridge of his nose, sighs. 'Forgive me for speaking plainly. But you know very well that your father kept you here at Merl for your own safety. If the king realises that you are, for all practical purposes, flightless –'

'I am *not* flightless.'

'We've discussed this. You cannot shift your shape; not at the moment. If the king asks you to transform for some reason –'

'Why would he? Nobility is not put to the test; it would be considered an outrage.'

'But if he did –' Lancelin glares at me over the top of his spectacles – 'you won't be able to comply. And you know what will follow.'

Disgrace and death. The flighted rule; the flightless do not. A Protector who could not fly would automatically be stripped of power and banished, no matter who was on the throne. To be sent away from Atratys would be bad enough. But Lancelin tells me I wouldn't even live long enough to grieve. With my claim on the throne, no prudent ruler would leave me alive.

'It isn't fair.'

'But it is the law, Your Grace. The Elders spoke, and the Decrees are what they are.' A stock phrase, used by parents to silence children, or by those in authority to explain why something cannot change. I heard my father use it often enough.

'But it must be nearly two years since my cousin the prince lost his arm. And he has not been banished. Or assassinated.'

'No, he hasn't. Not yet. But only because Prince Aron is protected by the king, and the king's pride.' Lancelin eyes me a little warily. 'And I'd like to remind you, Your Grace, that the prince has been cut out of the succession since his accident. Moving you one step nearer to the throne. Putting you more at risk.'

'I've no desire to become queen, you know that.'

'But does anyone else?' Lancelin ignores my scowl and

continues. 'I'm sure you've read my reports on the situation at court: your uncle the king's new wife, the rumours of factions, of a power struggle.'

'Yes, I read them.' I raise my eyebrows. 'What's your point, my lord steward?'

'My point is, things change. Even in the kingdom.' *The kingdom* – that is how Solanum is always described, in books or in speech. As if the rest of the world does not exist. Or is, at best, unimportant. 'The current political climate makes the Silver Citadel even more dangerous. Your father did his best to shield you. Everyone here has worked hard to keep your secret. But really, it is impossible to know what words might have been whispered into the king's ears. And to put yourself into harm's way, when it is not required, when your uncle has not sent for you, when your father specifically asked you not to go . . .' He throws his hands in the air as if despairing at my stubborn stupidity.

Anger lends acid to my tongue. 'You do not need to remind me what my father said as he lay dying, Lancelin. It was only six weeks ago. I remember his words quite clearly.'

My steward does not answer. He seems absorbed in straightening the papers stacked on the desk.

I clamp my mouth shut. Bite down on my irritation. Manage – just about – not to stamp my foot. 'Really, Lancelin, if the political situation is as you say, then all the more reason for me to go to the Citadel – someone needs to protect the interests of Atratys from those who might scheme against us. We've heard nothing from my uncle the king since his letter of condolence. I do not trust his silence.'

Through the window next to me I can see fields full of early crops, and brightly coloured fishing boats rocking gently in the harbour. Further off, looking landward across the causeway that links Merl Island to the mainland, are the straggling stone buildings of the nearest town, dominated by the copper-roofed sanctuary, the tapering chimney of a tin mine, the tall masts of ships docked in the port at the end of the next headland. Just a tiny fraction of my Atratys, but so heavy with life and history and expectation that I sag forward, bracing myself on the window frame as the weight of my inheritance, my home, bears down upon me. There is almost nothing I wouldn't do to defend my dominion. Almost nothing I wouldn't give up to protect what my parents were trying to build here, to keep Atratys free from the oppression and poverty that stalk some of the other dominions.

Almost nothing.

A huge rose bush scrambles up this sheltered side of the castle. If I stretch down from the window my fingertips will just brush the tops of the highest, pale green buds, but in a few weeks' time this section of wall will be veiled with deep pink roses, my mother's favourite flower. She and my father used to walk in the rose garden every afternoon during the summer months. I was often with them, and I remember darting along the paths between the flower beds, gravel crunching beneath my feet, breathing in the scented air, collecting up the silken rose petals that had fallen to the ground. I remember looking back to see my parents strolling, hand in hand, behind me. Or sometimes sitting, her head on his shoulder, his arm tight about her waist.

My father never returned to the rose garden after she was murdered. For him, there seemed to be no more summers.

'Why did my father stop visiting his brother?'

A shadow crosses Lancelin's face. 'Your father never took me into his confidence. I only know that he became more reclusive after your mother's death, burdened as he was with grief. Grief, and anger, at his own inability to find and punish the culprit . . . I believe he held the king in affection, when they were younger.'

Strange, then, that my father should never even talk about him. But I suppose there were a lot of things we never discussed. Whether it was my mother's death, or my requests to be allowed to leave the castle, my father's response to unwelcome topics was always the same: fly into a rage and lock himself in his laboratory.

There's a painting on the wall above the fireplace: my parents holding me as a baby, my uncle standing next to them, looking at me. Or perhaps at my mother. Likenesses captured to commemorate the celebration of my fledging, images of the living side by side with those now dead.

A cold gust of wind makes me shiver and I shut the window.

There are plenty of portraits here at Merl. Plenty of ghosts. But no answers.

'I'm going to court, Lancelin.' I don't intend to explain myself to him. To try to make it clear why, after all these years, my hunger to know the truth about my mother's death still rages unabated. Or why I think I'll find that truth at the Silver Citadel. But, as he gazes at me from his slightly hooded eyes, I decide he probably understands.

Another moment passes; my steward, finally, bows his head in assent.

'As you wish, Your Grace. I will, of course, accompany you –'

'No. I need you here. There's no one else I would trust to take care of Atratys.'

He bows again. 'Thank you, Your Grace. There is indeed much to deal with.' Moving back to the desk he lifts a sheaf of papers from the top of one pile. 'We've had a report of more people crossing the border into Atratys from the Dominion of Brithys.' His nostrils flare. 'And demands from the local Brithyan lords that we should round them up and send them all back again.'

I can't help groaning. 'Must we? From what I know of Brithys, I can't blame its inhabitants for wanting to live elsewhere. And there's plenty of work for them here. The port master at Hythe was complaining only last week about the shortage of labour.'

'The situation is causing a certain amount of political friction with Brithys. But I will do my best.' He picks up a lump of red quartz that serves as a paperweight, turning it over and over in his long, thin fingers. 'It would still be as well for you to take an adviser to court, in addition to your servants.'

'But why?' I turn away to pace the room. 'I've studied hard, my lord. I've learned everything about Atratys that you or my father would teach me. Spent more hours than I can remember watching him deal with treaties and land disputes. Am I not qualified to represent my dominion?'

'I'm not questioning your ability, Your Grace. You know Atratys. But you do not know the court.'

I can't argue with him on that point.

 12

Lancelin clears his throat. 'Do you remember meeting my son, Lucien?'

I have a very vague memory of gangly awkwardness and dark hair, but I can bring no other image to mind. Lucien has never lived at Merl, but he visited a few times while my mother was alive; I must have been about nine when I last saw him. 'A little.'

'After spending three years at the Citadel, he was sent to Frianland as part of our diplomatic mission.' The steward's stooped back straightens a little. 'He has a gift for languages, it seems. But he has now been released from service and will return home shortly. I'll send for him if you wish. Lucien knows the ways of the court. He knows who to trust and who is best avoided. You may even appoint him your clerk, to give his position formal status. I'm sure he will be happy to accompany Your Grace.'

And I am equally sure that he will not be happy at all. Despite my inability to picture him, I have a sudden, strong recollection of at least one outburst of rage. The Lucien of my memory does not seem especially . . . biddable. But perhaps the last eight years have mellowed him. 'Very well. I will take Lucien, and Letya. As to what clothes and so on –'

'Your Grace may leave the arrangements to me. I suggest . . .' Lancelin plucks a notebook from his pocket and flicks through the pages. 'I suggest that you leave the day after your eighteenth birthday. That will give us five or six weeks to prepare – the minimum necessary, I would say – and you should arrive just after the midsummer celebrations. Assuming . . .' he hesitates for the merest fraction of a breath, 'that you are proposing to go by coach.'

Unless I suddenly recover my ability to fly, we both know a coach is the only way I'll reach the Citadel.

'Yes. That is exactly what I'm proposing.' I speak firmly, hoping this is the last I will hear on the matter.

The next three weeks pass in a flurry of appointments: with dressmakers, dancing instructors, weapons masters. Over a year has passed since my last formal lesson in wielding a sword; as unlikely as it is that I will be required to use a blade, I choose not go to court unprepared, and spend hours working on my riposte. Any time not spent brushing up my skills is taken up by Lord Lancelin, hurrying through as much estate business as possible, any decision that might need my authorisation. I have to meet tenants, arbitrate disputes between minor lords and sign trade agreements. There is no spare moment for riding or reading. No time for worrying about leaving my home, about the court or about how I'm going to get there. But finally, one afternoon when the sunlight is glinting and dancing on the surface of the estuary below the castle, and the swifts are chasing each other about the battlements, I rebel.

'I'm going out.'

The dressmaker kneeling by my feet, pinning the hem of a lilac satin over-gown, glances up. 'But we're not finished, Protector. There's still the grey silk after this one, and then –'

'It can wait until tomorrow.' I gesture to one of the maids hovering nearby. 'Find Letya, tell her I'd like to go riding. And get me some comfortable clothes.' Thirty minutes later I am hurrying downstairs to the stables, in a baggy, faded old dress with coarse leggings underneath, my hair tucked up into a wide-brimmed hat like the countrywomen wear for working in the fields, and the prospect of at least a couple of hours of freedom ahead of me.

Letya is waiting just inside the main gate of the castle and brings her horse into step with mine. There's no need for me to speak: my friend knows when I wish to be silent. She's only a year older than me, and practically grew up with me. We even learned to ride together on the horses that carry us now. Animals on the whole are nervous around shape-shifters. They find our presence, even in human form, uncomfortable. But Henga and Vasta were introduced to me when they were too young to know any better, and Henga is used to the leather caparison she has to wear beneath her saddle to protect her hide. For perhaps an hour and a half, Letya and I ride contentedly through the maze of narrow lanes that thread the fields between sea, river and hills. But as the air grows warmer and more still, filled with the buzz and chirp of insects, the tall hedgerows either side of the path seem to close in on me.

'I need some space. Let's go to the beach.'

Letya hesitates. 'The beach? The one past the caves?'

'Obviously. What other beach is there nearby?'

'I'm not sure that's a good idea . . .'

'Why not?'

'Well –' she frowns down at her saddle, fiddling with a lock of blonde hair that has escaped from her hat – 'there have been rumours about cows going missing from the farms over that way. And one of the farm-hands. And then Fris told me that her cousin's friend was looking for moon-clams on that beach one night a few weeks ago and she heard this terrible, unearthly –'

'Enough.' I hold up a hand. 'I don't care what my maidservant's cousin's friend thinks she heard. And you should know better than to listen to gossip.'

'But the beach could be dangerous . . .' My glare must be effective, because my companion falls silent and screws her mouth up into a pout. Still, when I turn Henga's head towards the beach, she sighs and follows me.

By the time we get there – Letya, for once, has not spent the intervening minutes commenting on my reckless indifference to endangering my life – the low tide has exposed a wide expanse of black sand. I can feel the heat rising from the ground, but there is a breeze here, creaming the distant sea into a mass of white-crested waves. We set off, racing to the end of the beach, to where the sand tapers away and the land begins to rise into the cliffs that I see from my bedroom window.

Letya has the lighter horse and she accelerates quickly, glancing back to smirk at me over her shoulder. But I ride harder. Soon I draw level, then overtake. Still, it's only a narrow lead. So I lean low over Henga's neck, tightening my knees a little around her girth, urging her forward as loose strands of hair whip around my face. Her hoofs strike the hard, damp sand and every forward plunge jars my whole frame, but I don't care; the spar of rock that marks the end of the beach is so close now. Almost close enough for me to jump.

Faster now, Henga. Faster –

Henga bucks and twists and rips the reins from my hands, and there's space surrounding me, and salt spray . . .

The force of my landing drives the wind out of my lungs, sends stars wheeling across the blackness inside my eyelids.

Silence. Until –

Until I gasp, sucking in air, and the world comes back again. 'Aderyn?'

Every muscle and bone in my body throbs. When I open my eyes, Letya is crouching above me, her face white. 'Aderyn, are you hurt?'

'Um . . .' I flex my fingers and toes. 'Just bruised, I think.' The ache in my shoulder makes me flinch. 'What happened?'

'A sand mole. It shot up right in front of Henga, but I don't think she's injured.' A bit of luck, that – sand moles have fangs as long as my hand. Letya is scanning the ground anxiously. 'I knew we shouldn't have come here. And what is Lord Lancelin going to say to me, when he finds out?'

I sit up, wait for the dizziness to pass and try to stand. Too quickly – a bolt of pain shoots the length of my leg and sends me sprawling.

'Aderyn . . .' Letya holds out her hands. 'Here, let me help you.'

I shake my head. Letya is my best friend – my only friend, in truth – but she is flightless. One of the ruled, not one of the rulers, brought to Merl to be my attendant after my mother died. And I cannot safely touch her. Anything but the lightest brush of my skin against hers could hurt her. 'No. Not unless you have some spare gloves.'

My companion stiffens and huffs with irritation. 'Of course I do.' She pulls a pair of gloves from her pocket and drops them into my lap. 'Your Grace.'

17

I ignore her sudden attack of formality and drag them on. 'May I?'

'Yes! Just hurry up.'

I take hold of her gloved hands, she pulls me upright and, though I'm gritting my teeth with pain, I manage to limp to a large flattish rock nearby.

'I'll get help.' Letya wags a finger at me. 'Don't move, Aderyn, please. I'm going to be in enough trouble as it is.'

An unnecessary injunction; other parts of me are beginning to hurt almost as much as my leg. Letya and the horses are soon out of sight, so I switch my attention to the sea. The tide has turned. I try to distract myself from the pain by counting the seconds between each ebb and flow, thinking about the phases of the moon and the tidal bore on the River Rythe, in the west of our dominion; my father took me to see it once, many years ago. I don't notice the heavy grey clouds creeping across the sky, and the first fat drops of rain take me by surprise. There's still no sign of Letya. No sign of anything much: the beach seems oddly quiet, missing the usual flocks of sandpipers and true gulls. Wincing, I shift position, wondering where the birds have gone, wondering whether the sea will reach this rock before my rescuers –

Shock jolts me back to the present. To the inexplicable, impossible solidity of a rock dragon, lurking in the cool darkness at the foot of the cliff, its marbled grey-and-white scales blending into the background.

I hold my breath. Try not to blink.

Perhaps the creature hasn't seen me: its yellow eyes are sunken, rheumy, and it twists its head as if it can't quite focus.

It looks old, and more than half starved. But it could still crush me. Or rip me to shreds. Even its blood is toxic, supposedly. And yet . . . The creature stirs in the shadows, and the faint chime of metal on metal tells me my eyes aren't deceiving me. Someone has put an iron collar around the dragon's neck; a broken length of chain dangles towards the ground.

The path to the top of the cliffs is about five wing-spans away. Maybe I could crawl. Or maybe . . . Maybe I could transform. That's what I should try to do. I have no weapon. The dragon's scales are doubtless too thick for the creature to be hurt by my touch while I'm in human form. But as a swan, the power that runs beneath my skin is hugely magnified. And of course, I could fly away –

Too late. The sun breaks through the clouds, lighting up the rock on which I'm perched. The dragon sees me. Drops forward into a crouch. And as it begins thundering across the sand, and I sit there, paralysed by fear, some part of my brain starts screaming at me, cursing my own stupidity: would I really prefer to die here than shift my shape?

Apparently so. As the creature bears down on me I can do nothing but stare, mesmerised, at the strands of saliva dripping in anticipation from its huge jaws –

The black-feathered bird – a rook or a crow, I think – drops out of nowhere. Not a true crow – the bird's massive wing-span, the size of its outstretched claws, proclaim it to be a shape-shifter. The dragon feels the force of the crow's approach and skids round, bellowing in discomfort seconds before the crow first rakes its talons across the creature's back. Again and again the shape-shifter strikes, gouging the dragon's eyes, tearing its armoured hide, while the dragon snaps its jaws in vain, closing only on empty space. As the air fills with a mist of blood and the dragon's screams get louder and louder, I cover my ears and screw my eyes shut –

A thump – the earth shakes – followed by silence.

'You can open your eyes now.' The voice of a young man. But not one I recognise, even when I look at him. He's walking towards me, his feet stained red. I switch my gaze carefully to his upper half and I'm surprised – and embarrassed – by a flutter of admiration in the pit of my stomach. The boy's shoulders are broad, his chest and arms contoured: the result of much time on the wing, despite the fact that he can only be a little older than me. He's pale, for a member of one of the corvid families. But his hair and his eyes are a deep, iridescent blue-black. When he draws nearer, I see that there's an arrogance to his expression, as if he is well aware of his worth. 'Are you injured?'

'My horse threw me, and my leg –'

'Stay completely still.' Without asking he rips two wide strips of fabric from the bottom of my dress and wraps them around his hands. Then he starts running his fingers down my injured leg, carefully avoiding the exposed flesh of my ankle; he takes me for one of the flightless, who would be damaged by his touch. Blood burns beneath my skin.

'Stop it.'

He ignores my request. 'Can you move your foot?'

'A little. And I order you to stop touching me.'

'Order me?' There is a definite edge to his voice.

I straighten up as much as I can, given my aching muscles. 'I am the Protector of Atratys, and you're on my land.'

'You're the Protector?' He sits back on his heels, looking me slowly up and down. 'A Protector who is completely unattended? Who wears homespun and gloves like a servant?' He laughs – his face softens, for a moment – and shakes his head. 'If you're the Protector of Atratys, I'm a princess. Perhaps you're a liar, or perhaps you're concussed. Either way, you need to move from here: the tide is coming in. Be careful not to touch me.'

Ignoring my protests, he slides his arms beneath me, holding me out away from his chest as if I weigh no more than a bundle of feathers, and carries me up onto the tumbled boulders at the edge of the beach. From here I can see the castle, red-walled in the afternoon sun. Part of me wants to keep arguing with him, but I'm starting to feel sick, I've got sand in my hair and inside my clothes and somewhere along the way I've managed to lose a shoe. I really just need him to go away so I can cry in peace.

The boy is watching me. 'I'll send someone down from the castle to make sure you get home. You're welcome, by the way.' He gestures to the carcass of the rock dragon.

I can't repress a shudder. 'Thank you, Master Crow.'

'I'm not a crow. I'm a raven.' He grunts and pushes his hair out of his eyes. 'I'd like to know who managed to chain up a rock dragon. And why. And where it came from – they don't even breed around here.' Perhaps he takes my silence for fear, because he adds, 'Don't worry: you're not in trouble. No one is going to blame a child.'

A child? I open my mouth to reply, but he has already turned away and is climbing the path towards the top of the cliffs.

21

* * *

My tears have dried by the time Letya returns down the same path with servants and a doctor, but she stops short when she sees me and puts her hands on her hips. 'You were supposed to stay still! Look at the state of you. And bleeding too.' She gestures to the side of my head, then spots the dead dragon. Her eyes widen. 'What in the Firebird's name . . . ?'

'I'll explain later.' I put my fingertips to my head; sure enough, my earlobe is tacky with congealing blood. 'Just remember you're my friend, not my nursemaid. Or my bodyguard.'

Letya shoots me a long look. 'I'm your paid companion. The lord steward pays me to keep you company and to wait on you. I have certain . . . responsibilities.'

'So, you wouldn't – Ouch!'

The doctor stops prodding my leg. 'You've sprained your ankle, Your Grace. Quite badly, I'm afraid.' She gestures to two servants, who are waiting nearby with a sedan chair.

Once I'm settled I turn back to Letya. 'Do you think I look like a child?'

'What?' She frowns, confused. 'Of course not. Though . . .'

I raise my eyebrows, waiting.

'I suppose you do look quite young, dressed in those clothes. And covered in dirt. Why?'

'No reason. Would you really not come riding with me if Lord Lancelin didn't pay you?'

My paid companion crosses her arms and tilts her head. 'Well, I probably would. I've grown quite fond of you over the last five years. Besides, there's a certain entertainment to be gained from watching you risk your neck on an almost weekly basis.'

I've never talked to Letya about why I have to take such risks, but I suspect she understands. 'I love you too, Letya. I'll love you even more if we can keep this a secret from Lord Lancelin.'

She chuckles, a little reluctantly. 'He won't hear of it from me.' But her gaze returns to the dragon carcass. 'Did you kill it? Or did someone –'

'It died. It was old, I suppose.' A wave of nausea makes my head spin; I sink back into the cushions behind me, glad of an excuse to end the conversation. I don't want to talk about the raven boy. I don't want to think about his identity, or whether I'm ever going to see him again.

Please let him not be who I think he might be. Please . . .

Two

For the next three days I keep to my rooms, doing as the physician orders, nursing my bruised ribs and swollen ankle. I do not tell Lord Lancelin what happened, and he does not ask me about it. I wonder if he's trying to make a point: at the Silver Citadel I won't have the freedom to go where I like or wear what I like. Left in peace, I spend some of my time working through the various letters and petitions that Lancelin gives me. But every time my attention wavers I am back on the beach, watching the rock dragon, wondering where it came from and who could have wanted or needed to fasten an iron collar around its neck. How, indeed, such a thing was even possible. I turn the problem over and over until my head aches.

The dark-haired raven boy unsettles my dreams.

By the fourth day, the thought of remaining in my apartment for one moment longer makes me want to scream. After breakfast I get dressed, bully my doctor into giving me a crutch and limp off towards the library. Not to read – it's a cold, hard-edged room, furnished more for display than comfort – but to consult the chronicler, who is usually at work there. I want to find out if there have been any other reports of rock dragons in the dominion, and I need a more reliable source than my maid's cousin's friend. But as I reach the library entrance I hear voices through the half-open door. Not the chronicler: Lord Lancelin, and someone else. Someone angry.

'You had no right. Without consulting me, without even considering what I might wish, to make such a promise on my behalf –'

'And why should I not?' Lord Lancelin's tone, in contrast, is calm and measured. 'Do you not owe Her Grace your allegiance? To say nothing of your duty to me.'

'But it's not fair! You may have been content to waste your life in the shadow of the late Protector's wing, but I have other plans. I want to see more of the world – the world outside of Solanum. And there are so many improvements we could make to our own estate, if you ever spent any time there.'

My heart sinks – I know that voice. Even from here, I can tell that he is gritting his teeth. And pacing: footsteps ring on the marble floor. I force myself to lean forward, to peep through the crack between the door and the frame, and have to bite my lip to stop myself from swearing.

It's him. The young noble from the beach. The raven boy. Properly dressed now of course, in a red velvet tunic, dark leather trousers and knee-length boots. His hair is sticking up in tufts as if he's been dragging his fingers through it. And he's scowling. 'And what shall I say to Mother? After you've neglected her for so many years, that I am to be sent away again? To serve a Protector who is barely worthy of the name? And now you tell me that the idiot girl won't even travel as a swan, that we have to go by coach like a couple of flightless commoners –'

'Nevertheless –' Lancelin begins to reply.

But I'm too angry to wait to hear what he says. I push the door open and hobble forward.

'Nevertheless, you will do me the courtesy of accompanying me to court and remaining there until such time as I release you from my service. I do not imagine that will be far distant.'

The boy's mouth has fallen open, and his black eyes are wide with disbelief. There is such shock and dismay on his face that the urge to laugh bubbles up through my fury.

My steward moves forward and bows. 'Your Grace, may I present my son: Lucien, Lord Rookwood.'

I nod infinitesimally, drawing myself up as much as I can. 'Lord Rookwood.'

Lucien shuts his mouth and bows. 'Your Grace, I . . . Of course. I will endeavour to be of service.'

There's not really much else he can say. But I want to make him suffer for a bit longer, so I limp around him slowly, as if inspecting him, thinking about whether I should tell his father how we met the other day, how he disbelieved me and then abandoned me on the beach. It's very tempting. But better to have him in my debt, perhaps. I look him up and down one last time, enjoying my power. 'Very well. You may leave us, Lord Rookwood.'

Lucien bows again, nods at his father and makes his escape. My shoulders sag.

'Nicely done, Your Grace.' Lancelin's smile gives way to a sigh. 'My son's service abroad appears to have taught him many things, but perhaps not when to hold his tongue.'

'He's correct though, isn't he?' I look my steward in the eyes. 'If the people could choose a Protector, they wouldn't choose me. Despite all the books I've read, all the papers I've studied, I'm still . . . unprepared. To put it mildly.'

'You're young, my dear. But you are your mother's daughter; the people would hold you in affection for her sake, if nothing more. Besides, you have plenty of time ahead of you to learn.'

I hope he is right.

Later that night, alone in my rooms, I take off my clothes and look at myself in the full-length mirror. With my petite frame and my black hair I favour my mother. Though she could transform into a black swan, whereas I transform – or I used to be able to transform – into a white one, like my father. I have his blue eyes too, and the same stubborn-set jaw. Twisting round, I examine the scars on my back, running my fingers across them as far as I am able. It's been five years – no, closer to six – since the attack that left my skin so disfigured. And nearly four years since I last tried to shift my shape. Given the danger I put myself in at the beach, perhaps it is time for me to try again. I take a deep breath, ignoring the bubble of panic beneath my ribcage, and close my eyes, recalling what my mother taught me. I focus on the current running underneath my skin, the power to transform that only nobles possess, that sets us apart from the flightless majority. I envisage the contours of my body, the glowing outline that would be left if you stripped away flesh and bone, concentrating on its flexibility, thinking my way into that state of pure energy that sits between each physical configuration.

And I can feel that it's working, that my form is beginning to alter, to melt from one shape to another, the bones lightening, lengthening, the skin morphing into feather –

Pain flares from the ragged nerve endings in my scarred skin. Terror follows, as bitter and violent as I remember. As swift as the hawks – two transformed nobles – who dropped out of the clouds and fell upon my mother and me, killing her and ripping my back apart.

Two hawks. There in the sky, above us. I know what I saw.

I was talking to my nurse, because my father's grief had rendered him speechless.

You're mistaken, my lady. It can't have been hawks, because there are no hawk families, not any more. You saw some other noble in flight, and you're confused, my poor pet . . .

But I'm not confused. I know what I saw –

My chest seizes up and, as I struggle to breathe, the glowing outline in my head disappears. My human body reasserts itself and snaps back into existence, solid and undeniable, leaving me gasping naked on the floor.

Lord Lancelin's words come back to haunt me: *You are, for all practical purposes, flightless . . .* As I lie there, the carpet rough beneath me, I wonder for the first time whether I'm making a mistake. For years I've chafed against my father's restrictions, against the physical walls of the castle and against the wall of silence he retreated behind. I've fantasised about leaving Merl and seeking justice for my mother. But to risk my dominion, my life, for what may be no more than a dream . . .

Will I be able to survive in the world that I'm about to enter, if I can't even prove that I am truly one of them?

It's late, and I'm tired. My injured ankle is throbbing. I crawl into bed with the question still unanswered.

After another two weeks of frenetic activity, the day of my departure finally arrives. Lucien and I are standing in Merl's great hall, ignoring each other; we've not been alone together since that afternoon on the beach.

A servant approaches. 'We're ready, Your Grace.' He bows and returns down the stairs towards the landward side of the castle, where the coaches are waiting. Three for our baggage and a fourth for Lucien's servant, Turik. Despite my arguments, Letya is insisting on travelling in this coach too. There are armed outriders to accompany us, though they will have to turn back at the border with the Crown Estates: Protectors are not allowed to bring their own guards within the monarch's personal domain. Lucien and I are travelling together in a fifth coach so that he can start my 'lessons' in court etiquette and so on. The journey could take as little as two weeks or as much as three, depending on the weather and the state of the roads, so I'm torn. Now it comes to it, I don't particularly want to get to court any sooner than I have to. But the thought of an extra seven days shut in a small space with Lucien leaves a bitter taste in my mouth. It's a relief when Lord Lancelin appears.

'Your walking stick, Your Grace.' He hands me a – totally unnecessary – cane. 'It will not do to overtax your strength until you are fully recovered from the rock dragon's attack.' Lancelin's idea: to exaggerate the severity of the injury I suffered at the beach in order to provide me with an excuse for travelling to the Citadel by coach rather than flying. Humour glints in his dark eyes. 'Send me word if there is anything you need, and try not to worry: the court has its pleasures as well as dangers. I'm sure you'll be well prepared by the time you get there.' He raises an eyebrow at his son. 'Lucien. I trust you will conduct yourself appropriately. Be wary, take care of Her Grace and remember you are representing our house.'

'Of course.' Lucien kneels for a moment and receives Lancelin's blessing, before standing and embracing his father. 'I'll wait for you outside, Your Grace.'

Left alone with my steward, I look around the main hall of the castle, drawing out the moment of farewell, trying to ignore the voice in my head that is whispering to me that perhaps I will never return. In the bright morning sunlight, the stained-glass windows cast fractured rainbows across walls, carpets, furniture, every item almost as familiar as my own face. 'Take care of everything while I'm gone.'

'Of course, Protector. My only desire is to serve.' A form of words, but I actually think Lancelin means it. 'Here, I have something for you.' He produces a small leather-wrapped packet from his pocket. 'I suppose I should have given it to you yesterday, but –'

'I understand.' My birthday celebrations had been somewhat understated, overshadowed by packing and leave-taking. I unwrap the package. Inside is a slim rectangular box about the same size as my hand, made of some polished wood, with a small silver catch. I open it. 'Oh . . .' What I'd taken for a box is actually two frames, hinged together. A diptych. On one side, a painting of Merl castle. And on the other –

My family. My parents, and me as a small child, sitting between them. All three of us smiling and staring directly out of the portrait. As I study the image a memory darts to the surface of my mind: my feet dangling from the sofa on which the three of us were seated, my father's leather-clad legs on one side of me, my mother's green velvet skirt on the other. My hands held warm inside theirs. I swallow down the lump in my throat. 'I'd forgotten about this.'

'Your father gave it to me before he died. But I think it should be yours. I've had them reframed, as you see.'

'It's beautiful. Thank you.' I take a last look at my parents before closing the diptych and clutching it to my chest. 'I suppose I should go.'

Lancelin bows and leads the way downstairs. The coaches are there, the horses wearing large blinkers to distract them from my and Lucien's presence. The footman opens the door of the lead carriage and I get in. Lucien is waiting, sitting with his back towards the driver. Once the servant has put up the steps and shut the door, he leans forward.

'May I speak frankly, Protector?'

I study his face; he looks tired, but the haughtiness I noticed the first time we met is still there. 'I don't suppose I can stop you, princess.'

His lips twist in what might be a smile. 'Well, then. My father has asked me to help you, and I will, to the best of my ability. So here is the first lesson: not everyone in the kingdom is happy with the way things are. There are plenty of people who would seize your power if they could: you are a target. You will be in danger from the moment we leave Merl. So it would be best if you learn not to take unnecessary risks.'

31

'Like riding without a guard?'

'Exactly. You were alone on that beach. I could have killed you, if I'd been minded to. Letya could have killed you.'

'Ridiculous. She's my friend. We spend hours alone together every week.'

'Then why did she leave you there?'

'Because she is flightless, as you know very well. She had gone for assistance. She could not have helped me safely on her own. And she depends on me. Why would she kill me?'

'Perhaps because someone persuades her to. Or pays her more money than she can earn from being your companion. Or applies some other sort of pressure. The only person you can truly trust is yourself, Your Grace. No one else.'

'What about you, Lord Rookwood? Am I not to trust you either?'

The coach starts suddenly, throwing me forward, and Lucien catches me by my upper arms. Holds me there as his gaze roams my face.

'Well, my lord?'

He releases me and shifts to sit further away. 'I said no one, Your Grace, and I meant it.'

I turn to the window. This is no grand gateway. The causeway that links Merl Island to the mainland is used by the flightless: servants, people making deliveries and so on. The marble and gold are reserved for the castle, and especially the landing platform that stretches from the first floor out above the sea. But there is a statue here that I've always loved, of a swan and a cygnet. The limestone is worn and pitted by rain. I watch it as long as I can, until my vision is blurred by tears.

* * *

For the next few days I don't get any lessons; both Lucien and I are too busy trying not to vomit. Neither of us has ever travelled by coach before, and the motion of the vehicle makes my stomach heave. I wouldn't mind so much if it was just me, but every time Lucien turns pale and retches I can imagine what's going through his mind: *All this, just because the stupid bitch refuses to fly . . .*

Occasionally we're allowed to get out of the coach, when the horses are changed or when we arrive at one of the infrequent inns along our route. At first no amount of rest helps with my travel sickness, but finally my body seems to adapt. The nausea passes, and I'm able to start eating again, to take some notice of the lands through which we are now travelling. Lucien rallies too, and on the seventh morning after leaving Merl he takes down a roll of paper from the luggage rack above his head.

'What's that?'

'Your next lesson. I think you need to understand more about the family you're part of; from what my father told me, the late Protector thought it best to keep you in ignorance in order to –' he shrugs slightly – 'protect you.'

'And I'm sure my father was right.' I don't think he was right at all – I wish every day that he had taught me, not just about Atratys, but everything I needed to know, instead of leaving me to study mostly what I chose: how to read the night sky, how to fight, how to ride. But Lucien needs to learn his place. I wave a hand towards the paper that he's starting to unroll. 'You can show me that in a minute. First, I have a question. What did you mean, the day we left, when you said I was a target?'

'Isn't it obvious?' The faint lift of his eyebrow mocks me.

'Humour me.'

'Very well . . . You are a target in two ways. First, you're a target for those in your own family –' he taps the paper roll with his forefinger – 'who would prefer the considerable wealth of Atratys to belong to someone else. I think this will help you understand.' There is a sort of folding table attached to one side of the carriage; Lucien pulls it down and spreads the roll of paper out, securing it with books at either end.

'It's a family tree.'

'Quite. Here is the ancestor of the current royal family: Cygnus I. As you can see, his son, Cygnus II, had a lot of children. A lot of potential claimants to the throne.'

I peer at the names and dates written in cramped letters across the paper: countless births, marriages, deaths. My finger finds the current king, my uncle, and beneath him two names: my cousins Aron and Odette. Next to the king is his younger brother Rothbart (my father), and below him, me. Third in line to the throne. No – second. Aron has been disinherited. 'So, if something happens to Odette, I would be offered the crown.' My nausea threatens to return at the thought of such a choice, so much responsibility. 'And what happens if I die?'

'If you die now, the Dominion of Atratys will revert to the crown, to be resettled as the king sees fit.'

'I suppose I'd better hope my uncle doesn't plan to kill me.' I speak flippantly, hoping for reassurance. But Lucien does not oblige me.

'Indeed. He may, of course, be planning to use you as a marriage prize, to be auctioned off to the highest bidder. One of your many cousins, perhaps.'

Which includes Lucien, if this family tree is correct. I suddenly wonder about Lancelin's motives when he suggested that I should employ his son as my clerk; perhaps Lucien was being honest when he told me not to trust him.

My companion grins, as if he guesses my thoughts. 'You're extremely valuable, Your Grace. Dead or alive.'

Bastard. I push the roll of paper away and lean back against the cushions. 'And what's the other way? You said there were two ways in which I'm a target.'

'Well, you may be a target for those who seek not a reallocation of power, but to tear down the whole rotten edifice entirely.'

'There are such people?'

'Yes. Among the flightless, and even a few among the nobility. Rebels, who would free the ruled by removing those who rule them.'

'But that's not fair! You know the changes my parents introduced in Atratys. Schools for the poorer flightless children, and the free infirmary at Hithe –'

'All well and good. But if you lose control of the dominion, if you're replaced by someone who wants only to exploit . . . You've seen the people of this area. There's no hope left in them.'

We left Atratys behind more than a day ago and are now passing through the Dominion of Brithys; the rumours I'd heard did not prepare me for the wretched state of the villages along the road. I remember the blank gazes of a flightless family we passed this morning, standing outside a cottage with unglazed windows and half the thatch missing from the roof. The children didn't even have any shoes.

Lucien shakes his head and looks out of the coach. 'Why do you think these roads are so bad?'

I frown, following his gaze, wondering at the change of subject. 'I don't know. Are they especially bad?'

'Yes. Full of ruts, without proper surfacing . . . They're barely roads at all. Not compared to the roads in Frianland. But nothing is done to fix them, because nobles so rarely travel by road. And the flightless don't count.'

For couple of minutes neither of us speaks. Half of me wants to shut the conversation down, to order him into another coach. But I just can't help myself. 'You're a noble too.' I drag the family tree nearer. 'And we're related: your name is here, just like mine. You're part of this . . . rotten edifice you seem to despise. And I actually know someone who is flightless. Letya and I spend most of our time together. I rely on her –'

'She tells you what to do?'

'Of course not. But I like having her near me.'

'Like a pet?'

I feel the anger flaming into my face. 'I won't have you speak of her like that. She's my best friend.'

'Really? So did you ask Letya whether she wanted to leave Merl and come with you to court? Do you ever ask what she wants, instead of issuing an order and just expecting it to be obeyed?'

'Do you ask Turik?'

'He is my servant, and I don't pretend otherwise. It seems to me that Letya is neither one thing nor another. I pity her.'

Is it anger, or guilt, that makes me itch to slap his handsome face? 'At least I know better than to touch Letya or any other flightless without asking permission.' My mention of his behaviour at the beach makes him blush. I push on. 'Why are you here, Lucien? You obviously despise me. Why not let me go to court alone, let me make some mistake that will get me killed? You seem to regret not killing me when you had the chance.'

'Stop being so dramatic. I don't despise you; I hate what you stand for. What we stand for. But I –' He breaks off, begins to put away the family tree. 'There are plenty of people who might do a worse job than you. For the sake of everyone who lives in our dominion, I'm going to try to keep you alive.'

Until when? Until he decides I'm no longer useful?

He's staring at me, his dark eyes full of shadow in the dim light, as if he's trying to see inside my head. Or perhaps he just expects me to be grateful for his forbearance.

I close my eyes and try to sleep.

At least we're lucky with the weather. Most of the next week is sunny, and we travel quickly over the dry ground. I spend some more time studying the family tree, trying to memorise names and relationships, though Lucien won't tell me much about the people I'm shortly to meet. He says I'll remember the details better after I've seen them in the flesh. His silence makes me nervous, and I wonder what he is trying to conceal. Occasionally I ask him about family history, probing for information that might help me find out who killed my mother, but he either doesn't have the answers I'm looking for, or doesn't want to tell me. The rest of the time – as much time as I can stand – he teaches me about the intricate conventions governing behaviour at court. For instance, as a lower-ranking noble, Lucien should not address me without express permission. I don't trouble to conceal my pleasure at that particular rule.

When we're not studying, Lucien and I contrive to ignore each other by reading. Lucien, I discover, prefers novels, while I work my way through a book on astronomy. Trying to understand some of the mathematical concepts is a welcome distraction, though one which proves less and less effective as we get nearer to the court. I find I cannot concentrate. The Citadel and its inhabitants cast an ever longer shadow across my mind, feeding my doubts about the wisdom of my decision, eating away at my confidence. But we've entered the Crown Estates; I can't turn back now even if I want to. I don't mention my worries to Lucien. Instead I spend some of my time just watching him read; he smiles more, forgets to glower. Observing him passes the time quite pleasantly, until one morning when he catches me staring and I force myself to stop.

I've brought a travelling Battle set with me. We play twice – both times I win, capturing Lucien's eagle – before my companion tells me he doesn't particularly care for the game.

So we go on, peacefully, if not comfortably, until our luck runs out. The weather changes. Sunshine is replaced by rain, coming down in sheets, slowing our progress to a crawl as the carriage wheels and the horses become mired in mud. Eventually we stop, stuck fast.

Lucien puts aside his book and glares out of the window, cursing under his breath. He's craning his neck round from his backwards-facing seat, trying to see the road ahead, but I'm not about to invite him to my side of the coach. Instead, I keep my eyes fixed on the pages of my book, trying to concentrate on a description of the elliptical motion of the planets, until the muttering reaches such a pitch that I can no longer pretend to ignore it.

'Is there something you wish to say, Lord Rookwood?'

He turns on me. 'This is ridiculous.'

'The weather? It's annoying, certainly, but hardly ridiculous, given the time of year. Crex is often a rainy month.'

'You know very well what I mean. We should be flying.'

I take a deep breath, gripping my book tightly. 'I know your feelings on the subject. You made them quite clear that day you were talking to your father in the library.'

He scowls at me. 'I thought only children or the flightless eavesdropped on other people's conversations.'

'I wasn't eavesdropping,' I retort, unable to stop myself, 'and if I was, it's your fault for talking so loudly.'

'You don't have to justify your behaviour to me. You obviously don't care what I think –'

'No, I don't.'

'But you should care what others might think. Or what they might do. And in case my father didn't make it clear enough: if it's discovered that you can't fly, you will be banished, and you will be killed. You're risking the entire dominion because of this . . . this inability to let go of the past.' He runs both hands through his hair in what I now recognise as a gesture of irritation. 'For the Creator's sake, Your Grace, it's been six years since your mother died. Surely by now –' He breaks off, staring at me.

I don't know what he sees, but what I feel is cold. Cold, as if a hoar-frost has settled on my skin, as if the air is freezing inside my lungs.

'You weren't there. You didn't see what those monsters did to her. You don't know about the nightmares, about –' The coach lurches forward as the wheels are freed, and there's a ripping sound. I glance down: I've been clutching my book so tightly I've torn the pages loose. A few float onto the rug at my feet. 'You don't –' My voice cracks, so I try again. 'You don't know anything.'

Lucien doesn't reply. There's an odd expression on his face, but I'm not going to waste my time trying to decipher it. Instead I pick up the loose pages and try to reassemble my book. It's hard because my hands are shaking, and the paper is so thin and translucent – as light as down – that I'm scared of doing further damage. I'm still busy with my task when I hear Lucien's voice.

'Look: we're nearly there. The Silver Citadel, and the city of Farne.'

I look out of the window. In the distance is a pale grey castle, looming over a city that seems to plunge down the sides of a steep valley towards the sea. I'm about to ask why it's called 'Silver', but then there's a break in the clouds and the sun comes out and I understand. In the late afternoon light, the castle glitters. 'It's beautiful.'

My companion leans back in his corner of the coach and shrugs. 'On the outside. But I wouldn't swap the entire place for a single stone of Hatchlands.' It's the first time I've heard him mention his home, and the intensity in his voice surprises me. But the next moment he smiles slightly. 'Try not to look so worried, Your Grace. You have an excuse for arriving by coach. And the king has no reason to suspect any more permanent difficulties. After six weeks we can return to Merl, if you wish.'

Six weeks. Too long for comfort, but maybe not long enough to find the answers I'm searching for. The clouds have shut out the sun again. I watch the darkening castle draw closer.

Three

We have to drive around to the back of the castle, to the entrance used by servants and flightless visitors. I feel the curious stares burning into my back as soon as I leave the carriage, and I'm relieved I have my cane for support. I wish I could hold on to Lucien, but my clerk does not offer me his arm, and I am too proud to ask. We walk in silence up wide stone steps, following the guest master, an elderly man upon whose uniform the Cygnus coat of arms gleams in silver thread. The tap of my walking stick echoes in the dimly lit stairwell. Behind us are six heavily armed guards in black chainmail, their faces concealed behind visors; *Dark Guards*, they're called, according to Lucien. I wonder whether all visitors are 'honoured' with such an escort. The staircase goes on and on; through doorways I glimpse kitchens and offices and grey-clad servants everywhere. But eventually we emerge into the dazzle of the entrance hall on the main floor; the glow of hundreds of candles, reflected in crystal, marble and glass, makes me squint. The Cygnus family motto is carved in gold inlaid letters a wing-span tall around

the edge of the ceiling: FROM OUR SERVICE COMES OUR POWER.
It's a reference to Cygnus I's origins – he was steward to the
previous ruling dynasty – that neatly glosses over his ruthless
seizure of the throne. I'm still twisting my head to look at it
when Lucien stops suddenly.

'Wait!'

'My lord?' The guest master pauses, head bowed slightly.

'We've had a long journey, and Her Grace was recently
injured. She will go straight to her apartment.'

'But His Majesty wishes to greet Her Grace without further
delay. Your servants have been sent to prepare your rooms for
you, my lord.' He turns away and continues walking, and we
have no choice but to follow. Doors are thrown open ahead of
us and suddenly we are in a room full of people. Lucien drops
back so he is walking behind me; even though I can just see
him out of the corner of my eye, the sense of being alone takes
my breath away. But the guest master is still moving forward,
so I have to keep moving too. The voice inside my head is
getting louder and louder: *You shouldn't be here, you shouldn't
be here, you shouldn't be here* . . . More guards are stationed,
watchful, in the gallery that runs around the top of the room.
There are murmurs from the brightly coloured crowd around
me, tones of surprise and scorn. Someone laughs. The sound
is hastily smothered, and I try not to react, keeping my gaze
fixed, focusing on what's ahead of me: a huge stained-glass
window depicting a swan with outstretched wings, and below
that a dais, upon which is set a throne of dark wood, ornately
carved with gold-edged feathers and the Cygnus coat of arms.
But I can't stop the blood flaming into my cheeks.

Finally we reach the space in front of the dais. The guest master hits the marble floor with his staff.

'Her Grace, Lady Aderyn, of the House of Cygnus Atratys, Protector of the Dominion of Atratys, and Lucien, Lord Rookwood.' The throne is large enough to seat two easily – the Kings and Queens of Solanum have always ruled in mated pairs – but currently there is a man lounging there alone. I hand my cane to the guest master and bow, sinking low before stretching my arms backwards to imitate wings – the correct procedure upon first meeting a reigning monarch. I sense Lucien, still at my shoulder, performing the same gesture.

For a few minutes the king stares at me, and I look back at him. I can see the resemblance to my father – the same blue eyes, the same stubborn mouth, the same long limbs and ash-blond hair. But the man in front of me is older, corpulent – for all he looks so small, compared to the enormous gilded throne – gaudily dressed in blue silks and velvets. His fingers are decked with heavy rings, and he wears an ornate gold and sapphire coronet on his head. It fits well with the opulence of his outfit, but it is not the Crown of Solanum. That – the ancient Crown of Talons, a plain iron band dark with age and set with talons carved from some polished black stone – sits on a worn plinth next to the throne.

The king shifts on his seat, waves a hand and servants approach us both, bearing silver goblets. I take the drink and, as my uncle raises his cup in a toast and takes a sip, mimic his action. The liquid in the goblet – some sort of wine? – is rich and spicy; tears spring to my eyes and I have to suppress the urge to cough. The king smiles slightly, but it seems I am allowed to put the cup down; the servant holds out the platter.

'So. My flightless niece has finally come to visit me.'

Flightless? The word – the instant realisation that I have been betrayed – lands on me like a blow. Stuns me: every muscle in my body weakens. Behind me, Lucien gasps softly. But the king is still talking; I force myself to conceal my distress.

'I am glad to see you again, Aderyn. It has been too many years since my poor brother shut himself away at Merl. I was much grieved to learn of his death.'

Somehow, I do not believe him.

I take a deep breath. 'I thank Your Majesty. My father's death was a misfortune for all of his people. The condolences we received from you and the queen were of great comfort.' These are the words Lucien told me to say, the words we agreed upon. 'But,' I continue, 'I am not flightless, uncle. I cannot imagine who would have told you such a lie.'

A risk, to challenge the king the moment I arrive in court. But if I lose this game we are apparently playing, I will lose everything.

'Really?' He leans back, studying me. 'And yet you arrived by coach . . .' Another swell of laughter from the courtiers around us, slightly louder than before.

'On the recommendation of my doctors, Your Majesty. I was injured recently. The coach journey allowed me to rest, and to see more of the kingdom. It is true that I have not cared much for flying since witnessing my mother's murder,' there is a ripple of whispered conversation behind me as I speak the word, 'but I am not flightless.'

A young couple moves towards the dais. The girl, wearing a simple white dress, is beautiful enough to take my breath away.

She has no crown – her mass of silver-blonde hair is stunning enough without adornment – but I know she must be the Princess Odette. Which means the boy next to her must be her brother, Aron. Both have the same hair colour, the same high cheekbones and sensuously moulded lips, though there is a stubborn arrogance to the set of Aron's jaw that is missing from his sister's face. He is dressed all in black – a striking contrast to his shock of hair – and it takes me a moment to see the empty sleeve pinned to the front of his tunic.

'Well, niece, here are your cousins come to meet you. Odette –' I bow, and the girl inclines her head and smiles at me, a little uncertainly – 'and Aron.' I bow to the prince, but he ignores my gesture, his expression contemptuous.

He turns to his father. 'My cousin claims she is not flightless. But Atratys is second only to the Crown Estates in importance. Our main ports are there, most of our iron mines, our forests . . . If she is indeed worthy to be Atratys's Protector, and to stand second in line to the throne, let her prove herself. Let her transform, if she can.'

Panic twists in my gut like a knife as a cold sweat springs up between my shoulder blades. If I am asked to disrobe here and now, to shift my shape –

The king is shaking his head. 'Now, my son? In front of the entire court? I would not hear of putting your cousin to such a test.' My shoulders sag with relief, although I'm sure my uncle is more concerned with his own reputation than my modesty. 'There is, however, another way in which Lady Aderyn may convince us of her status.' He looks at me and then points to the servant still standing nearby with the goblet. 'Burn him.'

'Father!' Aron steps forward. 'That's not what I –'

'But you're right, my son. There are rules. So you will oblige me, Aderyn, by touching this man's skin.'

Horror forces me to speak. 'But, Your Majesty, custom forbids –'

'Forbids?' The king's tone is soft, incredulous. 'Am I not the king? Do I not make the customs?'

I hesitate, just a fraction too long. 'Of course, Your Majesty.'

He raises one hand and twists it back and forth, looking at the play of light on the coloured gemstones of his rings instead of at me. 'Rumour travels more swiftly than a coach. Shall I tell you what rumours I have heard in the last few weeks?' Without waiting for a reply, he continues. 'It is rumoured that you are not who you say you are. That my niece was killed in the incident that claimed her mother, and that a flightless imposter was set in her place. That my brother, in his grief, was somehow deceived.'

'But you can't possibly believe that.' Despite myself there's derision in my voice. 'It's not true.'

The king lifts his eyes to mine. 'Then prove it.'

I turn to Lucien, looking for help, for a way out. But he shakes his head – a tiny movement – and lowers his gaze.

'We are waiting,' my uncle murmurs. One of the guards near the throne shifts, his fingers straying towards the handle of the throwing axe hanging by his side.

The servant is staring at me. His eyes are full of fear – but what can I do? I take the tray he is carrying and pass it to Lucien. The man is wearing gloves and a tunic with long sleeves.

47

'Roll up your sleeve. It will hurt less.' The man obeys and holds his arm out towards me; he's trembling. 'I'm sorry,' I murmur. Finally I place my hand against his bare skin, wrapping my fingers around his wrist. The man winces as the heat grows, his mouth clamped shut to keep from crying out, but the pain soon becomes too much. He begins to groan, fighting the urge to pull away from me, and I can smell the hair on his arm burning –

'Enough.'

I let go of the servant. He stumbles backwards, crying, clutching his arm to his chest, his flesh blistered and red. My stomach heaves.

No one is laughing now.

'Very good, niece. I, of course, had no doubt of your identity, so like your mother as you are. But it is as well you have settled the question, for the benefit of those more . . . suspicious than me.' My uncle smiles as he lies; he can't hide the trace of disappointment in his voice. 'You see, Aron? Her Grace is clearly not flightless. As for the injury that kept her from making her journey here as a swan, it is, I assume –' his smile twists – 'very nearly healed.'

My cousin's face is cold. 'Indeed. I look forward to seeing her fly, before long.'

As Aron turns away towards the side exit, the king holds his fingers out to me; I step onto the dark blue carpet of the dais and force myself to kiss them. 'I am glad to have you here, my dear. I have been considering your marriage. As Aron reminded us, the Dominion of Atratys is important, and we must make sure its future is assured.' He waves a hand towards the assembled courtiers. 'There are several of your cousins here who have already expressed their affection for you.'

Affection for my wealth and lands. I wonder which of the men staring at my back he is planning to auction me off to.

My uncle pats my arm. 'Go and rest now, niece. We will speak further at the feast this evening.'

I bow again and step off the dais, taking my walking stick from the guest master. The courtiers part as I move towards the door at the far end of the throne room. Again there are whispers and sideways glances; again I pretend not to notice. Another servant – one of the guest master's underlings, I guess – is waiting to conduct me to my apartment. We go up staircases and along corridors and all the time I stare straight ahead, keeping my eyes fixed, my face set. Then we are shown into in a room, and the servant is bowing and handing us some keys, and the door closes and finally, finally I am alone with Lucien.

'I can't stay here. I can't.' The room is huge but somehow there doesn't seem to be enough air; I rush to one of the windows and fumble with the catch, trying to force it open. 'We have to get out of here, go back to Merl. He's mad, he must be –'

'Your Grace –' Lucien catches my wrists in his hands, casting me a look full of warning – 'you're tired after the journey. You should rest.' He presses a finger to his lips, then walks softly back towards the door, his feet making no sound on the thick carpet, and flings it wide. The servant who brought us up here is crouched on the other side; shock sends him sprawling backwards onto the floor. Lucien kicks him. 'Go and fetch the Protector's waiting woman. Then get out of here.'

'Yes, my lord. My apologies –'

Lucien slams the door on the man's grovelling and returns to where I'm still standing. 'Next lesson: this place is full of spies.' He stands close, leaning in towards me, his voice low, almost a whisper. 'I don't know if that idiot is working for someone, or whether he was just hoping for any information he could sell, but it doesn't matter. Most of the lower servants, the housemaids and so on, can't read, and they're not allowed to learn, but they can still listen. You have to watch your tongue at all times, even if you think you're alone. And always remember the first thing I taught you.'

'Trust no one.' Either here or at home, seemingly. 'Who would have told him I was flightless, Lucien?'

He shakes his head. 'I don't know.'

No more do I. Some guest who attended my father's Last Flight, perhaps? But I was in deep mourning – no one would have expected me to fly. Someone who lives at Merl, then? I twist my hands together, running through names in my head.

'Your Grace, you passed the king's test: you should let my father worry about whose words provoked it. I'll write to him before this evening's banquet. But in truth, rumours of all kinds – plots, potential invasion, rebellion – have grown rife in the last couple of years. The king is ruled by fear. The kind of fear that leaves no room for right judgement. Or mercy.'

There are sofas and chairs scattered about the room, all gilded wood and rose-pink satin. I realise how badly my legs are shaking and sink down onto the nearest pile of cushions. 'But what he made me do . . . Why didn't you warn me?'

'I didn't want to scare you.' He sighs and sits down next

to me. 'Though perhaps I should have done, if it would have kept you at home. The king seems to take delight in suffering; there are stories about what he does in private to flightless women –' He breaks off as I press a hand to my mouth, my stomach churning. 'They may be nothing more than stories. But I wish the king was more like your father. It's hard to believe they were brothers.'

'It's impossible. My father was a good man, a kind man, and the king . . .' Bile rises in my throat as I picture my uncle, sprawling on the throne of Solanum, defiling it with his cruelty and greed. As I imagine him wearing the Crown of Talons, degrading that ancient symbol of our people by his unworthiness. I push the image away and think of my father instead, and pretend that he is here next to me, protecting me. Make-believe; but it gives me a little strength. 'And what about my marriage?'

'I doubt he's going to try to rush you into anything; the longer he can keep all the potential suitors dangling, the more favours he'll be able to extract. And remember, you're of age. He can't make you marry anyone.'

In theory. In practice, who knows what kind of pressure my uncle might seek to apply? I sink my head into my hands, digging my nails into my scalp and screwing my eyes shut. In that instant, the chance that I can do some good here – that I can somehow avenge my mother, or make amends for my father's long, lonely years of grief – seems so remote as to be ridiculous. 'What am I to do?'

I feel Lucien shift position next to me, but he doesn't attempt to answer my question.

51

There's a knock at the door and Letya walks in, followed by housemaids carrying pails of steaming, scented water. 'Time for a bath, Your Grace. You need to rest and change before the feast.' She turns to Lucien, her hands on her hips. 'Your servant is waiting for you, my lord. In your usual room, he says.'

Lucien accepts his dismissal without argument. He stands and bows to me. 'I'll see you in a couple of hours, Your Grace.' And then he is gone, and Letya – her hands protected by fine leather gloves – is unbuttoning my dress, humming one of our favourite childhood songs under her breath.

A warm bath in front of a large fire soothes my muscles, although it can't calm my mind. My bedroom is as enormous and grand as my sitting room. Too grand, after the faded comfort of my rooms at Merl. But the view from my windows is breathtaking: they open onto a sheer drop, where the castle is perched above the top of a fjord. Rising up from the centre of the fjord, some distance away, is a tall tower built of the same glittering stone as the castle. And in the other direction are mountains, crowded together like a mouthful of sharpened teeth. White-water streams rush down their sides, and I can see the blue-green edge of a glacier cradled in between the highest snow-capped peaks. Shape-shifters don't feel the cold particularly, but I notice that Letya has on a new dress of thick lavender wool. As I wait for my hair to dry, she selects a gown for me to wear to the banquet: flowing green silk, high to the throat, caught in at the waist with a band of gold embroidery that is repeated along the hem. Sleeveless, as is the fashion for evening. The train sweeps behind me as I walk, and Letya reminds me that it will need to be pinned up if there is dancing. She plaits my hair and twists it, clipping it at the nape of my neck. Once I've hung my mother's emerald earrings from my earlobes she walks around me, her head tilted.

'You'll do. Just try to look less terrified. Remember who you are.'

She's right, as usual.

'Where's my sword belt?'

'Noblewomen don't carry weapons. And it will spoil the line of the dress.'

But I'm not just a noblewoman. I'm a Protector; I'm entitled to wear a sword. 'Trust me: it will help me – and everyone else – remember who I am.'

Letya smiles. 'True. And at least it's gold. It won't look completely out of place.'

I fasten the belt around my hips and place my mother's sword into the scabbard, as Letya fusses with the fall of my skirts. Finally she surveys me again and nods approvingly.

'I wish I could stay here and have supper with you.' I stretch out my hand, careful not to touch her, just in case. 'I feel so . . . exposed.'

'Come, it's just a banquet. There's nothing to be afraid of.' She grins suddenly, deepening her voice. 'Unless it's the Dancing Demon . . .'

I laugh, remembering how Letya and I convinced my somewhat gullible nursemaid that Lord Lancelin's apartment was haunted by a demonic presence from the underworld. He was less than amused when he found her 'cleansing' his favourite possessions by throwing them on the fire. 'We got into so much trouble. But at least we were together; if only you could come to the feast too.'

'Don't worry about me. I'll have my supper in my own room and spend the evening sewing and reading, which will suit me very well.'

There's a knock at the door. Letya passes me my walking stick (we've agreed that it would be as well for me to keep using it, at least for a few more days), then opens the door to admit Lucien. He's dressed in a sleeveless grey silk tunic and trousers and has the gold chain of the House of Anserys around his neck. The clothes suit him; the grey brings out the hints of deep blue in his hair and eyes, and the style of the tunic shows off the muscles in his arms. 'Are you ready? The first bell has been rung.'

'I'm ready.' I straighten my shoulders as we leave the relative safety of my apartment.

My clerk looks me up and down; his gaze is appreciative in a way I hadn't expected, and I clear my throat, suddenly self-conscious. He inclines his head towards me. 'You look . . . appropriate,' he murmurs. 'Letya has good taste.'

A spike of annoyance punctures my embarrassment. 'You're too kind, my lord. I'll be sure to pass on the compliment.'

There are other nobles here, all moving towards the great hall, where the feast is to take place. Most are lords and ladies of Solanum. Some are visitors from other realms. Lucien tells me that a couple with vivid scarlet hair are members of an ibis family from the Kingdom of Gerda. A tall man with blue-tinged skin and green hair – a peacock apparently – makes eye contact with me and bows his head.

I grip my cane more tightly. 'I don't know who anyone is . . .'

'It doesn't matter. The king appears to have accepted you, and you outrank everyone but the royal family. Over the next few days, most, if not all, of the nobles here will approach me for an introduction. You don't need to do anything.' Two more men and a woman duck their heads as we pass, and Lucien's lips twitch. 'I suspect I'm about to become extremely popular.'

When we enter the hall I can't help gasping. It's by far the largest room I've ever been in, larger even than the throne room: double height, with a floor of red-and-white marble tiles. The ceiling is elaborately vaulted and surmounted by an octagonal glass lantern. Huge arched windows are set into the upper half of each wall, the glowing stained glass bearing the same symbols over and over. Symbols of power. The shield of the royal family of Cygnus sits in the centre, flanked by the shields of the families (my mother's included), that have controlled Solanum for the last two hundred years: the seven Houses of Cygnus. The lower walls are covered in tapestries that show the history of the royal house. I spot an image of Tavin of Chenorys taking the throne as Cygnus I, after the War of the Raptors wiped out the House of Aquila (who could transform into eagles) and most of their related families. There are tables laid out in the other half of the hall, the embroidered cloths almost obscured under masses of silverware, but the courtiers are gathering here, nearer the entrance, talking in small groups and glancing towards the doorway. The ever-present mail-clad guards are dotted around the perimeter. Lucien guides me towards the centre, and people make space for us.

'Why are we waiting here?'

'After the second bell the royal family will process in; no one else can sit down until they are seated. And then we take our seats in order of rank. You'll be seated at the highest table, with the prince and princess.'

'But what about you?' My voice comes out louder than I'd expected; the nobleman next to us raises an eyebrow. I move closer to Lucien. 'You're my clerk – can't you sit with me?'

He smiles grimly. 'My temporary status as your clerk doesn't alter my rank.' A bell sounds from somewhere up above us, and the people around me start to move, lining up either side of the pathway from the door to the high table. Lucien whispers, 'After dinner there will be a concert in the long gallery; I'll join you then. Just try your best not to say or do anything idiotic in the next couple of hours.' The smile disappears; his expression is grave. 'Remember, the most important thing here is not your future; it's that of Atratys.' He nods at me curtly and retreats into a crowd of lower-ranking nobles as the harpists in the gallery above the main door begin to play.

The king enters first, wearing white silk and a diamond coronet, a much younger woman on his arm – the new queen, I guess. She's very beautiful. Her hair is white with one long black streak and her skin has the silvery-grey tint characteristic of heron families. In her white silk gown, she could almost be carved out of ice. Beneath her coronet her face is impassive, though a slight puckering of the skin between her brows suggests she takes little pleasure in her surroundings. Still, as she passes she notices me looking at her, and gives me a quick, tentative smile. The king and queen are followed by Odette, wearing a more ornate version of the white dress she had on earlier, and then by Aron, still in black. I expect the prince to go past, but he stops next to me, holds out his remaining arm.

'Cousin.' My eyes widen in surprise, and he smirks.

But I remember Lucien's words.

For Atratys then.

'Cousin.' I bow my head – as small a gesture as I think I can get away with – and lay my hand lightly on his arm. Together we move towards the high table.

Four

The banquet is long and tedious. On one side of me is Aron, who once we are seated ignores me, either eating or chatting to the woman on his left. On my other side is a middle-aged, slightly jowly man who introduces himself as Patrus, Protector of the Dominion of Brithys. Like most of Cygnus I's descendants he is blond, but his yellow, rounded eyes and the feathering of tawny hair at his temples and forehead indicate owl blood in his lineage. Patrus tells me first that he is widowed, secondly that he is struck dumb by my beauty, before proceeding to talk endlessly about his dominion: how many houses he has, how many hunting lodges, how many acres of land. How many noble families owe him fealty. I would be tempted to ask him how many of his people starve to death each year – the poverty I observed while travelling through Brithys is still fresh in my memory – if only he left any silence in which I might speak. At least the food is delicious and plentiful: dish after dish is placed before me, many of which I don't recognise. But I know the fine, tall-stemmed crystal glasses from which we are drinking were made in Atratys. Proud of my dominion, I take a little more of the wine than I am used to. It makes my eyelids heavy, and I'm glad when the last course – sun-baked plums from southern Olorys – is finally removed, and the king and queen rise from the table.

Aron turns to me, interrupting the long-winded compliment Patrus has embarked upon. 'Come, cousin.'

I take his arm with relief.

From the great hall we process to the long gallery. Even here, rank and etiquette still prevail. There seem to be divisions within the gallery marked by different coloured marble floor tiles – pale pink at the lower end of the room, deep purple at the upper – guarded by servants in black and silver. Lower-ranking nobles are applying to these servants; sometimes they are admitted into the next area of the room, nearer to the monarchs, sometimes they are not. At the furthest end of the room, where tall arched doors open onto a terrace, a quartet of flightless musicians are playing lutes. It's hard to hear them over the hubbub of conversation as people mingle and stroll around.

Aron leads me to a small sofa near one of the doors. 'Let us sit for a while, cousin; you seem weary. Besides, I don't think either of us needs to worry about not using our legs enough.'

I glance at him, suspecting a veiled reference to my ability to fly – or my lack thereof – but his expression is neutral. We sit, and he turns to face me.

'The sword belt is a nice touch. Is it merely jewellery, or is there an actual blade attached to that hilt?'

His tone takes me by surprise, and I answer more sharply than I intend.

'A functioning blade, cousin. And I know how to use it.'

'I'm sure, though I doubt it will help you here. What did you think of Patrus? Scintillating, isn't he? And supposedly well ahead in the bidding.'

'Bidding?'

'For you.' He laughs – at my expression of shock, I suppose. 'It's not phrased quite like that, of course. My father has let it be known that he thinks you ought to marry, and various interested parties have, quite coincidently, been moved to offer His Majesty certain lands, or treasures, or what have you.'

There's a servant hovering nearby.

'So thoughtful of my uncle, to concern himself with my future.'

'Quite.' Aron winces and shifts position slightly, as if the loss of his arm still pains him. 'Of course, you could refuse. In theory.' He stretches his legs out in front of him, crossing his ankles. 'Think of it from my father's perspective. He was convinced you were flightless; it does happen, even in the best families. And Atratys is so very well endowed with natural resources and convenient harbours. To take Atratys from you and have it directly under the control of the crown would be desirable. But if that's not possible, why not sell you to another Protector in return for one or two of your most important ports, or mines?' Aron grins. 'His logic, you must admit, is flawless.'

I grip the back of the sofa tightly with one hand. 'So who else might I be sold to?'

'Well –' Aron scans the room, counting on his fingers – 'of the five other dominions, you've met Patrus of Brithys. Olorys will be inherited by Siegfried Redwing. A brainless beauty, at least according to my father, but even if you want him you can't have him: he's betrothed to my sister. Grayling Wren is twenty and will inherit Fenian –' he points at a slightly stooped young man hovering near the musicians – 'but it's a poor dominion, and his father is a wastrel. He probably can't afford you. Lancorphys will be inherited by Nyssa, Lady Swifting – the woman on the other side of me at dinner. Nyssa is a chatterbox, though amusing in small doses. But even if you did like her,' Aron continues, 'Protectors have to marry so as to allow the possibility of producing children. Whatever your personal inclinations might be.' He shoots me a questioning look, which I ignore. 'And then there is Dacia. Protector Arden fancies himself a military genius, and he's already married. Still, I wouldn't be entirely surprised if his rather unattractive wife met with an unfortunate accident now that he's seen you.' He pauses, observing my face. 'Wishing you had stayed at home in Atratys, cousin?'

Panic rises in my chest as the prince watches me, head tilted, as if he is determined to force me to answer.

'May I have something to drink? It's very warm in here.'

Aron clicks his fingers at the nearest servant. 'Iced cloudberry tonic for Her Grace.' After a few moments she returns with a silver goblet. The liquid inside is cold, fragrant and slightly herby; a pleasant antidote to the soporific effect of the wine. My cousin is still silent.

'My father wished me to come to court,' I lie. 'And if my uncle truly thought I was flightless, then it is just as well that I have proved I am not.'

Aron purses his lips. 'You've proved you're not flightless. You haven't yet proved you can fly. I wouldn't count your cygnets before they've hatched, cousin. You might still be disinherited.'

I grit my teeth, repressing the urge to pay the prince back for his needling by kicking him. But I can't resist trying to wipe the smirk from his face. 'And you would know all about that, of course. Tell me, cousin, did your father think about challenging the Decrees? Looking for a way around them? Or did he allow you to be cut out of the succession without so much as a second thought?'

For a moment Aron's cheeks flush, and he narrows his green eyes. But his scowl dissolves into laughter. 'A nice try, Protector. But I lost my arm two years ago. There aren't many insults I haven't already heard. Still, if you think of some new way of abusing me . . .' He half shrugs. 'The Elders spoke, and the Decrees are what they are.'

'So I've been told, Your Highness.' I sigh; there was just a trace of bitterness in his voice. Just enough to make me feel ashamed. 'Have you found any other exercise you enjoy, instead of flying? I started to ride, after my mother's death. It took me a long time to train a horse to carry me, but it was worth it. I have –' An enormous yawn swallows the end of my sentence. 'Forgive me; it's several nights since I've slept in a proper bed.'

'You were saying, you have a horse in the stables, named Henga.' Aron smiles slightly. 'There are no secrets in the Silver Citadel, Aderyn. And yes, I ride too. We will ride out together, once you've had a chance to settle in. But for now –' Aron looks over my shoulder and his lips twist into something like a sneer – 'Rookwood is trying to attract your attention. I hope your choice of horse is better than your choice of adviser.' He rises and inclines his head – his eyes not leaving mine – before disappearing through the door onto the terrace.

One of the black-and-silver-clad servants is bowing to me. 'Lord Rookwood wishes to approach Your Grace.'

The request makes me want to laugh, but I nod, trying to look dignified, and wait until the servant has walked Lucien to the sofa and gone away again.

'Good evening, my lord. Did you enjoy the banquet?'

My clerk sits down without waiting to be asked. 'Why didn't you send for me? You know very well I can't enter this part of the gallery without permission from you or somebody else.'

'How was I supposed to know when you didn't tell me?'

Lucien sniffs and crosses his arms. 'You look haggard.'

I raise an eyebrow, staring at the dark shadows beneath his eyes. 'I'm sure I'm not the only one. Are we allowed to leave?'

To my relief, he nods. Once I've bid goodnight to my uncle – he is deep in conversation and waves his hand at me vaguely – I am free to go.

Lucien accompanies me out of the gallery. There are Dark Guards stationed at intervals along the corridors, and servants going back and forth between rooms, so I wait until we are in my apartments to tell him what Aron said. He dismisses it.

'He enjoys making people squirm, but he's telling us nothing we didn't already know.' From the corner of his eye he glances at me. 'My father and I have both spoken to you about the risks you face here, Your Grace. Aron uses his tongue as a weapon, but he doesn't have any real power, not any more. And he's nothing like his father.'

'He seems to dislike almost everyone.' I look up at Lucien to see the effect of my words. 'He definitely doesn't like you.'

My clerk shrugs. 'There's no particular reason why he should. Though truly, I pity him.' Lucien is frowning, his gaze clearly fixed on some scene playing out in his head, and I wonder what exactly he is remembering. 'Try to be pleasant to him, if you can. The purpose for which Aron was raised has been taken away from him. And a flightless noble is –' He breaks off, blushing.

A flightless noble is an object of scorn. A source of shame. I know that is what he was going to say.

Under the weight of my stare, Lucien tries to make a recovery. 'As a flightless noble, Aron is in danger. He survives – is tolerated – because he is still a prince. But he is no longer relevant. It can't be easy for him to have you here.' He opens the door to leave.

'He wants me to go riding with him. There's no harm in that, is there?'

Irritation flickers across Lucien's face. 'Of course not. And there's no need for you to seek my approval for such things: as long as your leisure activities don't take up all your time, you may do as you wish.'

He's talking to me as if I'm a child again. 'I'm not an idiot, my lord. Do you know how many hundredweight of wood Atratys exports to the other dominions each year? Or the cost of the machinery we are importing from Ryska to support our iron-mining industry? Because I do.'

'I'm glad to hear it. But it's late to be discussing mining. You should go to sleep.'

I grit my teeth. 'So should you, Lord Rookwood. Send Letya to me.' I slam the door on him. The effect is a little spoiled by my train getting caught, and by my having to open the door again to free it. But it doesn't matter. Lucien is already gone.

I'm soon in bed. It's comfortable – a soft mattress, lavender-scented linen – but I would give almost anything to be back at Merl right now. Left alone, I run over Aron's words in my head. His comments about me having to fly, and about the king's desire for Atratys . . . whatever Lucien says, the prince could hardly have chosen a better way to scare me.

The diptych that Lancelin gave me is on the table next to the bed. I pick it up and study it, and my anxiety about the future is swallowed up in a surge of longing for the past: for my parents, and my home.

But my home won't help me now. I grip the frame tighter, forcing myself to remember not the happy cocoon of my early childhood, but my mother's broken body lying where she fell on the causeway at Merl. My father's screams of grief and rage when he found us there. To remember why I am here.

Anger displaces my longing. I'm convinced that the answers I'm seeking lie here at the Citadel, the beating heart of the kingdom. I'm not leaving until I've found them.

Over the next few days, I begin to wonder why Lucien mentioned leisure activities, since the schedule he organises leaves me no time to myself at all. Each day is taken up with endless meetings: with wardens, controllers, governors, lords and ladies of this, that and the other. I smile and try to be charming, to promise much – in terms of trade and so on – while actually agreeing to very little. Some of the people knew my father, or mother, or both, so I try to steer the conversations, to discover who were my mother's friends, who were her enemies. But Lucien ruthlessly puts a stop to such recollections: 'Her Grace finds it difficult to talk about her parents, given her recent loss – you understand, of course.' And so my visitors nod and move on to less personal topics.

Each evening is much the same as my first: three hours of having to make conversation with the same people I made conversation with the night before, trying to ignore the false compliments and insinuations of the men competing to become my husband. Lucien seems to enjoy his evenings more. When I catch sight of him, seated at one of the lower tables, he always seems to be smiling or chatting happily with someone, and after dinner he often spends time with Lady Nyssa, the heir to the Dominion of Lancorphys. He smiles at her too.

Each night, after Letya thinks I'm tucked up in bed, I get up again and try to transform.

I haven't been able to stop worrying about what Aron said: I've proved I'm not flightless, but not that I can fly. There's some part of me that begins to hope, as the days go on, that I won't ever have to prove it. But still, I'm afraid. So each night I take off my nightgown and try to relax enough to shift my shape. And each night I fail. I just end up reliving the afternoon that my mother died: the ache in my wings as we tried to escape, the slash of talons along my spine. But I never get past it.

By the time we've been two weeks at the Citadel, I'm exhausted. But finally my opportunity comes: an Ember Day, a day of abstinence and contemplation. A day, importantly, on which no business may be conducted. A day off. Tired as I am, I force myself out of bed early, consult the sketched layout of the castle that Lucien had made for me, and make my way to the library.

Clutched in my hand is a slip of paper that I found among my father's things after he died. There's not much on it, just a name and an address in my father's handwriting: *Deeks (?) Flayfeather, Crowsnest Court, off Long Ship Street, Lower Farne.* I failed to find any reference to a Flayfeather family in our library back home, but I'm hoping for something more here, in the capital of the kingdom, in the castle where my father grew up. The paper was in among letters he'd written seeking information regarding my mother's murder – before he stopped looking. Maybe that means it's important.

The library is empty when I arrive. Or mostly empty: I can make out the scratch of pen on paper coming from some nook or other, but the sound is too distant for me to worry about. I begin searching for the catalogue books. I've read that some libraries outside of Solanum organise their contents by subject. But here in the kingdom, family is everything. History, science, discovery – each event is related back to the people involved. When I reach the catalogues, chained to their shelves, there are five thick volumes for the letter 'F'. I drag the right volume onto the nearest reading desk and begin scanning the pages. The lists of names are handwritten in cramped letters, but eventually I find what I'm looking for: *FLAYFEATHER: minor branch of House of Accipta Olorys.* See *ACCIPTA: Raptor War; ACCIPTA: mercenaries . . .*

The entry goes on, but I don't bother to read the rest. I don't need to. Members of the House of Accipta were able to transform into hawks.

Hawks. To know after all these years that I hadn't misidentified our attackers, that I wasn't somehow to blame for my father's failure to find them . . . I glance down at the slip of paper, blinking away the tears that have sprung into my eyes. My hands are shaking. Is the name I'm looking at that of one of my mother's killers?

'May I help you, my lady?'

I spin around, crumpling the piece of paper quickly into my fist. A soberly dressed woman, a book in one hand, a pen in the other, is watching me narrowly. 'May I help you?' she repeats. 'I am the chronicler here.'

I see now that she has the same ink-stained fingertips as our chronicler back in Merl, but this woman's pinkish-grey hair marks her as a member of a dove or pigeon family.

'I'm looking for recent family chronicles. The last twenty years or so.'

'Of course.' She bows and begins leading me to some large bookcases in the far corner of the room. 'We have up-to-date chronicles for all the leading families. All branches of Cygnus, naturally, and Ardrieda, Corvus –'

'What about Accipta?'

In the silence that follows my question the wind whispers around the castle. I remember the whispering wing-beats of the hawks, and shiver.

'In the last twenty years? I think not, my lady. That house was destroyed in the War of the Raptors. Their chronicles ended more than two hundred years ago now.'

'But surely, the children –'

'No.' She points at a section of shelves. 'All our records on the war, including eyewitness accounts, are here. Accipta and Aquila and almost all related families were entirely wiped out. Anything else you hear is just scurrilous rumour.' Her tone suggests personal affront. 'History books don't lie, my lady.'

I want to point out that surely that depends on who is writing them. But the chronicler's gaze has strayed to the Protector's ring on my left hand, and her eyes widen as she realises who I am. So I incline my head in thanks and make my escape, anxious to avoid any questions.

I consider returning to my rooms. I'm going to head into the city, to try to find the address on the paper. Maybe find this Flayfeather too. I'd be more comfortable with my mother's dagger in my belt. But either Letya or Lucien or both of them might be waiting for me in my apartment. Lucien would doubtless pry into my reasons for leaving the Citadel, or try to forbid me to leave. Letya would probably want to go with me. But taking a risk myself is one thing; I'm not going to put my friend in danger. Instead I make my way alone towards the main entrance of the castle. I haven't got far before someone calls my name.

'Aderyn! Cousin . . .'

It's Odette. She hurries down the steps, dressed in white as usual, her silk skirts billowing behind her. But before she reaches me she stops short, seeming suddenly shy.

'I just wondered, cousin, whether you are on your way to the sanctuary?' She gestures to the cloak I'm wearing. 'I was going to go with Aron, but he is . . . he is not in good spirits today.' She looks at me a little anxiously.

'Um . . . I'm not going to the sanctuary, not yet. But I'll go with you later, if you'd like.'

'Yes, thank you.' She falls into step beside me. 'Where are you going?'

'Out for a walk. Into the city.'

'The city?' Her voice rises in surprise. 'But why?'

'Well . . . my father grew up here. He told me about some places he used to visit, so I thought I would try to find them.' A complete lie, but Odette seems to accept it. 'Do you know where Long Ship Street is? It's in Lower Farne –'

My cousin is already shaking her head. 'No. I've never been into any part of the city.' She glances at me and blushes faintly (though I'm trying to conceal my astonishment). 'I wasn't supposed to be queen, you see. So learning about the kingdom, and the flightless and so on . . . it never seemed important. And I'm not like Aron; I hate politics, and studying papers, and having to make decisions.' Lowering her voice, she leans towards me. 'I know there are things wrong, in the kingdom. But I don't know how to fix them. My husband will though. I hope.' Her colour deepens. 'Have you heard I'm to be married, cousin? To Lord Siegfried.' She grins suddenly. 'I don't know yet how much we have in common, but I shall enjoy looking at him. He's amazingly handsome.'

'Is he? I'm glad for you.' I'm not sure what else to say. We part in the main hall, and I take the staircase down to the courtyards behind the castle, to the stables and the delivery yards. From there, I make my escape into the city.

The broad, paved roads of Upper Farne are pleasant enough, filled with the sturdy stone mansions of lower-ranking nobles and wealthy merchants. There are gardens and trees, and I walk along more than one bustling shopping street. Still, I can't enjoy my freedom from the Citadel. There are Dark Guards here too, stationed on corners or patrolling the arcaded avenues. None of them seems to pay me any attention, but I put up the hood of my cloak and hurry onward, downward.

Gradually, the city around me changes. The roads become narrow lanes, many with open drains running down the centre, stinking and buzzing with flies. The buildings are of wood instead of stone, jammed together, and so tall that they block out much of the sky. I can no longer see the Citadel, and I begin to lose my sense of direction. There are no guards here, but lots of people. Ill-dressed, ill-shod – ill-fed, by the looks of them. I have to start asking for help to find my way. Those I approach reply helpfully enough, but they stare at me as though they're not really sure who – or what – I am. I press on. I have the feeling that I'm being watched.

Eventually I reach what one smallish boy tells me is Long Ship Street; there is no street name that I can see, but the inn at the corner of the road is called 'The Long Ship', according to its painted sign. I make my way past a few dingy shops, their wares – not-so-fresh fish, tallow candles, an assortment of pawned items – displayed on rickety tables. The rest of the street, as it twists its way down to the shore of the fjord, seems to be made up of badly maintained tenements erected around tiny, dank courtyards. There are piles of rubbish everywhere.

An elderly-looking woman is sitting nearby on the steps of one building, staring at me.

'Would you be able to show me where Crowsnest Court is?'

She doesn't answer. But there's no one else nearby. I check

my pockets – wishing I'd thought to bring more money with me – and show her a silver half-sovereign. 'I said –'

'I heard. And I might.' Her gaze switches to the coin in my hand. 'Yes, I might.'

Once I've dropped the coin into her palm, careful not to touch her, she gets up, beckons to me and begins to walk further along the street.

I follow.

The woman leads me off into a maze of even narrower alleys, nothing more than walkways between the tenements. It must be nearly midday, but down here it's twilight. At least the permanent gloom prevents me from seeing exactly what I'm stepping in. A few more minutes, and she stops in a dead end, pointing up at a soot-stained building rising above us on three sides. 'Crowsnest.' She leers at me. 'So pretty you are. What business have you here?'

'I'm searching for someone, by the name of Deeks Flayfeather. He lives here, I think. Or used to.'

'Searching for someone, is it?' She shouts something up at the building – I don't catch the words – and a moment later a red-headed, thickset man appears from one of the doorways, quickly followed by a younger man with a woman clinging to his hand. They both look half-starved, and the woman has a black eye. My guide summons them nearer. 'This fine lady's looking for a man name of Flayfeather.'

As the people close around me, my heart begins to race. I don't know why I'm scared – if I touch them, I'll burn them – but still, nerves jangle my stomach. 'I can pay you.' I hold up another coin. 'I just want to talk to him.'

The older man holds his hand out for the coin, looking me up and down as he does so. 'I heard as there was a fellow lived here by that name, a good five years back, maybe more. A fellow from Olorys. But he went off one day, up Farne –' he jerks his head in the direction of the upper city – 'and he never come back.'

I catch my breath: Olorys again. And possibly around the time of my mother's death.

The man steps nearer; there's greed in his eyes. 'Now, maybe I can tell you who he was going to see up there. Maybe I can even tell you what happened to him.'

I check my pockets: empty, apart from my key. 'I've no money left. But if you tell me what you know, I'll send a servant with payment later.'

'What about that ring you've got there?' He points at the gold Protector's ring.

I shake my head. I'm doubtful that the man has the information he's trying to sell, but even if he did, I would never give him my mother's ring. 'Payment later, or not at all.' I straighten up, trying to look braver than I feel; as I do, there's a tug on my skirt. The elderly woman has got a piece of the fabric between her hands.

'Fine silk – worth a lot of silver. We could take this instead.'

I snatch my skirt away from her. 'Thank you for your help. I'm going to leave now.'

The man laughs. 'Are you? Think you know your way?'

He's right – I have no idea how to get out of these alleys, let alone back to the main part of the city. As I turn around, hoping to catch a glimpse of the Citadel, I realise that a crowd has gathered at the entrance to the courtyard.

73

I'm trapped.

'I'm warning you . . .' I hold up my hands. 'I'm a noble. I don't want to hurt you –'

The elderly woman cackles. 'Noble, is it? To tell such lies, with such a pretty face. Whoever heard of a noble on foot, and in Lower Farne?' Her smile disappears. 'Whoever heard of a noble caring whether we hurt? We rot here, and die here, and they do nothing. And if you don't give me that ring, you'll die here too –'

She makes a grab for my fingers and screeches in shock and pain when her skin touches mine.

The other people – there is a crowd gathered around us now – back away a little, but they don't run. The red-headed man has produced a knife and a hammer from inside his clothing; he passes the hammer to his younger companion. But the woman holding his hand tries to drag him away.

'Let 'er go, Moss, please . . .'

'Stand your ground, Moss,' the older man shouts. 'If we let her go, she'll bring the guards down on us.'

'I won't, I promise –' I fling my arms wide, cursing my inability to transform, hoping I'll be able to grab one of them as a hostage, hoping I can do something to protect myself before Moss smashes my bones with the hammer.

Shouts, from the entrance to the court. The noise distracts me, and as I turn back I see the older man, his face full of hatred, his knife raised –

Five

Seemingly from nowhere, the axe spins through the air and buries its blade in the man's back; he drops the knife, groans faintly and collapses at my feet. Silence, for a heartbeat, followed by screams as two Dark Guards begin hacking their way through the crowd, and the flightless inhabitants of Crowsnest Court trample each other in their panic to escape.

'Your Grace, this way –' A third guard is in front of me, waiting.

'But . . .' I wave helplessly at the mayhem around me.

'Your Grace – now, if you please.'

I follow him. At the entrance to the court we have to step over a body. It's the young man the others called Moss, the hammer still clutched in his hand.

A minute's running and we are back on Long Ship Street – it seems wide and filled with light, compared with the maze of alleys behind – and Aron is waiting for me, sitting astride a tall chestnut horse, more Dark Guards around him.

'I can't help you up.' He is using his one hand to hold the reins. 'You'll have to put your foot in the stirrup.'

I clamber awkwardly onto the horse, careful not to touch the animal with my bare hands. Settling myself behind him, I put my hands on Aron's waist as he wheels the animal about and sets it trotting back up the street.

I'm safe.

A wave of nausea and exhaustion makes my head spin; I cling on to my cousin more tightly and close my eyes.

'You can get down now.'

I look around. We're back at the stables behind the Citadel. Aron has brought the horse to a halt next to a mounting block; I swing myself down. Manage, just about, not to stumble, despite my shaking legs.

Aron jumps down and hands the reins to a waiting groom. 'Come,' he says to me. 'You've provided enough entertainment for one day.' He gestures up at the windows of the castle; I guess there are other nobles watching, and shame makes me feel sick. 'Come and have something to eat.'

I keep my gaze lowered and follow him inside.

Aron leads me to a part of the castle I've not yet been to, one of the upper turrets, I think. There are Dark Guards either side of the door, but Aron knocks and is quickly admitted by a servant into a sort of tiled entrance hall. More stairs, winding up inside the tower, and then I'm in a circular sitting room, all silver gilt and fine white lace, ringed by tall glazed doors.

Odette is there. She jumps up as we come in. 'My dear cousin, what were you thinking? Come and sit down.' She leads me to a sofa and pushes a cup of warm chocolate into my hands. All of me is trembling now, but the sweet liquid soothes me a little.

'I'm sorry. I didn't mean to cause so much trouble.' A lump rises in my throat and I dash away a tear. 'And those poor people –'

'You mean the ones who were literally about to kill you?' Aron's voice is dry.

'Only one of them really wanted to kill me, I think.' I shudder as I remember the hatred on the red-headed man's face. 'If the Guards could have just scared the others away –'

A disbelieving shake of the head. 'Did you not want to be rescued? If you like, I can take you back there . . .' He laughs at my silence. 'Don't worry, cousin. I enjoyed being useful, for once. Today is the anniversary of my removal from the succession, and your little escapade was just what I needed. Besides, they were flightless and they threatened you. They broke a Decree. I've asked the guards to take no further action once the crowd has been dispersed – no point in adding more grist to the gossip mill – but by law every one of them should hang.'

A statement of fact. I can't tell from his voice whether or not he thinks that outcome would be desirable.

'Aron, don't.' Odette pours me some more chocolate and passes a plate of biscuits to her brother. 'It was lucky I mentioned to Aron where you'd gone. Though I suppose the Dark Guards would have reported what had happened. Eventually.'

I almost choke on my chocolate. 'They were following me? Then why didn't they intervene?'

'Oh, they wouldn't, not without a direct order from the

77

king. Or from Aron, because they like him.' She flashes her brother a smile. 'But really, cousin, what were you doing in such a place?'

I glance from Odette to Aron. I'd like to tell them the truth. They've both grown up here, just like my father did. They might be able to help.

But I can't ignore Lucien's warning. *Trust no one*, he said . . .

'I was looking for a place my father talked about. From when he was a prince here. But I got lost.'

'Your father mentioned Long Ship Street?' Aron is frowning at me. 'What could have possibly taken him there?'

I think quickly. 'A theatre, he said. Though I may have misremembered the street name.'

My cousin shrugs. 'You must have done. There are a couple of theatres in Upper Farne that I suppose your father might have visited. Though I can't imagine our father going with him . . .' He pauses, considering. 'You could ask Lord Hawkin. He's lived here his whole life. And he loves to talk.'

I set my cup down on a little silver table nearby and catch sight of the dirt on my skirts. 'I should change. Thank you. Both of you.'

Odette returns my smile. 'I'm glad Aron found you. And I've noticed you don't have your walking stick with you any more.'

Perhaps I discarded my prop too soon. 'My ankle is much stronger now.'

'So would you come flying with me? I know you said you don't care for it, but perhaps if we went together?'

Is this a trap? But Odette looks excited more than anything else, and I wonder whether she's lonely, despite having her brother here. 'My back.' I touch the bare skin at the top of my shoulders. 'It's the scar tissue, you see. I mean, I can transform, of course. But it hurts. I prefer not to.'

'Oh. Of course.' The excitement has gone, replaced by pity.

Aron sits forward in his chair, as if he's actually interested in what I've just said; his usual demeanour is one of boredom, or contemptuous judgement, or both. 'Too bad, sister. She'll have to come riding with me instead. If Rookwood allows her, that is.'

Lucien. It's impossible he won't find out about my 'escapade'. I take leave of my cousins, wondering exactly how angry he is going to be . . .

The answer is – not surprisingly – very angry indeed.

'I really cannot understand it, Your Grace. We are not in Atratys. This is not Merl Castle. And we've only been here two weeks. Two weeks! I can't believe you would put yourself in such danger.' Lucien was waiting for me upon my return from Odette's apartments. Now he is pacing up and down my sitting room, casting furious glances in my direction. The glances are a substitute for words; I have shamelessly refused to dismiss Letya – I know very well that Lucien won't say everything he really wants to say in front of her – so my clerk is having to control his tongue. Clearly, he's struggling. 'And you tell me you just went for a walk, and got lost?'

He doesn't believe me. But I stick to my story. 'Exactly. Perhaps, my lord, if you had allowed me a single moment of leisure in the last two weeks, I would not have been driven to such an extremity.' I lift my chin and give him back glare for glare.

'Well.' He scowls. 'Perhaps, Your Grace, you should have mentioned your concerns to me before deciding to sneak out of the castle.'

'Or perhaps,' Leyta observes, 'you should have thought a bit more of my lady's comfort before filling all her time up with meetings.'

Lucien flushes. But though he clearly heard Letya's words he seems determined not to acknowledge her, and looks only at me. 'You could have been killed. What would have become of Atratys? Would you betray your mother's legacy so lightly? And what of the flightless that did die this afternoon, all because you wanted to take a walk?'

His words – and the disappointment in his eyes – sting me. I can't tell whether I'm angrier at myself or at him. 'You forget yourself, Lord Rookwood. Whether you like it or not, I am Atratys's Protector.'

He opens his mouth, and I can almost see his retort forming: *Then perhaps, Your Grace, it is time you behaved like it.* But the words remain unspoken. He bows and leaves the room.

Letya draws breath. 'Well –'

But I interrupt her before she can give vent to what I suspect will be some fairly astringent criticism of Lucien. She sits in silence while I explain the real purpose of my visit to Lower Farne, only pressing her lips together and shaking her head slightly when I tell her how close I came to disaster. She's still silent when I finish.

I wait.

'Well,' she says eventually, 'I suspect there's no point in me scolding you. But Lord Lucien is right, you know. You want to find out why your mother was killed. All well and good. But you're Protector now. Surely she would say that was more important?'

She would. But I can't be the Protector – I can't look to the future of Atratys – until I'm able to let go of the past. Not really. And to do that, I need the truth about my mother's murder.

The truth, and maybe something more.

As I see again in my mind the red-headed man dying in front of me, Letya sighs and plucks at the skirt of my dress. 'It's ruined, I think.' Neither of us mentions the fact that some of the stains are blood.

Lucien's anger does not abate. He speaks to me as little as possible over the next few days, although he seems to take a grim pleasure in telling me of the rumours that are now spreading: either I went to Lower Farne to stir up the flightless population to rebellion, or I went because I am in fact flightless myself (my 'burning' of the servant on the day of my arrival apparently being part of a pre-conceived conspiracy). I notice enough sideways glances and whispered conversations to realise that my clerk is not just trying to scare me. I'm still busy; when I ask Lucien to arrange a meeting with Lord Hawkin, he tells me my diary is full for the next three weeks, and that Hawkin has in any case been away from court for the last month or more. Still, my feelings towards Lucien are softened when I discover that he has rearranged things so that I can have my afternoons to myself, though he does not give me any opportunity to thank him.

In my free time I start riding again, with Letya or with Aron. Despite the fact that he came to my rescue, my cousin still seems determined to try to make me squirm. He tells me about his childhood, and about the countryside around the Citadel, but he spends just as many hours describing the progress of the men competing to be my husband, or speculating on whether his father will find some other way of getting his hands on Atratys. Still, whenever he invites me to ride, I accept. Partly out of pity, I suppose. But also because, of all the people in the court, he is in some ways the one most like me, though I conceal my injuries and he cannot. The one thing we never discuss is flying.

When I'm alone, I try to work out what I should do next. Letya has not been able to find out for me when Lord Hawkin is due to return, and there's no other obvious line of enquiry for me to pursue. I consider and reluctantly discard the idea of asking Lord Lancelin to write officially to his counterpart in Olorys to seek information. I'm still turning the problem over in my head when I go to the great hall one afternoon, just over a week since Aron had to come and rescue me. In honour of the arrival of a new ambassador from Ryska, the queen has invited a famous troupe of ballet dancers from Frianland to visit the court and give a performance, and we are all assembled to watch. For once, seating is not dictated by rank; at the queen's request, this gathering is informal, and I can't help wondering what other changes she might introduce to the court if she were allowed. Chairs and tables and sofas have been scattered about the room. The queen sits with Odette and the ambassador, a small woman with deep-purple hair and violet-tinged skin. I end up in a little group, with Lady Nyssa on one side of me and a courtier I've not met before on the other – an elderly man, his sparse grey locks more feather now than hair. I have no idea where Lucien is. We watch the first half of the ballet in silence. But at the interval, when Nyssa goes to take refreshment, the man turns to me.

'Forgive my presumption, but are you the Protector of Atratys?'

'Yes . . .' I wait, wondering whether I'm about to be quizzed on my visit to Lower Farne.

'Ah, I thought I couldn't be mistaken. Tried to look at the seal on your ring, but my eyesight isn't what it used to be. You're so like your mother though, at the same age. That's why I took this seat. *Hawkin*, I said to myself, *that must be Lady Diandra's daughter*, and I'd heard of course that you'd come to court –'

I turn in my seat a little, hardly able to believe my luck. 'You're Lord Hawkin? I was hoping to meet you. You would have known my father too, I think.'

'I did. Not well though. Your father was a prince, as well as being twenty years younger than me.'

'Of course.' Disappointment dampens my excitement. I had assumed, from what Aron said, that Hawkin and my father were friends and contemporaries. On the other side of me, Lady Nyssa returns to her seat. 'And you knew my mother?'

'Before she was married, yes. She spent three years at court before she came of age, as everyone of quality does.' He blinks and clears his throat. 'I mean, almost everyone.'

'So you were –'

'Your Grace,' Lady Nyssa interrupts, 'would you care for one of these excellent little biscuits?' She's holding out a plate of decorated sweetmeats.

'So kind of you, but no, I thank you.' I turn back to Lord Hawkin. 'You were here when my parents met?'

'Yes, indeed,' he continues. 'Prince Rothbart and Diandra of Atratys. They made a very striking couple. Though of course they had to leave when they decided to marry. That's when they ran off to her dominion.'

'Why?'

'Well, His Majesty wasn't happy about it. Not happy at all. Refused his consent, though it was obviously because –'

'Oh, look, the dancers are returning!' Lady Nyssa leans across, addressing us both. 'Such a wonderful performance so far, wouldn't you agree? I had no idea the flightless could be so graceful.'

The orchestra starts tuning. But I don't know when I'll have another opportunity, so I ignore Lady Nyssa and lean closer to Lord Hawkin. 'It was obviously because of what?'

'Well, not many people remember this – not many people have survived here as long as I have –' he looks at me proudly – 'but the king proposed to your mother. I mean, before he proposed to Rosa of Dacia, who became his first wife. But your mother wouldn't have him. And then she ran off with your father.' He nods. 'Remember it like it was yesterday. Pity really – she'd have made a good queen.'

I stare at him open-mouthed. I knew my parents were devoted to each other; my father became a different person after my mother died. But I didn't know the risks they'd taken to be together. And I didn't know that my mother had had the chance to rule. That she'd had the throne in her grasp – the throne, and all she could have achieved there – and had given it up for love.

And my uncle . . . My gaze strays towards the front of the room, where the king has joined the group around the queen.

Did my uncle really love my mother?

Or was it always, really, about Atratys?

The king turns around in his seat, catches my eye, and smiles.

I don't notice the rest of the performance. The next thing I'm aware of is applause – the ballet has ended. Lady Nyssa has already moved from her seat, and I see her on the other side of the room talking to Lucien, their heads close together. I turn back to Lord Hawkin, hoping for some more reminiscences, but he seems to have nodded off. I'm wondering whether I should wake him or let him sleep – servants are clearing the chairs away now – when Lucien taps me on the shoulder.

'We're returning to your apartment, Your Grace. Now.'

The anger in his eyes shocks me, and I obey automatically. We are soon back in my sitting room. Lucien makes sure Letya is absent, then turns on me.

'By the Firebird's blood, what do you think you're doing, Aderyn?' His voice is low despite his temper, as if he's still afraid that someone will hear us. 'Nyssa told me what you and Hawkin were talking about. Are you trying to give the king reason to take Atratys from you? Are you really that idiotic?'

'I didn't do anything!' I speak under my breath, trying to

85

match Lucien's tone. 'Hawkin was talking and I was listening, that's –'

'Hawkin's an old fool. He's too unimportant to be at any risk. But you –' There's so much scorn in his tone. He begins striding up and down across the soft-hued carpet. 'To encourage him to gossip about the king, to repeat rumours about his relationship with your mother –'

'I hardly encouraged him. But I want to know who had her murdered, Lucien. And why. And I want –' My breath catches in my throat as I recognise the truth of the words I'm about to speak aloud for the first time. 'I want to make the person who killed her pay. Someone should suffer, for what they did to her. For what they did to my father and me.'

He shakes his head in frustration and whispers angrily, 'Don't you realise how precarious your position here is? Especially after what happened last week. Any other hint of scandal or treasonous behaviour will undo everything I'm trying to achieve.'

I dig my fingernails into my palms. 'And what are you trying to achieve, Lucien? All you've done so far is arrange endless meetings with –'

'Most of the people you've met are state officers or members of Convocation. They could be helpful –'

'Will Convocation stop the king forcing me into marriage? Will they help me fly again?' Lucien doesn't answer. I draw myself up, wishing (not for the first time) that he wasn't quite so much taller than me. 'It's all very well for you, my lord. You have friends here. Nobody is watching you, or judging you. But the only time I'm able to relax is when I'm alone or with

Letya. I spend almost every other minute wondering if the person I'm speaking to is going to try to kill me or take my dominion. While you seem to spend most of your evenings in some corner, flirting with Lady Nyssa –'

He stops pacing right in front of me, his handsome face marred by a sneer. 'Nyssa? Is that really what you think is going on?'

'What am I supposed to think?' I hiss back at him. 'I've seen how you look at her. You never even smile at me –' I stop myself. I'm supposed to be a Protector, not a whining child. 'She must be very fond of you, since she was kind enough to run to you and tell you everything Lord Hawkin had been saying.'

Lucien almost laughs. 'Yes, she was being kind. She's my cousin, and she wants to help me. And you, strangely enough. But while we're on the subject: at some point in the future, if I survive, I'll be the master of one relatively insignificant estate. I could not aspire to marriage with a Protector. And no ruler of a dominion would ever consider me.' There is challenge in his dark eyes and he holds my gaze for a moment – but I've no idea what he expects me to say.

'If you're trying to warn me not to fall in love with someone inappropriate, you needn't worry, my lord. I've seen no one here I could possibly consider marrying.'

His face flushes and he flings away from me, stalking to the other side of the room before turning back.

'I'm doing my best, Your Grace. But I can't protect you unless you at least *attempt* to curb this childish inclination to say and do whatever comes into your head.' His words sting, despite the low tone in which they're spoken. 'You need to concentrate on trying to regain your ability to transform. And as for these romantic dreams of revenge that you're entertaining, forget them. Your mother is dead and flown, and it's about time you let the past die with her –'

I slap his face so hard my palm hurts. My fingers leave a red imprint on his cheek. 'Has it ever occurred to you, my lord, that I'm also doing my best?'

Lucien is staring at me, breathing hard. He doesn't reply.

'I know you hold me in contempt. That you think I'm too immature, and that I shouldn't be Protector.' My voice is getting louder, but I don't care. 'I know you're angry with your father for sending you here. But at least your parents are alive. And you are not the only one who loves Atratys –'

Tears spring into my eyes. Whether they are the product of anger or grief I'm not sure, but I know one thing: I am not going to let Lucien Rookwood see me cry.

Letya opens the door to the room. For an instant she stands on the threshold, eyes and mouth wide with astonishment. 'What's happening here? Aderyn?'

I ignore her questions, push past her and escape into the corridor beyond.

Six

I hurry along the corridors without any aim or conscious direction. My only thought is to get as far away from Lucien as possible. I suppose I'm trying to walk off my rage and hurt, but it doesn't really dissipate, just settles like a leaden mass underneath my ribcage. Eventually I pause for breath and look around me.

I'm lost.

Nothing in this part of the Citadel looks familiar. I start walking again, slowly, trying to work out where, in the maze of passages and courtyards and towers, I've ended up. I'm on the point of giving in and asking for help when I see a staircase that I think I recognise – one that should take me back to the entrance hall with its emblazoned motto. Relief makes me light-headed. I pick up my skirts and dash down the curving, shallow steps until I finally emerge, not into the glitter of the hallway, but into blazing late-afternoon sunlight. Dazzled and surprised, I stumble, straight into the chest of –

Someone. A man, completely naked, but with a dark robe

89

clutched in front of him. Beneath my outstretched fingers his skin is warm, tingling with power from a recent shift of shape. I can feel the insistent beat of his heart. The blood flames into my face as I lift my hands and try to back away.

'I'm sorry –'

'Careful!' He grabs my wrist with his free hand. 'Look behind you.'

I twist my head, and gasp, and my knees start to shake. I'm standing at the very edge of a sheer drop, hundreds of wing-spans above the fjord below. And I realise where I am: on the landing platform of the Citadel, a huge expanse of grass studded with trees and a lake, jutting out above the water. There are the leather-garbed attendants, hooded and gloved, waiting to hand robes to nobles who have arrived at the castle in their transformed state. And in front of me, looking as if he's about to laugh . . .

'I was lost.' I can't think of anything else to say.

'And now you're found.' He grins at me. 'I'm going to walk backwards. If you walk forward at the same time, we'll find a safer place to have a conversation.' Still holding my wrist, he guides me away from the edge of the platform. 'There.' I drop my gaze as he shakes out the robe and puts it on. 'Now, we may be properly introduced. Siegfried Redwing, heir to the Dominion of Olorys, at your service.'

'Aderyn of Atratys.'

He bows briefly. 'Protector. I'm delighted to meet you. I must apologise for being so informally attired.' He grins at me again, and I can't help smiling back, a little.

'I was trying to find my way to the main entrance.'

'Luckily for you, I know the safest path.' He offers me his arm, and leads me towards a pair of crude gates that open onto another staircase. Siegfried rattles on about his first time at court and how long it took him to find his way around. I'm not sure I believe him, but I appreciate his attempt to set me at ease. My discomfort has mostly faded when he asks me, 'So, how are you enjoying your visit so far?'

'Very well, I thank you.' I'm mindful of Lucien's warnings, even though at that moment I hate my clerk. 'Everyone has been most welcoming.' Remembering Odette's description of Siegfried, I glance sideways. He certainly is attractive: silver-blond hair, tanned skin and dark blue eyes. Not quite as beautiful as Odette, and not as handsome as Lucien, to my mind. But still, Siegfried and my cousin will look, at least, as if they belong together. 'You are here to see my cousin the princess?'

'To assist with the wedding preparations, supposedly, though I expect I'll be in the way.' He shrugs. 'I don't really mind, as long as they keep things traditional. A royal wedding should be traditional, don't you agree?'

I open my mouth to tell him that I haven't really thought about it, but he continues.

'I was sorry to hear about your father. I met him, about six months before he died. He was a good man.' He glances away briefly. 'My mother died three years ago. I remember how it felt. If there's any assistance I can render . . .'

'Thank you.' A kind offer, though perhaps only lightly meant. We're back in the entrance hall now, so I stop walking and turn to face him. 'Did you know my father well? I don't remember you coming to Merl.'

91

'He came to see us at L'Ammergeia.' Siegfried tilts his head. 'Did he never mention it to you?'

I hesitate. My father had secrets; I've always known that, and the revelation of another does not surprise me. But it's bad enough having Lucien acting so superior. I don't want this handsome stranger to think my father didn't trust me.

'Cousin . . .' Aron is making his way across the marble floor. 'A word, if you please.' He acknowledges Siegfried with a faint lift of his brows. 'Redwing.'

'Your Highness.' Siegfried executes a flawless bow and turns to me. 'I hope to see you again this evening, Protector.' He flashes me another brilliant smile, then winks at me. 'Assuming you don't get lost . . .'

When he's gone, Aron murmurs, 'So you've met Lord Seed-brain. He has a pretty face. And I suppose my poor sister must marry somebody.'

'He seems pleasant enough.'

'Hmm. Your waiting woman is looking for you.' He glances down at me, curious. 'You had a fight with Rookwood, apparently.'

Vexation – with Letya, for being so indiscreet, but mostly with Lucien – makes me clench my fists. 'Nothing to speak of. But thank you for the message, cousin. I dare say I'll see you at dinner.' I bow and hurry back to my room, where Letya is waiting for me.

'Aderyn, I've been looking for you all over.'

'I'm sorry. After what Lucien said, and what I did . . . I had to get away. Where is he now?'

'He stormed off. Possibly because I threatened to write to

Lord Lancelin and tell him that his son's been bullying you.' Her lips twitch. 'He knows I'll do it too.'

'Oh, Letya.' Her care for me brings fresh tears to my eyes. 'What would I do without you?'

'Let's hope we never have to find out.' Her smile fades. 'I don't know. Maybe this place is bringing out the worst in Lord Lucien.' She tugs on one earlobe. 'It's too big, and there are too many people. And those Dark Guards give me the shivers.'

'Do you want to go home?'

Letya shakes her head. 'Of course not. I'll stay as long as you do.' She grins suddenly. 'That's what Lord Lancelin is paying me for.'

'Very well.' I sniff. 'But I think tonight I'm going to have a headache. We'll tell Lucien that I'm too ill to come to dinner, and I'll eat here with you instead. And after supper we can read and talk and play Battle, and pretend we're back home at Merl.'

'Are you sure?'

'Yes.' My spirits lift a little as I contemplate an evening without courtly rigmarole. Without the royal family or any of the other Protectors. Without Lucien. 'Yes, I'm sure.'

Letya and I have a pleasant evening, although I can't stop my mind drifting back to Lucien's words, to the mixture of shock and hurt in his eyes when I slapped him. Once I'm in bed I start wondering whether our relationship can be repaired; whether I want it to be repaired. I could ask Lord Lancelin to send me a replacement clerk. Someone who doesn't argue with me or glare at me or think he's entitled to tell me off. I could send Lucien away and never see him again.

The idea should fill me with joy, given the way he talks to me.

I fall asleep wondering why it doesn't.

Lucien comes to my apartment the next morning, just after breakfast. He is wearing a long, loose robe, of the sort that Siegfried put on yesterday. Which means he's either just transformed from raven to human, or he's planning to shift the other way very shortly.

'Your Grace.' He bows. 'I'd like permission to leave court for a few days. I've had word from Atratys, and there are matters at home that require my attention.'

That's it. No apology. No reference to our argument. I suppose I wasn't the only one lying in bed last night thinking about the future of our association.

'I see. You're returning to Hatchlands?'

'Yes.'

I wonder what game he's playing. Is he trying to prove to me how much I need him? Is his pride such that he cannot get past the fact that I struck him? Or is he abandoning me in the hope that I'll fail?

'You seem very certain that I'll give you my permission.' I gesture at his robe.

'If my absence is at all inconvenient –' His colour deepens. 'I would not ask, if circumstances were not such as to . . .' The tendons of his wrists are standing out from his clenched fists. He clears his throat, seems to master whatever is provoking his distress. 'I trust you will remember my warnings and behave appropriately, Your Grace.'

Does he wish me to dislike him? 'You need not remind me of my duty, Lord Rookwood. Take as much time as you require. Pray send my compliments to your mother.' I turn away, too angry to watch him leave. Angry at Lucien for daring to upset me. Angry at myself for becoming so easily upset. Taking a seat at the window, I stare out at the glittering water of the fjord. Behind me, the door closes.

I stay in my chair, brooding – over Lucien's behaviour, over the king and my mother, over the whereabouts of Deeks Flayfeather – until Letya comes in a little later. She is tidying in the bedroom (she refuses to let the castle housemaids anywhere near my clothes and jewels) and I don't pay much attention until I hear her exclaim in horror.

I look round. 'What's the matter? Is something broken? The clasp on my amber necklace seemed a little loose the other day, but I'm sure it can be fixed.'

'It isn't that.' She comes out of the bedroom, holding something in her hand. 'This was in one of the drawers . . .'

The object she's offering me looks like a sort of doll, crudely fashioned out of coarse cloth with long black threads stuck to its head to represent hair. The face has been painted on: blue eyes, red lips. It's obviously supposed to be me. A white wing feather – from a true gull, I would guess – has been bound to the doll with a length of narrow chain. And there's something else . . .

'What is that?' I point to a disc of silver metal sitting about where the heart would be, if the doll were a person. Wordlessly Letya turns the doll over: the end of a long silver nail protrudes from its back.

My stomach heaves. 'It's horrible.'

'It's a curse, Aderyn, that's what it is. An evil curse, meant to harm you –' She's shaking and crying and trying to mutter a prayer at the same time.

'Letya, calm yourself.' I get up and point to the chair. 'Sit there, and put that thing on the table.' She obeys, and I fetch her a glass of wine from the decanter that sits on the sideboard. 'Drink this.'

'But we have to destroy it, we have to burn it –'

'And we will. But first we have to show the guest master.' Though I'm not sure what he will be able to do. My skin crawls as I force myself to pick the doll up. It wouldn't have been hard for someone to get into my room. Housemaids come in and out every day, and the boy who brings the firewood. And Lucien has a key . . .

I shudder and push the thought away.

Letya is still crying.

'Don't upset yourself so much. It's just fabric and stuffing. It can't actually do me any harm.' Her face takes on a stubborn look, but I try again. 'This is no more than superstition, that's all. Honestly, what would Mistress Gleb say?' Our tutor – my tutor, in theory, but I had insisted Letya join me for most of my lessons – had often chastised my friend for some ancient belief picked up in early childhood.

I replace the doll on the table. I know it's not a curse, but it is a threat. Someone wants to frighten me. Someone who, perhaps, has guessed or discovered that I'm searching for information about my mother's death. Who wants to stop me before I dig any deeper.

But I will not be stopped.

Later that afternoon, Letya and I go to the guest master. He is shocked – distraught – while acknowledging that there is very little he can do. He offers to have a Dark Guard stationed at my door, but I decline. I don't want to make it even easier for them to spy on me. Afterwards, we go back to my rooms and put the doll on the fire. As the flames catch, I notice that whoever made the thing didn't trouble to give it any arms.

Curious. Still, the doll burns quickly. Soon only the silver nail is left among the ashes.

The weather changes. Rainstorms sweep down from the north and the Citadel is marooned on its high cliff, surrounded by mist and water. It's too wet for riding. Too wet for flying, even for my cousin Odette. Instead she invites me to spend the second showery afternoon with her and Siegfried. She seems a little put out to discover that I've already met him, but she's in high spirits, and her determination to love her chosen mate is obvious in every look and gesture. I'm not wholly convinced that Siegfried is as taken with Odette as she is with him. But he is respectful towards her, attentive, and, since I have no experience myself of this kind of relationship, I doubt my judgement. Siegfried is easy to talk to, and the three of us pass a pleasant few hours together. We meet again for lunch the next day. For the first time since I arrived at the Citadel, I feel as if I have found some friends.

The rain continues into a fourth day. After a long morning of meetings, weary of confinement, I make my way to a large cloistered garden near the sanctuary. I'm thinking about Odette and Siegfried, wondering what they are doing at that moment, wondering how I might contrive to speak to Siegfried alone, when he emerges onto the path just in front of me.

'Your Grace.' He smiles and bows. 'What a pleasant surprise. We missed you at lunch today; I hope you've not been working too hard. May I join you?'

'Of course.' He falls into step beside me and I take his arm when he offers it. 'I've spent the last few hours discussing trade agreements. Necessary, but tedious. I hope you and my cousin have been more enjoyably employed?'

'We've been in the sanctuary, discussing wedding plans.'

'Has a date been set?'

'Not yet. It's up to the king.' He smiles slightly. 'But I don't think Her Highness is in any particular rush. I'm not.'

I'm surprised by his words. 'Perhaps you underestimate my cousin's affection for you.' We walk in silence for a while, as the rain patters against the stone columns and splashes onto the edges of the marble tiles, switching places when Siegfried tells me he's worried about my gown getting damp. 'You don't wish to be married?'

'Everyone must wish to be married eventually. And to be selected by the heir to the throne, to be offered the crown . . . I don't think there are many who would refuse.'

'But you had a choice, surely?'

'I had a choice. But I had to think about the good of my dominion.' I realise he faced the same choice my mother faced, all those years ago. But he came to a different decision. 'I feel sorry for the princess,' he continues. 'As heir to the throne, she must marry.' He shrugs. 'Her choice was also limited. If I was her, I would have probably picked me too.' A sudden smile brightens his face. 'Does that sound terribly vain?'

I grin. 'Perhaps a little. Still, as handsome as you are' – he bows in acknowledgement of my compliment – 'I am sorry for her. To be forced to marry before you can rule the kingdom, to be forced, in those circumstances, to choose someone to whom you will be bound for the rest of your life . . . I don't know why the Decrees insist on it.'

'But they do. They Elders have spoken –'

'And the Decrees are what they are. I know.' My mind drifts back to my first conversation with Aron, and his description of Siegfried. 'Some people think you're nothing more than a handsome face, apparently.'

He laughs at this. 'I'm sure they do. But perhaps I don't mind.' The amusement in his eyes fades as he adds, 'We all do what we must to survive.' He studies me, running his thumb along the edge of his jaw. 'May I ask you something?'

I nod.

'Well, then . . . the discomfort you have in transforming; I believe I might be able to help you. Would you allow me to?'

I stiffen instinctively. Odette must have repeated what I said to her. I shouldn't be surprised. But still, to have the subject brought up in such a way, so openly. To be reminded by this relative stranger, even though he doesn't know the truth, of my continued failure . . .

'I'm sorry.' He lays a hand lightly on my shoulder. 'I didn't mean to embarrass you.'

'I'm sure. And I thank you for your offer of help. But I don't require any assistance.'

'As you wish, of course.' He smiles. 'And now it's your turn. Ask me anything you like.'

'Anything?' I smile back at him. 'Very well. I'd like to know what my father talked to you about, when he visited you.' The evidence I've discovered so far – the records in the library, the testimony of the red-headed man in Lower Farne – clearly links Flayfeather to Olorys. If anyone can help me find out more, it should be the man who is going to inherit that dominion.

My companion has screwed up his face in an effort of remembrance. 'Well, we discussed trade, as you've been doing. My father was suffering from gout, as I recall, so I was playing host. And we talked about music, books . . . and a little about you. He was very fond of you.'

I decide to take a chance. 'Did he happen to mention anything about survivors from the War of the Raptors? Members of the Accipta families, perhaps, still living secretly in Olorys?'

Siegfried looks taken aback for a moment, before he laughs.

'You think it's ridiculous?'

'Not at all. I'd be amazed if some members of those families hadn't survived somewhere. But your father didn't bring the subject up. It's hardly something that's discussed in polite society.'

The obvious curiosity in his glance forces me to attempt an explanation.

'My father was gathering material for a history of the kingdom. I thought I might attempt to finish the project, but his notes are incomplete.'

'I see.' He raises an eyebrow. 'You're very unusual, Aderyn of Atratys.'

His tone is warm, not critical, and the comment makes me smile again. 'I'm honestly not trying to be. Is there anything else you can remember?'

Siegfried frowns again. 'Um . . . he asked me about a book. Or about a writer, rather. An Oloryan by the name of Brant. Or Frant, I think it was. But I'd never heard of him. Which doesn't necessarily mean much.' Another quick smile. 'My younger years were nothing if not misspent, and I can't claim to be well read.'

A writer? I can see the library tower from where we are standing. Excitement stirs in the pit of my stomach. 'Well read or not, you've been most helpful, my lord. Thank you.'

Siegfried bows. 'I'm glad. I know it must give you pleasure to speak of your father with one who knew him, even slightly.'

We move on to other topics until we part at the entrance to the cloister. I make my way straight to the library.

It takes me a while to track down Gullwing Frant in the library catalogues: he was not from a particularly important family. But eventually I find him and the title of his book: *Tales of the Flightless of Olorys*. There's even a bookcase number, so I don't have to ask for help from the chronicler. The book is chained, like all the others, but it seems little read; it creaks as I open it, and although the spine is faded, the rest of the blue cloth cover is bright and unstained. I sit at the nearest desk, still in my cloak, and start reading.

As the title suggests, the book is a collection of stories – folk tales, some from before the war, some more recent. Stories of the flightless collected by one who could fly. Some seem fantastical, describing such impossibilities as a tribe of flightless who are immune to our touch, in hiding until the day they are summoned to the kingdom's aid. I skip over a tale about a flightless person travelling to the moon on the back of an eagle. But in almost every story, believable or not, we are the villains, the monsters, the stuff of nightmares. I read about hunts where the flightless are the quarry, famines where the flightless starve while the nobility hoard grain, servitude presented as expected and acceptable loyalty. The stories sicken me. But I keep turning the closely printed pages.

And towards the end of the book I find something intriguing. A more recent tale – from less than fifty years ago – of a noble hiding among the flightless, concealing his identity. It describes a man transforming into a hawk and hovering on the wind above a field of sheep. And it gives a location. I look around to make sure I am unobserved, then very carefully tear out the page.

When I get back to my apartment, Lucien is standing by the window, glaring at the fjord.

'Lord Rookwood. You've returned.'

He bows. 'As I said I would, Your Grace.' He runs a finger around the inside of the high collar of his tunic. 'I wish to apologise for my behaviour the day before I left. It was . . .' he clears his throat, 'unmannerly.'

'Very well. I accept your apology.'

'Thank you. Please, allow me . . .' Lucien walks over and reaches around my shoulders to unclasp my cloak and I breathe in the scent of him; he smells like the outdoors, and wide-open spaces, and the sea. His closeness as he stands behind me makes the skin between my shoulder blades tingle; I realise, to my annoyance, that I've missed him. 'How was your visit? Is all well at Hatchlands?'

There is just a wing-beat of hesitation before he answers, 'Yes, thank you. My visit was useful but uneventful.'

He places my cloak over the back of one of the sofas. The movement reveals a deep, red gash on the back of his neck, only partly concealed by his tunic. 'What happened to your neck?' I reach out in concern – the injury looks painfully sore – but Lucien steps back.

'Nothing. An accident, that's all. I was . . . clumsy.'

His expression is blank. But we're hardly on good enough terms for me to press for more information. 'Well, perhaps you are able to tell me about the ball this evening. I know how to dance, but I don't know the etiquette.'

'As with most things at court, rules of conduct at a ball are based on rank. You may invite anyone of equal or lower rank to dance with you. If someone asks you to dance, you may of course refuse, but it would then be considered ill-mannered to subsequently dance with another.'

'So, if I say no, I can't dance again for the rest of the evening?'

'That is correct.'

I think about this.

'Do you like dancing, Lucien?'

He shrugs, a faint smile on his lips. 'Not particularly. I can think of several ways I would prefer to spend this evening. But I will, of course, be in attendance.'

I'm supposed to be resting for the remainder of the afternoon, but sleep evades me. When Letya arrives I'm impatient to get dressed.

'I thought I would wear the grey watered silk this evening, with –'

'No.' Letya shakes her head, taking the grey silk firmly out of my hands. 'The blue taffeta will be better.'

I can't help rolling my eyes, but I trust Letya's judgement. She hands me a flowing dress of gradated blue: the deep blue of a magpie's wing at the neck, shading into the brilliant blue of a kingfisher. The skirts are embroidered with tiny down-daisies – the white flowers that bloom all summer long in the hills around Merl – picked out in silver thread. While I dress, Letya polishes a pair of sapphire earrings and a dozen silver clips set with diamonds. She twists my curls up into elaborate spirals, which she fastens with the clips; they sparkle like tiny stars against my dark hair.

It's only when she brings out a pair of shoes that I assert myself.

'I'm not wearing those.'

'But they're beautiful.' She's not wrong: the shoes are ice-blue silk embellished with sea-crystals. But the heels are taller than the length of my hand.

'Please, Letya, let me at least enjoy the dancing.'

She mutters under her breath, but she puts the shoes away and brings out a pair of flat, soft-soled satin slippers instead. 'You'd be taller in the other shoes.'

'I know.' Once I've fastened the ribbons of the slippers around my ankles, I stand to survey myself in the mirror. 'You're right about the dress, Letya. This is lovely.' Raising an eyebrow, I turn to her. 'Shall we?' She laughs, but comes to stand opposite me, the correct position ingrained from all the dancing lessons we had together. We start rehearsing the steps to a passepied, bringing our hands close (but never close enough to touch), threading around each other as I mark time out loud. A knock at the door interrupts us: Lucien, in dark green velvet, waiting to escort me to the great hall.

The room looks different, and I realise the tables have been removed; food will be served later in the long gallery. As usual, we wait for the royal family to arrive. Instead of the harpists, a small orchestra is assembled in the gallery above the main door. Siegfried and Odette are to open the ball – it is held in honour of their betrothal – but I'm not entirely surprised when Aron asks me to join him for the first dance, a slow and elegant pavane. For once, he's not clothed in his customary black. He's wearing blue instead: a blue-and-silver tunic that might almost have been designed to match my dress. The thought flits across my mind that Letya may be attempting some sartorial matchmaking. After Aron, I dance with Odette, who moves as elegantly as I expect, and then with Grayling Wren. He doesn't say much – as usual – but he dances well, and I'm happy to promise him a country dance later in the evening. Unfortunately my promise means I also have to dance with Patrus. He steps on my feet, his hands are sweaty and he talks the entire time about the cost of his ballroom back in Brithys: the windows, the carpets, the mantlepieces. When our dance finally ends I notice Lucien leaning against a wall with his arms crossed. Glowering at the world, as usual.

'Lucien, will you dance the next dance with me?'

His eyes widen. 'I'd be honoured, Your Grace.' He takes my hand – for the first time, I realise – and begins leading me back to the dance-floor.

'You were supposed to say no,' I whisper.

105

'What?' Irritation sharpens his voice. 'If you don't want to dance, why did you ask me?'

'Because I was trying to be nice. You were supposed to say no. Then you wouldn't have to dance with anyone for the rest of the evening.'

Understanding flits across Lucien's face, followed by some other emotion I can't read. He opens his mouth to reply – but is interrupted by Siegfried.

'Do you mind if I cut in, Rookwood?'

A brief pause, then Lucien bows. 'Of course not, my lord.' He walks away before I can work out whether his tone is one or relief or regret.

Siegfried must read my vexation in my eyes. 'I'm sorry; I hope you and Rookwood will both forgive me. But I couldn't resist seizing the opportunity. I'm particularly fond of this dance.'

'Why?'

In answer, he slips one arm about my waist, pulling me in close to him.

'What are you doing? Why aren't you standing opposite me?'

'Don't you like it?' He raises an eyebrow, but his lips are quivering as if he's trying not to laugh.

'That's not what I asked.'

'I've asked the orchestra to play a new dance from Celonia: the lavolta. You dance just as a couple, not in a line.'

I scan the room. He's telling the truth: all around me are other pairings, standing in the same position as us (including the king and queen, though Her Majesty looks uncomfortable in my uncle's embrace). And I don't dislike the sensation of having Siegfried hold me.

'But I don't know the steps.'

'It's easy. I've been watching you – you dance well. And I have a feeling you're a quick learner, Your Grace.' He takes my right hand in his left and settles his other hand in the small of my back, smiling down at me. 'You'll pick it up.'

There's no time for me to argue. The orchestra starts playing and Siegfried begins guiding me around the floor. Luckily the steps are straightforward enough, and I fall naturally into the rhythm of the music. Every so often Siegfried tightens both hands around my waist and lifts me high into the air, and I can't help laughing. It's the nearest I've come to flying for a long time.

The ball ends in the early hours of the morning, and I feel as if I've barely been asleep when the castle bell wakes me. It is tolling insistently, over and over: a deep, resonant chime that echoes among the towers and vibrates through the foundations of the building. Rubbing my eyes, I go to the nearest window and unlatch the long shutters. It's early still – very early. The sun is only just above the horizon, gilding the clouds in the eastern sky. Someone knocks on my bedroom door.

'Come in.'

It's Letya, bleary-eyed and wearing her dressing gown and nightcap. Lucien is hard on her heels.

'What's happening?'

'You need to get dressed.' He drags his fingers through his hair. 'We've been summoned.'

Seven

I wrap my arms across my stomach as it seizes up, but Lucien shakes his head. 'Not just us – I mean, the whole court.' Letya is going through my wardrobe. 'Hurry – Her Grace just needs a robe, or something to go over her nightdress.'

Letya pulls out a grey satin overdress; I slip my arms into it and do up the buttons as she fastens a belt around my waist.

'That'll do.' Lucien takes my hand and starts walking briskly; I have to jog to keep up with him.

'You still haven't told me what's happening.'

'A punishment. The court has been summoned to the arena to witness it.'

'A punishment? For what reason? And who?'

'You'll know soon enough.' He stops abruptly in a corridor, glances from side to side and takes me by the shoulders. 'Whatever you see, Aderyn, don't say anything, or do anything. Don't react at all.' He's gripping my shoulders so firmly it hurts. 'Please – will you promise me?'

'I promise.'

There are voices approaching. Lucien grabs my hand again and we hurry onward. More and more people join us, all moving in the same direction. Eventually we emerge onto a railed balcony, open to the cool morning air. The balcony stretches along one side of the Citadel, and there's a smaller, higher balcony at a right angle to it. Both overlook an open space: a natural, grassy amphitheatre in the side of the mountain upon which the palace is built. The flightless servants who work in the Citadel are crowded behind the fences that enclose this arena at ground level. The arena itself is empty at the moment. But my eye is drawn towards two tall stone pillars with various metal rings and sets of manacles hanging from their sides.

I clutch Lucien's hand tighter. He's trying to push through the throng to a space at the far end of the balcony, where it follows the line of the wall away from the amphitheatre. But before we can get there, someone calls my name.

A servant approaches us and bows. 'Your Grace, His Majesty has requested that you join him in the royal box.'

I turn slowly and find the king watching me, Odette and Aron next to him. He beckons. Letting go of Lucien, I join them on the smaller balcony.

The king nods briskly. 'That's right. Come and stand here, with your cousins.' He runs his hand down the curve of my back as I pass, and I hold my breath so that I don't shudder. Odette's eyes are red-rimmed.

Aron murmurs in my ear, 'Remember, cousin, there are no secrets here.'

'What's that you're saying, my son?' The king leans nearer.

'Merely wishing my cousin a good morning, Father.'

'And it is indeed a beautiful morning. Though not, perhaps, for everyone. We are here to see a punishment for treason, niece. Treason leads to instability, and instability threatens the entire kingdom. Tell me, my dear, have you heard of nobles having their wings clipped?'

'No, uncle.'

'It is an old punishment. But Cygnus I chose to retain it when he reformed the Honour Codes. Ah, here is the miscreant.'

Dark Guards appear from the rooms below the balcony. And held between two of them, his head bowed and bloodied, is Lord Hawkin.

I bite my lip, but my pulse is thrumming so hard that I'm sure the king must be able to hear it. One of the guards salutes the balcony. 'Shall I read out the charges, Your Majesty?'

The king waves a hand in consent, and the guard unrolls a scroll.

'Rees, Lord Hawkin, stands accused of malicious agitation against the crown and collaboration with foreign agents. Having confessed the same, he is hereby sentenced to have his wings clipped.'

'Have you anything to say, Lord Hawkin?' the king calls out. 'We will hear you, if you wish to beg for mercy.'

Hawkin lifts his head, though it seems he has trouble focusing on the royal box. 'I am an old man, Your Majesty. I have served the kingdom well. I have spoken nothing . . . nothing but the truth. If I have spoken to the wrong people, a true king would forgive my indiscretion –'

'Enough.' The king waves a hand, and Hawkin is gagged. 'Carry out the sentence.'

On the main balcony an elderly woman – Lord Hawkin's wife? – begins pleading for clemency, but no one pays her the least attention. The guards manacle Hawkin's shoulders and wrists to the pillars so he is stretched between them. Two more guards come forward with lit torches, and a third with an axe. The smoke from the torches drifts upward; the smell of it turns my stomach. I want to grip the railing in front of me, to hold myself up, but Lucien told me not to react . . .

Beside me, Odette's fingers brush against my own. A sudden burst of affection for my cousin steadies me; hidden by the folds of our gowns, we hold hands.

'Chins up, my dears,' the king murmurs. 'We will at least do Lord Hawkin the courtesy of giving him our full attention.'

I raise my head, fixing my gaze on a patch of ground just in front of the spot where Hawkin is chained, so I don't have to see what is about to happen.

But I can still hear. I hear him moaning in terror. I hear his shrieks of agony as both his arms are hewn off. Screams that go on and on, echoing off the mountainside, as the stumps are cauterized.

Until, suddenly, the screams stop. There is a long, drawn-out wheeze, and then silence, and the stink of blood and burnt flesh drifting upward on the breeze.

'Unfortunate,' the king observes. 'It appears the trauma was too much for him.'

I risk a glance towards Lord Hawkin's wife. She is slumped on the ground, unconscious, a clear space around her as if the other courtiers are afraid that something – his treason, or her grief – might be catching. Down in the amphitheatre the Dark

Guards are already dragging the body away, leaving smears of blood across the emerald grass. The hacked-off limbs are left attached to the posts; a true crow is already eyeing them hungrily.

And is this because of me? Because Hawkin spoke to me about my mother?

'Walk with me, Aderyn.' The king is holding out his arm. I take it, and we begin moving towards a door at the far side of the small balcony. 'I have . . .' He pauses, wincing a little, fingering a patch of red, oozing skin on the side of his chin. 'I have a special honour for you.'

'Thank you, Your Majesty.' I'm amazed that I can speak, that my voice sounds flat and everyday.

'You know your cousin is to be married soon.'

I nod.

'After seeing the two of you dance so delightfully together yesterday, I have decided that you shall be one of her maidens. It is not an onerous role. You merely have to fly with her to the sacred lake at the top of the mountain, spend the night there as a swan, and then fly back with her in time for the marriage ceremony. By custom, that takes place on the landing platform, at sunrise.'

He keeps talking, something about robes, and music, but I can't concentrate. That one word, *fly*, swallows up every other thought. It beats against me like wings.

'Aderyn, you do not answer me. I hope you are not insensible of the very great honour your cousin and I are extending to you.'

My uncle's face is bland, but there is no hiding the triumph in his eyes.

I swallow, and try to think about Atratys, and Lucien.

'Of course, uncle. I am deeply honoured. Has . . . ? Has a date been set?'

'The first night of Pandion, weather permitting. The early-autumn star showers are an auspicious time for weddings.' We have reached the royal apartments. I bow as the king leaves me and make my way automatically towards my own rooms. But my chest is tight, and I don't seem to be able to breathe properly –

'Take my arm.'

Lucien is next to me. I do as he says, leaning on him, concentrating on putting one foot in front of the other. Finally we are back at my apartment.

As soon as the door shuts behind us the words spill out of me. 'A few weeks, Lucien. That's all I have left. I have to be able to fly by the time of the wedding, and if I can't . . .'

'Calm down. We'll think of a way around it.'

'But you were right. If he can, he'll have me executed.' I remember the doll, with its missing arms. 'He'll claim Atratys and then he'll chain me to those posts and –'

'Aderyn, listen to me!' Lucien grips my shoulders. 'I am not going to let that happen.' His dark eyes are boring into me, as if he's trying to convince both of us that he really can magically solve this problem. 'I know what I said the other day, but you've done nothing wrong. Even if Convocation collectively lost their minds and allowed the king to proceed against you . . .' He trails off.

Because we both know that Convocation can't defy the Decrees. If it's discovered that I cannot transform, I may be

113

spared public execution. But the best I'll be able to hope for is banishment, and an assassin's blade not long after.

Or maybe the talons of a hawk . . .

'Atratys – I can't let him ruin it, Lucien.' I imagine Merl Castle surrounded by the slums of Lower Farne, the neat houses of Hythe replaced by the broken-down hovels of Brithys. 'I can't. You've got to help me.'

'We'll find a way to protect Atratys. I'll think of something. I promise.' He lets go of me and moves to leave. 'It's early still; you should try to get some more rest, my lady. I'll send Letya to you.'

'But, Lucien –'

Too late – he's gone.

And I am left staring at the door, missing the feeling of his hands on my shoulders.

I'm still standing there when Letya arrives. She helps me off with the heavy satin gown, brings me a cup of chocolate and sits on the sofa next to me.

'I saw what happened to Lord Hawkin.'

'I killed him, Letya. I made him talk to me about my mother, and now –'

'You didn't kill him. The king did, black-hearted monster that he is.' She sighs. 'I wish I could hug you. Properly hug you, I mean.'

I understand; she wants to be able to put her arms around me and hold me tight and not have to let go.

'I wish I could hug you too, Letya.'

My friend is wearing gloves. I am not. But still, she squeezes my hand briefly in hers.

* * *

The day of Lord Hawkin's death is an Ember Day. Thankfully there will be no banquet this evening, no requirement to assemble in the great hall. I take a bath and go to the sanctuary to light a candle for the homing of Lord Hawkin's soul. The rest of the day I spend with Letya in my rooms.

The next morning, I try to transform again. Perhaps because my need to fly is now a when, instead of an if, I fare worse than ever. The current runs beneath my skin as always. But I can do nothing with it. I can't even find the spark that triggers transformation, the tipping point from which the power that I possess by birth should almost force me into the shape of a swan. I try again and again, until I scream and smash my fist against the looking glass in the corner of the room.

It breaks.

Letya bandages my hand when she brings me breakfast. But when I ask her to find Lucien, she can't.

I don't suppose it matters; he can't help me anyway, not really. Not even if he wanted to.

But perhaps someone else can.

It takes me a while to track Siegfried down. I try the library, the throne room, the great hall and the long gallery. The guest master thinks that he saw his lordship entering the sanctuary. One of the Venerable Sisters tells me that he was there, but has since left. He is not in his rooms, and he is not with Odette. I even ask Aron; my cousin ridicules me for falling under the spell of Siegfried's charm, and tells me that he neither knows nor cares where the future king may be. Eventually I decide he must have gone flying. I pick up one of my books and go into the gardens, hoping to calm my nerves.

Siegfried is lounging on a stone bench in the herb garden. He has his eyes closed and his face turned up to the sun, as if he's asleep. I hesitate, and am about to retreat – after all, this whole thing is ridiculous; what can Siegfried or anyone really do to help me transform? – when he looks at me and smiles.

'Your Grace. I was just thinking about you.' He pats the bench next to him.

I sit down, still clutching my book to my chest. I know what I want to say. At least I think I do. But as to whether I should say it . . .

Siegfried clears his throat. 'I'm not well read, as I mentioned, but I believe you need to open a book if you really want to get the best out of it.' He taps the book gripped between my hands. 'Or so I've been told.' The humour in his voice is a pleasant change from Lucien's usual tone of barely disguised impatience and Aron's mocking contempt.

I force a smile. 'I'm sorry. I'm distracted.'

'No – you're distressed.' He frowns and peers into my face. 'Is there anything I can do, Aderyn?'

I rush the words out before I can change my mind. 'You said before that you could help me.'

He sits up straighter, suddenly serious.

'And I can.'

'How?'

The bench we're sitting on is made of red marble, with the imprints of sea shells somehow trapped within it. Siegfried traces the outline of one of these shells with his forefinger.

'What do you know of the study of potions and elixirs?'

'Not much. My father experimented, trying to create medicines. But he allowed me into his laboratory only a handful of times.' I see the room in my mind's eye: tables covered in notebooks and jars and glass vessels, the air thick with smoke and strange scents. It's been locked up since he died. 'Why?'

'I know someone – an alchemist of sorts. He works with plants from outside the kingdom mostly. Trying to find out how they can harm, how they can help. He discovered a rare herb, a couple of years ago now, and from this herb he developed a potion. When given to the flightless, this potion emphasises the dominant aspect of their personality: bravery, recklessness, whatever. But when given to our kind, it has a more extreme effect. If you take it, it will force you to transform. Your conscious mind will have no say in the matter.' He pauses, drumming his fingers the bench. 'Now, I don't exactly know what difficulties you are having. Odette mentioned pain . . .'

He waits, leaving the sentence hanging.

I press my hands against the uncertainty churning below my ribcage, studying Siegfried's face. His expression is open; there's no trace of deceit that I can detect. If I continue, I am putting my life – and the future of my dominion – into his hands. But if I do nothing, in a few weeks' time –

Lord Hawkin's screams of agony are too fresh in my memory.

'It's true there's pain. The skin on my back . . . it didn't mend properly. But I lied to Odette. It's not that I don't want to transform. It's . . .' I close my eyes as I force the words out. 'It's that I can't.' My voice trembles as I speak my secret. But there is also a sudden, unexpected surge of relief. 'Can you

117

really help me, Siegfried? And this potion – is it safe?' I know enough to know that these elixirs have side effects.

'I promise you, it is safe. It's been extensively tested. Would you like to try it?'

I don't reply. The very first thing Lucien told me was to trust no one. This could all be part of a plan to kill me, or cripple me.

'I understand why you're nervous,' Siegfried says quietly. 'The canker that sits at the heart of our kingdom is a threat to us all. But soon I'll be married to the heir to the throne. I *can* help you. I can protect you. But only if you'll let me.'

We look at each other.

'Very well.'

He nods. 'I'm glad. And I'm honoured by your trust in me, Your Grace.' He lays his fingers lightly over mine. 'Keep trusting me. You'll have no cause to regret your honesty.'

I sigh, hoping he is right.

'Do you know the lake in the far corner of the gardens?' he asks. 'The one planted round with juniper trees?'

'Yes.'

'The moon is waxing. And it looks as if we'll have a clear evening. Slip out after dinner and meet me there.' He squeezes my hand. 'Tonight, you'll fly again.'

I don't know how I get through the rest of the day. I try to study, but I can't concentrate. I pick up the latest letter from Lord Lancelin, asking for my decision on a boundary dispute that has arisen back home, but I find myself reading the same line over and over again. Eventually I give up and sit, staring out of the window, until it's time to dress for dinner.

Lucien escorts me as usual. I don't ask him where he was this morning, and since he doesn't ask me about my day I'm spared the necessity of lying. Aron notices my lack of appetite and draws attention to it, asking which of my suitors I'm pining for, exposing me to the obsequious attentions of Patrus. But finally the banquet ends. Once we are in the long gallery I make an excuse about my head aching, and slip away.

First I return to my rooms, where I swap my teal-blue evening dress for a long robe and lock my mother's ring away in my jewel case. I've already told Letya not to wait up for me. By the time I get down to the gardens, having taken the most circuitous route I can think of to confuse the watching guards, the tendons in my neck and shoulders are singing with tension. The lake is a forty-minute walk from the upper terrace behind the palace. My feet crunch too loudly against the gravel. Every shadow among the trees and flower beds seems as if it might be concealing an enemy.

To my relief, Siegfried is already waiting for me. His silver-blond hair glimmers in the darkness; like me, he's wearing a robe.

'You came.' He sounds a little surprised.

'I said that I would.' There's a small glass vial tucked into his palm. 'Is that it?'

'Yes. I'm afraid it doesn't taste very nice. The antidote –' he taps a small leather pouch hanging from a cord around his neck – 'is a little more palatable.'

'Antidote?'

'To reverse the transformation. I'll administer it to you when we return. Don't worry: I've tried them both. You'll be fine.' He walks to the edge of the lake, and I follow. Together we wade a little way out, until the water comes nearly to our knees. He turns to face me. 'Shall we?'

My breath suddenly seems to be lodged in my lungs. I knew I would have to disrobe – it's possible to transform while dressed, but definitely not advisable. Now it comes to it, though, the thought of uncovering myself before him terrifies me. 'It's been so long –'

'I understand. Shall I go first?'

Without waiting for an answer, Siegfried undoes the fastenings of his robe and lets it slip into the lake.

Under the moonlight, his skin shines like marble. I try to keep my eyes fixed on his face. 'My back . . . it's very scarred, from the attack –'

'It doesn't matter.' Perhaps he sees that my hands are shaking, because he walks behind me and reaches around to the clasps of my robe. 'May I?'

I can't speak, but I nod and close my eyes, until I feel the fabric lift from my shoulders. The cool night air brushes my body.

'There. That wasn't so bad, was it?' Still behind me, Siegfried passes me the vial. 'That's one dose. Drink it all.'

'And then what?'

'And then the potion will do its work.'

Quickly, so I can't change my mind, I lift the vial to my lips and tip my head back. The potion is bitter and earthy. I swallow it in one draft, trying not to breathe, and wipe my mouth on the back of my hand. Siegfried takes the empty bottle. And then –

And then, I feel as if a fire has ignited inside me. It's like the warmth that comes with wine, but far more potent: it penetrates my core and pounds through my veins and seems to spill outward from my skin, enveloping me, lifting me up. Perhaps I stumble, because I feel Siegfried's hands on my arms, his breath on my neck.

'Steady, Aderyn.' His voice is soothing. 'There's really nothing to fear. The elixir will simply compel you to be what you were born to be.'

I take a slow, deep breath, and then another, and then –

A brief, far-off echo of pain and terror, as the moment of transition comes upon me. Too far off to disturb me, detached as I am, pinned in the warm embrace of the potion. A far quicker transition than I remember when I initiated the process myself: rapid – breathless – a sudden lengthening of arms and lightening of bones and eruption of feathers through skin – a shift of balance, a falling –

An instant of panicked struggle against wind and water as some memory lodged deep within my muscles seizes control –

I'm flying. My human mind – submerged, looking out from eyes that have become alien through disuse – knows that I am flying. I feel my wings, beating away the air, lifting me higher. I recognise the twisting streets of the city and the dark waters of the fjord spread below me. There ahead of me is a large white swan, moonlit against the night sky: Siegfried. I hear his voice in my head and my heart races with the jolt of remembrance. How could I have forgotten the secret, speechless communication of flight? But I obey Siegfried's directions, I follow him, without any act of will, with no conscious control over my actions.

We soar above the Citadel, my wings seeking out the air currents, sweeping wide over the fjord before turning back towards the city. The landing platform, with its long, bright patch of water, is beneath us, and Siegfried is leading me down . . .

Water beneath me, and my wings folding. Siegfried, already back in human form, is stepping onto the grass that covers the rest of the landing platform. A hooded servant hurries forward, holding out a robe. Siegfried shrugs himself into it and takes another.

'Come, Aderyn.' I glide towards him. The leather pouch with the antidote is still hanging from his neck. He tips cold liquid down my throat, and as its chill spreads through me, my body shudders painfully back into human form and I'm on my hands and knees, gasping, in the shallow water.

Siegfried grasps my upper arm, helps me stand, places the robe around my shoulders.

'I flew!'

'You did, Your Grace. Are you happy?'

He's watching me, waiting for an answer. And I am happy – if happiness can be found in relief. I'm relieved the potion worked, that there is a way for me to evade the sentence that will be passed upon me if my inability to transform becomes public knowledge. I'm relieved, too, that the flight is over. The experience was nothing like I remember it.

But that's hardly Siegfried's fault.

'Yes, I'm happy. Thank you, my friend. You've saved me.'

He breaks into a grin. 'You're welcome, Aderyn.' We start walking back into the Citadel. 'And thank you for trusting me. You really have no idea what it means to me.'

'I'm glad I did.' My muscles are tingling, twitching, as if part of my brain still thinks I should be able to leap into the air and soar away.

Siegfried puts an arm around my shoulders. 'Careful now – I don't want you taking a tumble into the fjord.' The warmth of his body next to mine is pleasant; the chill of the antidote seems to be gradually deepening, seeping from my skin into my joints and muscles.

'How long will I feel like this?'

'For a couple of hours, probably. The cold may get worse before it gets better. Shall we try again tomorrow night? The sacred lake is far up in the mountains. Flying at such a height will be a challenge.'

So I'd better keep practising. 'Yes, please.'

'After dinner then. We can stay at the lake in the gardens for a while. When you're feeling confident we can come back here, in the daylight.'

'Must we?'

'Of course. You should show people that the rumours about your inability to transform, to fly, are false. Or at least –' he quirks an eyebrow – 'you must make them think they are false.'

Because the potion is a deceit, of course. I've already lied – to the king, to Aron and Odette – so I don't really understand why this feels different. Worse.

'Don't worry, Aderyn.' Siegfried leans closer until he's

whispering in my ear. 'I will never betray you to the king. You just need to trust me.'

I nod. 'I know. And I do.' I look around, taking in our surroundings. 'I can find my way from here.'

'Until tomorrow then. If you don't mind my advising you –' he smiles at me warmly – 'try to get some rest. Goodnight, Your Grace.'

As Siegfried turns up a nearby set of stairs, I walk back through the corridors to my own rooms. It's late, and I know I should sleep. I get as far as changing into my nightgown. But I find it impossible to settle. Whether it's because I'm cold, and therefore uncomfortable, or because of some other side effect of the antidote, I can barely keep still. After nearly an hour of prowling about my room, I can't stand it any longer. I put on my cloak and head back down to the gardens.

There's no one around. I ramble among the pathways, enjoying the solitude and the space and the way every flower is silvered by the moon.

Until I hear voices coming from behind a nearby hedge. Puzzled, I slow down and edge closer, treading carefully on the grass verges.

Lucien. And the second person, I think, is Turik, his manservant. It sounds as if Lucien is dictating a letter.

'. . . much worse than we expected. Convocation continues to increase taxes on the flightless, despite the fact that many have virtually nothing to live on. Any suggestion of reform is now rejected out of hand. I believe, if there is to be a chance . . . no, if we are to succeed –' He sighs. 'I don't know. I'm too tired to think. We'll stop there for now, Turik; I'm sorry we didn't start earlier.'

'I don't mind, my lord. I hope you had a good evening? Did you enjoy your talk with Lady Thressa? I dare say your father would be pleased if you brought her home to Hatchlands.'

'I dare say. But I don't think we would suit.'

'Ah, I'm sorry to hear that, my lord. Though of course, she's not as high-ranking as Lady Aderyn. I remember you were very much taken with Her Grace, when we first went to Merl.'

'I think you are remembering wrongly, Turik.' Lucien's voice is cold. 'And besides, Lady Aderyn . . .'

'My lord?'

'It doesn't matter. To be honest, I pity whoever weds her. But it won't be me.' Silence falls – silence during which I wonder why Lucien's words should hurt me so much, and then he adds: 'Well? You obviously still have something to say on the matter.'

'Forgive me, my lord. But it worries us, who Her Grace will marry. If she should contract with someone like Patrus of Brithys . . . I know what a Protector like that means: hunger, and fear. We barely escaped with our lives. I thought Atratys would be safe.'

'It is safe.'

'For now. But . . . You'd make a good Protector, my lord. If there was a way, maybe, that you could persuade Her Grace to step aside –'

'That's not how it works, Turik. And you're worrying unnecessarily. Her Grace cares deeply for her dominion.'

'If you say so, my lord.' Turik sounds sullenly unconvinced.

'I do. You're just going to have to trust me. My first loyalty is always and only to Atratys, not to its ruler. If I'm wrong, and Lady Aderyn does anything to endanger our dominion, if it came to a choice between protecting her or protecting Atratys, then I promise you: I would sacrifice her. I'd sacrifice her without a second thought.'

Eight

He'd sacrifice me?

I strain my ears, not wanting to believe what I've heard.

'It's late. We should return to the castle.' Lucien's tone sharpens. 'And I don't want to hear another word on this subject, Turik. You presume too much on my tolerance.'

'Yes, my lord. My apologies.'

The voices are moving closer. I pick up my skirt and sprint back along the paths, into the castle and back to my own room, where I lock and bar the door. And then I sit on the edge of one of the sofas, staring at the locked door, too shocked to move.

I don't understand.

I've come to rely on Lucien. To trust him, despite his warnings. And only two days ago, he told me he wouldn't let the king hurt me.

For what? So that he can hurt me himself, if he decides I've somehow failed?

I know he's not my friend.

But I didn't know he'd cast himself in the role of my judge. Or my executioner.

There's a headache building behind my eyes. The chilling effect of the antidote is getting steadily worse. Cold bites deep into my bones. Begins to cloud my thoughts.

Perhaps – perhaps Lucien was just saying what he needed to say to calm Turik's fears. Turik, who only just escaped from somewhere – Brithys? – with his life . . .

My teeth are chattering. The embers of the fire are still glowing on the hearth, so I blow on them and add some more wood, crouching as near as I can to the flames, trying to rub some feeling back into my almost-numb hands. It doesn't help much. I can't stop shaking. My body is freezing and my chest aches and, despite everything, I wish that Lucien was here, so I could beg him to wrap me in his arms.

But he isn't here. I'm completely alone. And all the terror that the potion allowed me to avoid earlier – it's just been waiting for me, hiding in the shadowy corners of my room. I try to think about how it felt when I was flying with Siegfried. To recall my experience of flying as a child.

All I can remember, though, is that last flight with my mother. But now I can hear her voice in my head once more, and I can't shut it out. I'm compelled to listen, over and over, as she tells me to flee, screams defiance at the hawks who pursue us, screams in pain as they strike her down . . .

'Aderyn?'

'Hmm?'

'Aderyn, are you unwell?'

I open my eyes. Letya is peering down at me, her expression anxious. My arms and shoulders ache horribly. The skin on my back is sore, my nails sting, even the roots of my hair hurt. And for some reason I'm lying on the floor of my sitting room. I push myself up, groaning.

Letya gasps. 'I'll fetch the doctor –'

'No – I don't need a doctor.'

'But, your back . . .' She points to my shoulders.

I struggle upright and walk to the huge gilt mirror hanging on one wall. Above the neckline of my nightgown there are purple bruises fanning out across my collarbone and my shoulders. Another thing I had forgotten: how hard it is on the body when you first begin to shift your shape.

'It's just bruising, Letya, it'll fade. I transformed last night. It . . .' I prod the bruises and wince. 'I found it tiring. I must have fallen asleep in front of the fire.'

'You transformed? The Creator be praised.'

'I'll tell Lord Rookwood, but as far as the rest of the court is concerned, I never lost the ability. Be sure you keep it a secret.'

As soon as the words are out of my mouth, I regret them.

Letya flushes. 'As if I would ever say anything that might put you at risk, Your Grace.' When we're alone, she only uses titles at me when she's angry. I open my mouth to apologise, but a ripple of pain sends me snatching at my shoulder. My friend sighs and shakes her head. 'Get into bed. I'll have a housemaid bring some hot water for the bath. And a high-necked gown today, I think . . .'

With Letya's help, I feel a little less ruffled by the time I have to face Lucien. He's waiting in the sitting room with his notebook at the ready. When I walk in, he looks me up and down.

'You look as if you've been in a fight.'

'You don't look much better.' He can't deny it. There are dark shadows beneath his eyes, he's unshaven, and from the state of his clothing it's quite possible that he got dressed in the dark.

'I was working late on . . . on a proposal that we're presenting to the Clerk of Markets regarding reduction of tariffs on tin exports.'

'Is that so?'

For a moment I think about challenging him. I could tell him that I heard him in the garden with Turik. I could accuse – condemn – dispatch him. Protect myself by sending him back to Atratys in disgrace. I stare, hoping to read in his face some sign that what I heard last night was a mistake. That I can still trust him. But his expression is as carefully composed as always.

I stare for too long.

'Is there something the matter, Your Grace?'

'No.' Better, perhaps, to keep him where I can see him. 'I look forward to reading your report.'

He frowns ever so slightly. 'May I enquire what *you* were doing last night, Your Grace?'

'I was transforming into a swan.'

My statement has as much impact as I could hope for. My clerk's jaw drops and he gazes at me, silent, for a full half-minute.

'But – but, how?'

I hesitate. On the one hand, I am not about to tell Lucien, of all people, about the potion. On the other, if I am to keep flying, it's impossible that Lucien won't eventually realise that Siegfried is, somehow, involved. I shrug. 'Lord Siegfried was able to help me. With his . . . encouragement, I found that I could overcome the difficulties that I've been experiencing. We even managed a short flight.'

The excitement has faded from Lucien's face, leaving it cold.

'How fortunate. I wasn't aware that his lordship has such a gift for teaching. Perhaps the two of you should take a flight in public; it might silence the rumour-mongers.'

I resist the temptation to tell him how little his tone of disdain suits him. 'Not yet. Not until my flying is stronger.'

'As you wish.' Lucien bows and opens his notebook. 'I believe, as soon as the wedding is over, that we should return to Atratys. If you're in agreement, I'll seek permission from His Majesty's secretary. We could leave the very next day.'

So soon? Despite the danger I'm in, despite the fact that the king disgusts me and terrifies me, I can't leave yet. I haven't found the place mentioned in Frant's book. I haven't discovered what happened to Flayfeather. But I can't explain any of this to Lucien. I wave him away.

'I'll consider your suggestion.'

'Thank you, Your Grace. At least our return journey will be easier, now you can fly.'

He leaves, and I close my eyes and massage my temples. The headache I had last night is threatening to return. I suppose Siegfried could give me the potion and start me on my journey back to Merl. But someone – Lucien? – would have to know to give me the antidote. And how am I going to keep flying after that?

131

These questions are still weighing on my mind when I retire to dress for dinner eight hours or so later. Before Letya arrives, I try to transform again. I do my best to recapture the sensation of change that the potion gave me last night, to bypass that part of me that keeps reliving the attack, but it doesn't work. The fear – and the pain – are as unbearable as they have always been. For now, at least, I am wholly dependent on Siegfried's goodwill.

To begin with, my flying lessons go well. I seem to get stronger. The bruising and pain of transformation fade a little, and the chill caused by the antidote grows less intense. But towards the end of the second week something seems to change. I find it harder to concentrate. My mind, during flight and immediately afterwards, seems dull and disobedient, shrinking to the immediate moment, the next wing-beat, the mere mechanical sensation of wings moving against wind. And I grow forgetful: a couple of times, as we are flying, I struggle to bring to mind the names of the features beneath me. One evening, as we walk back through the gardens, I reluctantly mention my concerns to Siegfried.

'I can't afford to stop flying. But what if this potion is affecting me in some other way? And what if it's permanent?' I chew my bottom lip, thinking about the flight we've just taken. 'I should be able to remember the words "hill" and "lake" without any difficulty.'

Siegfried puts an arm around my shoulder. 'Don't worry. I'll contact my friend, see if there's something we need to add to the potion, or some adjustment that should be made to the dose. He's a clever man. He'll find a remedy.'

'But what if he can't?'

'He will.' Siegfried flashes me a smile. 'I choose my friends carefully.'

'Perhaps I can meet him. I could describe the symptoms . . .'

'I'm afraid not: he doesn't even live in Solanum any more. A pity, since I'm sure you'd get on well. Here –' he plucks a perfect red dahlia from the flower-bed next to us and passes it to me – 'a gift, from one friend to another. You trust me, don't you?'

'Of course.'

'Well, then. Carry on practising, and let me worry about the side effects.'

I don't really have any choice. My strange forgetfulness, the limitation of my thoughts while I'm on the wing, does not improve. But at least it doesn't get any worse.

About three days after I disclose my struggles to Siegfried, he suggests a daytime flight. We choose an early hour of the morning, when most of the court will still be in bed from the previous night's revelries, and we take off from the landing platform. The experiment goes well. Too well: perhaps because my mind is fogged, perhaps in the surprise of seeing the sunlit countryside beneath me, I forget to be cautious. After we land and transform back to our human shapes I walk with Siegfried, still robed, back towards the entrance hall.

Aron is waiting there. His mouth twists into a sneer when he sees us. And only at that point do I remember that I had arranged to go riding with him.

'Aderyn. I see that you are perfectly happy to fly –' he glances at Siegfried – 'given the proper incentive. I congratulate you.'

'Cousin . . . I'm so sorry! I didn't mean to –'

'To deceive me and my sister? Or to keep me waiting here like a flightless lackey until you have time for me?'

I can't think of a response.

Aron's face flushes red. 'No matter.' He begins to turn away. 'I certainly don't need your company, cousin.'

'Aron, wait –'

He keeps walking.

'Forget him,' Siegfried murmurs in my ear. 'He's powerless and irrelevant, and he knows it. He's just jealous that you've recovered your ability, and he never can.'

The unkindness of Siegfried's remark shocks me.

'But I shouldn't have let him down. And I haven't recovered my ability, have I?'

'No one but me knows that. You forgot an appointment, that's all. And really, you don't have time for riding any more. We still have a lot of work to do to build up your strength.' He brushes his fingers against the back of my hand. 'Don't worry about Odette; I'll talk to her.'

'But –'

'Don't worry.' He winks. 'I'll see you at dinner, Your Grace.'

Back in my rooms I write a note of apology to Aron, but he doesn't send a reply, and I'm left wondering what kind of revenge he will seek; I know my cousin well enough by now to know that he won't let it go. I'm prepared, when I go down to the banquet, for the whole court to know I've been flying with Lord Siegfried. As Aron has repeatedly told me, there are no secrets here. But what I'm not expecting are the whispers and sideways glances that greet my entrance into the great hall. I'm definitely not expecting the lecherous gazes I receive from some of the male courtiers.

'I don't understand,' I whisper to Lucien as we wait for the royal family to arrive. 'Everyone else transforms. Why should the fact that I've been flying cause so much . . . speculation?'

'Give me a moment.' Lucien disappears into the crowd of courtiers clustered near the door. When he returns a few minutes later, he looks embarrassed.

'Well?'

'Apparently a rumour has spread that you and Lord Siegfried . . .' He clears his throat and tugs awkwardly on his tunic. 'That you're sleeping together.'

I clutch my arms to my chest. 'But it's not true.'

Lucien stares at the marble floor. 'It's really none of my business.'

'But it isn't. I swear by the Firebird's blood.' A man I barely know, a minor lord of some insignificant island, is peering at me through a quizzing glass. I glare and turn my back on him. 'Am I in trouble? Will the king –'

'No. It would be considered unacceptable for the princess to take a lover. But male members of the royal family – and future members, I suppose – are given more latitude.'

Somehow that doesn't surprise me.

Lucien is fiddling with the chain that hangs around his neck, still not meeting my gaze. 'Try not to worry. Everyone will forget about it in a few days. And perhaps I can find out where the rumour started . . .'

He is silenced by the entrance of the king and queen – there are bandages on the king's arms, but they can't entirely conceal the lesions that seem to be spreading rapidly across his skin – followed by Siegfried and Odette. Aron stops next to me, offering me his arm as usual; his smirk tells me everything I need to know.

The next day I go to see Odette. I want her to know that the rumours about Siegfried and me are baseless; I'm prepared, if necessary to tell her everything: about my inability to transform, and about the potions. But when I bring the subject up, she cuts me short.

'I really don't care, cousin. And Siegfried has already explained it to me.'

'He has?'

'Of course. I understand that you don't fly often, and that you were worried about having enough strength to make the journey to the sacred lake, but really, you could have told me. I could have helped you, you know.'

Siegfried's talked to her, as he said he would. But he hasn't told her the truth.

'In any case,' Odette continues, 'the court is full of malicious tongues. My brother's included, unfortunately. I simply refuse to listen to them. I despise gossip.'

'As do I, cousin.' I lean forward, trying to emphasis my point. 'But the rumour isn't true. I would never –'

'And I believe you.' She half smiles and stares down at her hands, tightly gripped in her lap. 'I'm not blind, you know. I realise that my betrothed does not – yet – have the same strength of feeling towards me that I already have for him. But in time ...'

'Of course.'

Her eyes meet mine. 'As the heir to the throne, my choices are limited, cousin. I have to love Siegfried. So I have to trust him. And you.' She takes my hands in hers. 'I like having you here. And I don't want to think about unpleasant things. I'd rather talk about what you're going to wear for the wedding, and where we can fly together, and when I can come to visit you in Atratys. Though I hope you'll stay at court for a long time.' A smile lights up her face. 'I love Aron, but I always wanted a sister.'

I leave without mentioning Siegfried's elixirs.

That night I have strange dreams. I'm with Odette by one of the lakes in the gardens, and there's a man with us, but I can't see his face clearly. Sometimes I think it's Siegfried, and sometimes it's Lucien. Odette keeps asking me over and over, *Who do you trust, Aderyn? Who do you trust?* When I wake in the morning I'm more tired than when I went to bed, but at least I've come to a decision. I've trusted Siegfried this far. And I'm never going to be the sort of Protector Lucien wants me to be unless I do this first. I scribble a note and ask Letya to take it to Siegfried.

Half an hour later he is in my sitting room, walking with me up and down across the carpet, and I show him the page I tore out of the book in the library.

'This place that's mentioned – it's supposedly somewhere in Olorys. Do you know it?'

He frowns at the page. 'I'm not sure . . . Where is this from?'

'From the book my father was searching for: *Tales of the Flightless of Olorys*, by Gullwing Frant.'

'Ah yes, the history project.'

'Well . . .' I fiddle with the pearl buttons on the front of my dress, 'that wasn't exactly true. I'm not interested in history in general. But I'm very interested in finding out who murdered my mother.'

A pause, before Siegfried asks, 'So, these would be the hawks that you were asking about?' His tone is serious, but not sceptical.

'Yes. I think they were from the Flayfeather family. One of them at least was here in the city around the time my mother died. And I think they're living somewhere in Olorys. Hiding. The story Frant collected was from fifty years ago apparently. If it's true, then perhaps this –' I tap the place name on the thin leaf of paper – 'is where they came from. And perhaps they went back there.' A sigh escapes me. 'Maybe it's wrong, Siegfried, but I want them to pay for what they did, if they're alive. And if not . . . I still want the truth. Who told them to attack us? And why?'

Siegfried takes the page and squints at the small print. '*Dauflore* . . . . I don't know. It could be a misspelling, I suppose. There's a small town near the coast called Deaufleur. We'll go and have a look.'

'Really?'

'Of course. It's too far to fly there and back in a day, but I have a manor house nearby. We can rest there and return the next day. I'd like the chance to show you some of my dominion, Aderyn.'

I twist my mother's ring round and round on my finger. After all this time, the possibility of finally taking action against my attackers excites me. But it scares me too. Especially after what happened to Lord Hawkin.

I need to be careful.

Siegfried bends his head nearer. 'I heard a rumour that the king is going to try a water cure next week, at the spa at Lamming, hoping it will help with his skin. He'll be gone for a night. We'll leave the same day and return the following morning. No one will even realise we're missing.' He passes the page back to me and grins. 'It'll be fun.'

But when Siegfried has left it isn't any anticipation of fun that dominates my thoughts. I find myself imagining a confrontation with the two men who killed my mother, imagining what I might say to them, what I might do. Anxiety blooms in the pit of my stomach and sits there, a permanent background sensation to every waking moment for the next few days. It doesn't matter if I'm riding, eating, trying to work or to sleep. Even while I'm flying, with Siegfried's potion coursing through my veins, I'm still slightly aware of it.

Still, the time wears away, and the morning of the king's departure arrives. After Letya and I run over our story again (she knows where I am going, but will try to conceal my whereabouts from Lucien or anyone who asks), I go to the sanctuary. To my surprise, Lucien is there, talking in a low voice to the Venerable Mother. There are lines of tension in his face and his bearing. Despite what he said to Turik, part of me feels sorry for him; he looks wretched. But I leave without trying to speak to him. When the time finally comes for me to take the potion, I drain the vial with relief.

* * *

It's a long flight to Deaufleur, the longest I've made so far. I'm nervous, after the problems I've had concentrating, that the flight will be too much for me, but Siegfried is reassuring. Once I've transformed I'm barely aware of the time passing – of anything much, beyond the gradual warming of the air – until I'm crouched, naked, in a shallow, weed-choked lake. Siegfried unties the waterproof bundle he's been carrying and hands me a robe.

'Welcome to Olorys, Your Grace. Your presence lends new beauty to my dominion.'

Another stock phrase, though Siegfried delivers it well. I laugh. 'Why, thank you, my lord.'

We walk the short distance to the town walls. As soon as the guards see Siegfried they back away and bow deeply.

'Your lordship, we were not expecting you.'

'We're here to speak to the alderman.'

'At once, my lord.' There is a hasty exchange of glances between the guards. The older one says, 'Adain here will take you to the alderman's house, my lord. We are honoured by your presence.' He nudges his colleague. 'Gloves, boy. Quickly!'

Adain runs to the guard-house behind the gate and returns wearing gauntlets. 'This way, my lord. And my lady.'

We follow the guard into the town. The streets are narrow, but stone-paved, lined with arched doorways. Some of the red-tiled buildings seem to be houses, some are shops. There are stalls displaying bolts of fabric, bowls of spices and dried foodstuffs, glassware. A few of the arches open into courtyard gardens. I catch glimpses of trellises smothered in deep purple flowers and small trees bearing some kind of fruit that I don't recognise. The news of our arrival spreads quickly. Those we pass bow and edge as far away as they can. People fall silent, and mothers call their children inside.

The alderman's house overlooks a central square with a fountain in the middle. Adain leads us up a short flight of stairs to a covered walkway that surrounds the first floor of the house, and bangs on the door. It opens and he has a hurried conversation with someone inside, which results in a woman emerging from the house. She bobs a curtsy as she wipes her floury hands on an apron.

'I beg your pardon, Your Lordship, but His Honour isn't here. He's over at the Guildhall with the sheriff, seeing about a party that's arrived from –'

Siegfried cuts her off, turning to Adain. 'Take me there. Aderyn –' he leads me a little way from the guard and the housekeeper, lowering his voice – 'perhaps you should wait here while I see the alderman. I might get more information from him alone.'

'But –'

'I know how important this is to you. But really, I think it's for the best. You trust me, don't you?'

It's hard for me to argue. He knows his dominion, and I don't. 'You know I do. I'll explore the town a little.'

'I won't be long. You –' he points at the housekeeper – 'show Her Grace whatever she wishes to see.' Siegfried takes my hand, as he has done before, but to my surprise he turns it over and kisses my palm before he and the guard stride off.

Why did he do that?

141

'Your Grace?'

I realise the woman has asked me a question. 'What did you say?'

'May I fetch my gloves, Your Grace?'

'Oh, of course.'

The woman is back again within a couple of minutes, breathing hard. I guess she's run up and down at least one set of stairs.

'What would you like to see, my lady?'

'I'd like to know the names of some local things. There was some curious blue glass on a stall, and a sort of pinkish fruit . . .'

She nods and leads me down into the square. At first, I enjoy my tour. I owe my knowledge of the world outside Merl almost entirely to books, and I've a long list of places I want to visit for myself. Sights like the Pyre Flames north of Fenian, and the ruins of the city of Palia, on the island of Marris. Seeing a new place with my own eyes is fascinating. We find a glassblower, who tells me that the blue colour of the glass comes from the addition of a type of metal called *goblin*. My guide takes me to a lacemaker, a silversmith, and a grocer, where I discover that the pink fruit is a *citrine*. All the people I meet seem prosperous and healthy.

And yet, they are also, clearly, terrified of me. They answer my questions because they must. But they won't look at me. They offer me their goods and seem confused when I decline because I have no means of paying for them. I'm confused too, until my guide explains local custom: the nobles in Olorys are not required to pay for that which they take from the flightless.

My lack of knowledge about the rest of the kingdom shames me. Perhaps Turik is right. Perhaps Lucien would make a better Protector than me. I decide to return to the house and wait for Siegfried there, and begin telling my guide as much, when I'm distracted by shouts and cries coming from the courtyard of a large building nearby.

'What's that?'

The housekeeper twists her apron between her hands. 'It's only the justice house, Your Grace, nothing you would wish to see.'

'But what's going on?'

'The court's been summoned today, Your Grace, so perhaps we should –' She stops, pressing her hand to her chest as a child's voice rings out above the noise.

'Mother! Mother, please don't let them –'

The cry catches at my heart. I run towards the doorway. The guards there call out for me to stop, but I ignore them: they recognise what I'm wearing and don't dare to detain me. The people thronging the courtyard don't notice me at first, but I order them to let me through, throwing as much authority into my voice as I can. They look around and realise I'm a noble and scramble out of my way, and I'm soon at the front of the crowd.

There is a family there, ringed by guards. I can tell they're a family – the two children are an obvious blend of their parents – but each of them is bound to a stake, with logs and kindling piled at their feet. Bound and gagged. Even the youngest child, who can be no more than three or four. Two of the guards carry flaming torches.

'What is going on here?'

'I think the question, Your Grace,' someone calls out, 'is what you are doing here?'

I recognise the voice. But surely, surely it can't be . . .

Patrus of Brithys, my would-be husband, is sitting in the gallery overlooking the courtyard. Next to him is a glum-faced man with bright orange hair, yellowish skin and blue eyelids – a member of a gannet family. He looks from me to Patrus, bewildered.

I ignore him and address Patrus. 'Will you please tell me, my lord, why these people are bound like this?' My limbs have begun to tremble as the cold of the antidote worms its way into my core; I clutch my robe tighter around me and hope that no one will notice.

Patrus rises and makes his way down from the gallery to stand in front of me. 'There is no need for you to be concerned, my dear lady. These flightless were accused of breaking a Decree, they confessed to breaking a Decree and they are to be punished accordingly. Since the offence took place on Brithyan territory, I am here to see the sentence carried out.'

I glance at the young woman tied to the second stake. She can't be much older than me, and she's staring at me, weeping silently. 'What Decree did they break?'

'The man was found to be in possession of a bow, complete with arrows. A capital offence, as you will be aware. Fortunately Brithyan guards are highly trained. I hope to have the chance to introduce similar standards to Atratys one day.' He bows and simpers at me.

I bite my lip, wondering what I can do. Patrus is correct:

possession of a bow is punishable by death. It always has been. But I also know, from what Lord Lancelin has told me, that the flightless who live in the countryside will often take the risk; a bow enables them to catch game that otherwise would escape. And if the choice is to hunt with a bow or starve . . .

'But why are his wife and children condemned?'

'The punishment allotted is that the transgressor should witness the execution of his entire family before being put to death himself. The Decree is quite clear on the matter.'

'But no one enforces the Decree that way, not any more! And to execute them in such a manner . . . In Atratys –'

'Ah.' Patrus holds up a stubby finger. 'But we are not in Atratys, Your Grace.' His smile fades. 'You have no authority here.'

'Neither do you – we're not in Brithys either.'

Patrus merely nods at the nearest torch-bearer. 'Set them on fire.'

The anticipation in his voice sickens me. I run between the encircling guards to block the path of the young man with the torch. 'No further! I am a Protector – do you understand? I am niece to the king himself. And if you burn them –' I hold up my bare hands, threatening – 'I'll burn you.'

He stops. There's fear in his eyes – doubt – reluctance.

Patrus has gone red in the face. 'Carry out your orders, or you will all be punished!' He lifts the thick wooden rod he is carrying and brings it down across the back of the nearest guard. The man staggers and grunts in pain. 'Hurry up.'

One guard takes half a step towards me. 'My lady, please –'

'Aderyn?' Siegfried is walking through the silent crowd. 'Is everything well here?' For a long moment he stares at Patrus. 'Perhaps His Grace of Brithys would care to explain what he is doing in a town in my dominion?'

'The man was found with a bow, Lord Redwing. In Brithys. His local lord –' he flings his arm out to point at the orange-haired man crouching in the gallery – 'seemed inclined to leniency. I am therefore in attendance to ensure that justice is done.'

'Siegfried.' I walk towards him and the guards back away from me. 'They're just children. I know what the Decree says, but this is barbarous.'

He shakes his head. 'The Decrees are what they are, Aderyn. And the flightless must know their place.'

Patrus nods in agreement.

I'm silenced. I don't know exactly what I expected – that he would agree with me? That he would order a retrial? – but it wasn't this.

Siegfried sighs. 'Come, don't look at me like that. I cannot undermine the operation of local justice, especially in the borderlands. People must know that the Decrees will be upheld, or we risk a descent into chaos.'

The smallest child moans, a wordless, terrified plea.

'Please, my lord. At the very least, spare the wife and children. They are innocent. Their death serves no purpose.' I step closer to him, gazing up into his face. 'Siegfried, don't make me beg.'

A pause. Then Siegfried entwines his fingers with mine. 'Very well.'

'Lord Redwing, I must protest –' Patrus begins.

146

'You really mustn't, Your Grace. Not if you want to be welcome at court when I am king.'

Patrus, for once, is speechless.

Siegfried looks back at me. 'I'll spare the woman and children for your sake, Aderyn. I make you a gift of their lives.' He turns to the guards. 'Cut them free and get them out of here. Then dispatch the man.'

The guards hurry to carry out his commands. Within seconds the woman and her children are freed. She tries to go to her husband, but the guards drag her away, carrying the children after her. I can still hear her screaming his name when another guard thrusts a torch into the kindling piled up around the man's legs, setting it alight.

Siegfried puts an arm around my shoulders. 'We should leave. I would not have you witness this.'

I cover my ears and lean against him as we walk away. But it's not enough to block out the woman's howls of despair, or the dying man's shrieks of pain.

Nine

We don't stop until we are back at the lake outside the town. Siegfried has dismissed the guards who were trying to escort us. He hands me another vial of the potion and I drain it quickly, desperate to forget, at least for a little while, what I have just witnessed. Together we transform, and I follow Siegfried to the manor house he mentioned, down by the coast. It's not a long journey; we're soon at the landing platform, where a servant is waiting to hand us fresh robes. The building is of honey-coloured stone with large mullioned windows, a central tower and two wings stretching forward to enclose formal gardens. On the far side of the house the land falls away towards a beach of soft pink sand, and the sea beyond. Alone, we walk down to the entrance hall.

'It's a pleasant evening,' Siegfried begins. 'I'll have supper served on the roof terrace, I think. We have some fine vineyards here which –'

'How can you be thinking of food?'

He smiles. 'Because it's suppertime, Aderyn.'

'But that poor man . . .'

'He was a criminal.'

'He was probably just trying to feed his family. And no one should die like that. My parents would never have allowed it to happen.'

A flicker of exasperation crosses Siegfried's face, but he smiles again, and I wonder whether anything ever truly disturbs his self-control. 'You may not remember your parents' exact views on such matters. Are you so certain that nothing like that happens in Atratys? Have you visited every local landowner in your dominion and informed them how you wish the Decrees to be implemented?'

Of course I have not. I stay silent, but my stomach growls. My companion chuckles and tugs on a bell rope.

'You'll feel better after you've eaten. And tomorrow we must leave early and fly fast, so I recommend you take my advice and come to supper.'

I want to keep arguing with him, to slap him for his patronising self-assurance. But I am a guest in his house. So I clench my fingers into my fists and wait.

A gloved, solemn-faced serving woman enters the hall and curtsies to me.

'This is Gytha,' Siegfried tells me, before turning to the servant. 'Show Her Grace to the East Room, make sure she has everything she needs, then bring her to the top of the tower when our food is ready.'

Gytha nods and leads me along candlelit corridors and down a flight of stairs. The East Room is pretty; the walls are covered with blue-sprigged wallpaper, and there's a fire already burning in the tiled hearth. I sit on the window seat, hugging my knees, and look out to the horizon, where the sea and the sky are melting together into twilight. Gytha, still silent, lays out a change of clothing on the bed and fills a basin with hot, scented water. I wash, brush my hair and dress; the red gown is slightly off the shoulder and made of some soft, light fabric that clings. I wonder who in Siegfried's family it once belonged to. I comb out my hair, then pick a book from the selection available and read until Gytha comes to get me.

She leads me up almost to the top of the central tower before indicating with a nod that I should climb the last flight of stairs alone. I emerge onto a crenellated roof terrace. There's a table – already set with oil lamps and dishes of food – and silk-cushion-covered benches in place of chairs. It's dark now, but the air is still balmy, reminding me how much further south we are here than in the Silver Citadel.

Siegfried is standing at one of the breaks in the wall. He goes to the table as I approach, pours some pale amber liquid into a silver goblet and hands it to me. 'It's a type of sparkling cordial that they make on the estate here. I think you'll find it refreshing.'

I take a sip; citrus-sharp bubbles burst across my tongue. 'Delicious. Thank you.'

He pulls out a bench for me to sit down and begins placing food on a plate. 'I've dispensed with the servants this evening. These are all local specialities – I doubt you'll have seen them before, so I'll choose a selection for you, if you have no objection?'

Since he's already setting the plate before me, his question seems somewhat irrelevant. I wait until he has served himself and has sat down before asking, 'What did the alderman say? Did he have any information?'

'Yes. Though he was not particularly willing to divulge it. Hedged it around with all sorts of qualifications: someone *might* have seen something, someone else *might* know a location and of course it's been *so many years* since the last definitive contact . . . He left me wondering whether silence is being extorted from the local flightless population and perhaps bought from the local lord. I will have to send some of my people from L'Ammergeia to look into it.'

'So there are survivors from the Raptor Wars?'

'It seems as if that book you found is more reliable than I'd assumed.'

'Shouldn't we go after them?' I try to push the heavy bench away from the table. 'If they find out that we're looking for them –'

Siegfried holds up a hand. 'Calm yourself, Aderyn. Matters are already in hand. There's no need for you to concern yourself.'

'No need to concern myself?' My voice rises a little. 'But she was my mother. And it was my back that got ripped to shreds.'

'Matters are in hand.' He pours me some more cordial. 'We have to return to the Citadel tomorrow, and there's nothing to be done tonight. We may as well enjoy our time away from court. I like that colour on you, by the way.'

He turns the subject, begins speaking of something else. I'm unwilling to let it drop. But I realise, sitting there alone with Siegfried on the roof of his house, exactly how much I have allowed myself to become dependent on him. The people

I'm pursuing seem to be in his dominion. Unless he gives me his potions tomorrow morning, I won't be able to fly back to the Citadel, or return to my human shape. So I swallow my pride, my guilt, and we talk of inconsequential matters: local customs, music, our shared love of stargazing.

After we've eaten enough Siegfried turns down the lamps and we go to the wall to look out at the full moon silvering the sea. I'm not sure whether it's the monotonous, unceasing rush of the tide on the beach, or some effect of the drink, but I feel caught out of time. As if this moment is everything; as if I could stare at the moon riding the waves forever.

Until Siegfried's lips brush the bare skin of my shoulder. He slips his arms around my waist, tugging me sharply backwards so that I feel his body and the warmth of him through the thin fabric of my dress. I can't help gasping. Hastily I twist around in his arms.

'Siegfried –'

He crushes me against him and plants his lips on mine, kissing me deeply.

Shock immobilises me. Until I realise, with horror, that my body is beginning to respond. Getting my palms onto his shoulders, I push him away. 'No – stop!'

He lets go of me and drags the back of his hand across his mouth, breathing hard. 'But this is what we both want.' A statement, not a question. 'The first moment we met, I saw the loneliness inside you. And the desire. Tell me I'm wrong, Aderyn. Tell me that you don't feel the same way. That you don't want me as much as I want you.'

I open my mouth to tell him that he knows nothing of what

I feel, that we're friends, nothing more. But I'm suddenly very aware of how far I am from home, and from the Citadel . . . I focus on the one fact that is undeniable. 'Odette. You're to be married soon.'

He shakes his head and laughs, though there's no humour in it. 'Odette thinks she loves me, but how can she? We hardly know one another. Not really.' He shrugs. 'My relationship with her is a business transaction, organised by the king and my father. But you, Aderyn . . . When I agreed to marry Odette, I never expected to feel this way about anyone. I can't stop thinking about you. Every moment of every hour . . .' Reaching out for a lock of my hair, he twirls it in his fingers. 'There's no reason to be afraid of what we feel: thanks to Aron, everyone at court believes I've bedded you already. And no one really cares . . .'

'I suspect Odette may care.' I bat his hand away, grope for the words that will allow me a way out. 'Odette's my cousin, and I'm fond of her. And . . . And even if you don't care for her at all, you still agreed to marry her. We can't betray her like this.' I turn away from him, back to the moon and the sea.

Silence. And then he sighs. 'Well, perhaps you are right. I believe there is a way we can be together, though perhaps it is not yet. But I trust that once I have proved myself to you, you will find me more . . . deserving.'

I don't know what he means, or how to answer him.

'Aderyn, please . . . Will you not look at me?'

Reluctantly I turn to face him again. He takes my hands, kissing both palms as he did earlier in the town.

'I'm sorry. My passion for you is hard for me to master. Tell me you forgive me.'

'I forgive you.' How could I not? He is mistaken about my feelings for him. Very mistaken in his disregard for Odette. But he has helped me – is still helping me – and I can't help feeling both grateful and sorry for him. 'What do you mean, that there is a way we can be together?'

'I'll tell you soon.'

'But –'

He puts a finger to my lips. 'Soon. It's late. You should rest now. We have an early start.' There's a handbell on the table; he rings it, and Gytha appears almost instantly. I realise she must have been waiting there at the bottom of the stairs all this time, listening, and my stomach turns. 'Take Her Grace back to her room. And be sure to wake her in good time tomorrow; we leave at dawn. Goodnight, my Aderyn. Sleep well.'

I follow Gytha back down the stairs to my apartment. There's a nightgown laid on the bed this time; she makes up the fire, pours some more hot water into the basin and withdraws, all without speaking a word. I undress and wash and get into bed. I blow out the candle. But before I fall asleep, I realise something. Something that leaves me numb. When Siegfried was kissing me, at the instant that I began to kiss him back, it wasn't actually him I was thinking about.

It was Lucien.

At breakfast the next morning Siegfried makes no mention of what happened between us, and I wonder whether he regrets his behaviour, or has thought better of his assumptions. We leave the manor house just as a sliver of brilliant golden sun is peeping over the horizon. This is the first time I've flown such

154

a distance in one stretch, and I'm dimly aware of the ache of muscles and lungs, if nothing else. When Siegfried transforms me back to human I realise that it is mid-morning: the landing platform is busy with nobles coming and leaving. Hopefully no one will have noticed our absence, or that we've returned together. We walk inside to the point where our paths separate. There's a servant nearby, dusting the contents of one of the display cabinets that line this corridor.

Siegfried leans forward to murmur in my ear. 'I'm going away again tomorrow. Just for a few days, I think. To oversee the investigation that we've set in motion.'

'Do you honestly think your people will find them?' If these hawks really exist, and if they are the ones we're looking for, they've successfully concealed their existence for the last two hundred years or more. All we actually have to go on are rumours.

'I'll find them. And I'll bring them to you, Aderyn. And then . . .' His lips brush my earlobe – I manage, just about, not to flinch. 'Stay here. Be safe.'

'The potion –'

'I think you should stay earthbound, for the time being. It will do you good to rest.' He grins, pushing back his damp blond hair with one hand. 'We can't have you thinking that you can do without me, can we?'

A sweeping bow, and he's gone. I turn away to my own apartment.

Letya is in the sitting room; she is hopefully still the only one who knows where I was last night. There are various yellow woollen shapes spread out across her lap and the sofa.

'Good morning, Aderyn. How was your errand? Did you find what you were looking for?'

'Perhaps . . .' I sit down next to her, as close as I dare, and try, through a mist of tiredness, to review in my mind every interaction I've had with Siegfried, every word, every touch. How did he come to decide that I would be happy to give myself to him? Did I do or say something that I shouldn't have? We've spent a lot of time alone together, inevitably, but he was the one who offered me his help . . .

'Aderyn?' Letya is frowning at me. 'Is there something wrong?'

I press my fingers to my temples, not knowing where to begin, whether I should tell Letya about Siegfried's kiss, or about the man burned to death merely for trying to feed his family . . . 'What do you think about the Decrees, Letya? Do you think they're fair? Do you think Odette will be able to change them, when she becomes queen?'

My friend's eyes widen. 'Well, I can't say I spend much time thinking about it. The world is the way it is.' She peers at my face. 'You look exhausted.'

'I didn't sleep well, and it was a long journey.' I poke the yellow knitting on Letya's lap, not wanting to think any more about Siegfried, and his expectations, and whether I'm able to turn back along the path that I've been travelling. 'What are you making?'

'A dress, for my brother's youngest.' She lays out the woollen shapes. 'See, here is the front yoke of the dress, here is the back, the sleeves, the skirts.'

'It doesn't look much like a dress . . .'

 156

'It will when it's made up. And then I'll embroider skybells along the hem, in blue thread. My brother lives in Gartin, and they grow on the chalk escarpments there.'

I know I visited Gartin as a child, but I can't really remember it: a small town on a lake not far from Merl, mostly inhabited by ironmasters and their forges. 'Lucien thinks we should go home straight after the royal wedding. Should you like that?'

'Oh yes. To be back at Merl for the end of autumn, in time for the Blood Moon festival . . .' She trails off, and I know she's seeing the same image as me: the cliffs around the castle glowing red with crab-blossom. Each blossom falls from the tree after just a day and drifts down to the beaches and into the water. From a distance, it looks as if the sea is on fire.

Letya resumes her knitting, and I worry at a piece of dead skin next to my thumbnail, going over Siegfried's words to me. Does he love me? Is he perhaps reconsidering his marriage to Odette, hoping to marry me instead? Perhaps it might be an advantageous alliance, for Atratys. Better than being forced into a union with Patrus, or Grayling Wren. But I don't love him. And yet, if I turn him down . . . I press the heels of my hands against my eyes.

'You should get some rest,' Letya observes.

'You're right.' Needles of pain stab the muscles in my shoulders and back. 'Shall we go for a ride later on? I'd like to –' There's a knock on the door.

It's Lucien.

'Come in, my lord. I'm glad to see you.' It's the truth: I'm pleased to see another familiar face, a reminder of my home.

For a brief moment I study his face, trying to trace in his features some resemblance to my dear Lord Lancelin. But then I remember the thoughts I had about Lucien last night. And I remember his words to Turik. The spark of happiness fades, replaced by a churning mixture of guilt and anxiety, as I wonder whether spending the night away from court with Siegfried comes under Lucien's definition of endangering the dominion. I take a deep breath, preparing to deflect the conversation onto some neutral topic, but Lucien forestalls me.

'The king wants to see you. As soon as possible.'

My heartbeat accelerates. 'Why?'

'I don't know.' He rubs a hand over his face. 'You'd better get changed.'

Letya has already set aside her knitting and has rung the bell. 'I'll have the maid fetch you a tisane. Hopefully it will wake you up a bit . . .'

Half an hour later I'm walking alongside Lucien towards the king's apartments. I've not been in this part of the Citadel before; all the doorways here are watched over by Dark Guards. My clerk is silent, glowering at the ornate carpet covering the floor, but he remembers his role and gives our names to one of the servants when we arrive at the receiving room.

The man returns shortly with a reply. 'His Majesty is currently engaged, but he's requested that you should wait, Your Grace, if it's not an inconvenience.'

Deferring to my convenience is a formality, obviously. Maybe the king really is busy, or maybe this is a reminder that he has power here and I do not. Either way, we have nothing to do but stroll about the receiving room until my uncle decides to send for me. I wander over to a large book of maps displayed on a stand in the corner, thinking that I might at least look at the outline of Atratys, even if I can't be there. But Lucien follows me.

'Where were you last night?' he mutters.

I run my finger down the index page, giving myself time to think.

'Here. Why?'

'Don't lie to me, Your Grace.'

'If you think you know where I was –' I make a show of turning to the correct page – 'I wonder that you should take the trouble to ask me, my lord.'

'Letya is discreet. But Siegfried's servants are not. Either that, or he wants everyone to know that you spent the night with him.'

I stiffen, gripping the edge of the book. 'What do you mean?'

'I mean, it is already common knowledge that you were with Siegfried last night, and that you were not at court. As I said before, it's none of my business what –'

'Then why do you question me?'

'Because I don't trust him. And . . . And I care about you.'

I almost laugh. 'Now who's lying? You'd sacrifice me without a qualm if you believed I was a danger to our dominion.' I glance sideways to see what effect my words have.

'I am your loyal servant, Your Grace, as I hope you are aware.' His tone is dry, but he can't conceal the doubt in his eyes.

The servant approaches. 'His Majesty will see you now, Your Grace.'

I leave Lucien to his uncertainty and follow the servant through to the audience chamber. The king is lying on a daybed, wearing a loose robe. There is a servant – a physician? – applying some sort of poultice to a lesion on my uncle's leg. The air in the room is close, heavy with the scent of juniper wood burning in the hearth.

'You wished to see me, uncle.'

'Indeed.' The king holds out his ring for me to kiss. 'I would like to discuss – ouch!' He grimaces, seizes a bowl of candied plums from the table next to the bed and hurls it at the servant. 'Begone! No more treatment today.'

'But, Your Majesty –'

'Get out!' He picks up another makeshift missile – a silver-backed mirror – but the servant hurries away. The king slumps back against the couch, a sheen of sweat on his face.

The lesion on his leg is not isolated; there are more, on his arms and neck. The word at court is that this illness of the king's is an infection, born of his dissolute style of living. He certainly doesn't seem to have benefitted from the water cure he took yesterday. But I find I cannot pity him.

'Well, niece,' my uncle says, having recovered his breath, 'be seated.'

I obey, taking a chair nearby.

'Protector Patrus has been to see me. I think you can guess why.'

My stomach twists, but I keep my expression impassive.

'No, indeed, uncle. I cannot.'

'He has formally requested your hand in marriage.'

Just my hand? I have an urge to giggle, and glance down at

the limb in question. I'd rather chop it off and gift it to Patrus than marry him.

'And,' the king continues, 'I strongly advise you to accept him. He is anxious to celebrate your union as soon as possible, and since we are already arranging one wedding, I see no reason why he should wait. Yours can take place the following day.'

'I thank you for your concern, uncle, but –'

He pushes himself upright. 'Let me be clear, Aderyn. Your behaviour at court has left much to be desired.'

I freeze, gripping the arms of my chair tightly.

'First you seem to be unable or unwilling to fly. Then you show that you can fly, but you also begin this . . . this liaison with Lord Siegfried.'

'I have not –'

'Do not attempt to deny it. I had it from one of his lordship's own servants that you were with him last night.'

My blood burns beneath my skin, as if even my own body wishes to accuse me.

'Now –' the king picks up a glass of wine from the table and takes a sip – 'much may be excused by your youth and inexperience. But that is exactly why you should marry Patrus. He will provide Atratys with a steady hand. And you will provide him with heirs to both Atratys and Brithys. He has been singularly unfortunate in his choice of wives so far.'

Wives? I knew Patrus was a widower, but not that he'd been married multiple times. I swallow down the bile rising in my throat.

'But you are young,' my uncle continues, 'and attractive, and there is no reason to doubt your ability to bear children.'

Another sip of wine. 'You may not be aware of this, Aderyn, but there is a Decree that allows Convocation, together with the monarch, to remove a Protector in case of mental or physical incompetence. It has not been invoked since before the War of the Raptors. It would be a great pity if a need was found for it to be used again.'

He's smiling at me, watching me like a cat with a trapped mouse. Fury loosens my tongue.

'May I ask a question, uncle?'

'Indeed.'

'Which parts of Atratys has Patrus promised you in return for me? How many ports? Which mines? As you say, I'm young and attractive. I know Patrus wants to add me to his list of possessions. I do hope you drove a hard bargain.'

The smile fades into a sneer. 'Impudent girl. I'll give you twenty-four hours –' He breaks off, coughing and hacking, clutching at his chest. 'Twenty-four hours to come to your senses, or face the consequences. Your father underestimated me once; don't make the same mistake he did. Now leave me, and send the servant back in.'

Lucien is waiting for me as I return to the waiting room, but I don't stop for him.

'Your Grace? What happened?'

'Wish me joy, Lucien,' I snap. 'I'm to be married.' The air inside is stifling. I hurry down some stairs that I hope will take me to the gardens.

'Married? To whom?'

'Patrus.'

'But why? When?'

'Because Patrus has bought me from the king. And soon: the day after Odette's wedding. Unless I refuse. But then –'

'My lady, will you slow down –' he makes a grab for my arm – 'and talk to me.' I stop and glance around; we're outside now, nearly at the little garden near my rooms.

'Come with me.' I lead him into the green-hedged space. The pink flowers of the sweetbriar roses are fading, scarlet hips swelling in their place; the summer is coming to an end. 'The king says my behaviour is unsatisfactory. He thinks I'm sleeping with Siegfried, or he says he does. And he claims there's a Decree that allows Convocation to remove Protectors who are unfit for office. I've never heard of a Decree like that. Have you heard of it?'

'Yes – it's in one of the Charter Rolls dating from the Audax period. Though it hasn't been used for over three hundred years.' Lucien sees me rolling my eyes – I can't help it – and hunches one shoulder, looking defensive. 'What? I'm your clerk. I'm supposed to know these things. But the point is, he's bluffing. Even if you are sleeping with Siegfried –'

'For the love of the Creator, I'm not!'

'But even if you were, Convocation would never apply the Decree in these circumstances.'

'What if he forces them?'

Lucien paces up and down, running his fingers through his raven hair until it's sticking up on end. 'The other Protectors won't want to see Patrus gaining control over Atratys as well as Brithys. He's already choking off the supply of timber and iron from his own territories, which is artificially inflating the price.' He swings back to me. 'You need to say no. Force the issue. I'm certain Convocation will support you.'

'Even if they do, won't the king just find some way of accusing me of treason?'

'If he does, we'll find a way to deal with it.' He puts a hand on my shoulder.

I shrug it away. I can't help it: my feelings about Lucien are so . . . tangled.

From Lucien's expression, you would think I had slapped him a second time. He opens his mouth – shuts it – turns away. When he faces me again his expression is more composed, though there's something like anxiety lurking in his eyes. 'The morning we left Merl, I promised my father I would look after you. I wasn't lying. I repeat that promise now, my lady. I'm not going to let the king hurt you. And I know you're brave enough to stand up to him.'

I gaze up at my clerk, trying to reconcile this Lucien, who is suddenly kind, who has actually complimented me, with the Lucien who told his servant he would kill me if I threatened the well-being of Atratys. Sighing, I reach up to touch his hair, half expecting him to step away from me. But he doesn't. 'You need a comb.'

One side of his mouth quirks upward. 'I'll be sure to amend my appearance in time for dinner, Your Grace.'

Lucien escorts me back to my apartment. I don't tell Letya about my planned wedding: I don't want to upset her, or risk having her sacrifice herself by stabbing Patrus with her knitting needles. Instead, I decide not to think about it, and we go for a ride together. I want Letya to see the sacred lake where Odette and her attendants will be spending the night before her wedding, but it turns out to be far too high up the mountain for us to reach before we have to return to the palace. There is another banquet tonight. I don't want to dress up for dinner – I can't stand the thought of Patrus looking at me, thinking that he's going to own me – but Letya has planned the evening's outfit carefully, so I go along with it.

Lucien takes me down to the great hall as usual. On the way there, he advises me to say nothing tonight; he is going to write a response for me to send to the king in the morning. So, when Aron accompanies me up to the high table, and makes jokes about my planned marriage, wondering aloud whether I'll last longer than Patrus's other wives, I force myself to ignore him. I'm seated as usual between him and Patrus, who sickens me with empty compliments – completely ignoring what happened in Deaufleur – while telling me about the new suite of rooms he is having decorated for me at his castle, and how well I will look in them. As if I am a painting he's going to hang on his wall. When I remind him that I haven't actually accepted him, he just laughs and turns the conversation to Atratys and his plan to inventory the entire dominion. It takes all the self-control I have not to pick up my knife and stab him.

The meal drags on. But finally, it's over: the last dishes are removed, and the king and queen rise from the table. We all stand and are preparing to follow them into the long gallery – I've already decided I'm going to confront Siegfried, ask him why his servants are gossiping about me – when my uncle clutches his stomach.

'Father?' Aron leans forward, taking the king's arm. 'Are you unwell?'

'Get off me, boy!' The king pushes Aron away, but he's panting with pain, and his skin has a strange, yellowish tint that seems like more than just an effect of the candlelight.

'Summon His Majesty's doctor at once.' The queen tries to guide the king into a chair, but he pushes her away too. She tries again. 'My lord, I beg you, you must sit down, you're not yourself –'

'Silence, woman!' He grabs her wrist so tightly that she cries out in pain. 'I won't have it, d'you hear me? I am the king, I am Solanum.' He gasps and clutches at the tablecloth, dragging dishes and glasses to the floor. 'I won't have it . . .'

Courtiers scream, servants rush forward, the queen swoons, and my uncle –

My uncle's eyes bulge as he collapses.

Ten

The atmosphere at court has changed. Three days have passed since the king collapsed, and all formal activities (the banquets, the concert planned to celebrate the king's birthday) have been cancelled. We exist on a diet of rumours and speculation: the king is worse – the king is recovering – the king is dying. It feels as if everyone at court is watching. Waiting. Trying to see into the future, to determine whether the power is about to shift away from the current royal house; whether some other descendent of Cygnus I will choose this moment of weakness to stake a claim to the throne. Through Lucien, I receive invitations to dinner, invitations to various country estates and letters seeking my patronage. Directly, I also receive an offer of marriage from Grayling Wren of Fenian and an offer of 'protection' from Arden of Dacia. I consult my clerk before replying to either.

'What does he mean, protection? Protection from whom? From Patrus?' I'm avoiding Patrus as much as possible; each time I see him, he urges me to fly to Brithys and marry him immediately.

Lucien shakes his head. 'You're thinking too narrowly. We're all playing a game here: hold on to the power you have, take it from others if you can, and whatever happens – whatever the cost – don't be the one who loses. Arden can't marry you himself, not at the moment. But with the king ill, he sees an opportunity to separate you from Patrus and from Siegfried, to align Atratys with the interests of Dacia.'

'But even if the king is ill, he has two children. And the queen.'

'She seems mainly concerned with her husband's state of health and with making sure Odette's wedding goes ahead; at least that way the Dominion of Olorys will stay loyal to the monarchy.' He consults his notebook. 'Which reminds me, you're to attend another fitting for your bridesmaid dress.'

'Don't you think the other dominions will remain loyal to Aron and Odette?'

'Aron is unfortunately irrelevant since he's been bypassed by Convocation. Odette . . .' He purses his lips and throws me a sideways glance. 'She's even less political than you are. She's a pawn. I'm not sure she'll ever really make a queen.'

'I think you're underestimating her. And her brother.' We both fall silent. Arden's letter is lying in my lap; I begin folding and unfolding one of the corners. 'What about Siegfried?'

Undeterred by the king's illness, Siegfried stuck to his plan and returned to Olorys. Part of me misses him, despite his misguided assumptions and his disregard for Odette's feelings. I can't stop my thoughts straying to where he might be and what he might be discovering about my mother's death. Still,

I'm relieved that I don't have to see him, at least for a little while. 'His leaving court now is a good sign, isn't it? I mean, that he has more integrity than the others?'

'It really depends why he's left.' Lucien's dark eyes are questioning, but I don't reply. 'He already controls Olorys, for all practical purposes. He's set to become king, which will give him control over the Crown Estates. And through your friendship –' he puts an emphasis on the word that I don't care for – 'he might attempt to control Atratys.'

I open my mouth, about to argue that Siegfried does not and will not control me. But of course Lucien is right. Unless I can find a way to transform without relying on Siegfried's potions, he absolutely does.

With the queen mostly sequestered in the royal apartments tending to her husband, the prince and princess are left more than ever to their own devices. I begin taking breakfast with Odette. After what Siegfried said and did, I'm worried about my cousin's future happiness. She deserves better than to spend her time dreaming of a romance that her betrothed seems unable to give her. I try to enquire, as delicately as possible, whether her wishes are unchanged. But Odette won't talk about her marriage, other than to agree that the queen should keep planning the wedding. She won't be drawn into any discussion of the future of the kingdom either, or the Decrees; she just laughs and says I'm too serious, and what does any of it matter anyway as long as we have clear skies in which to fly. I realise she is protecting herself, and I pity her.

My relationship with Aron is still unrepaired. But one morning he corners me in the entrance hall.

'Cousin. I'm guessing you won't be flying this afternoon?'

'No.' I feel as if I should offer an excuse. 'Lucien thinks there might be thunderstorms later.'

'So Rookwood is a weather expert now?' He arches an eyebrow. 'I had no idea he was so multi-talented. My guess was based on the absence of Lord Siegfried – I'd rather assumed that your sudden resurgence of interest in flying had more to do with his attractions, than the attractions of being airborne. But I suppose thunderstorms might deter you.'

I sigh and cross my arms. 'Aron, do you have an actual reason to speak to me, or do you just wish to insult me? Because if it's the latter, I really don't have the time.' He's still smirking at me. 'I'm sorry I forgot to go riding with you, but don't you think you've punished me enough? If you were trying to hurt me, you've succeeded.' I begin to walk away. But Aron calls after me.

'Cousin –'

'What?'

'Come riding with me this afternoon.'

'So you can spend an hour telling me what my life will be like when I'm married to Patrus, and how he's going to –' I break off; even thinking about Patrus sickens me. 'I don't think so. Besides, I have work to do. Verginie of Lancorphys wishes to consult me over another petition for the extension of representation to the flightless. May I go now?'

'Just . . . listen to me, for a moment.' Aron looks down at the empty sleeve of his tunic and starts tugging at a loose thread. 'I thought . . . I thought you were like me. I thought that, whatever you claimed, there finally was someone else at court who couldn't fly, someone who would understand how I felt. And then, when I saw you with Siegfried that morning . . .' He swallows and takes a breath. 'It made me angry – too angry to think clearly. I'm sorry. I'm sorry for the trouble I've caused.'

I bite my lip. Part of me wants to tell him the truth: *I am just like you. My recovery is a lie: I still can't transform, and I've ended up giving Siegfried more power over me than I ever imagined.* But I don't. 'I do understand, Aron.' He doesn't look up, so I touch his hand. 'What time do you want to go?'

'The eighth hour?' He grins suddenly, and for once I can see the boy in him, the person he might have become were it not for his dreadful father, and the way his future and his dreams have been ripped away from him. 'As long as Rookwood's thunderstorms haven't shown up.'

Despite Aron's apology, I'm not especially looking forward to our ride. But my cousin is on his best behaviour. He doesn't mention Patrus, or Siegfried, and saves most of his sarcasm for the queen, whom he accuses – on the basis of nothing more than his dislike, as far as I can tell – of somehow contributing to his father's illness. When I say that I feel sorry for her, that she may have had little choice in accepting his father's proposal, he scoffs and waves my words away. But he retains his good humour and invites me to dine with him and his sister.

Apart from the handful of times I've eaten with Letya, it's the most relaxed supper I've had since our arrival at the Citadel. Aron seems to be making an effort to be less caustic and not to spend *all* his time finding fault with people. With her brother there, Odette doesn't mention Siegfried, or the wedding, and she's surprisingly witty. Away from my uncle and

171

the oppressive formality of courtly banquets, both my cousins are more relaxed, more normal, than I've ever seen them.

As the days pass, and my uncle makes no appearance – although his physician makes frequent predictions that His Majesty will resume his duties the next day, or at the latest, the day after – we settle into a routine. On the days I eat supper with Letya, I ride with Aron. And on the days I ride with Letya, I have supper with my cousins. The only person I don't see much of is Lucien. Released from the requirement to escort me to formal court events, he seems – from what Letya tells me – to spend most of his time alone. One afternoon, after a letter for him has been included among my correspondence by mistake, I decide to use it as an excuse and go to hunt him down.

Despite Letya's gift for picking up gossip, I'm a little surprised to find that he is indeed in his room when I knock. He opens the door and his eyes widen.

'Your Grace. What's happened?'

'Nothing. I have a letter for you, that's all.' I hand him the envelope and he stands there, staring at it, as if there might be some invisible message that will become clear if he glares at it for long enough. 'It was delivered to me by mistake.'

'Oh. I see.'

Now he's staring at me, and I notice that his eyes are red-rimmed, as if he's very tired; or he's been crying.

'May I come in?'

Wordlessly he opens the door wider and moves aside.

His room is a mess. Smaller than mine, it serves as both bedroom and sitting room. The bed is made – a servant would have taken care of that – but there are papers scattered across the floor, piles of novels and notebooks, loose scrolls everywhere. I glance around, trying to find somewhere I can sit.

'Oh – let me move those.' He grabs a stack of books from a chair, searches for a clear space to set them down, and settles for adding them to another pile. The whole edifice totters precariously.

'Lucien, please tell me all this work isn't because you're my clerk. Surely you should have an assistant, or –'

'No. It's not to do with Atratys. I mean, some of it is, but –' he gestures to a painting of a handsome, square-built house propped up on the fireplace – 'a lot of it is to do with Hatchlands. My mother's health isn't good, and my younger brother is busy with his studies. Someone has to take care of the business of the estate.'

Guilt makes me squirm. Why did Lord Lancelin order Lucien to come to court with me in such circumstances? 'Your father . . . he can't be aware of how much is falling on you.'

Lucien's face hardens. 'My father is concerned only with Merl, and the administration of the dominion. It is his priority. It always has been.' There's a bitterness in his voice; the same bitterness I noticed when I overheard Lord Lancelin and him arguing in the library, all those weeks ago.

'It's my fault.' I look down at my hands, at the Protector's ring glinting accusingly on my index finger; the heavy gold band flares at the top into a square, deeply incised with the coat of arms of the House of Cygnus Atratys. 'When my father died, I didn't want to take over. I didn't want to have to spend my time judging disputes and negotiating treaties. I'm sorry, Lucien. When we get back I'll try harder, I'll –'

'It isn't you, my lady. From what I've learned, my father's allegiance was fixed long before you were born. Before either of us was born. When he and your father were both young men . . .' He shrugs and nudges a scroll with the toe of his boot. 'I suppose he shouldn't have married, but he did. He loves my mother, but never as well as he loved your father.'

All those years when I was growing up, and Lord Lancelin was living at Merl instead of at his own home . . . I had no idea. Did my father know how Lancelin felt? Did he care? 'I'm sorry,' I say again, because I can't think of anything else to say. Until I hear Lucien's stomach rumble. 'Come to supper this evening with me and Aron and Odette. We've been eating together in Aron's apartment.'

'No. Aron doesn't like me. It wouldn't be comfortable. And besides, I haven't been invited.'

'I'm inviting you.'

'But the meal isn't being served in your rooms.' His jaw is clenched; I can tell he's going to be stubborn.

'Very well. Then I'm going to get you an invitation.'

He shakes his head. 'Your Grace . . .'

I point a finger at him. 'I absolutely forbid you to disappear.'

I send Letya to check the stables first (the grooms don't take kindly to nobles turning up unannounced and spooking the horses). She returns with the information that Aron came in from a ride about an hour ago – he should be somewhere in the palace. I wander from room to room and through the gardens, and eventually find him in the sanctuary. I'm a little surprised; today isn't an Ember Day, and Aron has never struck me as particularly religious. He's standing in the large empty space that is the core of the sanctuary, staring up at the image on the ceiling: the Creator, in the form of the Firebird, flying out of the centre of a star.

'Beautiful, is it not?' He gestures up at the glittering mosaic that makes up the picture. '"And thus was the world in fire born, and thus will it end in flame."'

I recognise his words as a quotation from one of the Litanies, though I can't remember which one. 'It is beautiful. Though I'm not sure I want to end in flame.' The shadow of the nameless man burned to death by Patrus shifts restlessly in the back of my mind, mingling with the fire and smoke of my father's Last Flight. 'I have a favour to ask, cousin.'

He raises his eyebrows, waiting.

'Might I bring Lucien to dine with us this evening?'

A look of disgust flashes across Aron's face. 'Is that it? I thought you were going to ask me something exciting.'

'Like what?'

'Like, would I kill Patrus for you? That would be a definite yes, by the way. I may not be able to fly, but my sword arm is strong. Easily strong enough to slice through his flaccid flesh.'

'Well . . . I'll bear that in mind. But what about Lucien? I know you don't like him –'

'Wrong, cousin. I loathe him.'

There's so much resentment in his voice I am temporarily silenced.

Aron rolls his eyes. 'I suppose you may bring him. If you must.'

'Thank you. He seems so sad at the moment. I think his mother is unwell, and –'

'Spare me the pathetic details. I've said yes, haven't I?'

I execute a deep curtsy, which makes him smile. 'Until this evening then, Your Highness.' I return to the main door, but as I leave the sanctuary I glance back; Aron is staring up at the ceiling again.

Lucien has been tidying up while I've been gone; the books and papers are still there, but they've been heaped up in one corner of the room.

'Good news, my lord: you're now officially invited to supper.' He doesn't look very pleased. 'You may escort me to the prince's apartments at the twelfth hour.'

He bows his head. 'Of course, Your Grace. My only desire is to serve.'

I bite back the sarcastic comment that rises to my lips. Still, during the intervening hours, I can't help worrying that forcing Lucien and my cousin together might just end in disaster. Letya and I spend the afternoon together, but eventually she gets fed up with my pacing and tells me I should do something useful. Remembering my promise to Lucien, I turn to the piles of correspondence sitting on my desk. Answering letters, or making notes on those that require further consideration, forces me to concentrate. The twelfth hour comes more quickly than I expected.

Our meal doesn't start well. Aron is at his caustic worst and Lucien takes refuge in being wooden and monosyllabic. The burden of making civil conversation falls on Odette and me, and initially we struggle. Having discussed the weather, the king's illness and the reports of a possible war between Frianland and Celonia, two of our nearest neighbours, silence threatens. Desperate, I'm about to launch into the latest news I've received from Lord Lancelin – the development of a new steel pen nib by an ironmaster in Atratys – when Odette turns to Lucien.

'Do you remember that time when you and Aron stole Dark Guard uniforms and commandeered a barrel of ice wine?'

Lucien draws back – flushes – laughs. 'I could hardly forget. It was only four years ago.'

'Five,' Aron comments. 'We were both fourteen.'

'That's right.' Lucien stares out of the window, frowning. 'But what were we going to do with the wine? Did we actually have a plan?'

'We were going to get Siegfried's father drunk, and then get him to say something indiscreet, and then dress as guards and pretend to arrest him for treason.'

Aron and Lucien were once friends? My surprise is quickly followed by curiosity. But I don't want to derail the conversation. 'And you thought that would be amusing?' I ask, glancing at Odette.

She shrugs.

'He deserved it,' Lucien replies. 'Aurik of Olorys is one of the most unpleasant men I've ever met. There were always rumours about his behaviour.' He leans closer to Aron. 'Do you remember?'

'Indeed. That family has long had a reputation for violence. Supposedly they used to cut out the tongues of their flightless servants so that they couldn't repeat anything they heard. Though that's just hearsay of course.'

177

I think about Gytha and her unbroken silence, and shiver.

'Well –' Odette raises an eyebrow at her brother – 'I feel sorry for Siegfried. Can you imagine, growing up with such a father? It's amazing he's turned out so well.'

Aron and Lucien glance at each other, but Lucien merely says, 'It's hard to blame Siegfried for taking control and putting a stop to Aurik's court visits as soon as he came of age.'

'Doesn't Siegfried's father suffer from gout?' I look from Aron to Lucien. 'I thought that was why he isn't here.'

'My dear cousin –' Odette spears another moon-clam from the dish in front of her – 'he *always* has gout. It's the longest attack of gout in history. He hasn't been seen at court for three years.'

'I actually wonder whether Siegfried's killed him,' Aron says.

Odette kicks his ankle. 'Leave my betrothed alone and tell us what happened to the barrel of wine. Did you get Aurik drunk in the end?'

'No.' Lucien looks at Aron and smiles. 'We decided to try it ourselves beforehand. We tried a little, then a little more –'

'We got completely inebriated and passed out. I think. My memory is a bit hazy.' Aron rubs his hand over his face. 'Didn't you vomit into your Dark Guard helmet?'

'I think we both did.' Lucien laughs again. 'And then as punishment your tutor made us put them on –'

Odette jumps up and pulls the bell to summon a servant. 'That's enough: you're making me feel quite unwell. And I want some dessert.'

I knew that Lucien had been at court for several years as a teenager, but I hadn't thought about the fact that he must have grown up with Aron and Odette. I wonder again what happened between the two boys to break their friendship. Neither of them mentions it. And when I ask Odette the next day, she claims ignorance.

As my uncle's illness drags on, the four of us relax around each other. I almost forget about the king. Siegfried is still absent from court, leaving me waiting for news of my mother's murderers; I feel as if the moment of revenge, the moment I've dreamed of for so long, is nearly at hand. But I cannot see what lies beyond it. So I try not to think about Olorys, or about Siegfried. Unfortunately, it's getting harder to ignore Patrus. I learn from Lucien that he has tried to see the king, to get permission to marry me in the palace sanctuary without further delay. But the queen refuses to allow him in, so I don't attach much importance to his behaviour; it seems irritating, rather than dangerous.

One evening I'm up late: there's a star shower due to begin, and the sky is clear, so I'm planning to take my telescope – my mother's telescope – up to the top of one of the towers. A delight in astronomy was one of the earliest gifts my mother gave me. I clearly remember standing at the top of the highest tower at Merl as she pointed out her favourite constellations: the huntress, the cygnets, the diadem. And tonight, Lucien has said he might join me. There's a knock at my door and I assume it's him.

'Come in.' I'm carefully assembling the brass stand of the telescope, so I don't look up. 'I'm so glad you decided to come, Lucien. Even from the window the display is –'

'Good evening, Aderyn.'

179

'Patrus . . . What are you doing here?'

'Come to . . . to persuade you. Obviously.' The only thing that's obvious is that he's drunk. He's wearing a robe and carrying the wooden rod that he had in his hand at Deaufleur. 'It's time to . . .' He pauses, swaying slightly, and blinks at the telescope that is sitting on the table between us. 'What is this?'

'A telescope.'

'Telescope. You know what this is?' He points at the wooden rod.

'It's a stick. Please leave my apartment.'

'No. It's a rod of –' he belches – 'correction. For flightless servants. And disobedient wives.'

I remember his determination to inflict suffering at Deaufleur, and his dead wives, and Aron's insinuations, and a horrible suspicion crawls into my brain. I back away from him.

'I am not your wife, and I never will be. You're a monster. Now get out.'

But he doesn't move. Instead he raises the rod and sweeps the telescope, stand and all, onto the floor. Glass shatters, and scatters across the floor.

'What have you done? That was my mother's telescope, you –'

Patrus raises the rod again. '*My* telescope. Just like you're mine, and Atratys is mine. Now get changed. We'll fly . . .' he pauses, shakes his head, 'we'll fly from here. Get married in my castle tomorrow.'

He's even drunker than I thought, if he believes he can force me to transform. I glance at the bell pull on the other side of the room, and back at Patrus's swaying from. Surely, surely I must be able to get there before him . . .

I dart out from behind the table, flinging myself forward –

Pain flares in my shoulders and my hands as he knocks the breath out of me, knocks me to the ground onto the broken glass. Patrus's arm is raised for another blow, so I kick him in the groin as hard as I can and he drops the rod, bellowing, but as I try to get up he grabs at me, knocking me forward onto my knees, grabs again and I feel his nails scrape my skin as the back of my dress gives way. In front of me is a table, Letya's knitting lying on the surface. I glance behind me, and Patrus is reaching for the rod again, so I lunge for the knitting needles, snatch them up, swing my arm up and back as hard as I can as my assailant stumbles –

Patrus screams. Falls. The door to my apartment slams open.

'Aderyn!' Lucien runs to the bell pull and yanks it violently. Then he is next to me, his hands on my shoulders. 'Aderyn, look at me. Are you hurt?'

I burst into tears.

'Aderyn . . . I'm here.' He puts his arms around me and holds me tightly until my sobs have subsided. 'You're safe. Just tell me what happened.'

'He broke my telescope, and he wanted me to leave with him, and he hit me, so I . . . I . . .' I drag a hand across my cheeks. 'I didn't know what else to do.' Patrus is lying on his side, writhing and moaning, clutching his face. 'Is he dying? Why's it so cold in here?'

'You're in shock.' Lucien drags a coverlet off the nearest sofa and wraps it around my shoulders.

Letya appears in the doorway and gasps. 'Oh, Aderyn –'

'Letya,' Lucien orders, 'find the guest master. Tell him there's been an accident and we need guards and a doctor.'

She runs off, and I have nothing to do but wait; my arms and legs are shaking so badly I couldn't move if I wanted to. Lucien stays next to me on the floor, even when Letya returns with the guest master, a doctor and three Dark Guards. The doctor examines Patrus, and then he and the guest master approach us.

'Well?' Lucien asks.

'The eye has been damaged beyond repair and should be removed to avoid infection. However, I believe His Grace will otherwise make a full recovery.'

'Lucky for him.' Lucien beckons to the guest master. 'Get him out of here. And if the members of Convocation have not been informed of this attack on Atratys by the time I leave this room, I will hold you personally responsible.'

'Of course, my lord. May I say that I am deeply shocked that such an event could –'

'Go away.' I don't speak loudly, but the guest master jumps, bows and almost runs to hurry the guards carrying Patrus from the room.

'Your Grace . . .' The doctor is kneeling in front of me. 'May I examine you? If there is any dispute as to events here this evening –'

'How can there be any dispute?' Lucien puts his arm around me. 'He was in her room.'

'Lucien . . . I don't mind.'

He scowls at the doctor, but doesn't say anything as he helps me up onto the sofa.

'Now, I see there are cuts on your hands. I'm afraid I'll have to remove this glass . . .' I close my eyes tightly and grit my teeth as the doctor picks out the shards with a pair of tweezers. The pain seems to go on forever, but Lucien keeps holding me, and finally it does end. The doctor applies something cool and soothing and bandages my palms.

'Well done, Your Grace. Are there any other injuries?'

'My shoulders. He hit me, with that.' I nod towards the stick still lying on the carpet.

'If you'll just remove the blanket . . .'

I hesitate, glancing at Lucien.

'Aderyn? What's the matter?'

'My back's very scarred. I don't like people looking at it.'

'It's only me and the doctor. And it can't be that bad.'

A wave of exhaustion crashes over me and I yawn; I'm simply too tired to argue. Pushing the blanket back off my shoulders, I sweep my hair forward.

'Oh.' The doctor sounds shocked. 'I'm so sorry, Your Grace.' He clears his throat. 'But luckily the fresh wounds are only superficial. They should heal quickly, even over the scar tissue. I'll clean them, then mix up a salve that can be applied twice a day.'

'I can do that,' Letya offers. The doctor draws her aside, giving instructions in a low voice, and Lucien replaces the coverlet around my shoulders. He sits down next to me on the sofa. 'Why did you never tell me?'

'You knew I was attacked when my mother was killed.'

'Yes, but – I thought you'd escaped with a few scratches. I didn't realise how much they'd hurt you. Is it still painful?'

'Sometimes. If my skin gets too dry. It was agony at first, especially when I tried to transform, but now –' I stop, before I accidently mention the potion Siegfried's been giving me. 'The scars further down are from talons. The ones at the top are from a beak. One of the hawks caught hold of me, then started trying to . . . trying to . . .' I don't know why I can't say the words; when I close my eyes, I can still feel the talons piercing my lower back, while the beak tears strips of flesh away from my shoulders. 'I'm lucky really. My spine could have been destroyed.'

I look up and find Lucien watching me, a stricken expression on his face. I suddenly remember the way my father used to stand at my bedside and gaze at me when I was recovering from the attack, his face a mask of distress and grief. For weeks he was too frightened to touch me, in case it somehow made the pain worse.

'Don't look at me like that. I don't want you to pity me. At least I'm alive.'

He flushes. 'I pity the child that you were, having to deal with something like this. But how could I pity you now? I already knew you were courageous, but truly . . .' He lays a hand over mine. 'No other Protector has undergone such a trial. I think that people should know how brave you are. I think you should show your scars.'

I shake my head, clutching the blanket tighter. 'They'll just see that I'm damaged. Broken.'

'No. They'll see that you're strong.'

For the next couple of days, I keep to my rooms. The guest

master informs me that Patrus has been ordered to leave court; apparently he is a man with plenty of enemies and few friends. No one seems to grieve for him. I also receive a note from the queen assuring me of her sympathy and goodwill and asking me to take supper with her once I am recovered. Aron, Odette and Lucien are all with me when this note arrives.

'If I didn't know you better, cousin,' Aron says, twitching the letter out of my fingers and scanning it, 'I'd almost suspect that this was a deliberate move on your part. You've disposed of Patrus very neatly.'

I laugh, but Odette wags a finger at her brother. 'Aron, how can you speak so? Imagine if Patrus had succeeded in his aim . . .'

'But he couldn't have,' I observe. 'He couldn't make me transform just by the force of his will. And he hadn't taken the trouble to acquire any influence. If he'd turned up here with Letya and threatened to harm her, then I would have done whatever he asked.'

'What if he'd turned up with Lucien instead?' Aron asks, glancing sideways at my clerk. As I frown and tap my chin, as if the question is difficult, Lucien and Aron both laugh. Patrus's attack seems to have broken down the last remaining reserve between them.

The next night, determined not to miss all of the star shower, I borrow a telescope from Aron, go to the top of the tower nearest my apartment and watch the silver light rain down from above, drawing bright threads across the Firebird's Wake, the faint band of stars that bisects the night sky. It's late when I finally to return to my rooms, and the corridors of the castle are empty, apart from the Dark Guards on their endless patrols.

My mind is so full of the beauty of what I've seen that I've forgotten about Patrus, about Siegfried, about my continued inability to transform. The Silver Citadel itself seems almost insubstantial compared with the eternity of the heavens.

Until someone grabs me from behind and claps a hand over my mouth.

'Aderyn, it's me. Don't make a sound.'

Siegfried. He lets me go.

'You scared me,' I whisper. 'Why did you do that? And when did you get back?'

'I'll explain. But you need to come with me now.'

I hesitate. I have no desire to be alone with Siegfried, not until I've made him understand that he is wrong about my feelings for him.

'Surely tomorrow would be –'

'This cannot wait until morning.' He takes my arms and draws me closer. 'I've found him, Aderyn. I've found the man who murdered your mother.'

Eleven

I follow Siegfried back through the silent corridors. At first, I assume we are going to his apartment. But it soon becomes clear that I'm wrong. He's leading me downward, away from the parts of the Citadel used by nobles, towards the realm of the flightless: offices, kitchens, sculleries, dungeons.

Finally, we reach an area that seems abandoned: rooms stacked with old furniture, firewood, piles of mildewed fabric that might once have been clothes. In the jaundiced light cast by Siegfried's candle something gleams briefly in the shadows: a round shield, embossed with an eagle. We must be walking through the remnants of the House of Aquila, the previous royal dynasty. I suppose when Cygnus I took power, the castle was cleared, the belongings of the defeated inhabitants left down here to rot.

Siegfried hands me the candle while he unlocks a door to one side. I blink in the sudden brightness; there are lamps burning in the room we step into, and two men – guards, wearing the insignia of Olorys – are seated at a table, eating.

They get to their feet as we enter. 'My lord.'

'Bring him up.'

The guards pull on heavy leather gauntlets, go to a trapdoor in the corner of the room and heave it up. One takes a lamp, the other a pitchfork that is leaning against the wall, and they descend. I hear muffled voices, barked commands, swearing. The lamp-bearer reappears. Behind him, stumbling up the stairs, his arms bound behind his back and his upper torso covered with a leather cape, a grey-haired man; his face is swollen and disfigured with bruises. The second guard climbs through the trapdoor and shoves the man in the back with the pitchfork, sending him sprawling at Siegfried's feet, where he lies groaning and twitching.

Siegfried gestures to the man. 'A shape-shifter, and a surviving member of a goshawk family. Someone who, according to official histories, shouldn't exist. Another gift for you, Aderyn.'

I peer at the man, but it doesn't help: those who attacked my mother and me were transformed. This man could be one of them, but I can't tell. 'How do you know it was him?'

'Tell her your name, filth.' The man launches into a long, inarticulate string of snarls and curses, until Siegfried kicks him in the stomach. 'Tell her your name.'

'Deeks . . . Deeks Flayfeather.'

The name on the slip of paper. But still, I hesitate. There's only one way I can be certain. 'What did my mother say to you, just before she died?'

He ignores me. At a signal from Siegfried, one of the guards grabs him and hauls him up onto his knees; the other jabs the pitchfork against his neck.

'Ask him again,' Siegfried says.

'What did my mother say to you before she died?'

'What mother? My mother died.' He begins to mumble something in a tuneless, sing-song tone.

Siegfried grabs his face, forcing him to look up at me. 'Tell him who you are.'

'I am Aderyn of Atratys. My mother was Diandra of Atratys. She died six years ago, in an attack by two hawks.'

Flayfeather's left eye is swollen shut. But the sudden glare from the other, sharp and orange-irised, transfixes me.

'I remember you now. My talons in your back. Red blood against white feathers.'

'If you remember, tell me what my mother said to you before you killed her.'

'She said, "Spare my daughter, I beg you." And I said –' he giggles, licking his lips – 'I said, "Like the hawk I will fall upon them; I will rend their flesh from their bones."'

A quotation from the Litanies, the line that haunted my dreams for months after the attack. As he speaks the words, his voice echoes through my memory, my heart races and I stumble, steadying myself against the wall.

'Where . . . ? Where did you find him?'

'In the mountains not far from Deaufleur. His family were landowners there, once upon a time. The few that survived the war returned to a place where they knew they could hide. They continued the line for a while through inbreeding. But he is the last one left, as far as my people have been able to discover.'

I move closer to the imprisoned man and crouch in front of him.

'Why? Why did you do it?'

Flayfeather's gaze switches to Siegfried. 'Agarica.' He takes a long, shuddering breath. 'You promised me.'

'Agarica?' I ask. 'What's that?'

'A drug the flightless consume in some parts. Mildly addictive for them. Extremely addictive for our sort, it turns out.' He turns to the man. 'Answer her. Then we'll see.'

The man shrugs. 'He offered me money. Lots of money. And he took my sister as surety to make sure I did as I was told.' He blinks at me. 'You should have died. Cost me five hundred gold pieces, because you didn't die. Cost my sister an arm.'

'And the second hawk?'

'My brother. Went to work for someone in Brithys, two years back. Not heard from since. Poor brother's missing. Poor brother's dead and flown . . .'

'And the man who paid you – did he give you a reason? Why he wanted me and my mother dead?'

'Didn't ask. Didn't care.'

There's only one question left. Now it comes to it, I'm strangely unwilling to put a face to the person who ordered my mother's murder, to have my suspicions confirmed. But I force the word out.

'Who?'

The man grins, showing a mouthful of broken teeth. 'The king.'

My father's brother. The man who at one time, supposedly, loved my mother. I should be horrified. But I feel nothing apart from a dull ache beneath my ribcage.

Siegfried is watching me. I push myself to my feet. 'You knew?'

'I suspected. As did your father.'

Another secret he kept from me. But apparently discussed with Siegfried. 'What did he say to you?'

'He guessed the king wanted two things: revenge, for your mother having chosen your father over him, and Atratys.'

'But I didn't die. And there was no subsequent attack . . .'

'You were kept carefully guarded. You never left Merl. You were never sent to live at court, as all noble children are.' He shrugs. 'His Majesty convinced himself that you could simply be set aside, when the time came.'

The gnawing ache in my stomach grows. Why didn't my father talk to me? Why didn't he tell me his suspicions?

The prisoner tries to pull away from his guards, earning a jab from the pitchfork.

'What do you want done with him?' Siegfried asks.

I want him to die, I suppose. I've had it planned out for long enough: how I would kill him, if ever I found him. How I would take a knife and slice him open and let him bleed. A sacrifice to my mother's memory. The shadows creep from the corners of the room, while my father's ghost hovers nearby, waiting. This is why I came here after all. To destroy those that had tried to destroy me . . .

But I can't move. Can't lift my hand to grasp the sword one of the guards has left lying on the table.

Siegfried whispers in my ear. 'Say the words, Aderyn. What do you want me to do?'

The darkness edges closer.

'I want . . . I want you to kill him for me.'

191

Behind me, Siegfried sighs.

'Agarica.' Flayfeather spits the word. 'You promised.'

'I did, didn't I? Very well then.' Siegfried nods to the guard with the pitchfork, who puts down his weapon and drags a wooden chest from near the door to where the man is kneeling. Siegfried opens it – it seems to be filled with dried yellowish leaves – and pulls on a spare pair of gauntlets. He runs his gloved hand through the leaves, and the room fills with a woody, musty scent. 'Unprepared agarica. Very potent, but dangerous to eat as it is.' He picks up a leaf between his fingers. 'The underside is covered in tiny, barbed hairs that contain an acidic poison. If it touches your skin – especially somewhere sensitive – it causes immediate and intensely painful blistering and swelling.' All of us stare at the leaf he is holding up. 'Wonderful, isn't it, how something so small can be so deadly . . .'

'No!' The man tries to shuffle away, but both the guards are holding him now, gritting their teeth against the discomfort they must be feeling even through thick layers of leather. 'No, you stinking swan –' He clamps his mouth shut, but one of the guards covers his nose until he is forced to gasp for air. As he opens his mouth, Siegfried crams two handfuls of the leaves into it, then holds Flayfeather's jaw shut. The man's eyes begin to bulge, his greyish skin turns purple and he jerks and convulses in the hands of his captors –

And I do not look away.

Eventually Flayfeather's eyes turn upward, showing the whites. He stops twitching. Siegfried lets go of his head, closes the lid of the chest and removes the gauntlets. The guards drop the man on the floor and stretch, rubbing their shoulders.

'Get rid of that, then leave us.'

The guards drag the body to the trapdoor, open it, and throw the corpse into the darkness below. When they've left the room, Siegfried turns to me.

'I thought you'd be pleased, Aderyn. You don't look pleased. Aren't you glad he's dead?'

'Yes.' I nod. Siegfried's right: I should be pleased. But I feel nothing. No triumph, no sense of peace. I think about my mother, trying to stir the embers of my fury, but I cannot bring her face to mind. Siegfried is watching me, curious. 'How did you know? About the . . .' I point at the box of yellow leaves.

'Oh, the dungeon master that worked here under the previous regime used to keep meticulous records. I've studied them at length. With the correct methods of application, they could keep people in agony for days at a time.' He laughs. 'Flayfeather got off lightly really. If we'd had more time, I might have tried a few experiments.'

There's a tone to his voice, a certain pleasurable anticipation, that reminds me of something . . .

Patrus, looking forward to seeing the flightless family die.

And suddenly I seem to be back in Deaufleur, because I can hear the agonised shrieks of the flightless man as the fire takes him, and I can smell the burning of his flesh, but I can't see. I can't see anything at all –

Someone's arms are around me. Lucien, surely? I must have had a nightmare, after the stargazing. 'I was so scared.'

'There's nothing to be scared of, Aderyn.'

Siegfried's voice. I open my eyes, and I'm still in the room below the castle. It was all true.

He helps me to a seat and passes me a glass of water.

'I'm sorry.' I don't know why I'm apologising. Some instinct of self-preservation?

'Don't worry. You've taken the first step, but you'll get stronger. You need to be strong, Aderyn, for what lies before us. Strong for what we have to do to save the kingdom.' His dark blue eyes are almost black in the lamplight, but there's no concealing the intensity of his expression. 'We were discussing treason, that day in the garden: cutting out the canker at the heart of the kingdom. But can it really be treason, to make that which is sick whole again? Together, you and I are going to restore Solanum.' He begins striding up and down, punctuating his words by smacking his fist into his palm. 'We're going to make it how it used to be. No more intermingling with the flightless. No more talk of allowing them representation, or of relaxing our borders. No more immorality among the nobles. No more squabbling between the Houses. We will burn away all that is rotten, and then – and only then – will come the time for mercy.'

'But the king, and my cousins –'

'Trust me – the king will not trouble us for much longer.'

'He's getting better, isn't he? His secretary said so, only yesterday.'

'Lies. It is no illness that afflicts him. It's poison. A slow, subtle, undetectable poison.' Siegfried gives me a quick grin. 'Another gift from my friend the chemist.' He waves a hand. 'Aron is irrelevant. An embarrassment, in fact – poor, flightless prince. And as for Odette . . .'

I swallow down the panic building in my chest. 'You said that there was a way for us to be together. Are you planning to break off your betrothal to Odette?'

He turns back to me and takes my face in his hands. 'We will be together, my love. Eventually, you and I will rule Solanum side by side, equals, seated together on the swan-kings' throne. But first . . . first, I must marry Odette. I will claim the throne as her husband when the king dies, and I'll have to keep her for a while –'

'You're not going to kill her?'

'Of course not. I'm going to give her the one thing she really wants.'

The realisation that has been building, that I'm shut in an underground room with a madman, crashes over me. If I wasn't already seated, I would collapse. I take a deep breath, grip the arms of the chair, focus on the need to get as much information as I can. 'I don't understand.'

'Odette doesn't want to be queen. She doesn't care about the kingdom. All she really wants to do is fly. And the potion I've given you, in a stronger concentration, will not simply transform her into a swan, it will keep her as one. Permanently.' Siegfried crouches in front of me. 'There is one thing I need to apologise for, my love: I changed the dose I was giving you, to see how it would affect you – that's the cause of your forgetfulness when transformed, the reason you've been forgetting human things, like words, and the passage of time. I had to be sure, you see. Sure that it would work. Sure of you. You understand, don't you?'

I nod automatically, and he laughs and tucks a stray strand

of hair behind my ear. 'I knew you would. I'll take Odette to some remote lake when I transform her. Give her a strong enough dose that she will forget ever having been a woman. To everyone else, it will appear that she's vanished. After a fruitless search, and a suitable period of mourning, I will marry you. With Olorys and Atratys and the Crown Estates united, Convocation will never be able to stand against us. Neither will the other dominions.' He stands and draws me up with him. 'We will sweep away any resistance. And then we'll be able to do whatever we want.'

'But you can't –' The words escape before I can stop them.

Siegfried's eyes narrow. 'Can't?'

I'm not sure I can save myself, but I have to at least try to save my cousin. 'You . . . You can't expect me to wait so long to be with you. As you say, Odette doesn't want to rule. Marry me now, and I'll persuade her to step aside. Claim the throne as *my* husband.'

His face softens. 'You want this as much as me. I knew you would. It has to be the way I've described though: I will not risk division within Convocation, or war between the dominions. Too much noble blood would be spilled. But we don't have to wait. The King's Mistress used to be an official court position; as soon as I am king I'll revive it, and we will have our union blessed by the Venerable Sisters in the sanctuary. Then we can be together.' He kisses me on the mouth, and I don't dare resist. 'Come. I'll escort you back to your rooms.'

We don't speak on the way back up through the Citadel. But just before we turn the last corner into the corridor where my apartment is, he pulls me into a dark alcove. 'I'm returning to

L'Ammergeia in two days to attend to some business. We may not have much time together between now and the wedding, so remember: this is our secret. Not a breath of it to anyone. Just carry on as usual, and let events take their course. And don't forget what you owe me.' He pulls a vial of the potion from a pocket and holds it in front of me. 'I hold your life and your dominion in my hand, just as surely as I hold this elixir. One word to Convocation, and your deception will be laid bare. You'll lose everything, my love.'

'Please . . .' I barely murmur the word.

Siegfried smiles in the darkness and puts the potion away. 'You understand me. I knew you would.'

We continue on our way. Siegfried opens the door to my rooms for me and bows. I go inside, shut the door, lock it and stand with my back against it for a moment, before sinking to the floor.

But fear won't allow me to rest. I pull off my dress and my underclothes, determined to shift my shape; if I can transform on my own, Siegfried's main hold over me will be broken. Everything else is just his word against mine. So, by the faint glimmer of starlight, the darkness of the new moon, I try. I try again and again. But with each failure my despair grows and the point of transformation seems further and further away.

What have I done?

And what am I going to do?

The grey light of early morning finds me still awake, sitting in the chair that overlooks the fjord. I've not slept. Instead I've been planning – or trying to plan – and thinking. Thinking about power, mostly, and how men like my uncle, and Siegfried, and Patrus, use it to take whatever they want. How their power corrupts them, and everyone who comes within their orbit. For am I not also tainted? My uncle's action led me to seek revenge, and Siegfried's actions enabled me to take it. There is blood on my hands: the blood of the flightless who died in Lower Farne; the blood of the noble who died last night; perhaps others. Siegfried was right: there is a canker at the heart of the kingdom. But it is not just the king, for whom I can spare no pity. It is all of us.

Odette, I trust, will see the need for change, and take action. But I have to give her that chance. I have to stop Siegfried from seizing the throne. I have to protect my mother's legacy – protect the Atratys that she and my father fought so hard to create. My cousin will hopefully be able to save the kingdom. I just want to save my dominion. And perhaps, if I'm able to, myself.

The day passes. As Siegfried ordered, I spend it exactly as had already been planned. I keep all my engagements, and I am careful to say and do nothing that will excite any interest, or suggest that I am in anyway preoccupied. Each time I look at the clock I will the time to pass faster, so that I can be alone again and relax my guard. The hours drag on. But eventually my last appointment – with an artist: sketches are being made for a portrait of the wedding party – is over. I return to my room and ask Letya to send Lucien to me.

He arrives. I bar the main door behind him, beckon him into

my bedroom and shut and lock that door too. He blushes; I'd find it amusing if I wasn't so nervous about what is to come.

'I've something to tell you, Lucien. Something to confess.'

His blush deepens. 'If this is about you and Lord Siegfried . . .'

A ripple of annoyance makes me clench my fists. 'It is. Though it is not what you are so obviously imagining.'

He ducks his head. 'Forgive me, Your Grace. Please continue.'

I open my mouth – and pause. I'm uncertain where to begin. I'm reluctant to reveal things that must destroy whatever regard Lucien has come to have for me, things that might bring to mind the promise that he made to Turik.

But this is about Atratys now, not me. I want to save my cousins. But I *have* to protect my dominion. So I clear my throat and lift my chin.

'You wanted to know the reason that Siegfried left court just after the king fell ill; he was absent on business that concerns me. I found information that suggested a hawk family might still be alive and dwelling in Olorys. So, at my request, Siegfried went looking for the men who killed my mother.' Lucien has been watching me, but at this he turns away, shaking his head. I force myself to continue. 'Late last night, Siegfried returned. He took me to a room somewhere deep in the Citadel, where he had under guard one man – one survivor – one of the two hawks who attacked me and ended my mother's life. I talked to this man, asked him why he did it, and who sent him. He told me he was paid by the king. Then I watched while Siegfried killed him. Afterwards, Siegfried told me that the king is being poisoned by him and will soon die. He plans to marry Odette, dispose of her, then marry me.' Bile rises in my throat at the thought of it. 'He will directly control over half of Solanum if he's not stopped.'

Lucien is frowning down at the floor. There's a muscle twitching in the side of his jaw. 'The king? The king had your mother murdered?'

'Yes.'

He swears and runs his fingers through his hair, seemingly more angry than surprised. 'Why did Siegfried tell you all this? Are you sure it isn't a trap?'

'I don't think so. He believes I will support him. That I wish to be with him.'

'Of course he would think that.' His words are clipped. 'After he helped you take revenge for your mother's murder . . .' Finally, he looks back up at me. The disappointment in his eyes sinks my heart, makes me wish I could disappear. 'I asked you to let it go, Aderyn. You saw what happened to Lord Hawkin, just for mentioning your mother –'

'It's worse than that.'

He exclaims with disbelief. 'How can it possibly be worse?'

I swallow hard and stand up straighter. 'Siegfried has a friend who is a chemist. He created a potion . . . I don't understand exactly how it works, but it forces our kind to transform. Siegfried plans to give Odette this potion to trap her as a swan. In the meantime, he's been giving it to me. It's how I've been able to fly.'

Lucien draws away from me. 'You mean, your ability –'

'Hasn't returned. I can only shift my shape when Siegfried gives me the potion. I can only shift back when he gives me the antidote. Without him, I am still earthbound. Without him, I may as well be flightless.'

For a long moment, Lucien stares at me, as if he can't take in what I've just said.

'Well done, Your Grace.' He pushes away a chair that stands nearby, shoves it so hard it falls backwards against the hearth. 'Well done. At best, you've embroiled Atratys in attempted treason. At worst, you've handed the entire dominion to a monster.'

Twelve

'But what was I to do?' I spread my hands wide, pleading. 'I have to be able to fly by the wedding, or the king –'

'The king is, by your own account, about to die.'

'Well . . . but if I hadn't asked Siegfried for help, then who's to say that *he* wouldn't have done the same thing? He's still planning to marry Odette. He could force me to fly at the wedding, and claim Atratys when I can't.'

Lucien waves a hand impatiently. 'Could have . . . Might have . . . I'm not going to argue with you over things that haven't happened. The point is, you've pursued your own interests – as usual.' He thumps his fist against the wall and stands there, glaring at me. 'You've acted with no thought for Atratys, no thought for the people who are dependent on you, no thought for anything apart from your own immediate desires. If you had come to me –'

'I would have come to you, the day after Hawkin died. But Letya couldn't find you. And after the first time I flew with Siegfried, I wanted to tell you the truth, Lucien, I really did but I –' I break off. I'm not going to remind Lucien of what he said to Turik that night in the garden. He already looks as if he would happily kill me.

'You what?' His voice is glacial.

'Siegfried was kind to me.' Had seemed kind, at least. 'He talked to me, and spent time with me and offered me his help.'

Lucien drops his gaze. 'So you fell in love with him?'

'No. I never loved him. I thought we were friends, that's all. At least until that night in Deaufleur.'

'Deaufleur? What happened in Deaufleur?'

Weariness is making my brain foggy. I try to bring the conversation back to Siegfried's plotting. 'It doesn't matter. Nothing. What matters –'

'What happened, Aderyn? Did he hurt you?' Lucien strides nearer, his eyes blazing. 'I swear I'm going to kill him if –'

'Nothing happened, Lucien! He kissed me, I told him to stop, and he did.' I don't want to remember how I felt sorry for Siegfried, let alone talk about it. My shoulders are aching; I reach up and try to massage away the knots. 'Why do you care, anyway? I was stupid enough to go there with him.'

I glance at Lucien, questioning.

He shrugs. 'To offer insult to you is to offer insult to Atratys. I would have felt honour-bound to seek satisfaction.'

Lucien and his honour – I wonder if he actually cares about anything else. But I'm too tired to argue any more. 'You couldn't help me fly, Lucien. And I didn't know where else to turn.' He's staring down at the carpet and doesn't respond. 'Stopping Siegfried: that's what matters now. You can berate me for my lack of judgement afterwards, if we're both still alive.'

203

Lucien sighs and drags both hands through his hair. 'You're right, for once.' He picks up the chair but moves to lean against the wall, his arms and his ankles crossed. 'Well, Your Grace?'

'I've been thinking –'

'Not before time,' Lucien mutters.

'– there are two things we have to do. First, find some tangible evidence of Siegfried's plans. I could go straight to Convocation, but then it's just my word against his. And I don't think they'll listen to me. Not when everyone is convinced that Siegfried and I are lovers.' The word tastes bitter in my mouth.

Lucien clamps his lips together, as though he is only restraining himself from making an acidic comment through heroic effort. 'Quite. Can you find the room that he took you to last night?'

'I could try, but . . .' I shake my head. 'Probably not. I didn't know what he was planning, when we were walking down there, and afterwards . . .' I hear again the sickening thud of flesh on stone as the Oloryan guards throw Flayfeather's body into the cellar – guards who shouldn't even have been there. A ripple of remembered horror crawls up my spine. 'I'm going to search Siegfried's rooms instead. He told me he's returning to Olorys the day after tomorrow. I'll find a quiet moment and slip in.'

Lucien is shaking his head. 'It's too dangerous. If you're caught –'

'If I'm caught, I'll say that I forgot he was going away, that I wanted to see him, and that I decided to leave him a note; something like that.'

He looks at me doubtfully. 'But what do you think you'll find? He won't leave incriminating evidence scattered about his bedroom. Siegfried is clever.'

'He is.' I shake my head. 'How the king could have been so deceived as to have thought him stupid, I'll never understand.'

'He wanted to believe it,' Lucien replies. 'That's half the battle.'

'I suppose so. But I'm relying on the fact that Siegfried is arrogant too. He thinks he knows everything, controls everything . . . he might be careless enough to leave some trace of his activities. One of the leaves he used to kill the hawk, for example.'

'Leaves?'

'Some sort of dried plant. I don't . . .' I squeeze my eyes shut as Flayfeather's frantic moaning echoes through my head. 'I don't remember what he called it.'

Lucien's expression is solemn; no trace now of the sympathy he showed after Patrus attacked me.

I stand and walk to the window so I don't have to look at him.

'Describe it to me,' he says. 'I'll go and search Siegfried's room.'

'No. I have more reason to be there. And I want you to go back to Merl. Tell Lord Lancelin what is happening, get the key to the laboratory and go through my father's books. Look for a recipe for something called a counter-active, and bring it back here. I'm hoping it will protect Odette from the effect of the potion – if we don't manage to stop Siegfried before he gets that far.'

Silence. For a moment I wonder if Lucien will suggest that we give the medicine to my uncle too . . .

'Very well. I'll leave after the banquet tonight.'

No mention of the king; I'm glad. There remains just enough of my appetite for revenge for that.

Lucien comes and stands next to me at the window. 'Your Grace . . .' He pauses, running the edge of his thumbnail across the soft wood of the sill. 'My lady, if we survive this –'

'I know. I don't expect forgiveness. Or mercy.'

He frowns, the expression in his eyes unreadable. 'Well, then . . . until this evening.'

A bow, and he is gone. I have a while before I need to dress, so I go back to staring out of the window. But what I'm seeing is my mother, rubbing my back and watching me anxiously as I throw up the mildly poisonous berries I'd eaten in the garden in a rare unsupervised moment, and my father hovering nearby, writing in one of his notebooks and saying, *Don't worry, my love, I'm working on a medicine we can give her, if she does it again* . . .

Such care they'd taken of me. I clasp my hands together.

If you can hear me, help me put things right. Please.

The banquet this evening – the first since my uncle's collapse – is supposedly held by his order to mark the fact that it is now only two weeks until Odette's marriage. It's traditional: the thirteenth eve before a wedding is reserved to honour the groom; the seventh eve, the bride. I don't want to go, but I must: the important thing is to avoid drawing any attention to my growing horror of Siegfried. I have to convince him that I will go along with his plans. I'm getting out of my bath and Letya is laying out my clothes when there's a knock at the door. She goes away, and returns a moment later with a large, linen-wrapped package.

'What is it?

She lays the package on the bed and undoes the ribbons. 'Oh . . . You ordered a new dress?'

Inside the linen is a scarlet silk gown. A red dress. I remember Siegfried's praise of the dress I wore that evening at Deaufleur, and turn away.

'Aderyn?'

I can't put my friend at risk. 'Yes. I thought, perhaps, for the wedding banquets . . .'

She takes the dress out and helps me into it. The skirt is heavy with rubies sewn in intricate patterns onto the silk. To my disappointment, it fits perfectly. And I know very well that Siegfried will know it fits – Gytha must have taken the measurements from the dress she gave me. I stand in front of the looking glass, Letya next to me.

'Beautiful. I like the gold thread running through the silk. But it's very . . .' She gestures at the low-cut bodice.

'I know.'

'You sound as if you don't care for it, Aderyn. You have time to change.'

'No. I'll wear it for this evening.' Letya is still frowning; I force a smile for her sake. 'That will teach me to have a dress made up without consulting you first.'

When Lucien arrives to escort me, his eyes widen.

'Don't you dare say anything,' I murmur. 'Siegfried sent it.' If I survive the next few weeks, I will never wear red again.

Our walk downstairs seems to take twice as long as usual. I try to bow and smile as normal as we pass other courtiers, but I'm growing paranoid. I study each face, wondering who is

207

innocent, who has perhaps already been bought by Siegfried. It's a relief to finally reach the great hall. Out of deference to my uncle's continued illness, there is no music this evening: the gallery above the main door, where the harpists usually sit, is empty. But the hall itself is gorgeous with light and colour. There are huge stands of flowers everywhere: crimson roses, combined with spears of fiery-orange dragon's tongue: the colours of the Dominion of Olorys. I stare down at the skirts of my red dress, feeling as if Siegfried has somehow marked me. Claimed me. When my cousins enter – Aron in black, escorting the queen, and Odette all in white as usual, on Siegfried's arm – they look almost out of place amidst so many vibrant shades. Even the queen, her expression more animated than I've ever seen, is wearing Oloryan colours: a gown made up of layers of flame-coloured tulle. For the first time, I wonder where in Solanum she comes from. A footman approaches me and indicates that I should join the procession behind Odette and Siegfried. I walk in solitary state up to the high table, ahead of the other Protectors and heirs.

The king's place is left empty, so I am seated between Aron and – since Patrus is no longer here to trouble me – Grayling Wren. Grayling says nothing and flinches every time I speak to him; perhaps he thinks I make a habit of stabbing people with knitting needles. He makes no attempt to renew his offer of marriage.

My cousin, in contrast, talks too much, rattling out words like garbled prayers. At one point, under the guise of carving some meat from a haunch of venison, he leans nearer to whisper in my ear, 'I'm surprised Siegfried isn't already warming his arse in my father's chair. The House of Cygnus Olorys has got its talons well and truly into the crown.'

It is not an enjoyable meal. We retire to the long gallery, as usual, and Siegfried makes a speech. He thanks the court for honouring Olorys, wishes the absent king a full and speedy recovery and thanks him and the queen for honouring him, and pays tribute to Odette's beauty and virtue. At least he makes no false profession of love. Though Odette doesn't seem to notice the omission.

Siegfried spends most of the rest of the evening with her. They walk about the room, talking to the other courtiers, and as she leans on his arm she seems truly happy. And Siegfried . . . Siegfried looks happy too. Watching him smile at her, knowing what is in his heart, sickens me.

The only other person who appears less than content is the queen. She seems to be continually watching the young couple, following their movements with a slight frown, a faint downward turn of the lips, marring her perfect features. My heart lifts slightly; if the queen is suspicious of Siegfried, then she is a potential ally.

Siegfried doesn't try to talk to me until nearly the end of the evening. I've gone out onto the terrace to get some air, when I realise he is beside me.

'Don't look so angry, Aderyn; our time will arrive soon enough. I have to at least pretend to hold your cousin in affection.' He glances around to make sure we are completely alone, before brushing his fingers from my jawline down my throat and breastbone. I can't repress a faint shudder of revulsion, but Siegfried merely chuckles; perhaps he takes it for desire. I let him kiss my hands, smiling in the teeth of my loathing, relieved that he has not guessed the true reason for my earlier expression of dismay. 'You like the gown?'

'Of course,' I lie, 'it's beautiful.' He seems to be waiting for something more, so I add, 'And so thoughtful. Thank you, my lord.'

He nods approvingly. 'When I return from Olorys, I'll come and find you.'

Soon after this, I say goodnight to our host the queen – she embraces me, for the first time – and return to my apartment. I allow Letya to think I've gone to bed; once she's blown out the candles and left, I get up again, return to the sitting room and throw open one of the tall windows. Lucien said he would come and take his leave of me before he flies to Atratys; I hope the cool night air will keep me awake despite my exhaustion. In the starlight, everything is hidden. Secret. The water of the fjord glimmers softly as the breeze ripples across it, but I cannot make out the tower that stands in its depths.

'Your Grace . . .' Lucien shakes my shoulder gently. I sit up and rub my eyes as he lights a candle and closes the shutters across the window. He's wearing a long robe, his black hair dishevelled. 'I'm ready to leave. Is there anything else you need me to do at Merl?'

'No, thank you. Just the recipe for the counter-active. My father's records are in some disorder; I hope it won't take you too long to find.' I frown. 'Are you going to be able to carry the book?'

'Once I've found the recipe I'll make a copy. I have carried some heavy loads while flying, but it's not ideal. Trying to work out the adjustments that have to be made to maintain lift gives me a headache.' He smiles a little. 'If you insist on going through with your plan, please be careful. I still don't like it. I don't like you being here alone either. What are the chances that this counter-active will even work?'

'My father was a very skilled chemist. And I won't be alone. I have Letya. And my cousins.' I swallow hard. 'I am sorry, Lucien. You shouldn't be involved in this. If I could have done as you asked, if I could have left the past alone, I swear I would have . . .'

'I understand, I think.' Sighing, he rubs the back of his head. 'None of this is your fault, my lady. Not really. Your mother falling in love with your father – Aron's accident – the king's vengefulness – Siegfried's ambition: all these roads have led us here. A spider's web of events that we've both been caught up in.' He half stretches one hand towards me – but drops it to his side. 'We can't any of us out-fly fate.'

There's a heaviness to his voice that sends a shiver down my spine. Before I can question it, he turns away a little.

'I should leave now. If the winds are with me, and if I find the recipe quickly, I hope to return in three days. Four at the most.'

'Greet your father for me. And Lucien – good luck.' Before I can change my mind, my pulse quickening, I stand on tiptoe and kiss him on the cheek. 'Fly swift. Fly straight.'

'And may the Creator guide you.' He finishes the saying, gazing down at me with those burning black eyes of his, a hint of surprise – and something else, something I can't identify – lurking at the back of them. I blow out the candle and Lucien opens the shutters again, so that the pale black of the windows shows against the deep black of the surrounding shadows. 'Stand back,' he whispers in my ear.

I obey. From the other side of the room I can see Lucien only in silhouette. He removes his robe, places it on a nearby chair, crouches down a little – as if he's about to race – and runs. Runs at the open window in front of him, leaps through it –

For a feather's breadth I see him, stretched out in the air as if he is diving, but then he plunges downward, out of sight –

Rushing to the window, heart pounding, one hand clamped to my mouth, I'm terrified that I will see him falling to his death. See his body broken on the rocks beneath the palace.

But he's not there.

Not as a human.

Instead, an enormous raven, a swift black silhouette against the night sky, is already flying out to sea.

Siegfried departs the following morning. I decide to wait until the afternoon to make my attempt at breaking into his apartment; the castle corridors are usually less busy after lunch. The door will certainly be locked, but I have a plan. I'm going to make use of the gossip that has been spread about me for my own ends.

The elderly guest master is in his office giving instructions to various underlings when I approach.

'Your Grace.' He pushes himself up from his desk, hisses at a hovering footman –'Get out, Porrin!' – and bows. 'How may I assist you? I trust you are here on no serious matter?'

'No, nothing like that.' He hasn't seen me since he came to remove Patrus from my rooms. 'I need a key, that's all.'

'Another key . . . to your apartment?'

'No.' I lift my chin, ignoring the churning in my stomach. 'I need to borrow a key to Lord Siegfried's apartment. He is visiting Olorys, of course, but I've realised I left something in his room last night; a personal item of mine.' The guest master's face has taken on a rigid quality; he is certainly judging me, but equally clearly he cannot be seen to. 'I would ask one of his servants, but . . . you understand our position. So soon after the groomsday banquet.' I force a laugh. 'I feel, however, that I can trust in your discretion.'

My flattery works: the guest master manages to look disapproving and yet somehow gratified at the same time.

'Of course, Your Grace. Not another word is necessary.' He disappears into another room and emerges a couple of minutes later with a key in his hand. 'If Your Grace would be so good as to return it in due course . . .'

'Indeed.' I take the key, pressing a gold coin into his gloved hand, and leave.

The key stowed safely in my pocket, I go to the north wing and roam the corridors and public rooms near Siegfried's apartment for a little while, partly to get a sense of where the Dark Guards are stationed, mostly to build up my courage. Eventually I can't stand to wait any longer. Checking for the last time that no one is in sight, I let myself into the main room and lock the door behind me.

It's a sitting room, smaller than mine and facing onto the city, somewhat sparsely furnished. There's a desk between the windows, a harpsichord to one side, a tall bookcase in an alcove to my left and a couple of sofas and small tables. The

213

door in the far corner must lead to his bedroom. I decide to start with the desk. There are papers collected in the obvious drawers, but all seem to relate to the administration of Olorys: letters of introduction, requests for intervention in land disputes, the sorts of things that are sitting piled on my own desk at home. I begin pressing various decorated panels within the desk, hoping for the revelation of a secret compartment, but it seems to be a depressingly ordinary piece of furniture. And I know from the chimes of the clock that I've already been here a quarter of an hour. As I stand there, hands on my hips, trying to decide whether to check the bookcase next, or try the bedroom, the castle bell begins to toll. And there are footsteps, running in the corridor outside . . .

I hurry towards the door, but I can hear voices now – the sound of a key in the lock – in a panic I wedge myself into the alcove next to the bookcase as the door opens.

It's a youngish man, one of Siegfried's servants, I guess. I'm trying not to breathe, but my heart is thumping so hard it's difficult not to gasp for air. The man has his back to me; he sits at the desk, gets out some paper and a pen and begins writing. All I can do is wait.

The clock has just chimed away another quarter of an hour when the man gets up and disappears from view for a moment. My muscles are cramping, but I don't dare move. There's a knock at the door; the man – a letter in his hand – opens it, and I hear his voice: 'Take this to L'Ammergeia. Quick as you can; if you can catch up with his lordship, I expect he'll make it worth your while.' He must be talking to one of the pages who live at the Citadel – young, lower-ranking nobles who are employed as a messenger service. Perhaps, now the letter is written and handed over, the servant will leave.

He doesn't. Instead, he stays in the room and starts tidying. I begin to feel faint; there's a pile of books on a table nearby, and if he decides to replace them in the bookcase –

Another knock at the door. It opens, and a housemaid walks in, followed by some sort of workman. The maid drops a curtsy. 'We're to see about the loose floorboard in His Lordship's bedroom.' She nods to the workman and they move towards the door in the corner, as Siegfried's servant follows them and begins to dispute their right to carry out the work . . .

All three of them enter the bedroom, and the door to the corridor is standing open –

Walk, not run – act as if you belong here . . . To my relief, the corridor is empty. I make it back to my rooms – just – before I throw up.

Letya looks after me. She assumes it must have been something I ate, puts me to bed and goes to see my cousins, to tell them I will not be joining them for supper. My failed attempt has exhausted me. I fall asleep with Siegfried's key tucked underneath my pillow.

The next morning, after Letya has brought my breakfast, I send her back to the guest master. The keys are all so similar – just tiny variations in the arrangement of the teeth – that I am reasonably confident the old man will not notice my deceit. The key Letya gives him is not the key to Siegfried's apartment, but one of the spare keys to my own quarters.

I'm planning to make a second attempt to search Siegfried's rooms this afternoon, but anxiety is making my head ache. Anxiety, mingled with unreasonable disappointment that Lucien has not yet returned. My father's note-taking was meticulous but extensive; at his death, there were notebooks everywhere, strewn across tables, chairs, the floor. I had them gathered up and locked into bookcases, but in no particular order. It's hardly surprising if Lucien is struggling to find the recipe.

In an effort to clear my head, Letya and I go riding before lunch. The fresh air does me good. Still, I can feel my knees trembling beneath my long skirts as I head back to the north wing. I'm almost at Siegfried's apartment when the door opens and Siegfried himself emerges.

The shock nearly fells me. 'My lord . . .'

'Aderyn.' He smiles, but there's a faint hint of suspicion in his eyes. 'What are you doing here?'

'My waiting woman told me she'd heard you had returned. And I've missed you . . .' The ease with which I lie disgusts me; another symptom of the Citadel's corrupting influence perhaps. Still, my words appear to reassure Siegfried.

'Of course you have. Come.' He turns back into his room. 'I have a few moments.' With the door shut, I'm scared that he might try to kiss me again. But instead he takes my hand and leads me to a sofa as he starts talking about our future at the Citadel. How, once he is king, he will have me moved to an apartment next to his own with an inter-connecting door. How we will explore Olorys and Atratys together. Idle conversation, seemingly. But I am beginning to think that, with

Siegfried, every sentence – every word – should be weighed for double meaning.

He seems a little distracted and sends me away again before long. I return to my own apartment, the stolen key still in my pocket, wondering what I can do to be certain of gaining undisturbed access to his rooms. I've considered and rejected the idea of bribing one of Siegfried's servants, when I notice a letter that has been left on the sideboard. The wax disc sealing the folded paper is marked with the royal coat of arms – it's from the queen.

A twinge of excitement bubbles up beneath my ribs as I break the seal. Perhaps she has found out about Siegfried. Perhaps the wedding is cancelled . . .

I read the letter through twice as my excitement fades into doubt. The contents inform me that three members of Convocation were arrested yesterday – was that why the castle bell was being rung? These nobles, one each from the Dominions of Lancorphys, Dacia and Fenian, have been accused of high treason against the crown. The trial is tomorrow evening. And I am summoned, since I am a Protector, to play the role of judge.

Nothing to do with the wedding. Nothing, on the face of it, to do with Siegfried, though I seem to see his shadow everywhere.

I wish Lucien were here.

Thirteen

But the wishing does not help. The best part of another morning wears away, and Lucien does not come. Instead, I go in search of Aron.

I find him – eventually – in the formal gardens. He is sitting on a bench with a small knife in his hand, carving his initials into the trunk of a beech tree.

'That seems needlessly destructive,' I observe.

'That comment seems needlessly antagonistic,' he replies, 'since I assume you want something.'

I sit down next to him. 'I'm sorry. Perhaps I'm just here to enjoy your company.'

'Really?' Aron quirks an eyebrow, still digging away at the bark of the tree.

'Well . . . that could be why I'm here. I do like you, strange as that may seem. But as it happens, I also need your help.'

He laughs and puts the knife down. 'I am at your disposal, cousin.'

'It's about this trial.'

The smile drops from his face. 'I don't know any of the accused well, but I pity them. Their families will be left with nothing once they are convicted. Less than nothing.'

'You speak as if they've already been found guilty.'

'Innocent or guilty, it doesn't matter. Clearly they are perceived as a threat to the throne; therefore they will be swept away. In a wing-beat. Despite what you may have read, Cygnus I claimed the crown as much with guile as with might. And for the last five generations we've held on to it in the same way.' He glances up at the Citadel. 'I wonder if this is my father's doing? Perhaps he is losing his mind . . .'

'But I'm supposed to be a judge. That implies a choice.'

Aron picks up the knife – tosses it into the air, blade flashing – catches it again. 'You would think that. But your judgement, in this case, will likely only be required to determine the severity of their punishment.' He frowns. 'Why are you asking me about this? Have you and Lucien had another fight?'

'He's not here. I sent him back to Merl to fetch something.'

My cousin seems amused. 'Lucien the errand boy. I'm sure he was thrilled.'

I can't resist asking. 'What happened between you two? What did Lucien do to make you hate him?'

'What did Lucien do . . . ?' He sighs. 'I suppose there's no harm in telling you. It's a sad tale of young love, misdirected. Some of us, as you'll know, love only the opposite sex. Some love only the same sex. And some, myself included, are more generous with our affection. You understand, I think.'

I nod.

'All honourable forms of love, all sanctioned by Litany and

219

Decree. But, unfortunately for me, the first person I fell in love with was Lucien Rookwood.'

'You were in love with Lucien?'

'Yes.'

'But why was it unfortunate?'

'Because, my dear cousin, when I confessed my love, he rejected me. Oh, he was kind enough. Told me that he was flattered, that if it was at all possible for him to return my affection, he would. That he hoped we could still be friends. But it was still a rejection. And, as perhaps is the way when it comes to first loves, I took it very personally. Perhaps, in retrospect, too personally.'

'I'm sorry, Aron.'

He shrugs. 'It wasn't exactly his fault. And I find now that Lucien's company is . . . perfectly tolerable. I hadn't seen him for a couple of years before he returned to court with you.'

We both fall silent. I think about Aron and Lucien, and Odette and Siegfried, and the happiness that my parents knew with each other. The breeze catches my skirts, scattering gold leaves across the grass; summer is fading. Next to me, Aron is studying his knife, twisting the pattern-welded blade back and forth so it catches the light.

'What are you thinking about?'

He glances up at me. 'You really want to know?' I nod, and he continues. 'I'm thinking about whether I should stick this knife into Siegfried's back at the next banquet.'

I wait for a moment, thinking that he'll laugh, somehow turn the statement into a joke. But he doesn't. 'You'd be executed.'

'So? I don't trust him. I don't want him marrying my sister.

Odette is the only person who loves me for who I am. She's the only person at court who hasn't treated me like an outcast since I lost the power of flight, and I'd do anything to protect her. Including dying for her.' He shrugs. 'I'd kill him as he sits down to his meat, because I doubt I can get close enough to him at any other time.'

I put my hand over his, stilling the movement of the knife. 'Have you talked to Odette? Have you tried to explain why you don't trust him? Given your father's illness, perhaps together we can persuade her to at least delay the wedding . . .'

His eyes widen slightly. '*We* persuade?'

'Yes; you're the only family I have left. And I've grown fond of you over the past few weeks. Of both of you. Have you spoken to her?'

'I have. But as she pointed out, she has to marry someone. Besides, she's convinced herself that she loves Siegfried. And she still holds our father in enough affection to talk of duty, of retaining the crown in our direct line. Ridiculous, since she has no interest in ruling.' He thrusts the knife back into its scabbard. 'But do you, cousin?'

'No. Of course not.' I glance around to make sure we are still alone and lean closer to him. 'I think things need to change though. I've seen little enough of the kingdom, but what I witnessed in Brithys, and Olorys . . . it's not right, Aron. People's lives shouldn't depend on laws they can't change and the whim of whoever owns the bit of land they happen to live in. My parents made a difference in Atratys, but that's just one dominion. You and Odette could change everything across the whole of Solanum.'

'Me?' He raises an eyebrow and gestures to his missing arm.

'Odette then. But with your guidance, if she's unsure how to begin.'

'Easy enough to *tell* people to change things . . .'

'Odette is going to be the next queen. I'm not.' My cousin doesn't reply. 'Honestly, Aron, I only want to protect Atratys. That's all I've ever wanted.' I hesitate, debating telling him everything. But I have finally – too late, perhaps – learned to be cautious. 'Try talking to Odette again. But don't risk yourself yet.'

Aron narrows his eyes. 'Why exactly are you giving me this advice, cousin?'

'Because, cousin, I do not trust Lord Siegfried either.'

The trial is held in the throne room. When I arrive, the queen is already perched on the edge of the carved and gilded throne, shoulders hunched, hands clutched in the lap of her slate-grey gown. Six seats are set out for the judges. Two are reserved for Arden of Dacia and me. We are the only two Protectors currently at court; like Nyssa Swifting and Grayling Wren, Siegfried is still only an heir, at least in name. The four other judges are members of Convocation, chosen by lot. The queen will have the casting vote. I sit next to Arden; he is watching the queen, tapping the fingers of one hand against his thigh over and over. Tall candles on even taller silver candlesticks – taller than a man – have been set around the throne and the judges' chairs – three on either side of the throne – encircling us in light. According to Aron, the candles are supposed to represent a ring of truth and justice. The rest of the room is in darkness.

But I can just make out the courtiers, crowded into the gallery that runs around the top of the room. The candlelight glints on jewels and sword hilts, and on the armour of the Dark Guards stationed around the outer perimeter of our circle of light. Siegfried and my cousins may be in the gallery, but it is impossible for me to tell.

More guards accompany the three accused nobles – two men and a woman – into the throne room. Their hands are bound in front of them. They look dishevelled and bewildered, and one of them stumbles as if exhausted, but I can't see any obvious signs of mistreatment. They are brought to stand before the judges, facing the throne.

The queen clears her throat. 'Let the prosecutor approach.'

The master secretary enters the candlelit ring, accompanied by a flightless assistant carrying a folder of papers. 'Your Majesty, honourable judges, I have here evidence collected of the treasonable intentions of the accused. Letters between the accused in which the approaching marriage of the Princess Odette is debated and questioned. Letters in which the enduring nature of the Decrees is debated and questioned. Letters in which the very fitness of His Majesty to rule –' the secretary pauses, and looks up at the gallery as the courtiers murmur and exclaim – 'is debated and questioned. In all of these letters there are hints of an even deeper treason. Suggestions of a plot, as yet uncovered, to remove Your Majesties from the throne.' More horrified exclamations from the onlookers. 'Furthermore, the accused have confessed to having written the letters. Guilt is admitted. Punishment must follow.'

Aron was right. This trial is a sham. The six of us are not

223

judges: we are mute witness, gathered merely so that people can point to us and say that justice was done. I risk a glance at Arden; his face is sallow in the candlelight, and he is gripping the arms of his chair tightly.

The queen sighs and stares down at the enormous diamond ring on her forefinger. 'The traditional punishment for high treason is a lingering death in the arena for the guilty, followed by seizure of their lands and goods and the imposition of indentured servitude on their dependents.' One of the accused begins weeping. 'However, I have petitioned His Majesty, and thankfully he is minded to be lenient. If you provide us with the names of the people involved in the plot hinted at in your letters, you will be granted swift deaths and your families will be spared any further punishment. However, if you decline to cooperate . . .' She sighs again, as if the fate of these people pains her. 'It is, of course, your choice.'

One of the male prisoners lifts his head. 'Mercy, Your Majesty, I beg you.'

'Mercy? Oh, there will be a time for mercy.' The queen's voice sharpens. 'But only once we have burned away all that is rotten.' She waves her hand and the guards move to escort the prisoners back out of the hall. But the same man who spoke before begins struggling.

'My Lord Arden – Your Grace –' he shouts loudly enough, but Arden doesn't respond, just clutches the chair and stares straight ahead as if his life depends on it, '– my dear cousin, I beseech you, there is no treason here, no plot, we have done nothing –'

The doors are slammed shut, cutting off his voice.

* * *

Another restless night. When I do finally get to sleep, I'm woken before sunrise by Letya, bearing a summons from the queen. My companion's face is drawn; the story of last night's trial has already spread rapidly around the Citadel. The miasma of fear infecting the corridors was palpable even before I retired to bed. But the embossed card Letya hands me bears no indication of why I am required.

Ten minutes later I am in the queen's withdrawing room, standing on the intricately patterned carpet as the queen, in a pale blue dressing gown that enhances the silvery cast of her skin, paces in front of me. She seems to have some difficulty coming to the point; either that, or she is trying to make me more nervous.

'Well, niece,' she begins finally, 'you are wondering, perhaps, why I have asked you to wait on me this morning?'

I try to imagine how Lord Lancelin would advise me, if he were here right now, and incline my head. 'My only desire is to serve, Your Majesty.'

'I'm sure. It is so difficult for me to know what to do for the best, with the king as ill as he is.'

I almost ask, *How ill is he, exactly?* But silence seems more prudent.

She takes a few more turns about the room, twisting the diamond ring on her finger. I notice for the first time that the stone is cut so it rises into a sharp point.

'Still,' she continues, 'I must ask, I suppose. Lord Siegfried . . . how do you find him? Do you like him?'

'Well enough, Your Majesty.'

'And –' she takes a deep breath, fiddling with the lace that

225

edges her dressing gown – 'are the rumours true? Are you sharing his bed?'

The directness of her question throws me; perhaps the guest master's discretion was less to be relied upon than I'd hoped. The queen is watching me carefully. I take a deep breath and look her full in the face. 'No, Your Majesty. I am not. I never have.'

She sighs and smiles. 'Good. I'm so glad.'

What is this really about? Is she worried that, somehow, I'm going to disrupt the wedding?

More back and forth across the carpet. 'And tell me –' the queen throws me a sideways glance – 'what is your opinion of the princess's betrothal? I know you spend time with her. Do you think it will be a happy marriage?'

Here is my chance, if I want to take it: I could repeat to the queen exactly what Siegfried said to me, both at Deaufleur and on the night he killed Flayfeather. With the king ill – dying – the queen is the most powerful figure at court. Surely, if anyone can stop Siegfried, it's her.

And yet . . .

I hear Lucien's voice in my head, as clearly as if he were standing behind me: *Trust no one.*

'I would not presume to have an opinion, Your Majesty. I'm sure the princess is the best judge of her own happiness.' My guess is that the king ordered the trial I attended yesterday; it would fit with his paranoia and vindictive character. But I cannot be certain. And I do not intend to be the next person arrested.

'Very true.' The queen nods. 'Perhaps I am worrying for nothing. Thank you for your time, niece.'

I'm free to go.

It's not until I'm outside of the royal suite that I realise I've been digging my nails so hard into the palms of my hands that my skin is bleeding.

Letya is waiting for me. 'Thank the Creator. I feared –'

'Don't. So did I.'

As we walk back to my rooms, I try to work out what is going on. Because there is something else, something other than the skeletal plot that Siegfried shared with me. I don't for a moment believe anything that I heard at yesterday's trial. But somewhere – somewhere – there is flesh, and feather, and colour, if only I could see it.

Trust no one.

But that's not possible, not really. I need help.

Back in my sitting room, I ask Letya to sit down.

'I have to ask you to do something.'

'Anything.'

'I'd like you to collect information for me. You're more observant than anyone I know. If you can talk to the servants, try to find out whether there is anything unusual going on with regard to . . .' I hesitate, wondering what I should say, how much I can tell my friend without compromising her safety any more than I have to.

'Is this about Lord Siegfried, Aderyn?'

I glance at her sharply.

'Yes. You've heard something?'

'There's been a rumour among the servants for a while now, that he aims at more than just the crown. And Turik told me about what happened to his family. How they had to run away.'

227

Her reference confuses me. 'Turik? I thought he'd escaped from Brithys?' Or had I just assumed it was Brithys, that night in the garden?

'No. He comes – came – from Olorys. His mother got him and his sister out, but his father . . . Turik was only a little boy. But they made him watch his father die.' Her mouth twists in distaste. 'Over some Decree that had been broken.'

Owning a bow and arrow, perhaps . . .

'Lord Siegfried cannot be allowed to become king. But he is cruel and powerful, and to offer any kind of opposition is risky. My friend, if I'm asking too much –'

'Atratys is my home too, Aderyn. I saw the suffering in Brithys, just as you did. I've seen more than you, I reckon, of how the flightless are treated here. Did you know that the servants in the Citadel are not allowed to learn how to read? Of course, some still try. One of the housemaids got caught with a book a few weeks back. She got branded on the hand and turned away with no reference.' Letya's eyes flash. 'I saw her begging when I was in the city the other day; the poor thing looked half starved. So, yes, I'm willing. I'll do whatever I can to stop Atratys falling to someone like Siegfried, or turning into somewhere like this. I know Turik will say the same.'

'Thank you, Letya.' I lay my hand almost on top of hers. 'I wish so much that I could hug you.'

She gives me a wry smile and gets up. 'I know. Now, it's still early. Shall I fetch you some –'

There's a knock at the door. Letya opens it a crack. 'It's Lord Lucien. He's back.'

I study Lucien's face as he sits on my sofa, drinking a cup of chocolate. There's stubble on his chin and dark shadows beneath his eyes.

He notices my scrutiny and flushes. 'I apologise, Your Grace. I thought it best to come straight here.' He tries, not very successfully, to tidy his hair by running his fingers through it.

'Don't apologise, Lucien. You look exhausted, that's all. You should have rested longer at Merl.'

'I didn't want to delay my return any further. It took me more time than I'd hoped to find the recipe for the counter-active among your father's notes, and I wasn't ready to leave until last night.'

Last night? He must have flown at speed, and without stopping, to get back here so fast. I want to tell him how much I appreciate his help – I want to reach across and brush away the smudge of dirt on his collarbone too – but something stops me. Clasping my hands in my lap, so I won't be tempted, I take refuge in formality.

'Atratys thanks you for your efforts, Lord Rookwood.' He looks so surprised at my ridiculous sentence that I burst out laughing. 'I'm sorry. I mean, thank you, Lucien.' My laughter fades. 'You didn't have to agree to help me.'

He half smiles, raising an eyebrow. 'Can you imagine my father's reaction, if I hadn't?'

'You have a point.'

'May I ask whether *your* undertaking met with success?'

'Well . . .' I pour him some more chocolate as I describe my two attempts to search Siegfried's room, followed by the trial and my interview with the queen. By the time I finish, he is glowering at the carpet.

'What is it that we're missing?'

'You agree, then, that something else is happening here?' He nods, so I continue. 'If the queen knows that someone is moving to take the throne, but doesn't know who, then that might explain the trial. Perhaps she is hoping to flush Siegfried out.'

'Possibly. Or perhaps –' He breaks off to stifle a yawn. 'Forgive me.'

'Lucien, you should go and rest. We can talk about this later.'

'Of course.' He picks up a bracelet of mine from the table – fine gold filigree, made to look like a feather curling around my wrist – and twirls it in his fingers. But he makes no move to leave.

'My lord, is something wrong?'

He sighs. 'When I was in the laboratory at Merl, examining your father's books, I found something that . . .' his frown deepens, 'something that worried me.'

I wait for him to continue.

'My lady, has it occurred to you . . .' He stops again, still focused on the bracelet, a tiny shake of his head suggesting he is trying to dismiss some unwelcome thought.

'Lucien?' A coil of fear makes the hair on the back of my neck stand up. 'Please, tell me.'

'This chemist friend that Siegfried mentioned, the one who supposedly produced the poison that is killing the king . . .' He places the bracelet carefully back on the table and looks up at me. 'Your Grace, has it occurred to you that Siegfried's friend might have been your father?'

Fourteen

'My father? Don't be ridiculous, Lucien!' I jump up and prowl about the room, until my gaze alights on the book I'm reading at the moment; a slim volume of poetry my father gave me for my birthday one year. I snatch it up and clutch it to my chest. 'My father was a good man. He studied to be a healer, not a murderer.'

'I know that, but –'

'And besides, Siegfried says his friend created the potion that forces me to transform, as well as whatever is poisoning the king. If my father had developed such a potion, do you really think that he wouldn't have given it to me? That he would have taken that secret with him to the pyre? It's impossible.'

Lucien doesn't answer.

My chest tightens. My father certainly had a motive, if he did indeed suspect his brother of orchestrating my mother's death. And Siegfried himself told me that they'd met.

But it's still impossible.

I flip to the front of my book and read the inscription:

To my beloved daughter, for her fourteenth birthday – 'And where the stars sing, there will you soar. And where the stars fall, there will you be free.' Another quotation from the Litanies. 'My father loved me.'

'Of course he did. But what if this friend is actually more than one person? There's no reason we should assume Siegfried is telling the truth. Maybe someone else created the transforming potion. But your father developed the poison.'

I shake my head, impatient. 'Why are you saying these things?'

Lucien holds out a small package that has been sitting next to him on the sofa. 'I found this, in your father's laboratory.'

I take the package unwillingly, and look inside. One of my father's notebooks, though smaller than the ones he typically used. And as I begin to flip through it, I see that the layout is not in the same style as the rest of my father's books either. Usually he started with observations about a particular illness – symptoms, occurrence, rapidity of spread of infection and so on – and from that would then start concocting experimental draughts. But this book . . . It doesn't seem like a book of cures. I scan the page open in front of me: *Mountain scabious, slow-acting but method of delivery not clear, too obviously present for direct consumption . . . . Dolorous ant, very venomous but difficulty in extraction may not make it worthwhile . . .* Entry after entry in my father's cramped handwriting. I keep turning the pages until I come to a place where someone – Lucien? – has tucked a bookmark. The writing is more uneven here; I take the book to the window and tilt it towards the light, squinting at the words.

'. . . and since the rock dragon has survived the procedure, giving us the possibility of obtaining more venom, I have proceeded to the next stage of the experiment. I look forward (with some trepidation) to discovering how the compound poison manifests itself. I anticipate some damage to the skin – lesions or suchlike – may be the earliest indicator . . .'

The rock dragon on the beach, with the broken chain around its neck.

The lesions that I saw on my uncle. Similar, now I think about it, to the weeping sores marring my father's skin before his death. Is it possible that he had been experimenting on himself?

And who is the 'us' he refers to?

I slam the book shut.

Lucien is watching me.

'It can't be true.' I take a deep, shuddering breath. 'It can't be true, because . . .' Because if it is, then how much else that I thought I knew to be true is actually a lie?

I stare down at the book in my hands. It's evidence, perhaps, of my father's complicity in the king's illness. But I still have no evidence of Siegfried's involvement. All I can do is repeat what he's told me: that he is planning to seize the kingdom. That he believes me to be a willing accomplice. My heart beats faster. Would other people believe the same? There are certainly enough rumours about me. What if I'm brave enough to claim it as the truth?

'Turn me in.'

'What?' My clerk frowns, not understanding.

'Use this as proof. I'll write a confession – I'll say that

Siegfried and I have been working together, using my father's notes; that we planned to take the throne. Summon the Dark Guards to arrest me, and I'll tell Convocation everything Siegfried told me.'

'I'm not going to do that.' Lucien is shaking his head. 'You're in shock, Aderyn, but there's no reason to –'

'We don't have any other options, Lucien.'

'You're being ridiculous.'

'No, I'm not. Hand me over. If the queen is looking for some reason to go after Siegfried, this will provide it. Maybe someone will be able to find Flayfeather's body. And you'll probably be given Atratys as a reward.'

Lucien pushes himself up from the sofa and begins striding about the room. 'Madness! You know what they'll do to you if you confess to treason? They'll take you out to the arena and then –'

I talk over him, trying to focus on Lucien's future, not my inevitable execution. 'Of course, the Skein would have to be summoned –' to resettle a dominion would require the consent of the whole assembly: monarch plus Protectors plus Convocation – 'but I'm sure they would be happy to make you the new Protector.'

My clerk makes a sound – somewhere between a laugh and a groan – and drops his head into his hands. 'I don't want Atratys.'

'But why not? You'd be a much better Protector than me. Aron understands: there's no place in the kingdom for a noble who can't fly. And Atratys deserves better than a Protector who cannot transform, who cannot truly protect.' I run my tongue over my dry lips. 'You deserve better.'

234

'No.' Lucien looks up; to my surprise, his eyes are full of anguish. 'I'm not a traitor, Aderyn. And I –' He breaks off, breathing hard. 'You don't know what you're saying, what you're asking of me. And you're wrong. I doubt I'd do any better than you, in the circumstances.'

I put the book of poisons down next to the book my father gave me and press the heels of my shaking hands against my eyes. Perhaps my father was tricked by Siegfried, as I was for a time. Perhaps he meant only to scare his brother, to force him to some confession. He was a good man. But a good man can still do terrible things.

I, of all people, should know that.

'It was horrible, Lucien: the way Flayfeather died. And I was the one who told Siegfried to kill him. I stood there and watched him suffer. And I was glad.'

Lucien comes and stands next to me. Is he going to take me in his arms? Hold me, the way he did the night that Patrus attacked me? I wish he would. My heart – all of me – aches to rest against him. To feel protected, if only for a moment. But he just puts one hand hesitantly on my shoulder.

It's all I can reasonably expect, I suppose.

'It wouldn't have made any difference, Aderyn. Whatever you said or did, Siegfried was always going to kill him.'

'Perhaps.'

I'll never actually be certain.

With an effort, I put my father out of my mind. There is yet another wedding rehearsal later this morning – the last one, I hope – so I send Lucien away to rest and summon Letya and hope that the other participants will not notice (or at least not comment upon) how weary I look.

Letya bullies me into eating some breakfast before I leave my rooms, and I'm glad: the rehearsal drags on for nearly four hours. The Venerable Mother insists on taking us through every detail of the ceremony. We hear (more than once) the readings from the Litanies. We listen to the Responsories, sung by a chorus of flightless singers huddled precariously near the edge of the platform. We practise walking and kneeling at the right moments. For some reason Siegfried himself isn't there, and Odette has to make her vows to the Venerable Mother instead, but it makes it easier for me to slip away with my cousin when we are finally released.

Together she and I wind our way down the main staircase to the entrance hall, then out to the wide stone steps that lead to the inner courtyard; we are making for the sanctuary. The bridge that spans the courtyard – vaulting over a stream that runs from the mountains to the fjord – is being cleaned; there are servants, gloved as usual, scrubbing the white, crystal-flecked marble even whiter, in preparation for the wedding. They stop their tasks and bow as we walk past.

After the brilliance of the sunlit courtyard the darkness of the sanctuary blinds me; my eyes take a few moments to adjust. Odette has moved towards one of the side chapels. I follow, watching the motions of her body as she kneels briefly then rises to light a candle before the image displayed on the chapel wall. She's as graceful as one of the flightless ballet dancers we watched perform in the great hall, what seems like months ago now.

'Well, cousin, shall we walk?'

There's no one else here, as far as I see, so I link an arm though hers and we begin strolling around the edge of the main circular space. Our footsteps on the inlaid floor echo through the dusty shadows.

'How long have you known Siegfried, Odette?'

'Not long really, I suppose. He spent some time at court while he was growing up, as most nobles do. But he is a little older than Aron and me, and Aron never liked him. And I was too nervous to talk to him. I had to be content with admiring him from a distance.' She smiles slightly and glances sideways at me. 'Why?'

'Because he mentioned some things, during the time we spent alone.' I pause, frowning; I've made it sound as if he was discussing his favourite food. 'I mean, he confessed something.'

'Confessed?' Odette's brows arch. 'You're making me nervous.'

'You're right to be nervous.' I try to think of some way of softening what I'm about to say, but I can't. Instead I stop walking and face her. 'Siegfried is responsible for your father's illness, Odette. He means to kill the king. And later . . .'

'I suppose you're going to tell me he's planning to kill me too.' Her voice is light and flippant. 'Whatever Aron and Lucien may say, Siegfried is not his father.'

'No: he's far worse. He plans not to kill you, but to drug you. To trap you in the form of a swan. Permanently.'

She laughs in relief. 'Ridiculous. It isn't possible. He's been leading you astray, cousin. Or you're trying to frighten me.' Her smile fades. 'Are you that desperate to separate us, Aderyn?

Do you really think that if I break off the engagement he will turn to you instead?'

'No! I want nothing of the sort. If only you knew how many lies Siegfried has told. Even my ability to transform is a lie: it's a potion he gives me that changes my shape, not me. I was . . . I was utterly deceived by him, as you have been. Please, Your Highness, you have to listen to me –'

'But I don't, cousin. The only thing I have to do is get married.'

I clench my fists. 'Odette, I am trying to find evidence to support my accusations, but in the meantime, you must protect yourself –'

'I've always loved this window.'

Confused, I follow Odette's gaze and stare up at the huge stained-glass window. It must face south-west; the colours of the glass are glowing as if lit by fire. The window shows a map of the kingdom, but instead of the familiar borders of the dominions and the Crown Estates there are pictures: tiny, frozen images of Solanum. A snow-capped mountain; a green meadow; a turquoise lake; a golden-leafed oak tree. Too many for me to take them all in.

'Our kingdom is beautiful, is it not?' my cousin asks.

'Yes. It is.'

She turns to face me. 'You tell me to protect myself. But who will protect the people of the kingdom, if I do not?'

'Aron actually wishes to rule. If we could convince Convocation –'

Odette shakes her head. 'You know the Decrees, cousin. If I refuse to marry, I cannot rule. Aron cannot fly, so he cannot rule. And now you tell me that you too are flightless. If my father dies and I am not wed, or I refuse the throne, who will Convocation turn to? Who is next in line?'

I mutter the answer. 'Aurik of Olorys. And after him, Siegfried.'

'Exactly. Siegfried.' Her voice hardens. 'And I could name you a dozen courtiers who will be willing to marry him, murderer or not, for the chance to wear the crown.' She takes my hands. 'As I said before, I'm not blind, cousin. I know that my betrothed is not the kind of man I would wish him to be. I accept that you are trying to help me. And if you had this evidence of which you speak –'

'But if we tell Convocation, they could help. There is a body somewhere below the Citadel –'

'Cousin, you are a newly anointed Protector who cannot fly and who has spent only a few weeks at court. You have no support outside your own dominion. Convocation will not believe you.' She sighs. 'They will be too afraid of Siegfried to believe you. Unless the queen steps in, I will marry him. If what you say is true, once I am queen I will have the power to stop him. I hope.'

One of the Venerable Sisters comes in and starts adding more oil to the lamps. She smiles at us and inclines her head.

'As you wish, Odette. But if you think of any way in which I can help you . . .'

'Stay here. Don't return to Atratys. Don't leave Aron and me alone.'

Does she understand what she's asking of me? Perhaps not. But I cannot abandon her.

239

The castle bell sounds.

'Again?' Odette frowns. 'Not more arrests. Or –' she swallows, and quickens her pace – 'perhaps it is my father . . .'

Together we retrace our steps to the Citadel. The high-ceilinged entrance hall is full of courtiers, huddled in knots or glancing nervously around, while up above us the bell still clangs. A few people notice me and begin whispering.

'Look.' Odette points to the stairs: Aron is coming to meet us. 'Brother, what's amiss? Is Father worse?'

'No, his condition is unchanged.' Aron glances at me. 'But the members of Convocation who were convicted of treason have volunteered some additional details of this supposed plot, apparently. No arrests, not yet, but some people have been taken in for questioning.'

Odette slips her hand into mine. I ask the question, even though I am certain of the answer.

'Lucien?'

He nods, and my heart races in a sharp spike of panic . . .

But panic is not going to help. I take a deep breath. 'Where are they being questioned? And by whom?'

'Up on the top floor, south wing. There's a small hall, the Sun Chamber. The master secretary is conducting the interviews, assisted, apparently –' he raises an eyebrow at his sister – 'by Lord Redwing.'

Siegfried. If he is up in this Sun Chamber, he is not in his apartment.

'How long, do you think, before they are allowed to leave?'

'I've no idea. Some hours, I would imagine.'

'Thank you, Aron. If you'll excuse me . . .' I bow to my

cousins and hurry as fast as I can, without attracting undue attention, back to my rooms.

By the time Letya arrives, a few minutes later, out of breath – I guess she ran, after I jerked so viciously on the bell pull – I have my plan clear in my mind.

'Aderyn, I heard about Lord Lucien –'

'I know, but we have something to do that can't wait.' She looks startled, but I press on. 'You mentioned housemaids to me the other day. They all wear uniform, don't they? Are they all exactly the same?'

She nods. 'Shades of grey. Dark grey gown, light grey cap and apron.'

'Do you think you could get hold of one of the uniforms?'

'I should think so – I know the laundry mistress. But what would you do with one?'

'People don't pay any attention to servants.' Hurt flickers in Letya's eyes; I correct myself. 'I'm sorry, my friend. What I meant to say is, nobles – courtiers – we're used to not really seeing the people other nobles employ as servants. The housemaids in particular: all dressed the same, present in every part of the Citadel . . . No noble would give a second glance at a housemaid. I doubt many of the more senior servants would either.'

'True enough.'

'I need to get back into Lord Siegfried's rooms. I managed to keep a key, and I know that right now he is upstairs questioning people – it's the perfect time. If you can get me a uniform, even if someone does come in, it will just look as if I'm dusting.'

Letya's expression is sceptical. 'Aderyn, I love you, but you've

241

never dusted anything in your life.' She grins. 'I have a better idea . . . I'll be back directly.'

While I wait for Letya's return, I consider potential allies among my fellow Protectors and the other courtiers. Patrus – were he here – would presumably side with Siegfried, out of spite if nothing else. Grayling Wren will probably feel he needs to write to his father for instructions. If he doesn't just fly away. But Lancorphys, given Nyssa and Lucien are related, will undoubtedly align with Atratys. And Arden of Dacia might also think twice about allowing Olorys to control the crown; although I don't know exactly what kind of pressure is being put on him by his cousin's arrest. I decide to start with Arden. Tomorrow is the bridesday, and there is to be a tournament in the morning, but after that I will find a way to talk to him privately. Perhaps Odette is right – perhaps he will not believe me. But I am learning that, sometimes, truth matters less than convenience. Especially here.

'Here we are.' Letya puts a large sack down on the floor. 'Some cloths, and a broom, and two uniforms.'

'Two?' I begin to shake my head, but Letya just laughs. 'You've never swept anything either. At least one of us should look as if she knows what she's doing. It will be just like being back at Merl, when we used to dress up in old clothes and hide from your tutor.'

I doubt it's going to be anything like that. But still, this is not an argument I can – or want to – win.

By mid-afternoon the pair of us are making our way to the north wing. I'm already grateful to Letya: she stops me going up the wide, ornately carved staircase I usually take and guides me to Siegfried's floor using one of the servants' staircases ('menial stairs' she calls them) instead. Still, my theory is proving correct. In the main corridors no one gives us a second glance; we may as well be invisible. Reaching Siegfried's door, Letya knocks, but there's no response, so she lets us both in.

'Shall I lock the door again?'

'No – housemaids don't, do they? I want you to keep watch near the door while I look around.'

Letya takes up her position next to a table – duster in hand – while I tuck another cloth into my waistband and begin examining the bookcase. I find nothing remarkable there, or tucked inside the chimney breast, or hidden inside the harpsichord, so I switch my search to the bedroom.

There isn't much furniture in this room either. It doesn't take me long to look under the bed and in the various drawers and the wardrobe; Siegfried really has surprisingly few clothes and personal possessions, at least here. I stand with my hands on my hips, tapping my foot, trying to think: where would I conceal something secret?

Beneath me, the floor creaks slightly. *We're here to see to about the loose floorboard* . . . I gasp as memory flickers into life: me, hiding in the sitting room, as the maid and a workman walked in. The next moment I'm on my hands and knees, trying to wrench up the floorboards, hoping desperately that Siegfried's man sent them away before they could carry out the repair.

One of the boards shifts beneath the pressure of my nails. I prise it upward far enough for me to reach into the cavity below –

There's something here. My fingertips brush across paper. Letters, I see when I draw the bundle out. Shoving them into the pocket of my apron, I replace the board and leave the bedroom. Just in time: the main door opens and one of Siegfried's servants walks in, the same man I saw the other day. He groans.

'Always fussing. It's clean enough – get out, the pair of you.'

Letya curtsies silently and moves towards the door. I copy her movement and follow . . .

'You, girl –'

Dread almost takes my breath away. But I force myself to turn back, keeping my gaze lowered. 'Sir?'

'You forgot your broom.' He sighs and mutters, 'Halfwit.'

I snatch up the offending implement, bob another curtsy and escape. Letya and I hurry back to my rooms, silent until we are both inside with the door locked.

'Letya . . .'

'You forgot your broom!'

The relief is too much for us; we collapse with laughter. Eventually, though, Letya recovers herself and reminds me that the clothes and so on need to be returned to the laundry before they are missed. When she leaves, I summon Turik and ask him to send me word the instant Lucien returns to his room (I refuse to allow myself to consider the possibility that he could be arrested). Then I sit in my favourite seat and begin to examine my discovery.

The letters, eight of them all together, form a manual on how to poison the king. They address such topics as dose; timing; inventive methods of administration. Suggestions include impregnating his bedsheets or painting the venom onto the bedroom furniture. But the happiness that arose from our small strike against Siegfried quickly dissipates: it takes no longer than the first letter for me to recognise my father's style and handwriting.

I suppose I should be grateful to Lucien for showing me my father's notebook; the shock, the nausea brewing in my stomach, are less than they might otherwise have been. At least there are no pleasantries among the words my father wrote. No sign that he considered Siegfried a friend. Every phrase is businesslike and to the point. Even the way the letters are addressed . . .

Frowning, I scan the letters again. My father's signature is at the foot of each one. But there is no name at the start. They are all addressed to *My Lord*.

I sigh. I have more evidence than I had before, but still not enough. It will come down to my word, again, that the letters were in Siegfried's room in the first place, that my father was writing to him and not someone else. And it's still not clear how Siegfried accomplished his task, what mode of delivery he employed, how he gained access to the king's rooms. I chew my bottom lip, considering. Perhaps Siegfried's letters to my father still exist at Merl. And if I send Lucien to find them, at least he might be out of harm's reach. Perhaps. If. Might. The only certainty is that my father's part in this plot cannot be kept secret. To save my home, and my friends, I'm going to have to sacrifice his memory and reputation.

So be it. The living are more important than the dead.

The soft chiming of the clock on the mantlepiece draws my attention to the fact that Letya is not here – she should have been back long before now. Anxiety needles my spine. I jump up and yank on the bell pull, trying to ignore the fears that instantly spring into my mind – that someone saw us leaving Siegfried's room, that she too has been taken in for 'questioning'. Another half an hour passes, as I pace up and down across the room. I'm on the point of going in search of my friend when Letya finally comes through the door carrying a tray of food.

'Where were you?' I exhale some of the tension that is cramping my shoulders. 'I thought you'd been arrested.'

'I'm sorry. But I had to get you some supper. And then you asked me to keep my ears open for anything that might be useful. So that's what I've been doing, in part.'

'What have you learned?'

'Food first. You've not had a bite since breakfast, I imagine. I'll feel less guilty about taking wages from Lord Lancelin if I at least make sure you're being fed while I help you risk your life.'

I suddenly realise that I'm ravenous: the smell of the food – toasted cheese, a slice of fruit cake and a jug of apple juice – is making my mouth water.

'That looks delicious, thank you. Now, tell me everything while I eat.'

'Well, there was a delivery this morning. Food for the wedding feast, including some sort of fancy cakes and what have you from Olorys.' Letya pulls a face that suggests she does not have a high opinion of Oloryan delicacies. 'Anyway, when I left the laundry I went back through the kitchens, and the Oloryan cart drivers were sitting there eating and drinking, which I suppose is fair enough, them having driven a long way, and probably overnight . . .'

'Yes . . .' I nod, hoping to hurry Letya's narration along.

'One of them asked me to take a glass of wine with him, so I agreed, thinking I could ask him about Lord Siegfried –'

'But you were careful, weren't you?'

'Of course. And I actually didn't even need to ask; he just kept talking at me.' She smiles grimly. 'Like he had too many words in his belly, and if he didn't get them out his guts would explode.'

'But what did he say?'

'First he went on about how wild Lord Siegfried's father – Aurik Redwing – had been as a young man. And how Lord Siegfried was controlled, instead of wild, but how everyone was all the more afraid of him because of that. And then –' she pauses and lowers her voice – 'then he got to talking – about the queen. Saying there are rumours that she isn't really the daughter of the man who's said to be her father. That the queen's mother was secretly the mistress of this Aurik, right up until her marriage.'

I drop the piece of cake I'm eating and grip the arms of my chair, half-stifled by the sudden acceleration of my heartbeat. 'Then the queen, and Siegfried . . .'

Letya nods. 'If the rumours are true, she's his half-sister.'

I sink back against the sofa cushions. So many things that I didn't understand before now make sense. How Siegfried got access to the storage room where he was holding Flayfeather. Why Oloryan guards were allowed within the Crown Estates. I recall the trial, realising my failure to hear in the queen's words the echo of sentiments Siegfried had already expressed. And when she questioned me the next morning, she was actually asking me what I thought of *her brother*.

She was the one who arranged the trial, of course, sowing seeds of distrust and fear between the dominions. And she must be the one who has been poisoning the king.

My mind strays back to my uncle. He had my mother murdered – because of his jealousy, or his lust for power, or both – and all but destroyed my father. His own brother. I remember how the king mocked me: *Your father underestimated me once . . .* A bitter desire fills me: that the king should know, before he dies, that my father has exacted his revenge.

'Aderyn, where are you going?' Letya calls after me, but I don't stop. Instead I make my way up the seemingly endless stairs to the royal apartments. Out of breath, I arrive at the king's receiving room. But there are no guards on the door. No guards anywhere in sight. I hesitate for a moment, turn the handle and go in.

The receiving room is empty; it's early evening now, so perhaps the king's servants are all at supper. I clench my fists, trying to stop my courage slipping away, and walk the length of the room as quietly as possible. There is a doorway at the end that leads to the next, more private space, the room where my uncle told me I was to marry Patrus. I reach the door, rest my fingers on the handle –

A noise, from a narrow corridor opening to my right. I hadn't noticed it before. But now I hear voices. And a ripple of laughter. Hugging the shadows, I edge along the corridor to where it opens out into another room. Peer in.

Siegfried. And the queen. They're standing close together.

Siegfried whispers something into the queen's ear and she laughs again and puts her arms around his neck. He pushes her back against the wall, pinning her there, and he –

He kisses her.

Fifteen

He kisses her. Not in a brotherly way. He kisses her exactly as he tried to kiss me, and then he hitches up her skirts –

I clap my hand to my mouth and jump back into the shadows. But I think I'm too late. I think I gasped out loud. I think they heard me.

So I run.

I run back across the receiving room. When I reach the door, I pause; there's no sign of pursuit. Carefully, carefully, I open the door, shut it behind me, and run again.

But not back to my room. I run down. I don't stop running until I reach the stables. They're not expecting me: horses rear, the ostlers curse me, but I don't care. I don't stop running until I'm in Henga's stall.

She snickers in greeting. And the fact that I can't put my arms around her neck, that I can't bury my face in her mane – it rips my heart out. I slump down in the hay, my back against the wall of the stall, waiting for my breathing to slow. Henga tosses her head and watches me.

I remember the groomsday banquet, the queen observing Odette's happiness with narrowed eyes. She wasn't ever concerned about Odette's welfare. Not then, nor when she asked me whether I was sharing Siegfried's bed.

She was jealous.

'What should I do, Henga?'

In reply, Henga snickers again, pawing the ground with her front foot. She wants to get out of here. And it would be so easy. If I put gloves on, I could saddle her myself. We could escape from the Citadel, ride back to Atratys. Back to Merl. I could run away, just like my parents did. Run away, and hide, and wait for Siegfried to hunt me down. Without his potion, I won't be able to escape for long.

I reach for the long-handled brush hanging on the wall and begin running it across Henga's back, trying to control the anger that has started to boil through my veins. How long ago did Siegfried and his sister plan all this? Before she married the king? And Siegfried's attempt to seduce me – was that also planned between them, or was Siegfried alone playing that game? Standing with me on the roof at Deaufleur, telling me of the strength of his passion . . . No doubt he thought it would be amusing to find out just how much he could humiliate me. How much I could be persuaded – how much I would be willing – to surrender to him.

I grit my teeth and grip the brush so tightly the tendons on my hand stand out. It's that or smash it against the wall behind me.

Henga snorts and rolls her eyes backwards; she's wondering why I've stopped brushing her. Or maybe she's trying to dispel my tension. I apologise and start moving the bristles across her coat again, my muscles relaxing as my rage cools a little. The brush is made of wood, painted red. It reminds me of the red dress I used to love, the red dress I was wearing when my father died.

My father spent years hiding at Merl. Hiding his problems and hiding me. And for what? It didn't solve anything.

But I am not my father, and I have a choice.

I hang the brush up again. 'I'm sorry, Henga. I can't ride you this evening. I'll ask one of the grooms to take you out.' She neighs as if she understands. I hope she does.

I'm not going to run, and I'm not going to hide. I'm going to fight.

I'm halfway back to the main entrance of the castle when Aron catches up with me.

'Aderyn –'

'I was just coming to find you, cousin. What's amiss?'

'Nothing. Well –' he quirks an eyebrow – 'nothing more than usual. They've finished questioning Rookwood and have allowed him to leave. I thought you'd like to know.'

'Thank you.'

'Why were you looking for me?'

'There are some things I'd like to discuss with you.' I keep my face and my tone neutral; there are too many other people coming and going up the wide marble staircases, too many Dark Guards standing around nearby. And everyone is watching, listening, wondering where the accusations of treason will fall next. 'It's about my horse. Henga has been off her feed, and I am not sure I agree with the stable master's diagnosis.'

'Of course. So worrying, when one's mount is unwell.' Aron clearly understands my subterfuge. 'When would be a convenient time for you, cousin?'

I hesitate. I was hoping to speak to Aron, to tell him exactly what I've discovered, this evening. But it's getting late, and I need to see Lucien first. 'Tomorrow, I suppose. After the tournament?'

'Why don't you come to my apartment at the seventh hour? We can have lunch together.'

'Very well. Thank you, cousin. I'm sure you'll be able to set my mind at rest.'

In contrast to the entrance hall, the corridors of the Citadel are quiet. The mood feels like the air just before a big thunderstorm: so heavy with tension and pent-up energy that something has to happen. I go back to my apartment first. Letya is waiting for me, as I knew she would be. I reassure her and tell her to go and rest, that I will see her in the morning. She seems inclined to argue, but I remind her that I used to put myself to bed at Merl, and that she will be of more use to me if she's not exhausted. As soon as Letya has said goodnight, I make my way to Lucien's room. Turik lets me in.

'Your Grace – I was just coming to fetch you.'

'No matter, Turik – my cousin let me know.'

Lucien is sitting at his desk, writing a letter. He's barefoot in his shirt and trousers, his tunic slung over the back of the chair. When he sees me he stands and nods at his servant.

'Thank you, Turik. That will be all tonight.'

'Are you sure, my lord? Is there really nothing else I can fetch you? Perhaps some fruit, or some more wine?'

'I've hardly touched the first bottle you brought up. Really, go and rest.'

'Very good, my lord.' Turik bobs his head and hurries away.

I frown after him as he leaves. 'He seems distressed.'

'I suppose he was worried what might happen to him, if I wasn't released.'

'I think he was worried about you.' I walk further into the room. 'We all were.'

'Your Grace,' Lucien makes no move to sit down again, just fiddles with his pen, 'you shouldn't be here. It's dangerous.'

'Why? I'm entitled to come and visit my clerk. Besides, nobody knows I'm here, apart from Letya and Turik. There wasn't a soul around –'

'Someone will have seen you before this. Someone will have followed you. You took an unnecessary risk, as usual.' He sighs, and finally looks at me properly. 'I don't know why I was taken in to be questioned, but I doubt this is the end of it. You need – you *have* – to stay away from me. I don't want you caught up in whatever is going to happen next.'

'You forget, my lord, I'm already caught up in it.' I move a pile of papers off the nearest chair, sit down and stare at him as haughtily as I can manage. He rolls his eyes and shakes his head, but he goes to the side table, pours two glasses of wine and brings me one.

'Thank you. Did they hurt you?'

'No. I sat in a room for hours and finally they asked me lots of questions: where had I flown recently? Who did I still know in Frianland, from when I worked for the diplomatic mission there? That sort of thing. And then they let me go.' He rubs a hand over his face and I remember that he only got back here this morning after flying all night.

'You must be dead on your wings. I'll leave you to rest.' Tomorrow will be soon enough to tell Lucien what I saw in the royal apartment. If I'm going to send him back to Merl to look for Siegfried's letters to my father, he has to be in a fit state to fly. I rise and move towards the door.

'Your Grace, wait.'

'What is it?'

'May I ask you something?'

'Of course.'

'This morning, when you suggested that I should betray you, that I should allow you to confess to poisoning the king, and become Protector myself – what gave you the idea?'

Was it really only this morning? 'Well . . .' I tug on my earlobe, considering. 'It seemed logical. Remember what you always say: the important thing is Atratys. Not me. Not any one person. And I think you would be a good Protector.'

'That's it? You're sure that there was nothing else? No more . . . specific reason?' His voice is calm, but his eyes are full of anxiety. It's on the tip of my tongue to lie, to reassure him. But I don't want to keep another secret from him.

'The potion that Siegfried has been giving me has –' I sigh – 'some unfortunate side effects. The first night that I took it – the night before I told you he had helped me transform – I found it impossible to rest. Eventually I went for a walk in the gardens.'

255

Lucien's colour fades as the blood drains from his face. 'I heard what you said to Turik, Lucien. The promise you made to him: that you would sacrifice me without a second thought.'

My clerk staggers to a chair and drops his head into his hands. 'What must you think of me?'

I cross the room to stand next to him. 'I think that you're the most honourable man I've ever met. Honourable, and honest and . . . and brave.' Lifting my hand, I brush my fingers across his raven hair.

'But I wasn't being honest. I was angry. Turik spoke of my feelings for you, and I wished to deny them. To convince him – and myself – that I did not care for you.'

His feelings for me? Something that isn't nerves or fear flickers in the pit of my stomach. I take a deep breath to steady my voice.

'Still, you were right, Lucien. My duty is to protect Atratys. If I were to fail in that duty, then I should be sacrificed. I would not deserve anything better. I understand, finally: what I want is really not important.'

He shudders, as if he's under some great stress, and stands up. 'I was wrong about one thing, Aderyn. When I told you not to trust anyone, that wasn't right. Not entirely.' Picking up his sword from where it's hanging on the back of the chair, he draws it out of the scabbard. 'You can trust me, Your Grace. Before, I promised to serve you. But now, I swear it.'

As I watch, he positions the blade across the centre of his left palm, grits his teeth –

'Don't –' I place my hands flat on the sword. 'Don't, Lucien. I would not have you injure yourself. And I already trust you.'

256

In the silence, I can hear Lucien's breathing. He puts the sword down and leans forward, lifting one hand to caress my cheek. I mirror his movement, staring up at the dark fire in his eyes, at the curve of his lips, enjoying the sensation of his skin beneath my palm. I scan his face greedily, studying every detail, as he twists the fingers of one hand through my long hair. Then his arms are around me, pulling me hard against him, and his mouth is on mine, and he's kissing me, and I can feel my heart hammering so hard I think it might smash my ribcage.

'Aderyn . . .' His voice is husky, but I hear the question in it.

And perhaps he is right. Perhaps, given everything we've said to each other, this is not an appropriate relationship. Perhaps, given everything that is happening, this is not an appropriate time.

But I fear the time we have is running out.

'I choose now, Lucien. And I choose you.'

He kisses my head, sighing into my hair. 'Then, with your permission, Your Grace . . .' He picks me up and carries me to the bed. I sit on the edge and watch as he bolts the door and snuffs out all but one candle, every nerve ending in my body singing with anticipation. He plucks, uncertain, at his shirt. 'Shall I . . . ?'

'Yes. But let me help.' I stand facing him. 'I've already seen you naked, remember?'

It doesn't take me long to pull Lucien's shirt over his head, and then he removes what remains of his clothing. This time, I do not drop my gaze.

I help him unlace my gown – defying the shame that is

always waiting for a chance to taunt me over the appearance of my scars – and slip it and my undergarment off my shoulders. The fabrics puddle at my feet; I step out of them and lie on the bed, and Lucien comes to lie next to me. For a moment he stares down at me; I can feel his body trembling.

'What's wrong?'

'You already know I want you.' He brushes a hand across the curve of my hips. 'But now – now I find I need you, Aderyn. Like I need water. Or air. I need you to be near me. And it scares me.'

'Don't be afraid.' I draw him closer. 'I'm never going to hurt you.' With that, we both lose control. And amidst hungry kisses and tangled limbs and blissful yielding, all the fear and horror and tension of the last few weeks are lost as well.

Afterwards, we lie together in his bed, our legs warm beneath the bedclothes. Lucien's skin is gilded by candlelight, and I run my fingers across his chest and down his arm. 'You're beautiful, raven boy.'

'Not as beautiful as you, my lady.' He kisses his way down my throat to the dip between my collarbones, making me sigh with pleasure. 'Should I tell you how long I've been dreaming about this day?'

'I thought you hated me, when we first came here.'

'I wanted to hate you. It was childish. I wanted someone to blame for my father virtually abandoning us; someone alive, someone I could punish. But more than that, I thought that if I could make myself hate you, I would eventually stop wanting you.'

'Why did you want to stop? Did you think I disliked you so much?'

'I'd given you no reason to like me, and every reason to hate me. And you're a Protector; I didn't think that you would – that you should – ever consider taking me to your bed. But despite my efforts, my desire for you didn't wane. It grew, and my temper grew worse to match. When I think of the things I've said to you . . .' He closes his eyes, a tiny frown creasing the skin between his eyebrows.

'Then don't think of them. Though I can't blame you for scolding me. I gave you plenty of reasons to.' I turn around and snuggle against Lucien's chest. 'I like this. I like you holding me.' His arm tightens around my waist. 'My mother used to hug me, and I know Letya would hug me if she could. But my father . . . my father was not affectionate in that way. Six years it's been, since my mother died. I've so missed the feeling of having another person's arms around me.'

'Then I shall keep holding you, as long as I can. For as long as you want.' His lips brush the scars at the top of my shoulders. 'Whatever else he's done, I'm glad Siegfried killed the man who did this to you.'

'Don't remind me of it, Lucien, please.' I shake my head, trying to dislodge the images that always seem to be waiting at the edge of my memory, ready to take centre stage if I ever allow them. 'I've seen too much death. I don't want to think about it ever again.'

'Forgive me.' He nibbles the edge of my ear, making me giggle. 'Tell me what you'd like to think about.'

'Let's think about what we're going to do when we get back to Atratys.'

'Easy: I've already planned it. I want to take you to Hatchlands and show you my home. I want to show you the starflower wood, and the view across the lake and the gardens where my brother Zavier and I used to play. And then in the winter we can fly –'

He catches his breath.

I change position, so I can look at him. 'I can't shift my shape, Lucien. I can't –' A pang of grief catches me unexpectedly. 'Right now, I still can't get past the fear. I can't find my way to the point of transformation. What if I never can?'

For a moment he gazes at me. 'Then we will walk around the gardens of Hatchlands. Or you can teach me to ride.' He kisses me gently, lingering over it. 'We'll find a way, Aderyn. Together.'

When I wake, the candle on the bedside table has guttered out, and pale grey light is filtering round the edges of the shutters. Lucien is fast asleep still, lying on his back, one hand flung up above his head, the other resting on my hip. I slide away, wrap one of the blankets around my shoulders and pull the rest of the bedclothes up to cover him. There's no clock in this room, but from the quality of the light it's early morning; the sun hasn't yet breached the horizon. I open one of the shutters a little. From here I can see down into the town. The streets are empty, but there are wisps of smoke rising from a few of the chimneys, and the smell of baking bread drifting through the open window makes my stomach growl. There's a litter of papers and books scattered across the floor at my feet; the mess seems so much part of Lucien that it makes me smile. I pick up some sort of architectural drawing – plans for an extension at Hatchlands, by the looks of it – and try to imagine what the finished building will be like.

'Aderyn?'

I go to sit on the edge of the bed. 'I'm sorry, I didn't mean to wake you.'

Lucien smiles. 'I missed you. Come back to bed.'

'It's morning; I should go. The servants will be up and about soon.'

He catches my hand in his. 'Please? It's early still. Don't leave, not yet.'

'And risk Turik finding me in your bed?' I lean forward to kiss him. 'Or even worse, Letya not finding me in mine, and setting the Dark Guards to search for me?'

Lucien groans and slips his arm around me, drawing me into a deeper kiss; desire surges through my core, but I pull away. 'Lucien . . .'

'I'm sorry.' He sighs and releases me. 'You're right.'

'Of course I am. And we have lots of other nights to look forward to.'

'Tonight?'

I grin. 'Only if you perform your other duties to my satisfaction, my lord. Remember, you have a tournament to escort me to.'

I get back to my room, discard my gown, put on my nightdress and get into bed. There doesn't seem much point in trying to go back to sleep, so I read until Letya brings me in a cup of chocolate. She folds back the shutters and I glance out of the windows. A grey day; the tops of the mountains are veiled in cloud and the surface of the fjord is a sullen black.

Letya follows my gaze. 'They say it should brighten up later. It's meant to be good luck, for a bridesday to start in shadow and end in sunshine.'

I've heard the same grandmothers' tale. I hope it's true.

Lucien arrives as Letya is putting the final adjustments to my dress. While she's in the room he is as formal as I've ever seen him – so formal it makes me giggle. Letya gives me a look. But as soon as we are alone he crushes me into his arms and kisses me as though we've been apart for weeks, rather than hours.

'I've missed you.'

'I've missed you too. But we'll be late for the tournament if we don't hurry. Will you pass me my cloak?'

'Of course. Allow me.' He places it around my shoulders and starts trying to fasten the clasp. 'I've had a message from Nyssa's mother, by the way. She said to tell you that Atratys will not be left without allies. That Lancorphys stands ready, if it comes to it.'

I put my hands over his, stilling them. 'What do you mean? If it comes to what?'

'War.'

Surely I misheard him. 'What?'

'War, Aderyn. Siegfried wants the crown, but I'm convinced he also wants direct control of every single dominion. You know he does. Surely you're not prepared to hand him Atratys without a fight?'

'Of course not. I just hadn't . . . I hadn't thought about it ending in war.' Combating Siegfried through subterfuge – that's what I'd imagined. We've had peace within Solanum since the War of the Raptors. What will it do to the kingdom, if that changes?

Disengaging his hands, Lucien tilts my chin upward and kisses me. 'Can you survive without a servant for a couple of days?'

'Of course. Why?'

'Because –' he steals another kiss – 'I think we should leave the Citadel as soon as possible. Send Letya and Turik away first, then you. We ought to return to Atratys before Siegfried becomes king.'

'The fact that he's not king won't stop him coming after us.' I wonder if this is how my mother and father felt, planning their flight from the Citadel, away from my uncle. 'And what about Aron and Odette? I won't leave them, Lucien. I'm not going to run.'

He sighs and turns away, dragging his hands through his hair. 'You're right.'

'We need to find a way to challenge the Decrees. To put Aron on the throne, despite the fact that he can't fly. Or to put Odette on the throne unmarried.' For a moment I laugh at myself: me, a newly anointed Protector, daring to act as kingmaker?

Someone has to do it.

Lucien is shaking his head. 'Convocation will never agree. The Decrees are what they are, Aderyn.'

I hold out my hand to him as the bell sounds for us to make

our way to the jousting field. 'They are. But perhaps it's time that changed.'

I've not been to this part of the Citadel complex before – jousts are for winter, in general. Lucien tells me that in other countries the nobility compete. But in Solanum the nobility watch, and place bets on their favourite – flightless – riders. Six shields are displayed on the wall by the entrance to the stadium: one for each dominion.

'What are those things next to them?'

'Broken lances,' Lucien replies. 'Wins per dominion for the last season.'

Olorys has by far the most. Atratys has none. 'We don't seem to be doing very well.'

'We don't enter. Your father stopped taking part after your mother died.'

Inside the stadium, the stands are divided – as usual – by rank. Lucien has to go higher up. I have a place reserved with my cousins and the other Protectors and heirs. There is no sign of the queen, but Siegfried invites me to stand next to him. I smile at him, all the better to conceal the hatred in my heart.

'Your first tournament, I believe?'

He doesn't seem any different to the last time we spoke, three days ago, when he surprised me trying to search his rooms.

'Yes. Olorys is the favourite, I imagine.'

'I expect so.' He winks at me. 'The House of Cygnus Olorys doesn't play to lose.'

The joust itself is noisy, fast and brutal. Each dominion (apart from Atratys) has entered five flightless riders, who will gradually be eliminated through either the complex system of scoring or because they are killed or so severely injured that they can no longer compete. Still, most of the people around me seem to be enjoying the spectacle. The thunder of the horses' hoofs, the clash of lance on shield and armour, and the cries of the injured blend with the ebbing and flowing clamour of the crowd. Odette, as is the custom, has presented a favour to the captain representing her betrothed's dominion. Yet she seems to take no pleasure from the seemingly unstoppable progress of the Oloryan riders.

The joust lasts a couple of hours. I decide that after I've spoken with Aron I'm going to go to the library and actually find a copy of these damn Decrees that everyone keeps quoting at me. And then I'm going to go and see Arden of Dacia.

Lucien meets me at the gates to the stadium and offers me his arm. He smiles, but the lines of exhaustion in his face worry me. I can't ask him to fly back to Merl today.

'Perhaps you should take a nap this afternoon.'

'Two questions, Your Grace.' He nods his head to another courtier, then leans closer to murmur to me. 'First, is it your bed you're offering? Second, are you going to be in it?'

My shocked laughter draws a disapproving glance from an elderly noblewoman nearby.

'I feel that would be counter-productive, my lord. Besides, I am very busy this afternoon. Far too busy and important to be helping you rest.'

This time Lucien laughs. 'Perhaps you're right. But as your clerk I feel that I should be assisting you, Your Grace. I can sleep later.'

With Lucien next to me, Siegfried seems a monster more of shadows than of flesh and blood. We return to our conversation of last night, and are still planning what we're going to do once we've returned to Atratys when we reach the corridor where my apartment is.

There are Dark Guards waiting outside my door. My hand tightens on Lucien's arm as one of the guards bows.

'Your Grace.'

'What are you doing here? Do you have news from Atratys?'

'No, Your Grace. We are here for Lord Rookwood.'

Lucien steps forward. 'What do you want with me?'

'You are to come with us, my lord.'

'For what reason?'

The guard glances at me, though with his face covered I can't tell whether he is nervous or irritated at my presence. 'You're under arrest, my lord.' He gestures to one of the other guards who approaches with a pair of manacles.

I throw up my hand. 'No closer! Under whose order are you acting? And on what charges?'

'By order of the queen. Lord Rookwood is charged with high treason, and with the murder of the king.' He puts his right hand meaningfully on the shaft of the axe hanging from his belt. 'Please step aside, Your Grace.'

The king is dead, then. More guards press forward. I try to stop them, struggling for breath, but Lucien holds me back.

'Don't, Aderyn! Don't give them an excuse to arrest you too.' He gasps and flinches as his hands are manacled behind his back. 'Tell my father –'

'Lucien . . .'

The guards pull him round, so he's facing away from me, and begin to march him away.

My knees give way and I sink to the ground. 'Lucien!'

There's no reply.

Sixteen

The flagstones beneath my knees are hard and cold. Still, I
don't move. Two gawking housemaids hurry by with arms
full of bedlinen, but neither of them dares to approach me. I
remember Siegfried's words at the tournament: *The House of
Cygnus Olorys doesn't play to lose.* And I know now that he and
the queen did see me the other day. That together they have
acted to take Lucien – my adviser, my lover – away from me.

My breath shortens. In my mind I'm already at Lucien's
Last Flight, watching his body burn, as my lungs fill with acrid
smoke. I slump forward, gasping –

The gold Protector's ring on my forefinger scrapes against the
stone floor. I never asked for this – I don't want any of it. Rage
burns my throat and I scream as I try to rip the ring from my finger.

It won't come off. I tug until the surrounding skin is sore and
slick with blood. But the gold band doesn't budge. A trickle of
scarlet runs down the back of my hand and I lift my finger to
my mouth, sucking the torn flesh, the carved crest of Atratys
beneath my tongue.

My Atratys. And Lucien's Atratys, and Letya's.

It does not belong to Siegfried. And if it is within my power, it never will.

I force myself to my feet and let my breathing slow, steadying myself against the wall. The fury I felt a moment ago is still there. But it's cooling now, hardening into something strong and sharp.

Siegfried hasn't won this game yet. And it's my move.

In my apartment, I ring for Letya as the castle bell begins tolling. Something to do with the king's death, I assume. Though without Lucien, I don't know the exact significance or what we are supposed to do.

Letya arrives. Somehow she already knows what has happened: her eyes are wet with tears.

'Oh, Aderyn . . .'

'We need to be brave, Letya, if we're to save Lucien. And clever. I want you to go and find out what is happening in the Citadel, and what that bell means.'

She nods. 'Yes, of course. But –' she opens the door to the bedroom – 'if your uncle really is dead, you ought to be wearing black.'

While I change, she hurries away to gather what news she can. It doesn't take her long. She tells me that the bell is to mark the start of the seven days of deep mourning. Conveniently, the king has died – or at least his death has been announced – just in time for Odette's wedding not to have to be delayed, though the celebrations will be curtailed. The king's body is being taken to the sanctuary to lie in state, and his Last Flight will be on the morning of the seventh day. And that evening Odette and I and the other maidens are to fly to the sacred lake. If I'm still alive, and at liberty. If Siegfried gives me the potion that makes me transform.

I ask Letya to return later; I will need to write notes to every member of Convocation and beg them to meet with me, hope I have not yet been tarred with the brush of treason. But first, I have to try to see Lucien.

My clerk's room has been locked, and there's a guard standing in front of it. There's no sign of Turik. The guard tells me Lucien has been taken down to the dungeons. I order him to show me the way, and although he doesn't want to – he mutters unhappily about leaving his post – he doesn't dare refuse a direct request from a Protector. Unfortunately, it doesn't help. When we reach the dungeon, I am refused admission. The captain tells me that Lucien is forbidden visitors, by order of the queen. I have nothing to do but go away again.

Instead of returning to my apartment, I make my way to my cousins' rooms. The guards at Odette's doors say she has asked not to be disturbed. Possibly true, but now I seem to detect Siegfried's malignancy in everything. Unless Odette believes the lies that are being spread about Lucien. At least there are no guards at Aron's door. Not that there ever have been, to my knowledge; a symptom of his 'irrelevance', I suppose.

Aron opens the door to me himself. He is wearing black, but since he usually does, that does not tell me how he is feeling.

'I'm sorry for your loss, cousin.'

'Thank you.'

This morning's mist has solidified into leaden clouds and heavy rain. Aron pours me a glass of wine and holds it out to me; the candlelight in the darkened room gleams through the crystal, throwing crimson shadows onto my cousin's face. 'The queen – and her doctors – would not allow us to see the body.' I understand him. We both suspect that my uncle has been dead for more than a few hours. 'By the way, I took your advice.' He gestures to a litter of paper spread across a large table.

'My advice?

'Yes. The first evening we spent together. You asked whether my father had thought about challenging the Decrees. He hadn't, but I am. I've been studying them. I've not found anything useful so far, but . . .'

'I hope you do. And soon. Have you heard about Lucien?'

He nods. 'Did you know that his servant betrayed him? He found a notebook in Lucien's room. Lucien has allegedly been investigating poisons. The servant passed the book to the captain of the guard.'

Turik, a traitor? I shiver as I remember his distress last night. The distress of someone about to commit an act of betrayal. And I had allowed Lucien to take the book of poisons back to his room, to protect me.

'Lucien didn't poison your father, cousin – I swear that this has nothing to do with him. That book belonged to my father. He produced the poison, I admit it. But Siegfried administered it. Siegfried, and his half-sister. Your stepmother. I only found out yesterday.'

For the first time I can remember, Aron appears stunned by my revelations. 'The queen, Siegfried's sister? Impossible.

I know who her parents are.'

'Her mother was Aurik of Olorys's mistress.'

He stares at me for a moment. Forces a laugh. 'How very clear-sighted of me. I know I blamed the queen for my father's illness, but really, I had no idea –' His slender fingers curl around the stem of his glass and he smashes it into the fire, sending up a sheet of flame. 'By the Creator! How long have those bastards in Olorys been planning this?'

I wish I could answer him. 'Atratys will stay loyal to the crown. And Lancorphys –'

'It hardly matters, if the crown is on Siegfried's head!' He snatches up his sword and strides towards the door. 'By the Firebird, I'll hack that head from his shoulders before I see him seated on the throne.'

'Aron, wait –'

He swings the sword round and levels it at me. I drop my glass, step back – but there's a sofa blocking my way.

'Why should I wait, Aderyn? Is your concern for me? Or for Siegfried?'

'For you, obviously.'

'Obviously?' Aron moves forward until the tip of his blade is touching my neck. His grip on the sword is unwavering. 'You really expect me to believe that your father was involved in this plot and yet you knew *nothing*?'

'I swear, Aron . . .' My throat is so dry I have to swallow, and the sharp point of the blade pricks my skin. 'I swear, he kept it all a secret. From me, from Lucien. Think about it: why would I be here now if I was working with Siegfried? Why would I have told you any of this?'

Aron is scowling at me, breathing hard. He draws his arm back and I shut my eyes, bracing myself for the sword thrust into my neck –

There's a thud. The sword is lying on the floor. Gripping the sofa for support, I lean back against it. Wait for my heart rate to subside.

'I didn't like him.' My cousin's voice is strained, as if he's trying not to cry. 'I hated him, a lot of the time. But he was still my father. And now . . .' He rubs his hand across his face, and when he looks back at me his green eyes are wet with tears. 'I've hurt you.' He steps closer and brushes his fingertips against my neck; they come away red with blood. 'I'm sorry.'

'A scratch. It'll heal.'

'Can you forgive me?'

I manage a small smile. 'I'll consider it. I loved my father too, and yet the things that I've learned about him . . .' I push away the image of my father that forms in my head: him in his laboratory, concocting poisons; it hurts too much. Instead I focus on Lucien in the dungeon, and Odette locked in her tower. 'I've just as much to lose as you if we don't stop Siegfried. And at least now we have some evidence.' I tell my cousin about my father's letters to Siegfried, and how I was planning to send Lucien back to Merl to search for the letters Siegfried must have sent to my father.

'Do you think they still exist?'

'I believe so.' My father never threw anything away. And his private papers are largely untouched. 'Send someone to Atratys. Someone you trust. With my steward's help they might be able to find the letters.'

'Very well. What else?'

'Shall I summon Convocation? It is my right, as a Protector.'

Aron rubs his chin. 'Not yet. If we move without sufficient evidence, and give Siegfried an opportunity to weaken our claims, we risk losing everything.'

'What about Lucien?' My breath catches in my chest as I say his name.

'Leave it to me. I have friends among the Dark Guards; I've trained with them a little since losing my arm, and they accepted me when my own kind would not. I won't be able to get Lucien out. But if I can get you in to see him, I will.'

I suppose I will have to be satisfied with that.

For the next two days, I wait. Odette still hasn't emerged from her seclusion in the tower. I know that she must be there unwillingly, because Aron has also been denied admittance. Whatever her doubts about my loyalty, Odette would never separate herself from her brother by choice. At least during the deep mourning there are no court assemblies. No need for me to see Siegfried or the queen, no requirement for me to be civil. Instead, I keep to my rooms, while Letya tries to distract me. When she isn't with me, Letya roams the castle searching for Turik. But there is no sign of him. Finally, late at night on the third day after I went to see him, Aron comes to my apartment.

'I've arranged for you to see Lucien. But it has to be now. Someone I know is in charge of this shift, down in the dungeons. He'll let you in.'

'Thank you.' I kiss my cousin on the cheek. 'This means a lot to me.'

Aron waits, staring out of the window into the night, as I fasten a cloak over my nightgown and put on some shoes. We take a circuitous route down to the dungeons, going outside the Citadel at one point. When we arrive, the guards at the main entrance open the gates to us without saying anything. Inside is another guard with a torch; still in silence, we follow him.

'They're going to pretend we're not here,' Aron murmurs. 'Don't try to talk to any of them.'

There are torches in brackets spaced out along the walls, but they do little to disperse the gloom. The air smells bad: a combination of too much dirt and too little ventilation, I suppose. We seem to walk for a long time, and I wonder whether the dungeons are built out from the castle, whether we're beneath either the mountains or the fjord. Finally, the guard turns aside. We stop in front of a wooden door with an iron grille in its centre. The guard places his torch in an empty bracket on the wall and retreats back up the corridor.

Aron gestures. 'He's in there.' There's a key in the keyhole; Aron turns it and pulls the door open. 'I have to lock you in. You haven't much time.'

I step into the cell and wait for my eyes to adjust to the sparse lighting. Lucien, in his shirt and trousers, is lying on a bench set against one wall.

'Lucien?' I kneel next to him. 'Lucien, wake up.'

He opens his eyes and smiles at me. 'Aderyn. I hoped I would dream of you again.'

'This isn't a dream. I'm here.' I brush his hair back from

275

his forehead, taking in the bruises across his cheekbones, the welts around his wrists and the blistered skin of his neck. 'Oh, my poor Lucien, what have they done to you?'

He pushes himself upright, wincing. 'How did you get in here? It's not safe –'

'Aron arranged it. It's fine, but we haven't got long.' I sit next to him on the bench and put my arms around him.

He sighs and leans into me, resting his head on my shoulder. 'Aderyn . . . Turik betrayed me. He gave them your father's book.'

'I know.'

'Siegfried has been here, trying to force a confession out of me.' He laughs; the laugh of someone who is a feather's breadth away from screaming. 'Siegfried, with his box of dead leaves.'

I shudder and clutch him tighter. 'I'm going to kill him. And we're going to tell Convocation the truth, about everything. I'm going to get you out of here.'

He sits up straighter and takes my hands in his. 'No – you mustn't do anything. You're already at risk, Aderyn. Siegfried is trying to make it look as if the king's illness and death are all part of a plot by Atratys to take the crown. You have to get away from the Citadel as soon as you can.' He kisses me gently. 'Once I'm dead . . .' His eyes widen in fear. 'Once I'm dead, he'll come after you.'

'I'm not going to abandon you, Lucien.'

'You have to. I'm one person, Aderyn. You have to think of Atratys. That is your duty. Remember?'

I smile, trying to force an appearance of confidence and bravery. 'Is that any way to speak to your Protector?' He doesn't respond, so I try again. I place one hand lightly on his bruised face. 'Look at me.'

He lifts his gaze.

'I'm not going to let them murder you. I swear it, by the Creator's blood.' I lean forward, resting my forehead against his. 'I think I love you, Lucien Rookwood.'

'I know I love you, my lady.'

The door creaks opens. 'Very touching. But it's time to go.' My cousin's voice – Aron is silhouetted against the glow of the torch burning in the corridor – sounds oddly strained.

'Already?'

'I'm afraid so. Quickly now.'

'Lucien –'

'Go.' He kisses me briefly, fiercely, then pushes me gently away. 'Aron – thank you. I'm in your debt.'

'Which is where I like you, Rookwood.'

There's no time for anything else. I am outside the cell and Aron is locking the door. I press my hand against the rough wood in an invisible, futile gesture of farewell. My cousin takes the torch from the bracket, leaving Lucien in darkness. The guard is waiting further down the corridor. Silently, he takes the torch and the key from the prince and leads us back to the entrance. It doesn't seem such a long walk in this direction.

The well-lit rooms and corridors of the upper castle are so bright in comparison, even at this late hour, that I have to squint. Aron accompanies me back to my apartment. We pause at the door.

'Thank you, cousin.'

'It was nothing.' He scowls at the flagstones, scuffing them with the toe of his boot. 'I doubt you'll be able to see him again. You should try not to think about him. '

'Have you had any news from Merl?'

'Not yet.' Aron glances up at me. 'Lucien's trial is likely to be set for tomorrow night. If they find him guilty – which they will – he'll die the next morning. I'd advise you not to attend the execution.' For a moment his mask slips; he looks stricken. 'Oh, Lucien . . . I can hardly bear to think about what they'll do to him.'

He can only mean that it will be terrible – worse than what was done to Hawkin. Bile rises in my throat. 'Then we have to go to Convocation tomorrow. We can't wait.'

'We must. We can't give Siegfried the chance to mount a defence until we're ready.' He brushes his fingers against the back of my hand. 'I'm sorry, cousin. But Lucien was right. Your duty is to Atratys. There's more at stake here than the life of just one person.'

Aron is right too, I suppose. But it's not what I want to hear. 'I bid you goodnight then, cousin.' I go into my room and shut the door behind me before Aron can see the tears that are threatening to spill down my cheeks.

All the next day I wait for news from Merl, wait for the evidence that will allow us to move against Siegfried. But now the sun is dropping towards the horizon, and nothing has come.

'Aderyn, will you please stop pacing! You're going to wear a hole in the carpet. And you're making me anxious.'

I sit down, trying to appease Letya, but within moments I'm on my feet again. I go to the windows and throw them open.

I suppose it's cold outside, because my companion clicks her tongue and starts to drag a blanket from the back of the sofa to wrap around her shoulders.

There's a knock at the door – a messenger from Aron. My hands are shaking; Letya breaks the seal on the letter and reads it.

'Well?

'Still nothing from Merl. I'm sorry.'

'And the trial?'

'Tonight. At the sixteenth hour.'

As my cousin predicted.

Letya is watching me closely. The mingling of grief and pity in her eyes is like a whip to my back.

'He's not dead yet, Letya.'

'Aderyn . . . You need to think clearly. What would Lucien say, if he were here?'

I grit my teeth and kick over a small table. 'I know what he would say. I know that I'm supposed to do nothing. To let him die in agony –'

I gasp, unable to continue.

Letya picks up the little table and the dish of candied walnuts that was sitting on it. Then she pulls on her gloves and takes one of my hands carefully in hers, drawing me towards the sofa. 'Sit down, Ryn.' A nickname, from when we were younger. I've not heard Letya use it for years. 'I'll ring for one of the housemaids to bring some chocolate.'

'No – I don't want anything.'

'But you didn't have lunch either.'

'Honestly, Letya, I'm not hungry.' The yellow dress that

my friend's been working on is on the sofa between us. It's nearly finished now; she's been embroidering it with tiny blue skybells for most of this afternoon. 'How old is your niece?'

'Just turned two. I hope I've made this big enough; my brother says she's growing fast.' She begins to talk about dressmaking and fabrics, trying to diffuse the tension, to distract me – and herself – from what is happening in the Citadel. From what is going to happen to Lucien. My heart swells as I listen to her.

'I want you to go home.' I sigh and rub my eyes, itchy from lack of sleep. 'Not want . . . I *need* you to go home.'

Letya shakes her head. 'I'm not going anywhere, Aderyn. Not without you.'

'You have to. Don't you understand? Siegfried already has Lucien. I can't risk him taking you too.'

'He won't.' She waves a hand, dismissive. 'You treat me like an equal, but in the eyes of the world – in the eyes of someone like Siegfried – I'm a flightless servant. Nothing more. It won't occur to him that I have any value.'

'That's not true. He must know how important you are to me. Please – I want you to leave. Today. Take Henga and Vasta and get away from here. Head for Chantry, on the far side of the fjord. If Aron and I succeed, I'll send for you.'

'But . . . I can't leave you here alone.'

'You have to.' I search for the words to convince her. 'You know I love you. If I were to lose you as well as Lucien . . .' I dash away a tear with the back of my hand, 'it would destroy me. But if I know you're safe, then I'll be able to do what I need to do. I'll be able to wait for the evidence from Merl. I'll be able to wait out whatever happens to Lucien.'

Letya is silent, tugging on one of the stray strands of yellow wool.

'Please, tell me you understand . . . ?'

Her eyes are glassy with unshed tears. But eventually she nods. 'When must I go?'

'After supper – as soon as it's dark. That will give you time to gather whatever clothes you think you can carry with you.'

As Letya begins packing up her knitting, I go to my bedroom and get out the red dress that Siegfried sent me. My father's letters are here, sewn into the lining by Letya. It gives me pleasure to rip the fabric open and retrieve them. I ask Letya to take them to Aron before she goes to pack, and throw the dress onto the fire.

She leaves, and I go back to pacing.

Time hurries on – no word from Merl, or from Aron – and the hour arrives. Letya and I have had supper together, and I've forced down enough food to satisfy her. Now she's adjusting the strap of the small bag she has slung across her body.

'I've written you out a pass; the gates will be shut by now.'

'Thank you.' She tucks the letter into her pocket. 'Though I'm not planning to go out through one of the main gates. There's a small door round by the kitchen gardens that leads into the town. I'm friends with the doorkeeper.'

I've already pulled on a pair of gloves, so I grip her hands in mine. 'Oh, Letya . . .'

'We'll see each other again soon. The news you're waiting for from Merl will arrive, and you and Prince Aron will put an end to this.' She sniffs. 'If you see Lord Lucien again, tell him I wish him well.'

I nod. I can't say Lucien's name, can't even think about him, without a sharp stab of fear in my chest. 'May I kiss you goodbye?'

'Of course.'

I lean forward and brush Letya's cheek fleetingly with my lips. 'Stay safe, my friend. My sister.'

She leaves. And I am truly alone.

The clock on the mantlepiece chimes, reminding me that I have little time to grieve what I've lost. I'm about to risk myself, but at least my Letya should be safe.

In the bedroom, I go to the chest of drawers containing my jewels and other ornaments. My mother's sword is in here, together with the sword belt. But there's also her dagger. I take it out of the velvet bag in which it was brought from Merl – I've had no reason to use it or wear it, so far – and test the edge.

Still sharp.

Lucien's trial is due to start in three hours. I wait out one more of those hours in my apartment, hoping to give Letya time to get well clear of the Citadel. Then I slip the dagger into the pocket of my dress and make my way to Siegfried's rooms.

The main staircases and public rooms of the palace are busy. Despite the deep mourning, despite the late hour, the court is bustling with gossip about Lucien's arrest and the king's death. As I pass, people break off their conversations and gawk, before returning to their whispering with renewed energy. I lift my chin, give back stare for stare. Lucien's words run through my mind: *Remember, the most important thing here is not your future; it's that of Atratys.*

I try to think only of Atratys as I reach Siegfried's apartment and my anxiety builds. No guards, at least. I'm a little surprised, but I lift my hand and knock.

A servant opens the door; he bows, granting me admittance, and I force myself to cross the threshold. When the door shuts behind me, fear twists my guts. Siegfried is standing near the windows on the far side of the room. He dismisses the servant and turns to me. 'Aderyn.' His smile is the same dazzling smile I remember from the first day we met. 'To what do I owe this pleasure?'

'I've come to talk to you about Lucien. About the trial.'

He nods. 'Very good. I'm so glad you didn't try to insult my intelligence – or your own – by pretending ignorance. Or innocence. You wish to negotiate with me?'

'Yes. Lucien is innocent. We both know that. And I have . . . certain evidence, that will implicate you. If I make it public.'

A muscle twitches briefly in the side of Siegfried's face, but his smile doesn't disappear. 'Fairly weak evidence, I imagine. Given that you haven't yet shown it to Convocation. So the question is –' he tilts his head, walking towards me – 'what are you offering me, in return for Rookwood's life?'

'I'm offering my silence, and my cooperation. I'll say nothing about you and your half-sister. I'll become your mistress and, in time, your wife. Olorys will control the Crown Estates and Atratys and eventually the whole of Solanum. That's everything you wanted, isn't it?'

Siegfried is right in front of me now, too close for me not to see the greed and desire in his eyes. 'Rookwood means that much to you? You'll ignore my plans for Odette, and give yourself to me, to save him?'

I stare up into his face. 'Yes.' I barely breathe the word, but he hears me.

'Prove it.'

I close up the space between us, go up on tiptoes and put one arm around his neck, pulling him towards me. His head dips and our lips meet and I kiss him hard, flicking my tongue into his mouth, forcing him to respond, to kiss me back. His arms fold around me. And slowly, carefully, I edge my other hand down from his waist and into my pocket. My knife is there, solid and real – more real than what I'm doing, or where I am; I grip it, slide it out, tighten my hold on his neck and thrust the blade upward –

My dagger slips and twists aside and I drop it as Siegfried shoves me backwards onto the floor.

He starts laughing. And at first I think it's shock, that I've managed to hurt him; there's a tear in his tunic. But then he gets hold of the fabric and rips it and underneath –

He's wearing chainmail. 'Did you honestly think I would trust you, Aderyn?' The laughter fades, and he wipes his mouth with the back of his hand. 'Did you honestly think I would still want you, you Atratyan whore?' His handsome features are twisted with contempt. He picks up my knife. 'Get up.'

I struggle to my feet. He grabs my arm and jerks me forward, holding the blade beneath my chin, forcing my head up. 'Turik told me. He's been in my pay for weeks now; it wasn't particularly hard to persuade him to betray his master, especially once I told him I had his sister in my custody.' Siegfried shakes his head. 'The loyalty of the flightless so very rarely endures any real test. I know, therefore, that you've been in Rookwood's bed. That you gave him what you refused me. That your virtue is nothing more than a sham.' He spits in my face. 'And yet,' he lowers the knife a little, 'I still have a use for you.'

I struggle uselessly against his grasp. 'If you think I'm going to help you, you bastard, you're even more insane than I realised. I'd rather die.'

'Oh, I think you'll change your mind. Unlike Patrus – who really is incredibly dim-witted – I have taken the trouble to acquire some additional leverage.' Still gripping my arm, and with my mother's dagger pointed at my back, he marches me towards the bedroom. 'Open the door.'

'No.'

'Open it.' He presses the point of the knife against the soft flesh beneath my shoulder blade.

I turn the handle and push the door open.

Sitting on the bed, her hands tied behind her and a gag in her mouth, is Letya.

Seventeen

My courage withers. Why is she still here? Why did she not leave earlier?

'How?'

'One of my servants caught her as she was trying to escape the castle. You were sensible, sending her away. Unfortunate that your timing was poor.'

My mother's dagger is digging into my back. There is no way out, for me or for Letya, unless I can transform. I screw my eyes shut, hoping that somehow my desperation will be stronger than the fear and the pain; that maybe, finally, my body will obey me –

Nothing. Apart from Siegfried's mocking laughter. My shoulders sag. 'What do you want?'

'We can discuss that on the way. Turik.'

Lucien's attendant steps out of the shadows. I hardly recognise him: his eyes are glassy and there are bloody lacerations across one side of his face. When he sees me he jerks forward. 'Your Grace –'

'Enough of that, fool,' Siegfried snarls. 'Remember your place, and what you risk. Bring her.' He nods his head towards Letya.

Turik is carrying a sword. He drags Letya to her feet; her hands are tied with a long length of rope, like a halter. Turik holds the end of the rope and positions the tip of his blade against her back.

'Very good. Now, while we are making our way downstairs, you need to be silent, Aderyn. The slightest sound, and Letya will suffer. Do you understand?'

I nod.

Outside Siegfried's room we turn not towards the main staircase, as I had expected, but in the other direction. Ahead of us is the door to the menial stairs, the ones Letya and I took disguised as housemaids, and for a moment I think that we are going to go through it, that Siegfried is going to force us down to the dungeons. But we walk past that staircase too and come to a dead end.

Siegfried stops in front of a large but unremarkable painting, leans forward and slips his fingers behind the frame. He seems to be feeling around for something. Then, at a jerk of his hand, the entire frame swings outward.

Behind the painting is a dark, cramped opening. Siegfried steps through, and a few moments later reappears with a burning torch.

'Now,' he murmurs, 'you are going to carry this. Letya will walk directly behind you. If you want her to live, don't try to escape.'

He holds out the torch, and I take it and step into the darkness.

I find myself at the top of a staircase. There's a rope running along the wall at waist height; a necessity, since the steps are narrow, uneven and slimy. The air smells damp and dusty and it catches, bitter, at the back of my throat. When the painting is pulled to, sealing us inside, the flame of the torch burns with a blue edge.

'Get moving.'

We descend. The torch illuminates only a couple of steps in front of me. Since each stair looks almost identical, and there is no other variation in my surroundings, I soon lose all sense of time and place. I seem to be walking the same steps over and over again, a slow, never-ending plunge to who knows where. My leg muscles start to ache. Letya is crying.

Finally, just when I think my calves are about to cramp and pitch me down into the darkness, the air seems to change. It's fresher, carrying the tang of seawater. Another few steps and there is a flat floor in front of me. I sigh with relief and hurry forward, anxious to get out of the tunnel, whatever may be waiting at the other end. Behind me, Turik swears at Letya, ordering her to walk faster, a sharp note of hysteria in his voice.

The tunnel widens, turns, and without warning we're in the open and it's stony underfoot. The cool night air and the space around me make me feel as if I've escaped. But Siegfried plucks the torch from my hand, throws it into the water – we are by the shore of the fjord – and takes my arm, jamming the knife against my side.

'Into the boat.'

There's a rowing boat drawn up on the pebbles; a man is waiting next to it with a pair of oars. Letya and I are hustled into the boat and made to sit in the bottom of the hull in a puddle of dirty water. Letya is at the stern, Turik next to her on a bench, and I'm in the prow. The rower takes his seat in the middle. We wait while Siegfried strips off his clothes and replaces them with a long robe. He climbs in and sits on a wooden ledge beside me.

'We have a pleasant night for it, now the rain has passed.' He gestures at the cloudless sky above the Citadel, slowly receding with every oar-stroke. 'I imagine Rookwood's trial must be about to start. A pity I am not there, but my sister will ensure the correct outcome.'

'I don't understand how I ever liked you.'

'You liked me because I'm charming, and clever, and I seemed to offer a way to get what you wanted. Which was revenge on those who killed your mother, of course. For both you and your father.'

'You used him.'

'We used each other. He hated his brother, and I wanted the crown. A slow, painful death for the king suited us both.'

'That's a lie.' I clutch my stomach, digging my nails into my flesh to ward off the nausea that threatens to overwhelm me. 'My father just wanted to frighten him –'

'Is that what you've been telling yourself?' Siegfried smirks at me. 'I'm afraid not, Aderyn. It was he who sought me out. He asked me to use my access to the Citadel to poison the king. In return, he offered me your hand in marriage and the whole of Atratys. I suppose he thought I would protect you. And I would have wed you, eventually. You would have ruled Solanum at my side. But as it is, you've chosen to throw away everything – everything – for one night of sated lust in the arms of a –'

My fist gets halfway to his face before he blocks me.

'I don't think so, you flightless bitch.' He grabs my wrist and twists my arm behind me so hard I cry out in pain. 'Touch me again and I'll break it.'

'I am – not – flightless.' I force the words out through gritted teeth.

'You can say that as many times as you like, but it won't make it true. Do you know who told the king you were flightless? I did. And who do you think told me? Your father. *My poor, flightless daughter* – that's what he called you. He didn't keep you locked up at Merl merely for your protection. He was embarrassed by you.'

He lets go of me, shoves me forward; I catch myself just before my face hits the dirty water in the bottom of the boat. I want to scream. To tell him he's lying. That my father would never – *never* – have called me flightless, that he was a good man, not someone to plan murder. Not someone to sacrifice his only child in the name of revenge.

But the words stick in my throat.

Because obviously I didn't know my father at all.

Siegfried chuckles. 'It has been amusing, talking to you about my friend the chemist, knowing all along it was your father who made the poison that killed the king. Who made the potion that enabled you to fly again.' He leans closer. 'The potion that he gave to me, Aderyn. To me. Not to you.'

The icy water has soaked into my dress. There's a large wooden splinter stuck in the heel of my hand. I pull it out, stare at the trickle of blood that tracks down my arm. I should be feeling cold, or pain, or both. Something. But my centre seems to have been . . . excised. Like someone has taken a knife and cut away whatever it is that connects my emotions to the rest of me. Cut away my heart.

'Why haven't you killed me?'

'A reasonable question. And I will kill you. Or –' he waves a hand – 'watch you be executed, I suppose. But first, you're going to write a confession. You're going to tell Convocation that it was you – and your father, and your servants – who planned to murder the king and take the crown. The queen will suggest, as a reward for unveiling this plot, that Atratys should be annexed to Olorys. Your family shield will be disgraced and struck from the records. But you'll be dead, of course. You probably won't care.'

I'm about to give in. To tell him that I'll write whatever he wants, say whatever he wants, if he at least allows Letya to live.

But then he adds: 'I've never been to an execution for high treason. Apparently, they're going to bind poor Lucien by his wrists and ankles to one of the posts in the arena and flog him. Then, once the skin is bloodied, they'll place borer worms into the lacerations.'

I clamp my hand to my mouth as my stomach heaves.

Still Siegfried continues. 'Curious creatures, borer worms. From northern Fenian. They live by feeding on wounded animals. The scent of blood prompts them to produce an acid, which, in combination with several rows of very sharp teeth, enables them to eat through skin, muscle, bone . . . But they move slowly. It's a lingering, agonising, humiliating

291

death.' He sighs. 'I would have so enjoyed making you watch Rookwood die.'

The fire flares in my belly. Maybe I can't feel anything else, but I can still feel rage.

'Go to hell. And rot there. I'm not signing anything.'

My captor merely smiles. The boat bumps against something solid, and as the oarsman jumps out to tie it up I look around. We're at the tower that stands out in the fjord. Siegfried drags me upright and we clamber up out of the boat onto the rocks that form the base of the tower. There's a small door. Once Turik and Letya have joined us, Siegfried opens it.

It's like our journey down the staircase behind the painting, but in reverse. Again, Siegfried forces me to carry a torch. Again – apart from the small area illuminated by its flames – we are plunged into gloom. But this time we have to climb upward, circling round the inside of the tower. There are windows, but only at the top; looking up, I can't see any glimmer of light. The darkness sucks at my eyeballs. The stairs are steep and uncomfortably deep. Turik soon starts panting. Every so often I slow down too much, and Siegfried yells at me. But I can't help it. I'm so tired; all I'm aware of is the ache in my lungs and the throbbing pain in my injured hand.

Past the point where I feel like I can't take another step, I have to keep climbing. Until finally the staircase ends. There's a door in front of me. It's fastened with a padlock and three heavy wooden bars and can clearly only be opened from the outside.

This place is a prison.

Siegfried puts the torch in a bracket and unlocks the door. But the space beyond is not what I was expecting. There's a broken chair to one side. Nothing else. Just thick dust and cobwebs and ten wooden pillars, supporting the beams that make up the roof. The only windows are high up in the walls, just beneath the roof beams: narrow glazed panels, half opaque with dirt, half smashed. I can hear the scream of the wind and the sea beating against the rocks below. Turik binds Letya to the pillar nearest the door. When he is done, Siegfried waves him away.

'Wait for me at the bottom of the stairs; I'll want you to take back the keys.'

Turik doesn't move; he is staring at me, his mouth working slightly as if he wants to say something. Siegfried shoves him.

'Get out!'

With a sob, Turik flees down the stairs. The echo of his footsteps fades. Letya, Siegfried and I are alone with the shadows.

'Why did you bring us here?'

'To keep you out of the way – your absence will suggest your guilt. And to give you time to think. Rookwood will be taken for execution tomorrow morning. I will return tomorrow evening with a confession. Either you sign it and confess your guilt in front of Convocation, or you can watch your friend here suffer. If you still refuse, I'll find someone else you love. Your steward perhaps – Lord Lancelin will undoubtedly come to find out what's happened to you. And to plead for the body of his son, of course. Whatever's left of it.' He grins at me, and I'm reminded of a grinning skull, bone-white and fleshless.

'I'll be interested to see how much blood you're willing to spill before you give in.'

'I'm going to kill you.'

'How, exactly?' He moves towards the door, stopping next to the pillar where Letya is pinioned and holding the knife to her neck. 'Unless you want me to slit her throat, I suggest you stand well back, Your Grace. Against the wall there. And don't move.'

I obey, stumbling backwards until I can't go any further. 'What are you doing?'

'I'm going to give you something to think about, while I'm gone.' My friend is trying to twist away from him, but she can't. 'The flightless are so easily damaged. It would have been far better for this woman if you'd left her among the peasants, where she belongs.'

Siegfried places his hand on her neck, closing his fingers around her throat – holds them there as Letya begins to whimper.

'Stop it!'

He lifts his hand away and laughs. 'As you wish. Until tomorrow evening then. I look forward to describing Rookwood's sufferings to you. With a bit of luck, he'll still be alive, just about.'

I scream and run at him, my hands raised as if I could claw away his skin – his life – with my nails.

But I'm too late.

He hurries out of the door and slams it behind him, and by the time I reach it I hear the last of the bars drop into place. I beat my fists against the cold wood, kick it, throw the broken chair at it – the door barely shifts in its frame. Siegfried has gone.

It's hard, untying the ropes that bind Letya to the pillar. Siegfried took my mother's knife with him, so I have to use my nails. My fingers are bloody by the time the last knot is undone. Letya slumps to the floor and pulls the gag out of her mouth.

'Turik tricked me. He told me that he regretted what he'd done, that he could make things right if I would just wait for him and take him with me . . .' She covers her face with her hands, sobbing so hard that she can't speak, can hardly breathe. I take off the many-layered petticoat that's beneath my gown and use it to cover my hands and arms.

'Letya . . .' She leans against me. I wrap the fabric around her and hold her for as long as I dare.

She cries for a long time. But eventually her sobs quieten, stop.

'I'm so sorry, Aderyn. If I hadn't told Turik that I was helping you, and what I'd found out –'

'It's not your fault, Letya. None of this is your fault. May I see your neck?'

She sits up carefully. There's no colour here, barely any light, but I can just see how her skin has darkened and blistered beneath Siegfried's touch; she is branded with his handprint. Tears spring into my eyes. 'My poor Letya. I don't know what to do to help you.'

'It hurts. Especially when I move.'

'Here.' I bunch the petticoat into a makeshift pillow and help her to lie down.

'We're trapped, aren't we?'

'Yes. The door is locked from the outside.' But even if we could force our way out, there are no other boats here. I sit back down again by Letya's head, hugging my knees to my chest. 'I wish you weren't here. I wish I'd let you stay at home. I wish I'd never left Merl.'

Letya's eyes are closed but she smiles faintly. 'If wishes were feathers . . . that's what my mother used to say. "If wishes were feathers, the flightless would fly."'

'I've not heard that before.'

'It's probably not a saying among nobles. You can already fly.' Her eyes open. 'I'm sorry. I heard what Siegfried said to you. What he called you.'

'It doesn't matter now. And what he said was true. I just didn't want to hear it.'

'It's not true.' She shuts her eyes again, but her fingers – she is still wearing her gloves – grope for my hand. 'Your mother taught you to transform, Aderyn. I never met her, but you've talked about her. She would have taught you well. So you can fly. You just . . .' Her forehead puckers with pain.'. . . you just need to let yourself remember how.'

Oh, Mother . . . I stare into the shadows, as if she might suddenly emerge from the darkness.

I wish you were here. I wish you would tell me what to do.

But you know what to do.

The voice arrives unbidden in my head. A memory: my mother and I, at one of the lakes in the grounds at Merl. I am nervous about transforming, and she is encouraging me. I remember her smiling down at me, cupping my cheek in her strong hand.

You know what to do, Aderyn. The power is in your blood. You were born with it, and it won't ever leave you. It wants to change your shape. You just have to let it.

But I'm frightened. What if it doesn't work properly? What if I get stuck? What if –

So many questions.

She laughs and crouches down and looks me in the eyes.

You trust me, don't you?

Of course I do.

Of course. Because you are my daughter, and the daughter of Atratys too. And I trust you, Aderyn. Now you just have to trust yourself.

'But, Mother –' I've spoken aloud, breaking the silence of the tower. 'Mother?'

It's as if I've lost her all over again. I weep like I haven't wept for years – not even when my father died. I scream at the Creator for allowing her to die, at myself for not being able to save her, at my uncle for his wickedness. Letya can only watch me, sympathetic tears spilling across her cheeks. I rage and rage until I've worn myself out.

Until finally, with exhaustion, comes a kind of peace.

'Letya?'

'Yes?' Her voice is weak.

'I'm going to fetch help.' I stop, laugh at myself. 'I mean, I'm going to try. If I don't manage to transform before I hit the ground . . .'

'Aderyn, are you sure? Couldn't you . . . ? Couldn't you climb down first? Just a little way?'

'No. I have to go from here or not at all.' I lean in closer, so

I can look into her eyes. 'I don't want to leave you. I'll come back soon. If I succeed.'

She reaches up and touches my face. 'You will.'

I hope that I can find that same certainty when it comes to it.

But first, I have to get out of this room. I walk around the walls, running my fingertips against the stonework. It's rough, but not irregular enough for me to find any foothold. The length of rope that Turik used to bind Letya is still on the floor. I pick it up, weighing it in my hands, squinting up at the windows above me.

There are brackets of some kind, on the walls below the windows. Metal rods of the sort that tapestries may be hung from. Some of them are loose; the iron fixings have rusted away. The chance that one of them will take my weight seems small. But I can't think of any other way.

I take off my gown and undergarments. Pick a bracket that looks firm, tie the end of the rope into a noose. Start throwing it upward. It takes me an age. I get sweaty and tired and every time the noose misses its mark I want to scream with frustration. But finally, it catches. I tug on the rope as hard as I can; the bracket creaks, but it doesn't move. Gripping the rope in both hands, wincing at the pain in my injured palm, I start walking my feet slowly, slowly up the wall.

My progress is agonising. The rope grows slippery with blood and sweat. The muscles in my shoulders send bolts of pain down my arms and into my back, and I have to keep stopping as it gets harder and harder to force myself up. But gradually I climb higher. And higher. Until I winch myself up one last time and my feet are next to the iron bracket.

The window is just above me. Holding on to the rope with one hand, I grope blindly upward, grab hold of what is left of the wooden window frame and pull –

I'm hunched up in the opening that pierces the wide tower wall, clinging to the window frame. The breeze whips my hair around my head and brings my naked skin up in goose pimples. On one side is the room where Letya is still imprisoned. On the other, the rocks and water of the fjord. I don't dare look down.

The Citadel is opposite me, rising from the head of the fjord. It looks a long way away in the darkness; here and there are scattered gleams of light from windows, and a brighter patch where the landing platform projects out over the water. That's what I need to aim for.

But I can't transform where I am. I can't even try. There's not enough space.

The night Lucien flew back to Merl – I remember him leaping from my window, launching himself into the darkness. I have to do the same.

I have to let myself fall.

Closing my eyes, I try to ignore the wind, and the fact that I'm crouched high in the air above rocks and water. My first instinct is to try to remember everything my mother taught me about air currents and lift and speed of attack – but a flash of insight tells me that such details are not going to help. This isn't a problem that can be solved by memory or thought.

I have to feel, instead. To allow myself, finally, to feel everything, however much it might hurt.

My skin, first of all. The damaged as well as the whole, the scarred as well as the smooth. In my mind, I examine every contour of it, separating myself from it, letting go of the feelings of pain and shame until my skin is no more to me than a convenient covering for muscle and bone. Then I move on to the current that runs constantly beneath my skin. The innate power, flowing from my parents, my ancestors, flowing through my blood. I follow the current, embracing it as I let myself sink into my core, leaving behind my human shape. Deeper and deeper the current draws me, until I can sense that my form is drifting, fragmenting, becoming malleable. And then . . .

I jump.

The air tears past me, threatening to drag me back into solidity. And for a moment the scream of the wind becomes –

– the scream of the hawks, clawing their way back out of my memory –

– the screams of my mother as she dies, of my father as he gathers her broken body in his arms –

Image after image flashes through my mind as pain sweeps across my scarred back. But still I am falling, falling away from the hawks and the hurt, and the shrieks dwindle and fade. There is nothing but me and the wind.

And the wind and I belong to each other.

I open my arms in a wide embrace. Spread them out into strong white wings. Skin, muscle, bone: everything changes, lightens, and the wind catches me and bears me upward –

Sea spray, against my face. I open my eyes and I'm flying above the waves.

I'm flying . . .

The exhilaration is there, the exhilaration that I remembered, that was so absent from the flights I took with Siegfried's potion in my blood. But it's the joy that shocks me. So much joy that my heart might break from it, that my whole body might burn up in its fierce heat. With sudden clarity I recall flying between my parents, hearing both their voices in my head –

You're doing so well, Aderyn!

Come, daughter, let us see how swiftly you can fly . . .

How swiftly can I fly? I tilt my wings, stretch forward, rush across the choppy waters of the fjord towards the Citadel. The mountains above call to me as my flight feathers sweep the distance away; my heart beats faster at the thought of exploring them, of soaring above glaciers and snow-shrouded valleys. I long to see the beauty of this land from the air . . .

But I am in control now, and the landing platform is below me. I circle round once, twice, making sure there are no other nobles in sight, and I land.

Panic flickers inside me briefly, as I hit the water – panic that, having succeeded in becoming a swan, I won't be able to change back. But in fact I barely have to think about it. One moment I am settling my feathers and folding my wings; the next, I am crouched in the shallow water.

A hooded servant approaches, offering a robe. I take one – my hands are shaking, and my knees – and cover myself.

At least Siegfried won't be expecting me to be here. He thinks I can't fly.

But I'm not planning to find him. Instead I make my way to Aron's room and knock on his door.

There's no answer. For one heart-stopping moment I wonder whether he's fled, or has been arrested. I knock again, louder.

This time the door opens.

Aron is rubbing his eyes, as if he was asleep. He opens the door wider to let me in.

'Aderyn? What's going on?' His glance takes in my robe. 'Where have you been? And why weren't you at the trial?'

'Because Siegfried abducted me. Aron –' I reach out for him as a wave of dizziness throws me off balance. 'Cousin, I need your help.'

Eighteen

Anger ignites in Aron's eyes. 'You're injured . . . That bastard. What did he do to you?'

'It's only my hand.' I stagger; Aron puts his arm around me and leads me to a chair. 'And I've just transformed for the first time in years. It was . . .' I catch my breath, struggling to find words that can adequately describe how it felt. 'It was wonderful, Aron, but I hardly ate anything today – or I suppose it was yesterday, so –'

'What do you mean, you've transformed for the first time in years? You've been flying for weeks already – with Siegfried. I've seen you with my own eyes.'

I shake my head, my excitement fading, dreading the effect of another revelation. 'I'm sorry, cousin: what you saw was a lie. Siegfried deceived you. So did I.'

As Aron cleans my hand and helps me knot a handkerchief around it, I tell him about the potion that Siegfried gave me. That my father made. He fetches me a glass of wine and some biscuits, and I tell him everything: my attempt to kill Siegfried, the hidden passage, the tower. His expression grows more and more grave, but he doesn't interrupt. He just sits with his chin propped in his hand and lets me talk.

'. . . and now I'm here. But Letya is still in the tower. We have to rescue her and get a doctor to look at that burn on her neck. And we have to stop them executing Lucien.'

Aron sighs. 'I wish you'd waited, cousin. Or at least told me what you were planning. My messenger returned from Merl not two hours ago. We have the letters that Siegfried wrote to your father.'

My shoulders sag with relief. 'Then we must rouse Convocation immediately.' I glance at the clock on the mantlepiece; the night is already wearing away. Lucien is supposed to be brought for execution at dawn.

Aron is still watching me, frowning.

'Cousin? Don't you agree?'

He nods. 'Of course. And we will go to Convocation. But there is another factor to consider. What will happen to the crown?'

'I don't understand.'

'At the moment, Odette and Siegfried are due to be crowned as soon as they are married. Once Siegfried and the queen have been exposed, the marriage will obviously not take place. Odette will not be able to claim the throne. Neither will you, since you are also unmarried.'

'But I could marry –' Sudden embarrassment halts me. 'I mean, I could marry someone.'

'If you're thinking of Rookwood, you could of course marry him. But if you want to be queen, Convocation would have to approve the match. And they won't: you and Lucien are both from Atratys; it would concentrate too much power in one dominion.'

'I don't want to be queen. I just want to go home.' I sigh. 'Who's next in line after me?'

'Siegfried controls his father – assuming he's still alive – so once he and Aurik are both excluded, the throne falls to either Arden of Dacia or Thane of Fenian – Grayling's father. Both married, both – due to the complex intermarrying of their ancestors – with an equal claim. The kingdom might end up in a civil war.'

'I feel as if Arden is more likely to win.' I've never met Thane, but if he's like his son . . . 'Would Fenian contest the throne?'

'Hard to say, but to give up such a prize without a fight . . .' He smiles contemptuously. 'I doubt either of them would make a good king. Not that my father set a particularly high standard. Of course, as someone with a better claim to the throne, you'd be left in a somewhat awkward position. As would my sister.'

He means we'd be at risk, of course. At risk of being forced into marriage. Or imprisoned. Or worse. A lifetime dealing with the sorts of threats I've had to face for the last three months. I take a sip of wine, hoping its warmth will dispel the chill of panic that just assailed me.

'This is ridiculous. I know Odette doesn't want to be queen. But you've been brought up to rule. And you want to rule. Did you honestly find nothing in the Decrees that would restore you to the succession?'

Aron stands and walks to the large table in the centre of the room. 'I did find one thing. But –' he laughs – 'I would need your help, cousin.'

'Of course I'll help, if I can.'

'You may not want to, when you understand . . .' He hands me a roll of parchment. 'I've marked the relevant passage.'

I study the words that Aron has underlined.

The flighted rule; the flightless are ruled. Thus will the kingdom be guarded. No flightless man or woman may ascend the throne.

So far, the Decree seems clear. But it continues.

Between them, the monarchs must defend the kingdom. The monarch must be first in flight, and last in retreat. The Elders have spoken.

'The monarch must be first in flight . . .' I glance up at my cousin. 'I can see how Convocation were able to challenge your right to rule. But . . .'

Aron sighs and points to the parchment. 'Look again. The monarchs – plural – must defend the kingdom. But the monarch – singular – must be first in flight. You see?' He stares at me intently. 'As long as one of the two monarchs can fly, the Decree is fulfilled.'

Realisation dawns. And dread blooms in the pit of my stomach.

'But to defend the kingdom –'

'You don't have to be able to shift your shape to defend the kingdom. It's at least as much about politics as brute strength.' He sits in the chair next to me. 'What you and I are doing now is defending the kingdom. Yet neither of us is transformed.'

I stare back at the paper gripped in my hands. But my vision is blurred by the tears in my eyes.

'You understand me, I think.' Aron's voice is gentle, but

there's excitement there too. 'I want to be king, Aderyn; it is my birthright. You want to save Lucien and protect Atratys. And we both want to take down Siegfried and the queen. The surest way for us to achieve our ends is for us to present the evidence to Convocation together. To give them an easy choice as to who should rule next. They won't even need to change the date of the coronation.'

'And if I . . . can't?'

He sits back in the chair and crosses his legs. Sighs wearily. 'I'll give you the letters. You can go to Convocation, and they will probably believe you. Lucien will probably be saved, and Siegfried will probably be imprisoned. As to what will happen then . . .' He shrugs.

He'll give me the evidence I need. But he won't come with me or support me. He won't use his influence with the Dark Guards.

Lucien and I might be free to return to Atratys together, which is all I want.

We might be left in peace.

Might . . . Probably . . . I bite my lip, trying to calculate the odds.

The room is silent apart from the ticking of the clock and the crackle of the fire in the hearth.

Aron clears his throat. 'You know what Lucien would say, if he were here.'

'Shut up, damn you.' I glare at my cousin. 'I'm trying to think.' Trying to think of a way around what he is suggesting. Of a way I can protect Atratys, and save Lucien, and still get to be with him. And I realise I'm facing almost the same choice as my mother had: do what is best for the kingdom, or what is best for me. 'What you're asking of me . . .'

'I know. I heard you together, down in the dungeons.'

I laugh, though I don't know why. 'We'd started planning what we would do together. Once we get home –' The word cuts through my throat like a knife as I try to imagine Atratys at war. Merl under siege.

Aron is getting down on one knee in front of me. 'I will try to be an agreeable husband, Aderyn. We're making an alliance. I would ask, for the sake of Solanum, that you honour the vows we take, as I will myself. Unlike my father, I would have a kingdom built on truth and honesty, not upon a web of deceit. But I swear I won't . . .' He colours and drops his gaze. 'I won't expect anything of you beyond that. I won't attempt to force myself on you. I know you don't love me.' He looks up at me again; to my surprise, there's both pain and anxiety in his eyes. 'What do you say, cousin? Will you marry me?'

Everything around me seems to slow down. All I'm aware of are the contractions of my heart, each beat shaving away the time I have left. The time Lucien has left.

I drag some more air into my lungs and place my hand into Aron's. 'Yes.' I can't say another word.

Aron grips my fingers tightly and smiles. It's the closest to joyful I've ever seen him. He kisses my hand, gets to his feet and pulls the bell rope to summon a servant.

'I'll send for the Venerable Mother. She knows my fears for Odette, and my suspicions of Siegfried. She'll marry us quickly.'

A servant arrives shortly and is duly dispatched. While we wait, Aron walks about the room, tapping his fingers on the side of his leg. But I . . . I can't move. There seems to be a great weight on my chest, pinning me to the chair. The Venerable Mother arrives, out of breath, with a cloak covering her nightgown and her long grey hair loosely plaited. While Aron talks to her in a low voice I stare into the fire, watching the logs burn into ash.

'Cousin?' Aron is waiting next to me. 'It's time.' I look around and realise there is another person in the room, a young nobleman I only know by sight; the pointed tips of his ears mark him out as a member of an owl family. 'This is Lord Tarl. We need a witness, and he owes me some favours.' The man blushes and ducks his head to me briefly. 'Come.'

Aron helps me to my feet, entwining his fingers with mine, and I cling on to his hand, leaning against him, numb. The Venerable Mother is in front of us holding a large leather-bound book.

She peers into my face. 'You look distressed, my child. Are you sure this is what you wish?'

I take a deep breath and force myself to straighten up.

I'm doing this for you, Lucien, and for Atratys. I hope you understand.

'Yes. Yes, this is what I want.'

She nods and begins reading the ancient text of the wedding service. The words wash over me, but I find I am able to respond in the right places, to answer the questions put to me without stumbling. My hand shakes a little when I sign the marriage pledge, but only someone who knows my signature would notice. Surely many brides are nervous. And soon – sooner than I would have thought possible – it is done.

The Venerable Mother joins our hands and binds them lightly together with a silver chain, each link of which is fashioned to resemble a feather. 'You are mated for life, as our nature and our customs and our holy laws demand, pledged to each other in a bond that only death may dissolve.' Removing the chain, she holds her hand up in front of us, five fingers spread out to represent the sun. 'I wish you joy of each other, long life and many young. Now, seal your union with a kiss.'

Aron and I turn to face each other. I close my eyes, lift my face and feel the brief pressure of his lips against mine.

The clock chimes one.

'Lucien –'

Aron nods. 'We have to hurry. Tarl, take my servant and a Dark Guard and get to the tower in the fjord. There's a flightless woman imprisoned there – you'll need to break the door down. You'd better take a doctor too.'

Tarl's eyes widen, but he bows. 'Yes, Your Highness. I'll see to it.'

The Venerable Mother is refastening the strings of her cloak. 'I must return to the sanctuary, but I will be ready if Convocation send anyone to question me about this marriage.' She glances at the lightening sky outside the window. 'It's dawn.' The bell of the Citadel starts to toll, summoning the court to watch Lucien die. 'You'd better go straight to the place of execution.'

Aron passes me a cloth-wrapped package. 'All the letters between Siegfried and your father.' He lifts his brows. 'Neither of our fathers is going to have much of a reputation left by the end of this.'

'I think they'll both be left with exactly the reputation they deserve.' I clutch the package to my chest. 'Let's go.'

We run from Aron's rooms down through the palace. But the corridors and stairways are full of people moving in the same direction, and our progress is slowed as we get nearer to the two doorways that lead to the balcony overhanging the arena. I look around, trying to identify members of Convocation, but the crowds make it impossible.

'We're going to be too late –'

'I know another way.' Aron takes my hand and drags me away from the balcony to another set of stairs. On we hurry, past the entrance hall, down into the gloomy rooms where the flightless mostly live and work.

The bell has stopped. 'Where are we going?' My voice is sharp with anxiety. 'There's no time –'

'Out into the execution space itself. Not much further.' He pulls me along another corridor. Round the next corner is a room full of Dark Guards. Off-duty, I guess – it's the first time I've ever seen any of them with their helmets off. Aron has a hasty conversation with one man, a captain by his insignia; the man puts his helmet on and leads us forward. Together we run along one more corridor and down another flight of steps, and then there is daylight, and a doorway –

There, on the far side of the grassy space, are the two stone posts. Lucien has his arms wrapped around one of the pillars as if he's embracing it, but then I see his wrists and ankles are shackled to metal loops sticking out of the stone. He's naked, and there are bloody red welts criss-crossing his back, and as I watch, one guard lifts the whip above his shoulder and another picks up a fat, grey worm in a pair of pincers –

'No!' I snarl and hurl myself forward, aware of nothing but my desperate need to save Lucien, pulling off my robe and transforming into a swan while I run. The power pours out of me. It burns away my human shape and I leap, claiming the air, spreading my feathers wide. The guards buckle, driven to their knees, screaming and clutching their heads as the field generated by my body rips through them. Diving at the two men nearest Lucien, I strike them with my wings, knocking them through the air, away from him. They smack into the boulders at the edge of the grass. Neither gets up. I land next to the pillar, shift my shape back to human and crouch there. Breathless. Trembling.

Silence surrounds me.

'Aderyn.' Aron is next to me. He wraps my robe back around my shoulders and helps me up. We position ourselves in front of Lucien, shielding him.

'The letters?'

'I have them.'

Together, Aron and I face the court.

On the upper balcony, the queen is standing between Siegfried and Odette. Siegfried is staring at me, eyes and mouth wide open, stunned. Turik, behind him, looks as if he might be sick. But the queen's face is twisted with rage. She clutches the railing in front of her. 'Traitors! Murderers! Seize them!'

A guard starts towards us, pulling his axe from his belt.

'Stop!' Odette's voice is shaky but clear. 'As your future ruler, I order you to stop. No one is to touch them.' The guard hesitates for a moment – steps back.

Aron points at the queen. 'The only traitor here, stepmother, is you. You and that man next to you. Siegfried of Olorys. Who is also your half-brother. And your lover.'

There is a shocked murmur from the onlookers on the main balcony. A louder outburst from the flightless servants gathered beyond the fence of the arena.

Siegfried laughs. 'Lies. The reckless lies of an unimportant, flightless boy who wishes to take back the throne he has rightly been denied. See –' he turns to address the courtiers – 'the treacherous Protector of Atratys stands at his side.'

'We have the letters, Siegfried.' I take the package from Aron and hold them up. 'The letters that you and my father wrote to each to other, planning the king's murder. And who, not knowing the relationship between you, would have suspected the queen of poisoning her own husband? You and she and my father are the guilty ones. Lord Rookwood found one of my father's notebooks and brought it to me, that's all.' I glare at the court, daring them to disbelieve me. 'He is innocent.'

'Ridiculous.' Siegfried laughs again, but his voice is strained. 'You expect us to swallow this elaborate confection of fantasy?'

'I expect Convocation to examine these letters. I call upon them to assemble, as is my right as a Protector. And then I will give evidence. I will tell them how the king planned the murder of my mother, and how her death led my father to seek revenge. About the potions my father concocted and shared with you. About your plans, once you were king, to dispose of Odette and marry me, in order to gain control of Atratys and the Crown Estates as well as Olorys. I'll tell them about the king's assassin, the hawk, whose body lies in a cellar beneath this very Citadel –'

'And I will tell them,' Odette's voice is stronger now, 'how you have imprisoned me since the death of my father, and how you threatened the life of my brother when I told you I would no longer marry you.'

A babble of confused noise – shouted questions, arguing – erupts from the main balcony, distracting me, but my attention is drawn back to the royal box by a gasp of pain. Siegfried is gripping the top of Odette's hair with one hand. In the other he holds a knife, the edge of its blade against Odette's neck.

'Aron –'

Silence descends as the rest of the audience realises what is happening.

'Take your hands off my sister, you coward.' Aron has drawn his sword, though he must know we're too far away to do anything. 'Come down here and fight me.'

But it is the queen who answers. 'I think not, Your Highness.' Now her initial fury has passed, her expression is calm, her voice oddly amused, and I see for the first time the resemblance between her and Siegfried. 'Lower your blade and stay where you are, unless you want to lose another member of your family.' Aron swears, but obeys. A trickle of blood runs down Odette's neck onto the white fabric of her dress.

One of the Dark Guards at the edge of the royal box inches forward, but the queen turns on him, pulling a dagger from her belt. 'Get out, all of you, or the princess dies.' The guards back away and the queen locks the gate between the royal box and the main balcony.

Siegfried sneers at me. 'Are you pleased with yourself, Aderyn? You, and that one-armed whelp standing next to you? Enjoy your victory and Rookwood's caresses while you

314

can.' As he forces Odette backwards towards the door in the side of the balcony, the one that leads directly to the royal apartments, the queen faces the court.

'The crown will be ours. Stand against us if you wish, but the whole of Solanum will pay the price. I promise you: this is far from over.'

'Let my sister go.' Aron's voice is hoarse.

The queen laughs. 'Kill her, brother.'

I can just hear Odette's whimper: 'Please, Siegfried, no . . .'

Siegfried's mouth twists into a snarl –

He shoves Odette away from him and onto the ground, at the same moment as Turik launches himself forward. The queen, with a shriek of rage, strikes her brother – her diamond ring leaving a bloody gash across Siegfried's face – raises her own knife, her arm outstretched, and plunges the blade downwards towards Odette –

Turik grabs the queen's arm. For a moment he holds on, screaming as her skin burns him, but Siegfried hauls him off and the queen thrusts her dagger into his chest. Siegfried drags his sister away, through the door to the royal apartments. Slams it shut behind him as the Dark Guards begin to break down the gate.

'After them, now!' Aron yells at the guards nearest us. After an instant's frozen confusion, they begin charging towards the castle.

And finally, finally, I can think about Lucien. 'Release Lord Rookwood, instantly.' As one guard hurries forward with a set of keys, I demand the cloak of another. 'Help me with him.' Lucien moans as I cover his lacerated back with the cloak. When all four shackles are undone, the guards support Lucien so he doesn't collapse and lower him slowly onto the grass. I pull the cloak around him, covering him, and rest his head in my lap.

'Lucien? Can you hear me?'

His eyelids flutter open, his cracked lips move, but no sound comes out.

'Water!' I snap at the guard who gave me the cloak. He runs off, returning a few minutes later with an iron cup. I raise Lucien's head a little and help him drink.

'Aderyn . . .'

My shoulders slump and I stroke his hair back from his face. 'You're safe now.'

'You saved me.' His voice is barely a whisper.

'I told you I would.'

He smiles. 'So you did . . . And now we can go home to Atratys, together.'

I don't respond.

Wincing, Lucien lifts his fingers to my cheek. 'Why are you crying, my love?'

'Because –' But I can't tell him that I'm married. Not yet. Instead, I bend my head and kiss him. 'I'm crying because I'm happy. I'm happy that you're still alive, and Siegfried is gone.' I smile through my tears, because both those things are true.

'Your Grace . . .'

I glance up. There's a doctor waiting nearby, and servants with a litter. I nod, and the servants – wearing heavy gauntlets, just like the Dark Guards – lower the litter and lift Lucien carefully onto it. I get to my feet. 'We'll take good care of him,' the doctor assures me, watching me anxiously.

'Of course. I expect to be regularly informed of Lord Rookwood's progress.'

The doctor nods and leads the servants back into the castle. And I wonder whether I will ever kiss Lucien again.

The Dark Guards nearby are watching me. 'Get back to your duties. And someone –' I point at the tub of writhing borer worms, feeling my mouth twist in disgust – 'destroy those creatures.'

Seven hours have passed. Or it might be eight; exhaustion is clouding every faculty. But somehow – probably due to the uncertainty poised like a blade beneath my ribs – I am still awake. And properly dressed. I sat for a while with Letya, and after speaking to the doctors about her neck I've dispatched one of the pages to Merl to get the recipe for a cream we use there on burns. Whatever else my father may have been, he was an excellent chemist.

Meanwhile, Convocation has gathered and has begun examining the letters I handed over. They questioned me for nearly three hours. Based on my description of the room, someone has been sent to look for the body of the dead hawk assassin. Others have been given the job of searching the queen's apartment and Siegfried's rooms for further evidence; the murderers themselves took flight before the guards could catch them. Their clothes were found by an open window, but that was all.

Turik is dead.

Messengers have been dispatched to Brithys, Fenian and Lancorphys, summoning their Protectors to the Citadel; the

Protectors as well as Convocation are required to consider the question of the succession, and to decide what steps should be taken against Olorys.

I fear war is coming, whatever we do.

I have sent another letter home to Lord Lancelin, asking him to join me here as soon as possible. I want his advice. I also want him to be here to take care of his son. Lucien has suffered enough, physically. And I'm about to hurt him even more. He shouldn't have to hear it from someone else.

Lucien is sitting up in bed reading when I peek into his room.

'I thought you might be asleep.'

He puts the book down and grins at me. 'I have been, for most of the day.'

I'd hoped that would be the case. I smile back and sit on the edge of the bed. The bruising on his face still looks fresh, and there are bandages encircling his torso, as well as his wrists and his neck. 'How are you feeling?'

'I'd be lying if I said my back didn't hurt.' He pulls a face. 'All of me hurts. But the doctors gave me something to help with the pain. To make it less . . . painful.' He takes my hand. 'When you arrived, and I saw you transform . . . I thought I was dreaming. That I'd finally become delirious from thirst and torture. But I was glad. Because even if it was a fantasy, it meant I got to see you again. In a way.'

'I've finally found my ability again, Lucien. Without the help of Siegfried's potion. You're right though. Everything that's happened in the last twenty-four hours has felt a bit like a dream. Or a nightmare.'

'But we're here now.'

'We are. And . . .' I swallow, 'Aron helped.' I describe everything that happened, from when I left him in the dungeon up until I arrived in Aron's room. More or less; I gloss over any detail that I think might upset him. I don't tell him what Siegfried called me, or what he did to me in the boat. When I reveal that it was one of Aron's servants who found Siegfried's letters, Lucien whistles and looks up at the ceiling.

'Another thing I owe Aron. He's going to enjoy having me in his debt.'

'I think . . . I think he might consider that debt to be repaid.'

'How?' Lucien frowns, but he's still smiling. 'What promise have you made on my behalf? What am I going to have to do?'

'It's not something you have to do.' I drop my gaze and begin twisting my Protector's ring around on my finger. 'It's something I've already done.'

'Aderyn? What have you done? You're making me nervous . . .'

I don't dare look up. 'He gave me the letters. But he wouldn't help me in any other way, unless . . . He talked about civil war, the dominions fighting over the crown, and he said . . . he said he'd found a way he could rule, if I would agree to . . .'

Lucien doesn't respond.

'I did it for you, Lucien. I had to be sure I could save you. And save Atratys. And marrying Aron –' Lucien flinches as I say the words – 'was the only way. Please . . .' I half reach out for his hand. 'Please, say something.'

He bites his lip and nods a little. 'Well . . . we can find a way. It's not what I wanted. What either of us hoped for. But we're both alive, and we can find a way. Aron can't be so unreasonable

319

as to expect you to . . .' He stops, flushes, slips his fingers into mine. 'I mean, you don't love him. You love me. You're married to him, and you can rule with him, but that doesn't stop us being together the rest of the time.' He lifts his eyes to mine. 'It doesn't, does it?'

I remember Aron asking me to honour the vows I was about to take.

I also remember the look in his eyes. The expectation of hurt.

'I'm sorry, Lucien. I never wanted to cause you pain. But I am married. I'm bound to Aron until one of us dies. And I made a promise –'

'But, Aderyn . . .' He shakes his head, helplessly. 'Surely . . .'

I don't answer him. But I don't need to.

Lucien slides his hand away from mine. There's a tear tracking its way down his cheek. 'Of course. I'm sure you did the right thing, Your Grace. I'm . . .' His lip trembles, before he regains control. 'I'm very grateful for your care of me.'

'No one else knows yet, but it didn't seem fair for you to keep on thinking –'

'Of course. I thank you. And I hope you and His Highness will be very happy.'

'Lucien –' I lean towards him, swallowing the sob of anguish caught in my throat, refusing to add my own grief to his burden – 'you know I won't be happy. How can I ever be happy, without you?' For a moment I stare at him, pleading silently. Not for forgiveness – I'm not sure I can forgive myself – but for understanding, for anger, for *something*.

'Please, Aderyn . . .' Lucien's face crumples, and the agony in his voice is like a knife twisting in my chest. 'What do you expect of me?' He turns his head away. 'Please, just go. Now.'

There's nothing else I can say. Nothing I can do. I leave the room and shut the door quietly behind me. Somehow, I make it back to my own apartment before I collapse.

* * *

It takes another five days before all the members of the Skein – an interregnal Skein, technically, a meeting of Convocation and Protectors in the absence of a monarch – are gathered. But now they, Aron, Odette and I are in the throne room. The Crown of Talons is missing, stolen or destroyed by the queen and Siegfried. The ancient, gold-flecked throne that dominates the far end of the room is empty. Waiting.

With the exception of Aron, who is wearing his usual black leather tunic and trousers, all of us in the Skein are wearing the long, dark robes used after or just prior to transformation; the confirmation of a new monarch is traditionally followed by a ceremonial flight. But above us the gallery is crowded with brightly dressed courtiers, just like it was for the trial staged by the queen. Aron's idea: after the lies and deceptions of the last few months, everything should not just be done, but be seen to be done.

Lord Lancelin is among the crowds, and I have secured a space for Letya too; she is the first flightless person, apart from the Dark Guards, to witness the Skein. But I search in vain for Lucien. Perhaps he is still too ill to leave his room.

Once everyone has come to order, Lord Semper Corvax, an elderly member of one of the crow families and current leader of Convocation, addresses Odette. 'So, Your Highness, we come to the question of your marriage. To take up the throne it is required –'

'Yes.' Odette nods curtly. The wound on her neck is healing, but it's likely she will bear a scar for the rest of her life. 'I know what is required.'

'Then have you given any other thought as to whom you might marry?'

'There is no one else I can consider marrying.' My cousin takes a deep breath. 'My feelings for Lord Siegfried, irrational as they may appear, were nonetheless real. I am not ready to contemplate marriage with anyone else.'

Lord Corvax clears his throat. 'That is of course understandable. But still, as heir to the throne –'

'I don't want the throne. I never wanted it. In front of the Skein, in front of all Solanum, I solemnly renounce my claim and ask that I be removed from the succession.' Odette smiles at me, and I realise Aron must have told her our news. We haven't informed anyone else so far.

Arden of Dacia raises his hand.

'We all know the Protector of Atratys is next in line. But she is also unmarried, and extremely inexperienced. Perhaps Convocation would consider an alteration of the succession –'

'I object.' Grayling Wren's father has raised his hand, but the objection comes from Patrus; he has returned to court wearing a patch over his empty eye socket, but otherwise behaving as if absolutely nothing has happened. 'To fulfil the Decrees, Convocation should require the Protector of Atratys to marry someone older, someone who has the necessary experience . . .'

Next to me, Aron groans and shakes his head, pinching the bridge of his nose.

I can't help smiling as I raise my own hand.

Lord Corvax nods to me. 'The Skein will hear from the Protector of Atratys.'

'Thank you. I wish to inform the Skein that I am already married.'

Corvax bangs his walking stick on the floor to silence the murmuring of the assembly and the less restrained reaction from the gallery. 'A marriage to Lord Rookwood would, unfortunately, mean that –'

'I am not married to Lord Rookwood.' I take a deep breath, trying to ignore the regret surging through my core. 'My husband is Prince Aron. The Venerable Mother has the marriage pledge. She conducted our wedding an hour or so before Siegfried and his sister fled.'

'But . . . but, my lord,' Arden pushes further forward, 'we already know that the prince cannot rule –'

'Is that so?' Aron walks up to Lord Corvax and hands him the scroll with the relevant Decree. 'One monarch has to be able to transform. Not both.'

The noise level rises, unabated, as Corvax and the rest of the Skein pass around the scroll and discuss it. Aron and Odette and I wait, a little apart.

'Thank you for what you've done,' Odette murmurs. 'I hope you can be happy.'

I nod. I can't force myself to say anything else, even for Aron's sake: it's too soon. When I close my eyes, I can still feel Lucien's lips against mine, his hands on my body.

Odette kisses my cheek. 'It's selfish of me, but I'm glad you'll be staying at the Citadel. As I said, I always wanted a sister.'

I jump as Corvax bangs his walking stick on the marble tiles. 'The Skein has considered.' He glares until all present are silent. 'And, in the absence of a ruling monarch, our decision is final. The kingdom is in danger, and we will not add to that danger by leaving the throne empty. We therefore agree that Aderyn, of the House of Cygnus Atratys, being married, is the rightful inheritor of the throne.' Aron's hand finds mine. 'And furthermore, we agree that Prince Aron may rule alongside her, and by her right.' With a grunt, leaning on his stick, Corvax goes down on one knee in front of Aron and me. Odette copies him. And one by one, every other person in the room does the same.

Aron turns to face me, and kisses my hand. 'I wish you joy, my cousin, my wife, my queen.' He too drops to one knee. 'Long live Queen Aderyn.'

The acclamation is taken up by the others, on the floor and in the gallery. It echoes round the throne room, and as we process out to the landing platform I hear other voices, inside the Citadel and out in the courtyards and in the city, shouting out the same words. Calling them over and over until the noise makes me want to cover my ears.

I don't, of course. Instead, I turn to my cousin – my husband, as I suppose I must learn to think of him. 'Aron –'

'Go. I'll be waiting here for you, when you return.'

Odette stays close to me as we hand our robes to the waiting guards, and I'm glad. Together we enter the water. Together we kneel, transform – no difficulty any more, it's as natural as drawing breath – and together we launch ourselves into the deep golden blue of the late-afternoon sky. I hear Odette's exclamation of delight as the rest of the Skein transform and follow us. And below me . . .

Below me, the Silver Citadel sparkles. The city of Farne spills down to the open waters of the fjord, and I can see the upturned faces of the people crowding the streets. Banking, turning, revelling in the cool wind slipping across my feathers, in every strong downbeat of my wings, I lead the Skein upward. Up towards the pine-clad mountains and the blue-green glaciers cradled amid the crags.

The high peaks are snow-clad, their white tips stained crimson by the light of the setting sun. An omen, perhaps, of imminent bloodshed.

Still, in this moment, I'm not afraid. The fierce joy of flight – a joy so deep it is almost agony – overwhelms every other sensation. Borne up by the wind, I look down to see the towns and fields of the Crown Estates spread out like a living map below me. A patch of glitter on the edge of sight marks the sea. And somewhere, off in the distance, lost on the hazy horizon, lies Atratys . . .

When our enemies return – and they will return – I must be ready.

This is my home now.

This is my kingdom.

Acknowledgements

We officially started working on *A Throne of Swans* shortly after *The Witch's Blood* (the final instalment in The Witch's Kiss trilogy) was published in March 2018, though the story had been bubbling away in the background for nearly a year before that. Leaving behind our first family of characters was hard. But at the same time, we were really excited about the prospect of writing a high fantasy novel, with all that might entail. Our hopes weren't disappointed: it's been a joy to venture beyond the leafy suburbs of Surrey (the main setting for our previous books) and into a world of shape-shifters, palaces and dynastic feuds. Once again, our characters have completely stolen our hearts. We just hope the story we've created gives as much pleasure to you, our reader, as it does to us.

As with our previous books, *A Throne of Swans* has been a team effort. It wouldn't have come into existence without the input and continuous encouragement of the following people.

Claire Wilson (Rogers, Coleridge & White) continues to be the best agent ever (and yes, that is a hill we're prepared to die on) and one of our biggest cheerleaders. She's always available to calm our jittery author nerves, and her continued rock-solid support for our writing means the world to us. A shout-out and thank you to the ever-helpful Miriam Tobin too.

The team at Hot Key have been an absolute joy to work with, and we are both amazed and delighted by their boundless enthusiasm. We can't say a big enough thank you to our brilliant editors, Emma Matthewson, Carla Hutchinson and Talya Baker, or to our marketing and publicity gurus, Roisin O'Shea, Amy Llambias and Molly Holt.

Our unbounded gratitude goes to Alexandra Allden and Steve Newman for designing our stunningly beautiful cover. Thank you to Sally Taylor for giving our kingdom a map and for the other artwork within the book. We'd also like to thank Jamie-Lee Turner for creating crests to adorn our website.

Over the three-plus years since our first book was published, we've made some wonderful and supportive friends amongst the writing and blogging communities – too many to list in this limited space, but hopefully you know who you are. Thank you; we couldn't keep going without you. Special thanks and love to Perdita Cargill, Peter Davey, Sinéad O'Hart, Lu Hersey, Vic James, Kiristina Perez and the Feminism 2.0 gang.

Finally we'd like to thank our family for putting up with us, particularly our partners, Neill and Nick. Dinner's on us.

Katharine and Elizabeth Corr

Katharine and Elizabeth Corr are sisters, originally from Essex, now living in Surrey. When they both decided to write novels – on account of fictional people being much easier to deal with than real ones – it was obvious they should do it together. They can sometimes be found in one of their local coffee shops, arguing over which character to kill off next. Katharine and Elizabeth are authors of the spellbinding series The Witch's Kiss.

@katharinecorr
@lizcorr_writes
Instagram: katharinecorrwrites / lizcorrwrites
www.corrsisters.com

The flight continues . . .

A
Crown
of
Talons

Coming in 2021.

Read on for an extract . . .

PROLOGUE

Winter has caged my kingdom in ice.

For the last month the snow has been relentless: an endless fall of frozen feathers, too thick to fly through. The glass-panelled octagon of the great hall creaks with the white weight of it. But this evening, at least temporarily, the clouds have dispersed, and beneath the cold gaze of the stars the inhabitants of the Silver Citadel are celebrating the midwinter feast of the Deep Dark, the first Solstice of my reign. Pine logs crackle in the fireplaces. The scented smoke mingles with the aroma of the delicacies heaped upon the tables. Roasted venison, still sizzling from the spit; winter roots tossed in spiced flour and fried in salted butter; sugar-iced plum cake and thirty or more other dishes. A thousand candles blaze in ornate crystal chandeliers in an attempt to dispel the darkness of this long, frostbitten night

Dressed in a cloth-of-gold gown, with a gold and diamond circlet set in my dark hair, I'm dancing with Aron, my cousin and co-ruler. My husband, at least in name. I'm surrounded by servants and courtiers, all of whom have sworn loyalty to me.

Many of whom claim to love me. But in this glittering throng, my thoughts and feelings are focused entirely on one man. A man who has been ignoring me, and flirting with others for the last three hours.

With every laugh, with every look – Lucien Rookwood drives another dagger into my heart.

Aron takes advantage of a pause in the music to lean forward and whisper to me: 'You look tired.'

'I didn't sleep well.' It's true. I have many reasons to lie awake, and I haven't slept well for weeks. The violence of this winter is bringing sickness and fear of famine to my people. I'm tired of being cooped up by bad weather, unable to take to the sky. And I'm tired of the protectors and the nobles through whom I rule. Of their stubborn resistance to the reforms Aron and I want to introduce that would grant greater protection to our flightless population. Of their blind insistence that Siegfried and Tallis, the Oloryan half-siblings who nearly succeeded in seizing the throne, are no longer a threat, merely because they seem to have vanished from the kingdom. I cannot forget for a single day Tallis's promise: that she and her brother would return to exact revenge upon Aron and me, and that the whole of Solanum would pay the price for our defiance . . .

I have many reasons to worry.

But tonight, at least, every other concern is consumed by my misery over Lucien.

My feet take me through the steps and turns of the minuet while I concentrate on not allowing myself to look at the man who was – so briefly – my lover. Three months have passed, but my heart fractures a little further whenever I think about the one night we spent together, about our last meeting. Whenever I silently murmur his name. Lucien left court straight after my coronation. He came back only a week ago, and that only because of the Solstice. Because I specifically invited him to the celebration. Insisted, in fact, that he should come.

'Aderyn?' Aron has raised one white-blond eyebrow; the dance has ended and he's waiting for an answer to a question I didn't hear.

He sighs. 'I said, do you want to dance again, or rest?'

I become aware of the flightless musicians, bows poised above strings, waiting for me to decide whether I wish to continue. Of the dazzlingly clothed nobles observing me. 'I'll rest.'

'As you wish.' Aron kisses my hand as I leave the floor. He walks over to his sister, Odette, and leads her back into the dance. As the music resumes, I return to my seat on the dais and let my eyes stray towards Lucien. His dark hair – the same iridescent blue-black as the raven into which he can transform – is a little longer now; it curls against the edge of his collar. But otherwise he's little altered. He's still handsome and broad-shouldered. He's even wearing the same sleeveless grey silk tunic he wore on the night we first arrived here – less than six months ago, though it seems like another lifetime. A life in which I was merely the Protector of the Dominion of Atratys, hoping to find answers about my mother's murder, hoping to survive the intrigues of my uncle's court. A life in which Lucien was merely my clerk.

But now . . . Now I am the Queen of Solanum. And Lucien seems more remote than ever.

Another dance begins. Aron is still with Odette, so I take a sip from the goblet of mulled wine a servant has placed at my elbow, grip my courage between my teeth and rise, making my way down the room to where Lucien is standing, chatting to his dance partner. Courtiers part and bow as I pass. The heavily armoured Dark Guards patrolling the edge of the room stand to attention, and household servants – now clad in the blue and silver of my house, Cygnus Atratys – drop their gaze. Yet Lucien does not appear to notice my approach. He is talking and laughing loudly, and doesn't stop until the woman he is with bows and backs away.

'Your Majesty.' He ducks his head. His expression is calm, but his dark eyes are hard, glittering too brightly. 'May the Creator grant you safe passage through the dark season.'

A well-worn expression. His first words to me since he told me to leave his room, after I revealed my marriage to Aron. They are appropriate to the time of year. Still, I'd hoped for something more, given what we had been to each other. I swallow my disappointment and force a smile.

'I'm glad to see you back at court, Lord Lucien. Will you do me the honour of being my partner in the next dance?'

His face flushes – whether with surprise or vexation, I'm not sure – but he cannot refuse my request. I place my hand on the bare skin of the arm he has offered me, try to ignore the surge of desire in my belly as he leads me back to the centre of the hall.

While the orchestra tunes up and we wait for the other dancers to assemble I make conversation, asking about news from home – his estate of Hatchlands lies within Atratys – about the health of his mother, his father, his brother. About anyone

I can think of who is connected to him, since I cannot ask the questions to which I actually want the answers: how he is, and whether he has forgiven me.

The brevity of his responses, the cool tone of his voice, tell me more than his words. Anger sparks inside me as we begin to dance. I want to shake him, to ask what choice he thinks I really had. To remind him that I married Aron to save the kingdom. To save Lucien himself. But I don't. Instead, I focus on my steps, wishing that I hadn't forced Lucien to come back to court.

Aron, I know, is watching us.

Finally the dance ends. I sweep away from Lucien before he has finished bowing, making for the full-length windows that lead out onto the terrace. I need some air – clean, cold air, not stuffy with woodsmoke and the scent of wax. But before I reach the windows the heavy doors at the far end of the great hall are flung open. There are cries coming from the entrance hall. The Dark Guards stationed at the edges of the room swarm towards the source of the commotion.

'Aderyn!' Aron is hurrying towards me, his hand held out. Together we return to the dais, other guards taking up position in front of us. Aron has a sword belted to his waist; I regret that I have not. Both my ceremonial swords are locked, useless, in my rooms.

We don't have to wait long. One of the guard captains runs across the ballroom towards us. 'Majesties . . .'

'Speak, Hemeth.' Aron gestures the man closer. 'What's amiss?'

'Nobles, from Celonia.'

'An invasion?' I ask, my heart racing. 'Has Siegfried launched an attack?'

'No, my queen.' The captain hesitates. 'They claim there has been a rebellion, that the flightless of Celonia have risen up. The nobles are here seeking refuge.' He gestures behind him. 'Those who survived.'

The flightless seizing control of an entire country? The word *impossible* rises to my lips. But I can't disbelieve my own eyes. People, some robed, some still naked from transformation, are crowding into the ballroom. Some are limping, many are injured – a woman with long, matted red hair clutches one hand to her face as blood wells between her fingers.

A man who seems to be leading them drops to his knees. 'Mercy . . .' He clasps a young child, bundled in a robe, to his chest. 'Mercy and shelter, we beg you . . .' His words are punctuated by rapid, shallow breaths.

One of my courtiers pushes forward – Nyssa, Lady Swifting. Lucien's cousin. 'What of my betrothed? Where is Lord Bastien?'

The man stares at her, uncomprehending.

'Bastien of Verne,' Nyssa repeats. 'Where is he?'

'Behind us. I hope. We were separated . . .' The child in his arms begins to writhe and cry, a high-pitched keening that makes me wince in sympathy. I'm about to step forward and take her from him when Aron's fingers curl around my wrist. Whether to protect me or to remind me of my position, I'm not sure. Instead, Nyssa helps the noble lay the child on the floor.

'Aron . . .'

He nods, moves his hand briefly to my shoulder before

turning away to begin issuing orders. The injured must be tended to. But I saw in my husband's eyes my own fears: Solanum is about to be plunged into more uncertainty. More danger.

I leave Aron to organise the servants and summon doctors. I am the queen: my role is to be seen to rule, to be in control. So I walk briefly among the injured, dropping words of comfort here and there, counselling patience to my own nobility. Like Lady Nyssa, some here have family and friends in Celonia, but I would not have anyone fly off in rage and get killed. I remind them of the enduring nature of Solanum, of storms that we have weathered before. But I know – everyone here now knows – that the world is shifting beneath our feet. Whether we like it or not.

Finally I feel my work is done. Back in my own rooms, my maidservants help me out of my heavy gown, relieve me of the diadem, bracelets and rings that have been weighing me down. They depart. Naked – alone – I make my way out onto the private landing platform that is tucked away at the back of the royal apartments. I need to feel the wind beneath my body, to lose myself in the consuming joy of flight. To get as close as I can to the stars that burn above the surrounding mountain peaks. Wading into the frigid water of the lake, I give in to the power that is always waiting just beneath my skin. Hair morphs into feather, muscles shift and bones lengthen and lighten as I let myself transform from girl into swan.

I spread my wings and claim the cold night sky.

HOT KEY BOOKS

Thank you for choosing a Hot Key book.

If you want to know more about our authors and what we publish, you can find us online.

You can start at our website

www.hotkeybooks.com

And you can also find us on:

We hope to see you soon!